The Temporary Typist

A Novel

Also by TIMOTHY MERRILL

*Winkies, Toilets and Holy Places: One Family's Story of Life on a Sabbatical
— Europe, Istanbul and Bethlehem*
Published in both print and electronic format by iUniverse, www.iUniverse.com,
and available on Amazon, www.Amazon.com

The Temporary Typist
© 2013 by Timothy Merrill
All Rights Reserved

Cover art by Ying Tiun, Shanghai, China; and Darren Raber,
Raber Graphic Design, Wooster, Ohio

ISBN 978-0-9897890-0-4
First Paperback Edition.

Dedicated to the memory of

FRANK DEXTER MERRILL, 1879-1957

The Temporary Typist

A Novel

by

Timothy Merrill

Prologue

Spring of 1929
Chicago, Illinois

IF IT WEREN'T FOR PROHIBITION, CHICAGO just might be the most boring city on the face of the earth. What's there to do in this town anyway? It's a big city, alright, with lots of bright lights along the lakeshore, and Madison Avenue. And you got your stockyards and stockbrokers, the Sox and Cubs, and Smokey Hollow. Don't forget Marshall Fields. But if the do-gooders and goo-goos have their way, the world is going to die of sheer apathy.

These were the mature sentiments of Mr. Joseph Craglione, bartender. He was a Young Man with Potential, enrolled at the University of Chicago. Of a philosophical bent, he was one of the few, apart from the teetotalers and Social Gospelers, who thought that Prohibition was a good thing. Craglione believed that the 18th amendment had injected new life into an otherwise banal existence. His view was that man is endowed with certain fundamental drives and that to curtail the free and creative pursuit of any of these urges is sheer folly. Further, he felt that bad laws generally invited creative disobedience, even if the sanctions had the blessing of the government.

Actually, there is but one primal urge, he believed, and that is LUST. But Lust is a hydra-headed beast appearing in different forms, mainly three: erotic lust, economic lust, and, for want of a better word, alcoholic lust. In other words, sex, money and booze. Dolls, dough and drink. He'd given considerable thought to the subject. Nothing is going to change, ameliorate or mitigate these basic, most fundamental drives. Man is helpless against the powers of these three demi-gods, the attempts of the church and one's mother to socialize mankind and to lift up the human condition notwithstanding. Broads, bread and booze. There it is, right there. The Holy Trinity, the Three In One. LUST the Broad; LUST the Bread; and LUST the Holy Spirits, to wit, whiskey, gin and vodka. That's why since the dawn of man there were three things one could always find without the slightest effort: a willing woman, a greedy man and a stiff drink. Or, a greedy woman, a stiff man, and a willing drink. Shoot, as soon as Noah got off the Ark after forty days of non-stop living with his wife and all those animals, he got drunker than a sailor on shore leave. The first thing he did was to make a nice red wine, and then he passed out like a Skid Row bum, stark naked right in front of the children! Even our Lord and Savior Jesus Christ kept the party going at Cana when he worked his first miracle. Isn't it curious that of all the miracles that the Son of God might have performed to announce to a fallen world that the Savior was among them, he chose to conjure up a Galilean grenache! Why, he could've healed a baby, or raised someone from the dead, or made a blind man see, or the lame to walk. But the first thing he does is to make sure everyone has a drink! So here we are, he thought, *trying to undo what Jesus did!* Ain't that something?! So, right now, thanks to the 18th Amendment, Chicago is not a boring town at all.

Craglione was about six feet two, blond hair, and a complexion as fair as a ripening peach. He was as slim as a willow and not bad-looking. He was wearing a long-sleeved white shirt that was flecked with a few red stains from maraschino cherry juice. His sleeves were rolled up. A green, St. Patrick's Day bowtie was snapped to his collar slightly akimber. He didn't have a steady girlfriend, but he was keeping company with Mrs. Patrick McAndrews, the childless wife of a Rush Avenue attorney. He was behind the bar of the back room of a blind pig known as the Blue Sky Lounge off Longnecker Street. The front room was moderately full of patrons. It was only 9 p.m. This room was decorated with large prints of the Chicago skyline, posters of the 1893 World's Fair, a large photograph of George Ferris' giant revolving wheel and some original oils brought in by local artists. The lounge served only non-alcoholic beverages—tea, coffee, iced tea, sodas, sarsaparilla—and sandwiches and tea cakes. Overhead were two large fans operated by electric pulleys. Behind the mahogany bar was a large mirror. Fat cats and painted women with pearls and gem-studded bracelets could sit at the bar and smoke their Chesterfields and read the paper, or huddle in groups around smaller tables and socialize in the dim yellow light.

But Craglione did not work the front room. He worked in the back room along with two goons hired by Gus Morley, the manager of the place, to keep order if necessary and run errands. His duties included keeping tabs on what was happening in the front lounge. This he did by sliding a small disk to the side which allowed him to peer into the room through what was the hub of Ferris' wheel in the photograph. In this manner, Craglione was able to ascertain at all times what was happening therein. The booze was in the back room. Morley kept the hooch in a vault and only certain amounts were brought out on the hour to meet the expected needs of the next hour. The back room was larger than the front and a whole lot noisier—all the people and music. An eight-record music box kept the air full of swinging sounds and, at the moment, "My Blue Heaven" was playing and three or four couples were swaying limply to the music on the dance floor. The patrons of the front room were also patrons of the back room. The house policy was that every patron had to spend some time out front, thus legitimizing the business to nosey parkers who might be walking by or the occasional cop on the beat. Sometimes the cops stepped inside. Craglione knew the cops by sight. And if a pair of officers dropped in uninvited or unrecognizable, Craglione knew when to get the booze back in the vault. And he always had five gallons of tea behind the bar in the case of emergencies.

Helping him at the bar tonight, as she usually did, was a quiet gal of medium height and a sad face. She wasn't just any doll, she was Morley's old lady. She always brought her kid with her, just a 6-month-old infant. Tonight he was sleeping in a pram parked in a dark corner by the back door and sometimes she'd go by to check on him and she'd rock the pram a bit to lull him to sleep if he was crying. She'd given him a bottle not long ago. It was Craglione's opinion that Gus was worthless as a father—and as a husband, for that matter. Morley was in the office, doing God knows what. Craglione popped in with a question and there was Gus, hunched over his desk which was awash with papers, betting slips and invoices. Gus was maybe ten years older than his moon-faced wife and growing fat around the middle, fat in his cheeks and under his eyes. He had a mole in the crease where the nostril meets the face. Craglione noticed the safe was ajar. Gus was counting money. He no doubt had a meeting with the Genna Brothers coming up soon. But he couldn't be sure. He stayed out of those things. He was just a philosophy major, which authorized him to be a student of human behavior and the human condition.

Craglione was still musing about the depravity of mankind when six or seven cops burst into the front lounge with revolvers drawn shouting "This is a raid! Everyone stay where you are!" But they made straight for the back hallway and the door leading to the back room, a door which was heavy, locked and barred. Someone must have tipped them off. It would only be a few minutes before they broke through; he saw that they were prepared with battering equipment to ram through Gus' defenses.

Craglione could also hear them pounding on the alley door. "Chicago police! Open up in there!" He sprang into action, shouting at shrieking patrons to pour out their drinks on the floor, and he started spilling tea into two-quart pitchers and getting as many of them to the tables as he could while at the same time getting the gin, vodka and other spirits into the vault as quickly as possible. The baby in the pram woke up and began to wail. Gus ran from his office to open the vault, hidden inadequately by a bookcase and was helping clear the bar of the booze.

"You ready for the smoke, boss?" Craglione yelled. Morley called for the smoke, and Craglione grabbed two smoke bombs from under the bar, and rolled them across the floor. The fog was merely an element of confusion. It could help some patrons slip by the officers. It also bought more time for Morley, Craglione and the goons to get their house in order.

Moments later, the cops pushed inside and stomped through the place like elephants on a rampage trumpeting obscenities and wreaking havoc. Guns blasted, glass shattered and the music stopped after a policeman took his Billy club to the music box. "Hey, we don't got no guns," Morley shouted. "No guns! Why you shooting at us? We got no guns! No guns!" The gunfire ceased.

"Hey, why you giving us the bums rush here, eh?" Morley yelled. "We're running an upstanding establishment here!"

"Yeah? So, what's with the locked doors?" asked the cop closest to Morley at the time. He was dressed in full uniform, with a panel of silver buttons running up and down the left side of his jacket. His cap was pushed down over his eyes, hiding them. "Why the back room, moron?"

"Because this here is the *noisy* room. We got a dance floor here, if you'd taken time to notice. The music is loud, so this room is not, you might say, conductive to conversation. You want conversation, you use the street room, officer."

The coppers ordered everyone to the wall. The smoke had pretty much dissipated, although the room was still hazy and smelled like sulfur. After the initial uproar, the place calmed down as the officers took control and assessed who, if any, would be arrested and on what charge. They began by frisking and patting down everyone in the room, giving special attention to the ladies who—evidently—could be hiding Derringers in daring and unmentionable places. Craglione himself was up against the wall, his arms above his head, legs spread. While he waited for his own pat down, he looked around, and noticed that the alley door in the back was open, and that the pram in the corner had vanished.

And so had Mrs. Gus Morley.

Chapter I

February 22, 1952
Bathington, Iowa

ON THE DAY THAT HE STARTS keeping a diary, Mr. Carlton Cooper, the erstwhile station manager for the Rock Island Railroad stands before a heavy oak door identified by a brass plate that reads CHURCH OFFICE. Slowly he removes a dimpled gray felt hat and straightens himself up to full height. Staring at the frosted glass window in the door before him, he takes a deep breath like anyone might do who is two steps away from beginning a new career.

He is dressed in a light blue serge suit, pressed Arrow shirt, starched collar, and a patterned bowtie. Brown Florsheims, worn but shiny. It is the way he dresses every day. *I must be out of my mind.*

He sighs. He grasps the doorknob, hesitates for a second, then twists and pulls and steps inside, closing the door behind him. Before him is a chest-high counter beyond which is a large desk behind which sits the Church Secretary, Violet Crenshaw, identified by a sign on her desk that reads in stacked rows: MISS VIOLET CRENSHAW, CHURCH SEC-RETARY. On the desk is a green blotter pad, and assembled at one corner of the desk are several framed photos. One is of a woman and a small girl. Another of two young women in twenties flapper outfits. And another is of an elderly couple, probably her parents, Coop thinks. Near the photos is a wooden crucifix, about seven inches high, affixed to a fine box. Both the box and the crucifix appear to be made of a hard wood, such as mahogany or cherry. Crenshaw is on the phone. She gives him a little fluttery wave. He leans forward and rests his elbows on the counter but then removes them and stands erect—waiting.

"Got to go, Penny," the Church Secretary says into the shiny black Bell receiver. "Mr. Cooper's here. I'm going to show him everything. Put him through his paces." She giggles. Pause. "Yes, yes, I am quite sure, it's time and no one's indispensable, you know that's what I always say." Her voice modulates up and down as though following a Bell curve. Sort of sing-songy that way. Pause. "You're sweet." Pause. "Okay, then, buh-bye, dear." She hangs up and stands up and walks around her desk to a Dutch door at the far end of the counter, the kind of barrier meant to keep out toddlers or fox terriers. "Come on in, Mr. Cooper," she says brightly.

Miss Crenshaw is one tightly put together package. Everything about her is pulled, tucked, pressed and severe. She looks very *holy*. She isn't unattractive, but no one would call her a beauty, either. Yet there is a simple goodness in the lines of her face that is appealing. Her face, pale and drawn, is heart-shaped with a wide forehead and narrow cheeks devolving to a diminutive chin. Her hair is pulled taut and sweeps upward and back into a simple chignon. Her complexion is waxy with a hint of rouge on the cheekbones. On her nose rest wireless eyeglasses. Her mouth is small, lips are narrow and pursed like she's just sucked on a lemon. From her face alone can be inferred a lifetime of earnest probity, utmost practicality and religious piety. She wears a long-sleeved white Antoinette high collar blouse with a pleated bib and frills at the wrists. Around her neck is a delicate gold chain from which hangs a small bejeweled cross. Her pleated black skirt extends to well below the knees. On her feet are T-strap black heels. Mr. Cooper can see she is wearing a girdle so firm you could crack a bottle of Dom Perignon on her backside like you were christening the Queen Mary. It makes his skin crawl the way she says "buh-bye" and "dear." He advances toward the welcoming Miss Crenshaw. "Reporting for duty, ma'am," he says cheerfully.

She shuffles some papers, takes up a No. 2 pencil and scribbles some notes on same. Coop takes a seat in a heavy wooden chair that has been shellacked a dozen times giving it a glossy jaundiced look. He rests his hat in his lap, reaches for a handkerchief in his suit pocket and wipes his brow and bald head. Then he folds the damp cloth into a tight square and tucks it away. His head is a globe of a noggin and not a strand of hair has survived above the equator. But around his ears and circling the back side of the hemisphere is a thatchy band of salt-and-pepper hair that is more than enough of an excuse to visit Doyle's Barber Shop at least once every other week. He reaches for his pocket watch, a railroad-grade, 18-jewelled retirement gift back in '48. Forenoon, 11 a.m. straight up. He slips the timepiece back into his watch pocket.

He looks around. He's been in the church office many times since 1932 when he and the wife first moved to Bathington. Not too much has changed over the years. The oak-paneled wainscoting is original, dating back to 1924. Behind Miss Crenshaw and to her right is a doorway which opens to a large storage room where open shelves hold reams of 20-weight paper, bulletin stock, Gestetner ink, stencils, glue, staples, poster board, construction paper, cases of filmstrips, flannel and flannel graph boards, easels, envelopes, stewardship supplies and the like. A table sits in the center of that room where bulletins can be folded or envelopes stuffed and prepared for mailing. This room also has a janitor's closet containing mops, buckets, brooms, heating oil, rags and other supplies.

The office itself is rectangular and painted in a grim white. To his left is a large double hung window that gives a view to Center Street. Under the sill is a two-shelf bookcase holding back issues of *Presbyterian Life*. A picture of Sallman's *Head of Christ* hangs on one wall, and behind and above Miss Crenshaw is Holman Hunt's painting of *Christ at the Door*. The wood-plank floors are covered with linoleum, one foot squares of alternating pale green and white tiles. He remembers when the Trustees authorized the linoleum a while back. Which makes him think of Cushing.

"I say, old boy, why would an old plow horse like you, a full 68 years old, keep on working?" the Reverend Archibald Cushing had asked, laughing, only yesterday. "Not that you're old ... at least not *frightfully*." They are in the Pastor's Study. The Reverend fattens his straight-stem pipe, and strikes a match. "I can think of at least three reasons," he says, "No, maybe four."

"Is that so?" replies the railroad man cautiously. He isn't sure he's ready for more of Cushing's badinage. The cleric leans forward out of the shadows of his wing-backed chair, pipe in hand, and replies: "Well, I'm just thinking out loud. Hear me out. See what you think. First, the old fellow could be under-financed and needs the money; or, two, he's under-educated and bored out of his mind; or, third, he's under-appreciated and feels useless—misses the harness, the yoke on his shoulders and all that, eh? Or you could say he needs to be needed. And, finally ... last ... — what was I thinking? I think I'm getting a wee bit balmy—" Cushing stumbles here. "Oh, yes! He's an over-achiever and needs the praise of his peers. You know the type, eh? Someone who's an adoration addict ...

or *adulation* addict. Oh! I like that, too." Cushing reinserts his pipe into his thin-lipped mouth and puffs, pondering the alliterative alternatives. Blue smoke curls slowly out of the bowl rising in a small swirl which becomes gray and then a cloudy cirrus-like layer of white before vanishing. "*Affection* addict." Puff. Puff. "So which do you think best describes you, Coop? Perhaps it's a combination of one or two, eh? Or—" His voice rises here—"I might have missed the *true* reason completely! What do you think?"

Cushing is only in his mid-thirties, but his thin hair is already graying and in retreat. His face is pallid and Calvinistically earnest, his features fine and unambiguous, and his gaze steady and assured, all in all lending to a general sense of ecclesiastical dignity.

"Oh, I don't know, really," Coop replies. He thinks it odd that as he gets older, he is plagued with all this codswallop as to how he'll stay "useful," as though being alive isn't useful enough. Being alive is useful to *him*. Every day he wakes up is a good day. He worked for the railroad for over forty years, not in order to feel useful, but because it put butter and bread on the table. Not that he didn't enjoy his job—but it wasn't about fulfilling any other need than to have a profession that kept him alive—the ultimate utility. Then Coop says what he's thinking: "I think that if you're alive you're of *some* use, or the Creator wouldn't have put you here in the first place, or keep you around past your usefulness. Are babies in the cradle 'useful'? Are madmen in an asylum 'useful'? You don't have to *produce* something to be useful, I don't think. But more to your point—I don't feel underappreciated, that's for sure; I really don't think it matters one way or the other. I just sort of know what's got to be done and do it. All the whys and wherefores, that's your job! That's why you're a preacher and I'm just an old railroad man who can type." They laugh.

"Jolly good!" Cushing cries. "But if you're not a man struggling against a feeling of uselessness, it's not going to make for a very good book now is it? And we want this to be a good book, don't we?"

"A good book?" Coop is puzzled.

"Yes!" the Reverend exclaims. "The book of your life. A book with no conflict is not much of a book."

Coop scoffs. "Well, then my life is not much of a book, certainly no best-seller because nothing happens. I guess other people would say it's been pretty boring—"

"But you've been happy, content, at peace with yourself and others, and as far as you know, with the Good Lord, too, right?"

He shrugs. "Yes, I guess that's one way of putting it."

"A good life is not a boring life, Coop!" Cushing says in a soothing voice, wanting his friend to properly value his self-worth.

"Yes, it is, but that's okay by me," Coop counters. "I guess if there's any struggle—since you're bound and determined to find one—it's not against uselessness; it's against powerlessness—"

"Aye! You are so right!" Cushing cries, clapping. His pipe nearly flips out of the corner of his mouth. "That's very perceptive, Coop!"

"Well, okay, but ... you know ... Remember a couple of years ago when Ducky Doyle was bringing the CNW No. 64 through and he was only going about 40 miles per hour, but he was pulling about 25 cars, maybe more, so there he was, had thousands of tons of iron and steel rolling behind him and when you got that much tonnage and you're going 40 per, it's hard to stop all that very fast, and then he comes through town, his whistle blowing like crazy, but—"

"—Hog Kramer had a truckload of pigs he was taking to Waverly, and he hit the tracks, or a pothole or something and the back gate sprung just as Ducky's making the curve."

"Yeah, and Hog got out and tried to get the gate back on and corral a hog that had fallen off ... but, that train kept a-coming, and Ducky says he saw what was happening and tried to stop, and Hog got in the cab, couldn't get the truck going, and finally bailed at the last moment before the train hit."

"*Good Lord!* I remember, a bad one, that was."

"We had bacon and blood for about a half mile ... but my point is that I think of my life that way ... my life has accumulated a whole bunch of cars I'm pullin' and the older you get the more inertia, and most of the time you just can't stop stuff. You try but you don't got the brakes for it. But you know I lose Antonia, then Johnny's killed in some rice paddy half way around the world, and there's not a darn thing I can do about it ... you just plow right through it and on down the track and hope there's not too much debris you leave behind. I do keep busy with what I do—helping Millie and the girls, visiting my friends—and now helping out in the church office, although whether I'll be much help remains to be seen."

That was yesterday. Here he is, offering to be of use to Miss Crenshaw and the Bathington Community Church. "Okay, then," says Miss

Crenshaw, placing her palms on the desk and looking at Coop directly. "Let's get started." She instructs him on the production process, how everything comes in to her office via the mail, a phone call, or from Reverend Cushing. He'd need to come to the office Friday afternoon or Saturday morning and put everything together. Cushing would have the Order of Worship completed. He'd also leave a list of announcements about "Upcoming Events." He might have an updated prayer list. "Don't get behind on the prayer requests," Miss Crenshaw says. Last month the list had included a request to pray for a certain Mrs. Louisa Stoddard on account of her being in the hospital after she'd taken a header in the bathroom. But she had died and was in the bosom of Abraham, her body cold in the ground, while they were still supposed to be praying for her recovery! He would need to monitor how much text he had and whether he could get it on the space provided. Usually an insert was required. When she first started, she typed up the bulletin normal-like, and then used it as a guide to make the stencil. She reviews how to cut stencils, shows him the dotted line that acts as a guide to cut the stencil in half so that each half will fit in the typewriter carriage. She reminds him to use the "white" setting to disable the ribbon, so that the keys will cut cleanly. She shows him where the cleaner is for the keys. She warns him that C and W keys tend to stick.

Coop listens intently. Being the Church Secretary is a *very* important position in the church. The person sitting at this desk has to have an eye for detail, an ear for gossip and a tongue that refuses to divulge the contents. There is only one person who has a more intimate knowledge of the ecclesiastical culture of the Bathington Community Church than the Church Secretary and that is the President of the Ladies' Aid Society. The Minister comes behind these two. Coop is well-suited for the job: his career with the railroad gives him experience with *minutiae*, reports, tables, facts and figures. He knows virtually everyone in town and his discretion is above reproach. Heretofore, the unwritten rules—given that the church secretaries had historically been *women*—were that the secretary could be neither too young nor too old; if the former, the threat of scandal was too great, if the latter the lesser risk of incompetence. If young, it was paramount that at the very least the Church Secretary not be *attractive*, and failing that, she should be married. Miss Crenshaw is eminently suited for the job inasmuch as she—although without a matrimonial attachment—is lacking in both youth and beauty, deficiencies which trump all other concerns. As a rule, the Session prefers someone who is of middle age, married and plain. If she has actual skills, so much the better. Coop has the one attribute that makes him an ideal, if not irregular, candidate: he is a man. And he can spell and type.

# # #

They spend the next hour together as teacher and pupil. She shows him where everything is stored. Then she demonstrates. She spreads the two stencil halves on the countertop, applies cement to one half and glues them together again. She tears off the cardboard backing. She shows him how to lift the cover of the mimeograph, insert one end of the stencil in the slots and then carefully let the filmy stencil drape over the drum as she turns the handle. It is a critical part of the process. If the stencil is improperly positioned, a fine wrinkle will develop and this will result in thin black lines spidering across the printed page. The machine needs to be inked, and, depending on the size of the printing project, it will need to be re-inked several times. She takes a white tube of black ink and squeezes a line of ink along the drum and then cranks the drum like she's starting a Model A until the thin line of the black goo is spread on the drum evenly. She inserts some used paper stock to run some test copies. She shows Coop where they keep the bulletin stock that comes from Chicago which already has two-color religious themes printed on the front.

"When the printing's done, the only thing left is to fold 'em," she says brightly. "Nothing to it." They are walking out of the storage room. Violet closes the door behind them and stands behind her desk as Coop moves toward the dog and baby gate.

He nods and shakes a finger at her: "I wish you hadn't said that 'cause there's always something to it."

"Spoken by someone who's afraid to fail," she says reprovingly. "Like I said before, you'll be fine!"

Coop picks his hat off the counter and prepares to depart. "You're right, I'll be fine. You've done a heck of a job here in this office over the years, Miss Violet. You're going to be missed."

"Very kind of you, Coop."

Coop pauses at the door. "So why now? "

Miss Crenshaw appears ready with an answer. "I'm tired of the winter cold. I have friends in southern California, and California seems to be where everyone's going these days, and I can't say I won't enjoy the warmer temperatures, the ocean, the fresh fruit and vegetables, you know."

"Yeah."

"And it's not like I have friends and family to keep me here, you know, like you, Coop—"

"—of course you do—"

"—you know what I mean, no children, husband—real *family*—to keep me here, so why not? I'm not getting any younger, you know. And it's been rough at the bank lately—that's another story. So, anyway, I got some savings and resources I've developed over the years. I'll be alright. And I can always find work. California is growing so fast, it's not hard to find a job—so they tell me."

They stood in silence awkwardly for a moment. "It's too bad, though," she said.

"What's too bad?"

"That you don't really value the friends you have until you have to leave them," she says, sitting down and pulling some notes from the desk top and placing them in a drawer. She slams the drawer shut.

Coop fiddles with his hat. "Yes, you're right about that, for sure. But around here, you don't think of such things, 'cause no one ever leaves and, if they do, it's probably a short trip—and a final trip—from the city to the cemetery. When are you leavin' anyway?"

"Oh dear! I don't know for sure," she says, fussing with papers. She's tidying up. "Moving is *such* a big deal, Coop. You just can't up and move. I got things to take care of, arrangements to be made, and it will be so much easier not having this responsibility at the church. I got to get this taken care of, one less thing to do later, you know." She pauses, and looks at Coop.

The new secretary pushes open the office door and gets one foot into the hallway. "I understand," he says.

"All you got to do," Miss Crenshaw says, "is to find another secretary."

"I understand that, too," Coop allows, tipping his hat to the lady and closing the door behind him. Through the frosted glass he sees the cloudy outline of Miss Crenshaw staring after him.

I got to find another secretary! And soon! Coop shakes his head, drops his hat on his head and walks down the hallway, down some stairs and out to the street. He glances at the sky, gray as winter fog, and looks up and down the streets. He shivers. The roads are clear, but snow is on the ground. He digs around in his inside suit pocket for a handkerchief and gives his nose a good blowing out. *And I'm going to start my diary. This is just too interesting, and there's no time like the present.*

It is 1952. February 22, to be exact—eleven days after his birthday. He'll backtrack to his birthday and officially begin to "number his days" from his sixty-eighth birthday. His ancestor, Thomas Bathington, had kept a diary and thereby told his story. He will likewise tell his.

Chapter II

FRIDAY, February 22, 1952
Washington's Birthday, 220 years old today!

Up at 7:15 a.m. Temperature outside 30°; Des Moines WHO says 28° there. Last night I inhaled the fumes from some Eucalyptus oil to fight off my cold but it didn't do much good. No school today for Millie and the kids, not sure how the girls spent their time, but Vickie is never wanting for something to do and Frankie I think was angling to go to a movie this weekend sometime, and a boy may be involved. She and her mother are at loggerheads too often it seems. Millie is going to do some Avon-ing, I believe. LATER: In the forenoon, walked to the P.O. for mail. Nothing for me but a belated bday card from cousin Alta in Omaha. To the house for lunch. Peeled spuds for supper later. Lunch consisted of chili, crackers and bread. In the afternoon I kept my appt at the church office with Miss Violet Crenshaw who showed me the ropes for creating a stencil and cranking out the church bulletin and newsletter until I can locate a new secretary. Not sure how I got this job, but I shan't have to do it long I would hope. She only works on Friday afternoons when she has off from the bank, and sometimes comes in on a Saturday morning. So it won't be time-consuming, I guess. Can't be sure why Crenshaw is leaving. I guess she has money. Says she's gg to California. Back to the Fremont where I listened to my "operys" and then be-

gan this diary by gg back to my bday and recollect-
ing as best I could. Then to the house, put spuds
on, helping Millie get ready for supper for which
she'd baked two cherry pies in honor of Washington
and his little hatchet. Back at the Fremont, went to
the bathroom and found Jules buck naked on the
floor. Said he'd hit his head or something. Didn't
want my help, but I got him back to his room. Read
some more of Chamber's book <u>Witness</u> regarding Alger
Hiss. Had heard the letter written to his children
and the world read over the radio the other—

Coop comes to the bottom of the page—a three-holed half page— and
now he pulls the paper out of the typewriter, spinning the carriage with a
zip! and lays it aside and pushes back from his writing desk. Sometimes
he would insert the page lengthwise and conclude his sentence up the
side of the page. Not tonight. He stands and pulls the delicate chain dangling like a necklace beneath the lampshade of the lamp on his desk. He's
wearing his topcoat over his striped pajamas. On his feet are old slippers
with matted sheepskin padding. He potters to the oil heater hidden in the
shadows of a corner, and lights a fire as he does every night during the
long, dark winter. This rectangular room is where a third to a half of his
life is played out. In the universe, it's just one infinitesimal speck of
square footage stocked with books, a bed, two chairs, a table and a commode—this is where he lives. This is what he now calls "home." A fox
hole, a lion's den, a bird's nest, an eagle's aerie, a badger's burrow—this is
a *human's* haven, his port in the storm. He likes it. It suits his require-
ments for solitude when he needs to chug on a glass of contemplation, or
chew on the heel of some crusty self-reflection. The room is not spartan.
He doesn't believe in the mortification of the flesh; at his age, he's sufficiently mortified as it is. He has his radio, his player, his records, his pens,
his writing paper. Above his secretary is a print of a 1914 Mountain class
165-ton locomotive. By it, hanging on a thumb tack, is his old switch key.
So Coop does not feel deprived, oppressed, marginalized or poor.
    He retrieves a book from his writing table, Daphne Du Maurier's *Re-
becca,* and then walks to the upholstered chair by the window and tosses it
to the lap of the chair. He returns to the commode, the top of which is
covered by a doily crocheted by his grandmother Lillian, he reaches for a

shot glass. He makes a mental note to get some Lysol for the slop pail. He pours himself a stiff one and heads across the hardwood floor for his chair. Peering out his fourth-story window he notes the glow of the HO-TEL sign which half lights up the snow-packed street below. The John Deere thermometer reads 28°. He turns to his chair and retrieves his book. The lamp is already on. He stands in front of the chair facing away from it, and then falls with a thud into the softness of the upholstery. The moment is perfect. All he is missing is a crackling fire in the hearth and a dog at his feet snoozing on the hooked rug. He puts his scotch down on a coaster on the end table by the chair and opens his book.

But he can't read.

Whitaker Chambers, Alger Hiss, Richard Nixon, Joseph McCarthy. Communists everywhere. Better dead than red. Loyalty oaths. Truman. America For Americans.

"I got to get a secretary," he says. He talks out loud when alone in his room, and has completely come to terms with it. He tries to understand it, as he does with most things that happen in his life, and he concludes that it is a sign of sanity rather than senility. Both the senile and the sane talk to themselves, but the former talks to no one in particular about everything in general, whereas the latter talks about nothing in general to someone in particular. The sane person addresses his *self.* When he talks to himself, Coop reasoned—and he does this aloud as well—the action itself somehow calls out to his alter ego and between the two selves confusion is clarified, action becomes focused, and arguments are brought to a conclusion.

He grabs his straight-stem pipe and some Prince Albert, and lights it. "So how shall I go about this?" He puffs. A thin wisp of smoked curls up from the bowl like incense. "First I need to make a list of possible candidates."

"Um-mh." More puffing. He cinches his overcoat a bit tighter around his neck.

"Then I got to talk to them to ascertain their willingness to take the job."

"Well, first you need to submit your list to Reverend Cushing for his approval. After all, he would have veto power or some reasons why a particular candidate might not be suitable."

"Of course, of course. And he might be able to suggest the best ones or the most likely candidates, and I would start with those."

"I suppose before you get to the 'interview' stage you'd need to create a job description so that they'd know what they're getting into." Coop puffs in silence as the conversation momentarily ceases.

Then, "But I can't really write up a job description when I haven't spent a day on the job myself, now can I?"

"Miss Crenshaw could write it—"

"No, no. I sat with Crenshaw for over an hour today and should know what the job requires. Besides, soon I will have experience enough."

"True, so then I interview the likely candidates ..." He pauses to puff and cogitate.

"What are the chances that more than one person wants the job? I would then give Reverend Cushing a short list of people who are willing to take it on and he can make the decision."

"Of course he may want your opinion."

"Of course."

His pipe fails. He looks across the room. In the opposite corner is an armoire in which are a couple of suits and a raincoat—most of his clothes were at Millie's. Along the far wall is his bed, neatly made, and above it on the forlorn papered wall is a faded cameo photograph in an oval walnut frame of his beloved Antonia, taken when she was 19. It is a profile. Her hair is done up in a bun. Her head is turned slightly toward the camera showing soft features and shadowed eyes. Her lips are closed; just the hint of a wistful smile.

"It's time to go to bed," Coop says. He removes his uppers and drops them into a glass of water on the nightstand.

"Tomorrow, I need to talk to Millie about this," he says to no one in particular.

Chapter III

BOTH THE RIVER AND THE RAILROAD serve Bathington and the farmsteads beyond that lie tucked in green and wooded hills like nests in a thicket. A highway leading south to Des Moines and north to Austin, Minnesota, slices through the town like the first cut of an apple pie. But the county road running east and west leads nowhere without connecting to other roads to Plimpton to the west or Garringer to the east and east of that, Dubuque.

Bathington is a sodden village hidden in leafy red elms, oaks and silver maples that shade its streets. Some are paved. Most are gravel and pocked with potholes or ribbed in washboard. Beyond the town square the gravel gradually disappears in the curbless lanes of West Bath, or Beverly Hills, as it is derisively called by East Bathingtonites. West Bath, home to the only colored family on either side of the Clearwater, has no gravel at all. Just Iowa dirt, and these lanes are rutty when dry and muddy when wet. The town's houses sit shyly back off old cement sidewalks that heave over the roots of elms and oaks like flattened tombstones in a cemetery. They are for the most part modest dwellings— a mix of bungalows, Victorians, Federal and others defying architectural description. The older ones sit on foundations of rock pulled out of the Clearwater just as their ancestors had pulled stone out of Massachusetts Bay. Every home has a basement and most a fruit cellar, and all with a veranda of some kind— except for Robert Ransom who has built a new house out on the edge of town in the so-called "ranch" style that was then becoming popular. Except for the Ransom house, the town has the feel of a New England village, and echoes of Puritan piety can even be heard in the cadences of the language and the occasional accent and tone of its speakers.

In autumn, the town's maple trees erupt into a conflagration of reds and yellows, and its branches drop leaves like flaming embers on to gutters, lawns and sidewalks. The crisp, curled leaves are raked into the

streets where they are burned or strewn into the winds by urchins running through them. And like many Midwestern towns, Bathington has a
square block off-center of town as a park and gathering area with a band
shell on a platform ten risers above ground. Plans are now afoot to refur-
bish the bandstand, park and all public areas in anticipation of the Centennial Celebration in August during which the sons and daughters of
Bathington will congregate to applaud the daring of their ancestors, the
achievements of their forefathers and collectively aspire to even greater
accomplishments in the century ahead of them.

The last Bathington in Bathington died in 1865 at the age of 65. His
name was Adonijah. He was survived by three daughters, one of whom,
Cora, married Emerson Harrison Cooper. They had a son, Edgar, who
with Lillian, had a son, Edward, who was united in marriage to Claire
Campbell, and it was of this union that Carlton Campbell Cooper was
born in 1884 in Ashland, Nebraska. His father was a silversmith before
moving the family back to Bathington when Carlton was young and after
a brief pilgrimage with Coxey's Army in 1894. Of the Coopers, only he
and Millie and Victoria Ashley and Frances Katherine remained. He is
now living in the Fremont Hotel wondering how many more years he has
left, and Millie is raising the two girls by herself.

# # #

At about 7:30 a.m. the next morning Mildred Allison Cooper, *nee* Morri-
son, opens her eyes. It's a brand spanking new day! she thinks. But she
doesn't jump out of bed. She lazes luxuriously for a while, stretching,
yawning and thinking, knowing that once she leaves her bed she'll not
have a moment's peace until she throws herself back into it at the end of
the day. This is the singular place where Millie is assured of privacy. Her
bed is her *sancta sanctorum*. Here she is not disturbed. So she lies by herself, in her big brass bed, her big *empty* bed. Her bed without Johnny. She
still—after two years—never wakes up in the morning without thinking
about him. She glances at the alarm clock: 7:40 a.m. Coop's on his way
down, she reckons. She stares at the ceiling of her second story bedroom.
She can see Coop, exiting the Fremont Hotel as he does every morning
dressed in his hat and topcoat and appearing on Main Street. He'll walk
past the Bathington State Bank and then the hardware store. He'll come
to the post office on the corner of Main and Poplar where he'll check for

the morning mail. He'll walk past the new-fangled telephone cabin, the only one in town, and check to see if someone has left a nickel in the change hole. Then he'll keep walking south for another two blocks, quickly getting away from the town center. He'll turn left on Maple, and a half block east will arrive at 149, the home of Mrs. John Cooper and girls. *He's going to be here any minute. I should get going. But then, what's the rush? Let him get here, and then I get out of bed and get started.* She rolls over away from the east window and pulls the sheet and Grandma Great's quilt high around her shoulders. It feels good to still be in bed at 7:45 in the morning.

She hears Coop enter the house, not by the porch and the front door but by a rear door that opens to the kitchen. Normally, he'd be at the house at 7 a.m. to help get the girls to school, but today is Saturday.

Three Cheerios are still floating in Coop's breakfast bowl when she comes through the door in her man-style pajamas, but wearing a pink terry-cloth bathrobe.

"Morning, gorgeous," Coop says. He's standing at the stove with a pancake griddle greased and warming up.

"Morning, Coop." She puts some bread in the toaster and heads straight for the coffee pot. She takes cream, no sugar. She sits down at the table with a white Formica top and shiny chrome legs on a chair upholstered in yellow plastic. She sits sidesaddle on the chair and crosses her legs, and tucks the bathrobe up and over her knee. Her legs are long, and Coop realizes that she is taller than you'd think just seeing her sitting there slouched in the chair. And she is thin. Her fingers are bony. She throws one arm over the back of the chair and grasps her coffee mug in her other hand while keeping watch on the toaster. Her face is austere when expressionless, but fortunately, it is usually animated—by something. Millie is a go-getter. Her eyes are deep and intelligent, her hair short and black. Nothing languid about her appearance, her present lassitude notwithstanding. Millie's face and her carriage suggest alacrity, sharpness, quickness and cunning. They exchange the usual questions and answers regarding the night's sleep and the weather forecast.

"Tired?" Coop asks. He slops some Aunt Jemima batter on the griddle.

"I'm always tired on Saturday mornings." The toast pops up. She arises and scratches across the floor to the counter, dabs some oleo and huckleberry preserves on her toast. "I start to relax you know and get some rest … and my energy back and then whoosh! Suddenly it's Sunday night and I got school the next day and it starts all over again."

"But you didn't have school yesterday," Coop says, spatula in hand, watching the flapjacks browning.

"No, but I had Avon deliveries to make, and had, well, to get the girls organized and so on." She returns to the table. "You know," she looks up at him, taking a bite of toast, "you know how that is." Then, "Hear you applied for a job," she says.

"Yup, I applied for a job and one of the first things I need to do is find someone to replace me at the job for which I was just hired!"

"Well, that's very good of you to volunteer to fill in. Good Lord, I think Miss Crenshaw's been looking for someone—unsuccessfully—so I don't know how you're going to succeed where she failed."

Frankie appears, also in pajamas. "Where's Vic?" her mother asks.

"She's hanging on the door again."

"Oh! For pity sake! Where did she get that idea anyway?"

"What idea?" Coop asks, his spatula dripping with batter.

"She thinks that if she hangs from the top of a door, she can stretch herself and be taller," Millie says, stepping quickly to the kitchen door. "VICTORIA! GET DOWN HERE RIGHT NOW! Tippy? Here, Tippy!" Turning back into the kitchen, she says, "We got a 6-year-old girl who hangs on doors and a 6-year-old dog who steals the neighbors' shoes."

Vic has her teddy bear. Tippy pads in behind her, tail wagging. Her pink tongue is hanging out the side of her mouth, draped over one of her incisors. She's a black and white mix who thinks of herself as a border collie. Her fur is medium length, curly and matted. Vic, the bear and the dog are the same age, about six. Vic sits down at the table. Frances sits immobile, elbows on the table and head in her palms. Her eyes are languid and colorless, her face fleshy and pouty, flush from the night's sleep. Her hair is still in curlers—one behind her right ear about to fall off, dangling and bobbing like a lantern in the wind. Vic sits straight up with her bear in her lap and looks up at her mother. Her face is round. Everything about it is round. Her green eyes round and wide. Her nose is an upturned button and her mouth closed in the form of a quiet smile. She is a dynamo and, even early in the morning, she is wound up and ready to go. Except she just sits there. Millie understands that they both will be sitting there until kingdom come unless she clarifies the routine: "Girls, get yourselves some milk from the icebox and Pops is making pancakes. What's it going to be this morning—little people? A dog? A cat? Let him know. And Vic, speaking of dog, you need to feed Tippy first, okay?"

Victoria bounces out of her chair and heads for the pancake chef at the stove. "Can you make a bird, like a robin? I'd like a bird!"

"Of course!" Coops says, laughing. "A robin redbreast it is! But you go feed Tippy and wash your hands." He flips the two pancakes on the griddle to a waiting plate, and then takes a soup spoon to carefully ladle the batter to the griddle. Coop is a pancake artist.

Frankie does not bounce up. Frankie is not in a bouncing mood. She seldom is. She is 16 years old. She hit puberty a few years ago like a truck hitting a brick wall and the wreckage is still smoldering. She says: "Mom, please let me go to the movie. Tink and Naomi are going. Their parents said they could go."

"But, Frankie, I'll bet there're other parents who said no."

"Who?"

"I don't know. You're saying that *two* parents said yes and that's not a large opinion sample, is it?" Turning to Vic: "Honey, close the fridge door, okay?" To Frankie: "Two parents are not too many or even *all* the parents of teenagers in this town. Probably *most* are saying no, don't you think?"

Coop interjects: "What's the movie?"

"*A Girl in Every Port,*" Frankie says, looking up. She thinks that in Pops she might have an ally. "It just came out."

"Who's in it?"

"Groucho Marx, Marie Wilson, I don't know. What difference does it make?"

Coop wipes his hands on the white dish towel wrapped around his waist as an apron and says: "Oh, Frankie, yeah I don't know about this one, pumpkin. *Marie Wilson.* Ooohlala. I saw her during the blackouts not wearing much more than lace mitts, I don't—"

"*Thanks*, Coop," Millie says in that certain voice. Turning to Frances, she softens her tone: "Frankie, let's skip this one. You know I don't say no too often. Why not have your friends come over to the house this afternoon?"

That suggestion falls flatter than a cow patty. Millie knows that a war is already in progress, a war of the heart against the mind—that is, Frankie's heart, and her mother's mind. It started some time ago. Frankie is attempting an ideological *coup d'etat*. The household has become a battleground for competing points of view. Frances Katherine Cooper is becoming what all 16-year-old girls become: a vortex of hormones, emotions, instincts and illusions. She's rising to the peak of her intellectual acuity, absorbing with incredible speed every day new data about her world, but is forbidden to engage in discussions about this world or participate in decisions concerning it. She's able now to bear children, but is forbidden to even touch or be touched by a boy. Millie knows that Frankie is already by temperament given to the dramatic (her maternal grandmother had several notable episodes of hysteria) and that her Emotions, aided and abetted by Passion, are a Force of Nature so strong that Reason is utterly powerless before it. That's why Millie had the *petting* conversation with Frankie even though she'd never yet—as far as Millie knew—been alone with a boy. "If you permit yourself to get into a situation in which the emotions can become aroused, it could very well be impossible to control them, like when a crack in a dam, you allow that crack to stay there, you see, the water's going to come crashing through. That's what could happen. You must *think*, Frankie! Think! That would be awful for you, Frankie, so you need to be prepared. You have to decide ahead of time that you won't allow yourself to get into a situation where the emotions can gain the upper hand."

They had been talking at this same table not that long ago. Frankie had looked her mother in naked astonishment: "Crack in the dam?" she asks, with just the whisper of scorn in her voice.

Millie stares at her uncomprehending. Frankie continues, her voice louder and impatient: "I'm a dam? There's a crack in my dam? There *might* be a crack in my dam? The water could come crashing through? Unless I take care of the crack in my damn dam?"

Millie remembered how shocked she was when her daughter had spoken like that. "Frances Katherine!"

Then Frankie says, "Mom, do you ever listen to yourself?" She leaves the table and goes to her room. She's not at all angry. It's more like resignation, the resignation of one who knows her mother still has so much to learn.

Millie had sat at the table after Frankie left pondering her daughter's last question. Yes, she did listen to herself. Actually in this case, the person she'd been listening to had been *her* mother who had had the petting conversation with *her* when she was Frankie's age. Her mother had framed the discussion differently. Millie's body is a *temple*—a sacred temple. This temple is holy. It must be kept clean *and the doors locked*. Not just anyone should come in to her temple to worship. She had said to her mother: "The doors locked?"

Oh, dear! Millie smiles. Gracious sakes!

So Millie had had the *talk*. It is her responsibility as Frances' mother. But she knows that all her words are as valuable to Frankie as Monopoly money. Her words are not the currency Frankie wants to spend. It's like trying to deal dollars in Denmark. Frankie inhabits another country where the language, culture and currency are different than anything Millie understands, but a country in which Frankie on the other hand is a naturalized citizen. She will go her own way—like all adolescents do—and somehow she'll survive her mistakes and build upon her successes. And Frankie will have more than one success, of that Millie is confident.

Vickie returns to the table with her milk and her pancake robin. "What's lace mitts, Pops?"

"Well—"

# # #

No further discussion ensues of the physical attributes of Marie Wilson or of her acting career. It is decided Frankie will not go to the movies, but will attend the roller skating party in Charles City sponsored by the CCYF, but she'll need to complete her homework as no homework is allowed on the Lord's Day, bake a cake for Sunday dinner dessert, do the vacuuming and color the oleo. Vickie has to clean up her room, do homework, gather dirty clothes for the Monday wash and pick up after Tippy in the yard. Perhaps she can go with her grandfather on some visits in the afternoon. Millie is going to do some Avon-ing, orders she'd been unable to deliver the day before.

"What about the writing contest?" Millie asks. "The entrance form is due next week, right?"

"It's almost done," Frankie says without emotion to show she is not angry, that she was in total control of her feelings—which is her invariable response when she is angry, and thus a transparent ploy easily recognized by her mother and Pops. "Except I can't decide on a topic."

"Do you have to decide now?"

"Yes 'cause they don't want there to be overlap. If there is they'll tell the kid they can't write about it 'cause someone else already has it."

"Um, you could write about what makes Bathington a great place to live in," Coop offers. He is on his third cup of coffee. The gas on the stove is off and Coop's pancake work is done. "Bathington has a lot of great qualities that makes it a swell place to live and grow up in."

"Or, hey," Millie adds, "Here's an idea! What about trying to identify one of the most important—uh, influential—figures in Bathington's history, and explain why you think he or she made the most important contribution to the city's existence."

Frankie listens expressionless. "Another idea," Coop says, "would be to predict what the next one hundred years might hold for Bathington. Maybe in 2052 it will be a city of 20,000 and every house will have one of those radios with pictures—"

"Televisions, Pops," says Frankie, wearily.

"Yeah, that's right. I know that! Televisions, and in color, too, and there won't be any more cars because everyone will have a flying machine—"

"Pops, it's speculation. I don't want to write about that. It's science fiction. It can't win."

The contest to which they allude is sponsored by the *Bathington Beacon-Gazette* as a part of the forthcoming Centennial Celebration in August. It is open to anyone 18 years of age or below, and the writers can enter in the Early Elementary division (grades 1-4), Upper Elementary (grades 5-8), or the High School division. No restrictions have been placed on subject matter, but obviously the winning entries will explore some connection to the town of Bathington on the occasion of the Centennial. The length of the essay can be no more than 3,000 words, no less than 1,500 for the High School division. The winning essay will be printed in the newspaper and the author awarded a cash prize of $50. The newspaper also reserves the right to publish an additional essay it considers to be print-worthy, but without a cash award.

They sit in silence for a few moments. Coop takes a sip of coffee. Millie munches on toast. And Vic fiddles with the pull string on the back of the teddy bear. "You like history," Coop says. "Perhaps you could write a general history of Bathington. That would be useful for generations to come."

"Yeah, well that's not too swell because it's been done before and the newspaper will have stories about the history of Bathington long before the Centennial even starts. It's too obvious. To have a chance at really winning I need to write something that will grab the attention of the judges before they even read a bloody word."

"Let's not talk like that," Millie says sharply.

"I heard Rev. Cushing say it," snaps Frankie. "Are you going to wash my mouth out with soap?"

"Frankie! Why are you so sassy this morning? You're being horrible. The Reverend has spent too much time in England, I think, sometimes I can't even understand what he's sayin'. He talks that way for fun."

"Frankie, your idea sounds good," Coop says, feeling put in his place. "What will get their attention then do you think?"

"What I'm thinking of doing is something on the *pre-history* of Bathington."

"The pre-history? Like the history before the history?"

"The story behind the story, or like the *real* reason behind the *apparent* reason, see, what everyone talks about. I read once about Thanksgiving and everyone believes—"

"—Roosevelt or Lincoln's Thanksgiving?" Coop asks, looking intently at his granddaughter so as to show more interest in her problem than he is actually feeling.

"Just a sec, Pops," Frankie says tartly. "If I may continue?"

"Please do," Coop says, amused. This child is an Emma Goldman with pimples.

"Everyone thinks it was started to celebrate the end of the harvest but the first one may have been to celebrate the massacre of the Penobscot Indians because they were savages after all."

"I've never heard of such a thing!" Millie exclaims, throwing up her hands, then pushing from the table. She goes to the toaster and inserts two more slices and turns to listen. Sunlight from the window above the sink catches the right side of her face, rendering half of her countenance dark and doubtful.

"That's the point. If I could write something no one's heard about maybe I'd have a chance at the fifty bucks. My essay would be about the people, our ancestors before they arrived in Bathington, who they were, what they did, and how they got here."

Millie returns to the table and begins to collect some of the breakfast dishes. She says, "Well that does sound *very* interesting, Frankie. I can't wait to read it." She pauses. "You're a good writer," she says.

"When's it gotta be done?" Vickie asks. She pops the bird's head, dripping with syrup, into her mouth and chews loudly.

"June 16."

"You're a cinch to win, sweetie! My money's on you!" Coop declares, looking about at the others with a triumphant glow. "Who are the judges, anyway?"

"The editor of the newspaper, Mr. Whatshisname—"

"Hughes."

"Hughes, and the old lady from church and some other people."

"Battleaxe Broughton!" Vickie yells, as though she's cheering, her arms in the air. Her dinner fork sticks out of her fist.

"Victoria!"

"What? That's what Frankie calls her."

"Frances! We don't talk like that about people. Mrs. Broughton is the President of Ladies Aid, and I guess she's chair of the Essay Judging Committee, too, isn't that right, Frankie?"

"That's right, ma'am," Frankie says, mocking.

"And she's the chair of the Centennial Committee, too," Coop notes.

"She's also a member of the state chapter of America For Americans committee," Millie adds.

"Hey, Pops," Vickie says, "you should get her to be the new church secretary!"

Everyone laughs except Frankie.

Vic sticks her finger in a little white plastic ring in the teddy bear's back. It is attached to a string. She pulls it out and releases it. The bear says, "Hello, my name is Teddy. What's yours?"

Chapter IV

Sunday, March 2, 1952

Up at 6:36 a.m. temp was 55° but the radio said it
could hit 65° and I believe it did. I'm sitting here
soaking my corns in Epsom salts. Today is the First
Sinday of Lent, I mean Sunday of Lent (the u and the
i are side by side, so that's an easy but revealing
error to make! Or appropriate error. Ha!). So I may
as well offer my mea culpas as far as the bulletin
is concerned. Actually, there were no typos or the
like that I know of. And I am sure they would've
been pointed out. The only problem is that I didn't
get a good seal on the stencil when I glued the two
halves together, and a black ink line showed up running up and down on the fold of the page. So that
wasn't good. But Millie foned to congratulate me on
my first one. I put a notice in the bulletin about
the need for a part time position in the church office the position being "Bulletin-doer." After
church, two people approached me, so I met with both
of them in the office. One was Mrs. Fredrika Solvig,
a stern widow. Her husband died in a farming accident. He was attaching a plow to the tractor on an
incline, and suddenly the tractor lurched back—it
might have slipped out of gear—hitting Sven and
throwing him off balance and those big back tires
rolled over him, crushing him. Funny how such absurd
things can happen. You wake up. The sun is shining,

the grass is green, the corn is growing, you're fit
and fiddle, but you don't know that you'll not live
to see another day. Shazaam! You're gone. Fredrika
still has family in Sweden. She speaks with a heavy
accent and is very proper. But I asked her how many
words a minute she could type, and she said she
weren't sure, about 20 she thought. Turns out she's
never actually typed anything, but she thought she
could learn how. She has a good heart. She worked
for phone company in Des Moines during the war and
her mother had a Halda typewriter on which she had
typed some letters she sent back to Stockholm. I
told her that the church was looking for someone who
had some typing skills already acquired, but should
this seem an impossible prerequisite I was sure we
would contact her later. She took this in a good
spirit. I am afraid with Mrs. Solvig typing the lit-
urgy would soon be in Swedish. The other applicant
was Gertie Johnson, a popsy in her thirties I would
say and has two very active little boys but a very
inactive husband on account of his being disabled
with a war injury. She has typing skills, 55 wpm she
said—although you can't type that fast when cutting
a stencil I told her. She wanted to know pretty
quick what the job paid, and I said $2.50 to do just
the bulletin. The job was thought to be something
one could get done in two-three hours. She was not
impressed with this rate and wondered if I could
talk the powers that be into giving her what the
church is giving me. I said Mrs. Johnson, I'm a volunteer! She said, "Well, for heaven's sake," and got
up and left. So as of today, I'm still looking for a
secretary. I've never looked this hard for a woman
since ... well, I've never looked hard for a woman.

# # #

While winter cracks and thaws its way into spring, ordinary life continues to be nurtured by its ordinary citizens doing what they do every ordinary day as they have for the past one hundred years, growing— inexorably— a town. The hamlet on the river became a village; the village a town; the town a town posturing as a city. It has matured like a maple, adding ring upon ring of pulp pushing its bark outward, spreading its branches wider and sending long tendrils into the substrata of the rich Iowa soil. Rev. Cushing is still preaching sermons, Carlton Cooper is still looking for a church secretary, Violet Crenshaw is yet preparing to blow town, Millie continues to teach school and Frankie is writing her essay. Vickie is still playing pretend, hopscotch or "Simon Says" when she's not skipping rope or spinning a top. Mrs. Clarice Broughton, chairman of the Centennial Committee, America for Americans, and the Board of Directors of the BSB, is never without something to do as well, and if there is nothing to do, she finds something about which she can at the very least voice an opinion or make a positive contribution. But there is no question right now that Broughton is preoccupied with only two things: the Centennial and communism.

The winter cold of February kept the ground frozen like the tundra in Alaska. The streets were covered in ice or packed snow. Saturdays Vic and the Waylon boy would trudge off to Hagee's Hollow with a sled and spend hours trudging up the hill and sledding down, only to return with Sisyphean optimism to the top and to do it all over again.

The universe in northern Iowa moved slowly in February. Nothing exciting happened in February except Valentine's Day, when there was a dance sponsored by the Lodge, and the high school had a dance, too. Millie was there as a chaperone to keep watch over a gymnasium of boys, their hair greased and proper and black shoes spit-shined, and the girls all dolled up in chiffon frocks or, more common, poodle skirts and saddle shoes. Other parents chaperoned as well, and even Rev. Cushing was present on account of he had been invited to say a prayer at the beginning. He didn't dance except for some bebopping and bunny hopping with Gertie Johnson, Millie archly observed. She didn't dance at all, although the marshal, Marshal Cutler, had invited her to take to the floor. Frankie did not attend because she hadn't been invited, except for the Harmon boy, who was a hood from West Bath—not that Frankie had anything against the hoods. Rondo was just a yuck of a person.

The feeling in February was that it was just plain cold, and the sun could pop up in the east and hang over the town as big as a yellow balloon and it wouldn't make no never mind. It just stayed cold, and on overcast days, the cold'd creep into your bones like a feral disease. Coop figures that for some reason—maybe it's their situation along the Clearwater River—February has more three dog nights than any other time of the year. He'd sit at his typewriter clattering out his daily dairy on these frigid evenings; but in this cold, typing a page on his Underwood is like pounding out a prelude on a Steinway in sub-zero temperatures. The fingers are clumsy, and the touch isn't there. Like he is wearing mittens.

Generally speaking, then, Coop's life has not been greatly altered since his interview with Crenshaw whom he seems to see more often coming and going out of the Fremont where she has a room on the second floor. He has greeted a couple of newcomers to the Fremont who are staying temporarily in rooms reserved for out-of-towners passing through. He often has lunch at Mary's Kitchen down the street, and he stops at the Snack Shoppe for candy for the girls. He helped Jules Joyce, who on weekends was usually goosed and in his cups, get to his fourth floor room across the hall by count five times in February alone. Once, he fell in front of his door and passed out cold. Coop could always tell how much Jules had had to drink according to the landing on which he collapsed. If Jules could get himself up the stairs to the top floor unaided, Coop knew that he hadn't tried too hard to get drunk.

And, every day he meanders down to Millie's, which, after all, was his and Antonia's house a long time ago.

During this time Frankie begins her work on the Bathington essay, spending hours at both the high school and town libraries. Some newspaper accounts still survive from the 50th anniversary back in 1902. From this she is able to develop a few paragraphs which she shows to no one except her best friend, Naomi. "You should show it to my dad," Naomi says earnestly one day as they are walking from school to Shimel's house across the river in West Bath. "He used to do theatre on weekends and stuff and read lots of scripts. And he's studied Torah. He's very smart." Naomi has dark straight hair, coal black eyes in which flashes of light can erupt like fire. Her skin is Palestinian tan and as smooth as stone. She prefers jeans to dresses, and wears a choker around her neck made of buttons of many colors and a silver bracelet on her left wrist. Like Frankie, she is *serious*. "Really, Frankie, it wouldn't hurt to have a professional look at it." Frankie says she'll show it to her teacher. But Naomi insists.

The Shimels live across the river in West Bath, as locals called it, where the houses are small, decrepit, patchwork boxes tucked into tufts of timber still standing from the Reconstruction; they sit back off the road under oaks and cottonwoods as though embarrassed to be seen. Every lawn has its peculiar ornaments, the detritus of accumulated life, such as car and truck tires, Valvoline oil cans, toilet seats, car batteries, wood piles, trash cans, and on the porch there might be a seat pulled from a pickup which could be used on mild evenings to relax and smoke. It is in West Bath that railroad coolies had lived and coloreds had squatted on the run en route to St. Paul. The Chinese and coloreds, except for the Watson family, have disappeared, but farmhands and others continue to populate West Bath. Naomi has a room of her own and lives with her parents, Mr. and Mrs. Joel Shimel (Ruth), on a small and narrow dirt lane that when the snow is gone is bounded by thin grass or ragweed. Their house comes with a small barn which once served as a livery and an all-purpose shed for a pickup or car, but Shimel parks his 1936 Ford on the front lawn and he has turned the garage into a shop where he sets up his sewing machines and stores bolts of fabric, working days and evenings making men's suits, dress trousers or dinner jackets. He can't make a living catering only to Bathington residents, so he's hired himself out as a farmhand, while filling orders from customers he still has in New York. Ruth takes in washing and ironing which she does while helping with some of the routine sewing chores in the shop. He receives mail orders with measurements filled out on a form and he sends the product back through the post. But his business grows, because people who had known Joel Shimel in New York have advertised his talents to friends in the midwest, and over the few years since they've been in Bathington, four years now, he has had plenty to do. He learned his craft from his father who worked in the garment district and, as a boy in New York, he had jobs pushing carts laden with suits, coats and dresses up the streets in midtown and soon was learning how to sew on a machine.

Frankie and Naomi have been friends since the Shimels arrived in town four years ago—a little more than a fourth of her lifetime. The only reason she knows that the Shimels are Jewish is that she heard Pops telling her parents that he'd invited the Shimels to church, but that they couldn't go because they are Jewish, which is why they go down to Des

Moines at least once a month to synagogue there. That's when Frankie sought out Naomi, who, like Frankie, is a junior in high school, if for no other reason than she was curious. And when she meets Naomi's parents, she realizes that they do not at all look like or even act like Jews. They are neither skinny nor swarthy; they don't have hooked noses and curly hair; neither one of them plays the violin; they've never been in the banking or diamond business. And they don't wear funny clothes.

The half born essay goes to Naomi's father. He is in his shop at a machine over which hangs a bright light. It is on a large table in the center of the room, on which are patterns, pins, pin cushions, measuring tapes, a yardstick, a T-square, snips and scissors. Frankie has never stepped inside this miniature factory. Against one wall are shelves on which are stacked bolts of fabrics of many colors and textures. There are several sewing machines, a pounding block, irons, hundreds of pegs on which are spools of thread. Boxes on the floor are stuffed with patterns. Overhead, electrical wires run spaghetti-like hither and yon. The scent, the smell of a tailor's shop, is something she's never encountered: Light aroma of cinnamon with a whiff of apple, she thinks.

Mr. Shimel takes the two pages from Frankie's hands. Shimel is wearing a white blouse with puffy sleeves, and over this, a black vest unbuttoned. He is stout and pudgy. His hands are fleshy and his fingers short like sausages. There is a reason he did not become a violinist. Black hair grows like brush bristles from the tops of his fingers. He does not consider himself bald, but this is the description others give of him. He denies it like he denies other things in his life, such as that his wife does not look at him with longing any more. His face is round and full and belligerent. His nose is thick and pocked and looks like it is affixed to his face by plumber's putty. His nostrils flare horizontally. He is not by any means a handsome man, Frankie thinks, but she senses that he is a good man and one who is accustomed to interruptions which he suffers with patience. And he must be a good man because Naomi loves him.

She steps back as he begins to read. She moseys around the shop like a tourist in a museum, inspecting, admiring, wondering, craning her head for better looks, refocusing her eyes to gain a perspective here or there, before moving on to something else.

The first of the Bathingtons in America was probably a native of Bristol, England, because in 1640 he mortgaged his farm to "Humphrey Hooke, alderman of Bristol." There may have been other Bathingtons in the New World before Thomas Bathington, but this is where the Bathington line of the Bathington, Iowa, Bathingtons begins. Our first forefather was born about 1595. Tradition gives him a doubtful grandfather, Richard, and a great-grandfather, William. In 1629, he came to Boston either with John Endicott or in Governor Winthrop's fleet, bringing with him four children and servants. No record is found mentioning his wife, on account of she no doubt passed before the migration to America and her death may have been a factor in the decision to leave.

So widower Thomas, or Goodman Bathington, as he was called, settled in Saugus, Massachusetts, and had sons and daughters and prospered. But later generations pushed to Paris, New York, and then on to Rockford, Illinois, and finally across the Mississippi to Iowa, settling on the Clearwater, and establishing trade for those passing north from Des Moines or Cedar Rapids, or to the same from Minneapolis or Austin in the other direction. That was about 1830 and by 1850 Bathington, as it was now called, had grown from an unnoticed village of fifty or sixty souls to a small town of more than two hundred. By then the Meskawki, Otoe, Ioway, Ho-Chunk and all the Indians, except for the Dakotas, had not only been cleared out of Clearwater County, but the entire state of Iowa.

In 1852, Bathington was officially incorporated in Clearwater County ...

"That's all I have right now," Frankie says when Mr. Shimel puts the pages down and looks up from his perch in his chair behind the sewing machine. She is wearing a simple brown pleated cotton skirt, white socks and saddle shoes, and a white collared blouse over which she'd pulled a loose-fitting V-neck sweater. Her hair above her left ear is pulled back and tied with a yellow ribbon. She stands expectantly with her hands in the folds of her skirt. "Very good, then … alright, a good start," he says, pushing his glasses up atop the ridge of his nose. "Of course it needs an introduction," she explains, "but I want to get the body of the essay on paper to see what I have, and then I can write an introduction and conclusion better tailored to the essay itself."

"Is it going to be interesting? Or is this a boring, stuffy essay that would, like … be in an academic journal or something?" Frankie stares at him blankly and realizes that she isn't really prepared to answer questions about her essay; she certainly had not thought she'd need to defend it. She regrets showing it to him.

"Father, really!" Naomi protests. She has been standing over his shoulder as he was reading. Now she steps around to face him and she snatches the papers out of his hands. Shimel looks at his daughter. "What? I can't express an opinion?" he asks with a shrug. "It's not a criticism, just a question. For me, this is not too interesting. It's history. It's HISTORY!" Addressing Frankie who keeps her distance, he says, gesturing with open palms, "The writing is very good. It's the content I am talking about. This is history. You like history? You must like history 'cause that's what this is. Now you probably need to provide some historical background before you get to the interesting part so that people will understand the context, right? But maybe, on the other hand, your purpose is to write something more scholarly that would interest people who are only interested in history. See some people, as you probably know, will read a fat book about, for example, the history of a Sumerian funeral dirge, because it happens to interest them. There are probably five such people in the world. That's fine. I think the writing is very good in your paper, Miss Cooper. And you know where you're going with this. I hope for the sake of those who are reading on the judges' panel and those who might read this in the newspaper that you can lighten it up a bit and get something in there that connects with people, you know?"

Frankie glumly concedes that he has a point.

The two chums trudge next door to the Watson's shanty. Ben and Molly Watson have two children, Jimmie, their 6-year-old son, and Tink, their 12-year-old daughter. Ben and Molly had very little schooling when they were growing up and Tink's education is limited. To rectify this situation, Naomi and Frankie have taken it on themselves to tutor Tink, hoping that within a year they can get her into school. Bathington is a northern town, but no coloreds have ever sat in a Bathington school, and Ben isn't of a mind to press the point. Times are changing, but the memories—the memories of fading traditions, well, those linger. Ben had an uncle who was lynched in Readlyn back in 1932. And a colored man who doesn't understand the way things are, is a colored man who will probably be taught a lesson. Not that anyone dislikes the Watsons. They keep to themselves and work hard and there hadn't been any trouble for a long time, except for when Frankie and Naomi took Tink to the movies. But that got resolved after the girls threatened to organize a boycott of the theatre. Ben can do just about anything whether it's changing storm windows, carpentrying a porch, shoeing a horse, delivering calves or lambs. "Why, Ben Watson is just about the most talented man in town," Coop told Frankie once. And Molly, like Ruth Shimel, takes in washing, ironing and mending, and sometimes she'll assist Joel Shimel with some of his tailoring projects. Tink's a *black* colored, as black as coal and teeth as white as ivory. When she smiles, the whole room lights up. Millie provides the girls with the curriculum—on loan from the school, she says— and they enjoy playing teacher and giving instruction. For her part, Tink is eager to learn. The three have a bond that goes beyond the racial and class distinctions of Bathington. Theirs is a sisterhood, and the three of them talk about everything from their parents to their periods; their friends and their enemies; the boys they like and those they despise; their hopes and fears.

Their high school is no more egalitarian than Bathington itself. The strata of the town are mirrored in the micro-culture of the classroom. The school has its rich kids, its poor kids, as well as the jocks and the eggheads or four-eyes. It is populated by the shy and withdrawing as well as the bold and brash; the hoods and slutty girls who hang out with them; the righteous goody-two shoes, and the irreligious and scoffers. Naomi and Frankie maneuver adroitly through this kaleidoscope of cultural diversity without giving it too much thought. They are gifted with an uncommon sense of individual freedom. They are beholden to their parents and to God, respectful of their teachers, but care little about what others think of them. "You can always do whatever you want," Naomi would say to Frankie and Tink, "as long as you're prepared to pay the price. That's right. Isn't that amazing? *Whatever you want.* But you has to be willing to pay the price. You better know what the price is, though, because sometimes it's pretty steep."

This cultural disconnect or failure to be socialized in any way approaching normal often manifested itself in surprising, sometimes shocking, ways—especially when the girls spoke their minds ... as, for example, when Frankie attended a meeting of the Centennial Committee.

Chapter V

CLARICE BROUGHTON IS QUITE UNAWARE THAT some of
the village children call her Battleaxe Broughton behind her back. Had
she been apprised of this information she would have smiled; the
knowledge would have confirmed her own view that Mrs. Harold
Broughton is a woman to be reckoned with. In a rare moment of sobrie-
ty, Jules once declared to Coop, when they traveled to Waterloo to attend
the Cattle Congress, that there are two kinds of women in the world:
Those who need money and must save it in order to spend it, and those
who have money and spend it because there is no need to save it. Mrs.
Broughton belongs to the latter caste. She is a woman for whom one
makes way, for she is of generous proportions with a florid, bejowled
face of soft, rather than angular, features. Her nose is pleasantly formed,
powdered and perfectly suited to her disposition which occasionally laps-
es into the amiable. Her eyes are bright and intelligent. Her mouth is wide
and gravity has unfortunately shaped it as an upside down half moon giving her countenance a dour aspect except when she smiles, and then her
entire face appears to lift and be altered in appearance as though she'd
donned a mask. Her lips are red and usually parted. Scarlet Passion is her
shade. Today she's put on earrings of topaz, and around her neck, falling
lightly on a white blouse, is a single strand of pearls—a gift from her late
husband who'd picked them up while in the diplomatic corps in Formosa
during the war. She is wearing a tailored blue suit of worsted wool, this
being winter. She has no spring wardrobe, for Mrs. Clarice Broughton
does not mothball her clothes from year to year. Her spring outfits are in
production at this very moment. Her hair, although thinning, is platinum
and waved, an effect that requires the talented ministrations of a cos-
metologist in Cedar Falls. She is the frequent subject of churlish gossip,
but this, too, does not surprise her but rather flatters her. She is accustomed to devoting considerable attention to herself and takes pleasure in

knowing that she is the object of grapevine *reportage*. This dedication to her appearance is not, in itself, a defect in her character, which, it is universally agreed, is sterling and above reproach. Although a woman of Rubenesque dimensions, she has become comfortable with her tonnage; but, knowing that her best feature is her head, she never fails to appear in public without a hat and today she is wearing a black straw weave hat with front netting and adorned with a chartreuse bow that matches her suit nicely. To her face she applies the utmost diligence, resorting to whatever cosmetic assistance is required so as to maintain her reputation as a doyenne of distinction.

In this latter role, she attends a meeting of the Centennial Committee. She is stunningly over-dressed, wearing attire more suited to a funeral than a committee meeting of farmers and mothballers. The group is meeting in the large oak-paneled parlor of the ivied manse. Two tables have been brought in for the occasion. They are crunched together. A linen tablecloth is thrown over both creating the effect of a single table. Attendees have already munched on desserts furnished by Millie and others, including Millie's three-layered frosted prune cake, Broughton's Depression salad, Fredrika Solvig's apple strudel and Hazel Hemming's delectable pork cake which hints of a double measure of brandy.

Coop and Millie are on the committee as is Frankie, by virtue of her being the president of the CCYF of her church—representing the youth, the future of Bathington, the leaders of tomorrow. Frankie and her grandfather mill about waiting for the session to begin. Coop points to three portraits hanging high along one wall. All three are of white-bearded men. "You know who they are, Frankie?" he asks, looking at her.

"Former preachers of this church?" she says quickly.

"That's right! How'ja know?"

"I've been here before, Pops."

"Yes sirree, that one on the left is Reverend Hiram Latham, 1925-1941. The man in the middle is Reverend Philip Lauten, 1914-1925. And the third one is Reverend Paul Crane, 1899-1914. Do you notice anything different about him, about the way he's seated?"

Frankie studies the portrait for a few moments. She shrugs. "I don't know."

"Look at his hands." She steps forward to get a closer look. Reverend Crane is a burly man with a short white beard, and long white hair, sharp features and deep-set eyes. His chest and stomach push out against a tight black vest. A gold chain swings across a row of buttons and disappears into a vest pocket. His chubby hands rest on his thighs. He is looking away from the camera.

"Nope," she says, turning back to look at her grandfather. "Don't see anything."

"The fingers of his right hand," he says.

"What about them?" Frankie asks, looking again.

"Well, see how his forefinger and middle finger are parted?"

"Yeah, what of it?"

"What of it?! There used to be a fine Cuban cigar in those fingers."

Frankie is surprised. "Really!? What happened?"

Coop chuckles and they turn away and walk slowly. "In the thirties, the fundamentalists thought that cigar shouldn't be there, so they had it painted out, that's all."

"That was stupid," Frankie says in her usual understated way.

"No, not stupid. Every generation seems to have its own sense of propriety. I wouldn't be surprised if another generation will paint it back in, restoring it to its original appearance."

"I'll paint it back in," Frankie offers.

Broughton brings the meeting to order. Cushing says a prayer. Broughton then asks Millie Cooper to read the minutes, which she does in her teacher's voice, after which the minutes are approved as read. Then reports are accepted, mostly updates, some of which requires brief discussion. Millie heads up the Publicity Committee and has created a logo contest among the upper elementary students that will be used in all publicity for the centennial. Some question the wisdom of placing the centennial in the hands of children who are so young, volatile and sprouting acne. She says she is still looking for a printer for posters and flyers. Coop is in charge of the pageant which for now has the working title of "Celebrating our Past; Preparing for our Future." It will not be too ambitious, in Coop's mind. Just some characters dressed up in bathrobes and towels, some songs and speeches. Joel Shimel has volunteered to make some of the important pageant costumes, Coop says, his reference to bathrobes notwithstanding, which will dignify the presentation considerably and, as he has had some acting experience off Broadway when in New York, there is a strong possibility he'll play one of Bathington's founding fathers. Following the pageant there'll be a dance featuring the Blue Moon Trio. But this is just the tassel on the corn. There is also the Centennial banquet, the golf tournament in Charles City, and the concluding picnic and pig roast Saturday afternoon complete with dignitaries from Des Moines and plenty of speeches.

"Old-fashioned family fun," says Dan Faulkner, a hog farmer five miles east of town who is donating the first porker but charging very little for the others that will be needed.

"I'm not sure we need to involve Shimel, do we?" The speaker is Art Bandy, Assistant Vice President and Senior Loan Officer at Bathington State Bank. He is a thin man with a narrow frightened face supported by a wobbly neck around which is a starched collar tightened by a tie which caused his chin wattle to hang like a piece of turkey grizzle. His comment is met with a murmur after which he adds nervously, "I mean, he's not a *Christian*, is he?"

"Don't know about vat, but he's an excellent tailor," says Solvig emphatically.

"No disrespect," says Bandy, "but he's sort of new here, too." His eyes flit back and forth and around like bats at dusk; he's looking for support from others around the table.

"No disrespect, Art," says Reverend Cushing crisply, "but he's an *American,* and a shirt's a shirt, a blouse is a blouse is a blouse. What's his religion got to do with it?"

"Well, he may be an American and maybe not," says Broughton, raising her body stiffly.

"What's that supposed to mean?"

"I don't mean to suggest anything unkind or outside the realm of facts, Reverend. I would simply note that he has not offered his signature on the Loyalty Oath, there are some questions about his experience in New York, and I think we all agree that he doesn't seem to fit in here, like a fish out of water, although to be fair, not fitting in is certainly no crime."

"I have not signed the Oath either, and won't, and as for fitting in, it seems to me that it's not his job to fit in with us, but our job to fit in with him. Our Christian duty is to welcome the stranger, not throw him out of town."

"Point taken," Broughton continues, clearing her throat, "but—since we're citing Scripture here—we're also to be aware of the wolves among us in sheep's clothing. And I understand there's a problem with the town regarding his business which he's operating out of his garage without a license. All this adds up to the perception—just a *perception* mind you—of a problem, a problem which under normal circumstances we can overlook, but which we might want to avoid during the centennial celebration … in the interest of harmony and unity."

Cushing rises to the challenge. His thin jaw is firm, his eyes narrow with intensity. He takes the measure of people around the table. "It's hardly appropriate to imply that Shimel is a wolf. He's a U.S. citizen, he resides and has resided in our town for several years, he does honorable work, and he's applied for the license, but the town has been remarkably slow to produce it. He's no different than any of us, who are all unique in our preferences, values, heritage and background. I'm still not clear on just what it is that would disqualify him from sewing some trousers and blouses for the pageant or playing a role on the stage. We're not asking him to make a speech or represent the town in some official capacity, although I would have no objection if we were."

"He's Jewish for one thing," counters Bandy, "and that certainly makes him different, and if you ask me, this country is becoming the Jewnited States of America as it is, together with its capital, Jew York, Jew York."

This comment, like a match thrown on a puddle of gasoline, results in an immediate flash fire of outrage and protest. "Oh, for pity sakes, Mr. Bandy," Broughton exclaims, exasperated, "that's quite enough." The stir and murmuring is such that it is impossible for any single voice to be heard above the rest, and Coop and Millie, Violet Crenshaw and others are speaking vainly into the din. Into this cacophony, Frankie mutters, "We all immigrants, anyway." But her comment is uttered at the very instant when everyone has stopped to take a breath before resuming the brouhaha and consequently her words are quite distinct and no one says a further word. Broughton, however, asks for clarification: "What did you say, dear?"

Frankie is silent, head down, eyes averted.

"Yes, Frankie? It's quite alright. I just didn't quite catch it. My hearing sometimes, well it comes and goes, and lately it seems like it's been going more than coming. Go ahead, speak up."

"Thank you, ma'am. It's just that I don't see any Injuns here today—in this room."

The murmuring rises again. "*Whatever* do you mean, child?" Broughton asks in a most kindly way, touching her hat casually as though to indicate to all that this discussion is nothing about which to be concerned and that indeed it is rather inconsequential.

"What don't you understand?"

Millie tries clunking her daughter's feet with her own under the table. She whispers urgently, "Frankie, pleeeease." Whereupon Millie's father-in-law uses one of his feet to tap on Millie's before saying *sotto voce*, "Let her be, Millie, let her be. I think she's on to something. This could be fun!" They were tromping and tapping below the table deck more vigorously than an organist playing a Bach fugue at First Congregational in Cedar Falls.

"I mean, Frankie dear," Broughton continues fulsomely, "that *of course* thar no ... Indians in this room!" There is a snuffle of laughter at this announcement. No one wants to giggle too much out of respect for Millie and Coop. "What does that have to do with the, well, the matters at hand?"

"Then, we are all, every one of us, immigrants, or at least the children of immigrants, right? Every one of us is here in this room right now because at some point in the past our ancestors left their homes—in Italy, Sweden, England, Germany, Russia, Palestine—because they thought America was a place where they would fit in and make a life for themselves. Every one of us. Unless one of us is an Injun. They's the only ones to whom this land rightfully belongs. Seems to me that if we reject Mr. Shimel, we're rejecting ourselves, that's all. What's so hard to understand about that?"

This soliloquy delivered from the mouth of a babe is met with stunned and guilty silence. And then Broughton answers:

"That's a *very* beautiful thought," she says evenly. Her fingers caresses her hat once again, but this time it is as though to adjust the crown, in a Victorian "We-are-not-amused" sort of way. She continues: "Yes, we are all immigrants as you say. It's a very novel idea. And I like it! Which is saying a lot for me, as most of you know that I usually don't care too much for a lot of so-called *novel* ideas that are bandied about these days. So much flapdoodle, if you ask me." The room fills with some appreciative chuckles at Broughton's attempt at self-deprecating humor. "Be that as it may, the truth is that times change, my dear, whether we like it or not. And Mr. Bandy's intemperate and ill-considered remarks notwithstanding, we have to consider what is right and proper for ourselves *today* in this *modern* era. And I should also say that I am hoping that we might be honored with the presence at our centennial of the honorable junior Senator from Wisconsin, and I think it might be awkward if our celebration were to be marred by the energetic participation of those who have not thoroughly embraced the American way of life. That's what I see. But I also see—"

"Begging your pardon, ma'am," Frankie says without understanding that she's just interrupted Mrs. Clarice Broughton, "if I may say so, as citizens of the modern era as you say we are, we'd better not forget the very principles upon which our modern state was founded and has made it great—I learned this in U.S. History class last year with Mr. Harbaugh—like Jefferson's idea, for example, enshrined in the Declaration of Independence, a document secured by the blood of our forefathers, that all men are created equal, or the French ideals of liberte, egalite and fraternite—ideas incidentally, which were borrowed from our own revolution—or even Jesus' words that we should love our neighbors as ourselves. I don't think there's any time in human history, *modern or not*, when we can forget or ignore these ideals—they made us the great country we are today—and if we do forget them … well, we're in big, big trouble, is what I say."

Millie realizes that she has scarcely been breathing as Frankie was speaking. Now she silently and slowly lets out her breath. Her face feels flushed. She looks at her hands resting on the table one inside the other. They are clenched. She relaxes. She is utterly astonished at what she's just heard, and not just the content, but the maturity of these words, and the form of expression, and the fluidness of their delivery. This from a 16-year-old girl! Who is this child? Millie thinks she has underestimated her, an idea which makes her cringe and feel as though she's failed as mother. Why should she worry about Frankie wanting to see *A Girl in Every Port*? It seems silly to her now. This child is advancing into intellectual frontiers that she herself has never thought of exploring. And she is amazed that her daughter apparently has no fear of speaking out, that she apparently feels not the least intimidated by sitting at a table with her elders, and not the least reticent in expressing her opinion as though she is an equal among equals. *Oh! If Johnny could be here right now!* She blinks consciously to disperse welling tears, but her cheeks are moist nonetheless.

Coop, meanwhile, watches the Chairman. He notices that, as Frankie is speaking, her eyes narrowed slightly and her eyebrows dropped almost imperceptibly, but to him it is clear. Over Broughton's face there has now appeared a cloud, or an air of stern regality. Like Millie, her hands lay on the table before her, one in the other, but they are completely relaxed, although she is playing absentmindedly with the large diamond on her wedding finger.

Cushing thinks he could not possibly have expressed his own opinion better than Frankie has expressed hers, and his mind conjures up the image of the 12-year-old Jesus schooling the Scribes and Pharisees in the Law and the Prophets. A nation of immigrants! He has never thought of the country like this. Interesting.

"Miss Cooper, that was expressed most beautifully. You certainly have a gift with words. And what you say is so ... so very true. So very true. But a truth uttered is not necessarily the truth completed," Broughton says censoriously. "While I could not agree more with the Jeffersonian principles of liberty, equality, and brotherhood, what concerns many in our country right now are those in our very midst, mind you, who abuse these democratic ideals, espousing dangerous notions and scurrilous political agendas which threaten to undermine the very truths you've so eloquently mentioned. I cannot but believe we are all agreed on this, and that the difference may only be a difference of emphasis not of substance. But, as I was going to say before you so *thankfully* interrupted me, is that this is a discussion we would be wise to table and refer to the Executive Committee, and if this body will delegate this matter and other similar issues to the ExCom, that would help smooth the process of ensuring that this wonderful celebration of our first 100 years goes smoothly. I would entertain a motion to that effect."

The motion carries.

The reports continue. Bandy says the bank is throwing in $100, and he already has pledges from fifteen businesses in Bathington and intends to solicit support from some enterprises in neighboring towns. Private donations are also sought, and no taxpayer money will be used for the celebration.

Other matters are discussed. Beulah Bradley offers a report of the Carnival and Fair Committee concerning the rides, games, and the temporary "jail" where citizens in violation of the centennial spirit—failure to grow a beard, for example—would be incarcerated for a brief period, unless bail money was paid, money which would be donated to charity. There would be street performers, jugglers, clowns, unicyclers, a stilt man, buskers, acrobats, strolling mandolin players, etc. Throughout the weekend, a fair would be in progress in which cooking, baking and gardening contests would be held and ribbons awarded as prizes.

The Parade Committee announces that some eighty-five floats had been entered for the parade. The high school band would march and play. There would be a glass lantern demonstration, a pancake breakfast sponsored by the Lodge, a photo board of families and old buildings. The Hospitality Committee is sending out invitations to dignitaries and will be responsible for providing housing for them during their stay. An Official Photographer will be hired. Sunday morning there will be a combined worship service, the Rev. Cushing presiding, a service which would be held in a large tent set up on the high school football field. The Equipment & Facilities Committee has secured the very tent in which the late baseball player turned evangelist Billy Sunday preached his first revival in Garner, and under the same canvas the first of his tens of thousands of converts hit the sawdust trail and knelt at the mourner's bench. All the churches in the area had agreed to cooperate except the Catholics and the Pilgrim Holiness group which meets in West Bath in a converted barn. The Fire Chief was in charge of Sunday night fireworks display, the event which would bring the weekend to a close.

# # #

Coop thinks that perhaps it is this unusual arctic cold that is responsible for his lack of success in the last week of February in drumming up any interest in the typist job. And March isn't any better, although he had some interest and a few interviews. In addition to Fredrika and Gertie, he was visited while working in the office on a Saturday morning by Mrs. Mabel Mang. His visitor was wearing a pale yellow dress with a wide plastic belt of the same hue cinched around her tiny waist. The dress had a collar that flared around her neck over which her hair—blondish—fell nicely. The lipstick was red, but subdued. Her face was perfectly proportioned and her eyes blue and earnest. She was wearing shiny yellow heels, and her hose was runless, and seams straight. Coop knew because of his work on the Membership Roll that she was in her 40s, but she could easily pass for 35. She was a simple, beautiful woman, Coop knew that. Beautiful, but simple. How often those adjectives seemed to be paired. Or, conversely, plain, but smart. Plain, like Crenshaw, but clever. Her vocabulary, Coop had learned, consisted of a mix of four words, sweet, adorable, cute and delicious, which were usually applied to babies, dogs or food. Mabel's husband, Max, was a doctor in General Practice in Charles City.

They'd raised two boys who were now grown and out of the house. But when Coop saw who his inquirer was, he knew immediately that she was unsuited for the position because Mrs. Mang had an unenviable reputation as the town tattler, Bathington's matron of mendacity, and it would be impossible to install this flibbertigibbet in an office through which many of the town's secrets passed. Before the morning was over—she stayed to help fold the bulletins—Coop learned that Widow Brown has not heard from her son, Roy, who's gone out to Wyoming to work the oil fields, for more than two years. That Hatty Nordman believes in UFOs. That Mr. and Mrs. Sid Wedeking are about to lose their house to the bank on account of his drinking. And that Shorty Hoffman went to the dentist to have his left molar extracted, and the dentist had pulled the wrong one.

"You understand that anyone working in this office must have absolute respect for the principles of confidentiality," Coop says. "Nothing said *here* can be repeated *there*," he says, pointing to the street.

"Oh my Lord, of course!" Mabel exclaims, throwing her hands in the air. "You are so *adorable!* Why do you think I've mentioned these things? If we cannot bring these concerns to the attention of good Christian people who care and who can lift these poor souls, bless them, to the Lord in *prayer*—and we know that there's power in prayer, don't we?— then what are we to do? I suppose it would not be good for the word to get out that there are so many sinners in the church, I can see that for sure. But that's what the church is for, right? It's like a hospital for sinners, is it not?"

"Good point, Mrs. Mang, but you don't want to offer a cure that's worse than the disease, do you? Sometimes it's best if the patient's disease is not known to the general public, because that could be hurtful to the patient and not particularly edifying for the public."

"Oh, I think you're so right, Mr. Cooper. That's where a body needs to have—what does Rev. Cushing call it?—*discernment!* A person's got to know when they need the full help and prayer support of the church community and when it's best just to let, well, to just let the professionals handle it, don't you think?"

Coop jigged the bulletins into two nice stacks and moved them aside. Mrs. Mang is seated at the table across from him. He looks toward the door and then leans in closer to her. "Let me give you an example, Mrs. Mang. I wouldn't tell this to anyone but you—on account of you being such a prayer warrior and all. But this is in the strictest confidence mind you, and must not be repeated to a living soul, understood?"

Mabel Mang cranes forward, their heads now earnestly over the center of the table. They look into each other's eyes. "Oh, yes! Mercy!" she exclaims. "Not a word! Not a word!"

"You know Bob and Hazel Goodnow?"

Mrs. Mang shakes her head. "The name sounds familiar, but I can't place them. But I don't know everybody in this town."

"They've only been in Bathington a couple years and they stick to themselves, that's for sure. They haven't been to church for some time now. And even when they came, it was very infrequent. He's a Fuller Brush guy and is out of town a lot—and well, that's another story, if you know what I mean—"

"—I do, oh, I do!"

"But they have a daughter, 17, name's Clare. They said that she'd gone back to Boston on a student exchange program. She's been gone since last September. She started school right here at Bathington High, but then this exchange opportunity came through. At least that's the story the *public*, the curious public we were talking about, you know—that's the story they're giving the public. But, truth is, the poor child was with child, and has since delivered, and is now making arrangements for the adoption. I assume we'll see her this summer, and that there will be an official account of her time with the exchange program, and she will finish her senior year beginning next fall."

Coop leans back in his chair. Mabel remains transfixed, her eyes wide and mouth agape.

"Those poor souls," she cries. "Oh my! How perfectly dreadful! Now *there's* a family that needs prayer! I'll bet it was that Harmon boy who got her in a family way."

"Can you understand that were the truth to be publicly broadcast about this tragic situation that it would be harmful to the girl and needlessly hurtful to the parents?"

"Yes, yes, yes!" She pushes back from the table and stands up and smoothes her dress. "Thank you ever so much, Mr. Cooper."

"May I call on you in case there's an emergency some time?"

He knows that he'll never call Mrs. Mang. There will never be an emergency so grave as to necessitate a phone call to a woman who never

met a secret she could keep. Whisper something into her ear in Bathington today and it would be a headline in Sioux City tomorrow.

Mrs. Mang leaves in a hurry.

# # #

Although his first worship bulletin published for the First Sunday of Lent
had only been marred by a black line running down the fold of the page,
the next few versions seem to decline in quality. The black line disappears
indicating that Coop has solved the problem of getting a good seal, but
now there are faint black lines that flow across the page looking like rivers and tributaries on a topographical map. This indicates that he's had
trouble getting the stencil laid on the drum smoothly and without wrin-
kles. Mistakes also appeared. IMPORTANT ANNOUNCEMENT was
IMPOTANT ANNOUNCEMENT. Rev. Cushing becomes Rev. Cuss-
ing, untied for united and trinty for trinity, Sun for Son and so on.
Meanwhile, Gertie Johnson has taken to circling the mistakes in red and
leaving the proof marks on his desk in the church office. Coop takes all
this in stride, but the mistakes are vexing. Of course, it is not as though
he has not seen some of them prior to print. But upon discovering a mistake, he faces a three-fold choice: One, he can use correction fluid and
attempt a revision. This method has the advantage of alerting the reader
that the typist has at least spotted the error and has endeavored to amend
it. Unfortunately, many times, the correction appears as a small black
blob on the printed page, like a tiny Rorschach test. Second, he can type a
another stencil so as to type the misspelled word correctly on the re-do.
This, however, has the disadvantage of providing yet another opportunity
to make a different mistake while amending the original one. Third, he
can leave it as it is, warts and all, and beg pardon. By and large, Coop opts
for the third choice. And by and large, the congregation is sympathetic.
After all, he is no Violet Crenshaw.

Violet herself is the most soothing in her treatment of the railroad
man *cum* typist. She always speaks to him after the service with high
praise and appreciation. Coop is happy for the encouragement. Her praise
is never so effusive, however, as on March 23, the Third Sunday of Lent,
when the worship bulletin appears in the hands of the parishioners—and
it was a full house—without black lines or ink blots. Gertie Johnson had
not been able to spot a single mistake.

That evening, Coop comes down the stairs in the Fremont Hotel and is passing out of the lobby when Miss Crenshaw calls out to him. He is wearing a winter suit, brown wool, and has his topcoat over his arm, and his hat in hand. He looks toward the voice that has called his name and sees Violet sitting in the corner of the parlor in a chair by a lamp. She has a book. She closes it and gets up. She is wearing a dark full skirt, and a patterned blouse, and also has a coat with her, a scarf and a handbag. Coop thinks she looks less holy, somehow, than usual. Her hair, for one thing, is let down. They exchange greetings during which it emerges that Coop is en route up the street a block to Bud's Tavern where he thinks he might celebrate his error-less publication by perhaps committing an error or two in a pub. He also wants to see if Jules is there as he suspects, and if he is, he is quite sure his good friend will need help getting back to the Fremont. So his is an errand of mercy, he said to himself earlier during an *entre nous* conversation in his chambers. He invites Miss Crenshaw to join him, thinking it will be an invitation she'll reject, and if not, an invitation he'll regret. She accepts with alacrity, and Coop pushes aside his misgivings. He feels gregarious and magnanimous. They step out into the night. It is cold. A few flakes of snow are falling. Des Moines has forecast a spring storm that might bring one to two inches of snow.

Jules is on a bar stool when they arrive. Coop and Violet take a table in the back. The crowd is thin, but it is early, although Sunday nights are never as busy as Fridays or Saturdays. The jukebox is playing Cab Calloway and "The St. James Infirmary Blues." They order a couple of Pabst Blue Ribbons.

"So you're celebrating a clean bulletin?" she says smiling at him.

"Well, I guess it's as good a reason to have a drink as any," he replies nervously. He is rarely in public with a single woman.

"Good for you!" she exclaims. "You're doing a swell job and I know you will find someone soon."

"Maybe," he said, looking at her closely. "And what are you celebrating?"

"Oh, I don't know. I'm leaving Tuesday for Los Angeles. Pulling up stakes. So I guess that's a reason to celebrate—or mourn."

"Which is it mostly?"

"Probably mourning, because with the Los Angeles thing, that's more of anticipation or excitement, not something to really celebrate, you know. But leaving Bathington, that's not something to get excited about. It's such a lovely town, and I have so many good memories here."

"I've been to Los Angeles," Coop offered, "a couple of times in fact. That's a big place, so much to see. Antonia and I went to the Chinese Grauman Million Dollar Theatre—this was back in 1919 I think—to see a movie, that was before talkies of course, and once we saw Tom Mix driving down Sepulveda Boulevard in his convertible. That was before the arthritis got to her so bad, in fact it was shortly after that she went into a wheelchair and didn't get out till she died."

They continue in this manner through one beer and then a second. The saloon has filled up so that all the tables are occupied, and patrons take to standing around pillar and post, many with a beer in one hand and a woman in the other. Coop keeps an eye on Jules. Occasionally he can make him out telling a bad joke and laughing, or arguing loudly with the bartender about the weather or something equally important. "A lot of people in here tonight," Violet says. She sounds nervous.

"Afraid someone might see you?" Coop teases.

Violet waves off that suggestion. "Oh no, why should I be? Thought I saw someone I knew is all." She finishes that sentence with a dismissive chortle.

"You know that in a small town there's not much you can get away with. Remember that burglary a couple years ago at Newton's house? When the account appeared in the paper the following week it mentioned that among the items stolen were a couple bottles of wine, vodka and whiskey. Which is neither here nor there, except that the Newtons are God-fearing, Baptist teetotalers—at least everyone thought they were!" Coop laughs. "No use pretending when you're in a small town. There's no anonymity in a village. Now you want to go some place where no one will notice you, well then you go to a place like Chicago. Here, everyone knows your name. It's both the blessing and curse of a small town like Bathington. You're blessed because everyone knows you and knows your business and watches out for you, and you're cursed for the same reasons. I think that's why—as a general rule mind you—small town people are better people than most city folks. They have to be. You can't trust a city person unless you really get to know them—which is hard in a big city. Here, if you're dishonest, everyone soon knows it and no one will do business with you. If you're a cranky, bitter and vindictive son-of-gun, well, people will let you know and you either mend your ways, or you end up spending a lot of time by yourself. There's sort of an incentive, a moral imperative—Cushing would say—for decent living in a small town that you won't find in a big city and I know cause I lived in both."

"Oh no, I don't care who sees me with a beer, or in a tavern, or even with you!" They laugh together. "That's the real threat to my reputation, right there, Mr. Cooper! Being here with you! But—" She takes a sip of her lager. "—the problem with the very thing you describe is that the small town life of *apparent* transparency fosters what I think is perhaps the biggest sin of all. You know what that is, Coop?"

"No, you tell me."

"Hypocrisy. Most people don't really like to be saints, but they're not willing to be considered sinners, so they play the role of a saint. I've found that small town saints are also big time sinners, and often you can't really know who they are or what they're thinking. All we see is the role they're playing in public. Whereas in Chicago, people can be rude and mean-spirited, but at least you know that's who they are, and because there's no moral imperative as you put it, Mr. C., to live like a saint, when you *do* find a saint, it's quite likely you got the real deal. Here, you don't know what the hell you got, excuse my language."

"That's quite perceptive of you, Miss—"

"—And, sorry to interrupt but I had one additional thought, wherever the need to be righteous is the strongest, that's where you'll find the largest the number of hypocrites. And where, besides a small town like Bathington, is righteous living valued more highly? In the church of course! And that's why you find more hypocrites per square yard in a church than in any other geographical location on the planet! That's something that if you didn't know before you started working in the church office, you certainly know now, huh?"

"You make a strong case, Miss Crenshaw," Coop says thoughtfully. He wonders if Violet drank often.

"Oh, pouff! Just thinking out loud is all … the thing is—" She leans toward him and glances about nervously. "—Art Bandy's not to be trusted, speaking of phonies, Mr. Cooper. Do not trust that man. There's some shady stuff going on, and that's all I'll say now. And if this blows up, and it will, he's going to blame Jews and Negroes. He's an awful man, that Bandy, but there he is every Sunday, going to church, sitting there with his pretty little wife, and his two petticoated girls." She leans back now, and reaches into her handbag and retrieved a large fancy box. "Enough of that. I have something for you." She gives him the box. Coop thinks it is fancy because the walls of the box are covered with a fine fabric with a floral pattern, predominantly red, and the box has a lid which is secured with a small string to which is attached a piece of bone which hooks into a loop. He watches with amazement as she sets the box down in front of him. He slides his beer across the table to have a better look.

"Here, I want you to have this. Something from my Chicago days," she says.

"Chicago, huh? I guess I knew that, didn't I? I forgot. My first job after Antonia and I were married was in Chicago. Western Union office. We lived down near Hyde Park."

"My time was probably later than that. Someday I will have to tell you my life story," she said somberly.

"What is this?"

"Take a look, silly" she says, smiling. He takes the box, and pushes the bone from the latch and lifts the lid. Inside is a crucifix carved out of a dark wood, anchored to a pedestal and lying in a preformed notch on a bed of red satin. He lifts it out and sits it on the table. Its total height is probably about seven inches. He recognizes it as the one he'd seen on her desk the day he'd first received some instruction on the mimeograph.

"Well, lookee that," he says. "It's beautiful." He removes his hands from it and then bends over to peer more closely.

"The wood's teak, and it was handmade by a Mr. Hu, a Chinese woodcarver I knew when I lived in Chicago. I've always treasured it, but I would like you to have it, and it gives me pleasure to think that something I enjoyed so much is still in Bathington and is now being enjoyed by someone else. Look here, look at the eyes of Jesus. What do you see?"

Coop took the crucifix in his hands. "He's got slanted eyes! This is a Chinese Jesus! Well, I'll be!"

"Isn't that clever?" Violet exclaimed. "Mr. Hu was a Christian. He had carved it originally for his pastor in China, but then during the civil war, the Communists closed the church, seized the pastor, and so Mr. Hu grabbed this crucifix before they destroyed it and kept it safe, and brought it with him when he got out of the country. Of course now, since Chairman Mao's started a new country, who knows what's going on in China!"

After this, the conversation winds down. She would be leaving Tuesday on the evening Rocket for Cedar Rapids, and from there to Des Moines and a flight the next day to Denver, and on to Los Angeles.

"So you're from Chicago where you could live like a sinner, and you move to Bathington where you've either been a saint or a hypocrite, and now you're going to Los Angeles." He pauses. "You planning to live like a sinner again?" They laugh loud together again. "I'll never tell," she says.

"You know, I need to use the Ladies' Room. Will you give me a minute?" She pushes back from the table, and makes her way through the throng. Tony Bennett is singing "Because of You." Coop stands up and wanders to the end of the bar to take a look, to see if the box had "If I Could Be with You (One Hour Tonight)." Didn't look like they had many songs from the 1920s. He looks for Jules, but he isn't at the bar. He surveys the crowd. He doesn't see him, but he can hear him—"There once was a gal from Nantucket, who—" Just then Miss Crenshaw appears at his side. "Coop, we need to go."

"There you are," Coop says. "Are you alright?"

"I'm fine, I'm fine. I just want to get out of here." She looks back to the Ladies Room.

As she looks left over her shoulder from whence she came, a tall man appears on her right, bumping briefly into Coop, creating some space between Coop and Crenshaw and he says, "Hey, Lizzy. Elizabeth Morley, isn't it? I'll be damned! It *is* you!" He's beaming. "Lizzy!"

Violet whirls round to face the stranger and as she does, she inserts her hand through Coop's arm, coupling the two of them together.

"You remember me, don't you Lizzy?" His smile appears as genuine as his affection seems … affected. He's more than six-feet tall, his frame lanky and his blond hair thinning, almost white. As he talks, he leans forward. He's dressed in a smart blue double-breasted suit, and carries a topcoat over his arm, and holds his hat in his free hand.

"I'm afraid I do not," Violet says quietly. "You have me mistaken for someone else. My name is Violet Crenshaw."

"Come on! It's me, Joe. Joseph Cragilione! We had some good times back in Chicago, didn't we?"

Violet looks away briefly and then says: "Well, I used to live in Chicago, that's true, but you have the wrong person, I'm sorry."

"Oh, I don't think so, but I suppose it's possible."

"Really, Mister … Mister … I'm sorry, the name escapes me—"

"Craglione."

"Mr. Craglione, I am occupied right now. By the way, this is my very good friend, Mr. Carlton Cooper. Carlton, this is someone who thinks he knows me." She laughs nervously."

Coop says, "Pleased to make your acquaintance."

"Right, right, likewise, I'm sure." A pause swells up between them, and then Coop says, "Small world, you running into someone who reminds you of an old acquaintance after all these years. What brings you to Bathington?"

"Aw, I'm on my way up to Minneapolis, a philosophy bash, lectures on everything from neo-Platonic Thomistic philosophy to the new existentialism, you know, Jean-Paul Sartre, Camus, et cetera, et cetera. Anyway, had a flat a ways back and bumped on into town, going to spend the night at the Fremont, and then head on up tomorrow, if the old rattletrap will get me there."

"The Fremont?" Coop explains, "Why—"

"Really, Mr. Craglione, I am sorry I am not the person you thought I was, but now I must beg your pardon for leaving, as I have some matters to attend to." She pushes off against Coop, causing him to take a quick step to keep his balance. She steers him back to their table.

"Alright then, Miss Crenshaw, you say? It's been a pleasure. Perhaps we will meet again soon, real soon."

Back at the table, Coop says, "What's the matter with you?"

"Nothing, nothing," she says. "It's nothing. Haven't you ever had someone mistake you for someone else?"

At their table, they find Jules gazing closely at the crucifix. They sit down quickly.

"Jules," Coop says. It is more of a question than a greeting. Jules lifts his head and rolls his eyes. His face is flushed and fleshy and covered with a two-day growth of salt and pepper whiskers. His eyes are round and protuberant; his hair white but thin and greasy and his scalp red. "This is a swell little Jesus," he mutters. His speech is deliberate. Coop knows he is trying to appear sober. Playing that role is very difficult for Jules. Coop gently lifts the crucifix out of his hand. Jules' gaze follows the cross in Coop's hands until it disappears into its box. "Where'd you get that?"

"It's a gift, Jules."

"It sure is swell. Are you going to finish that beer? Would you like to hear a limerick, Miss Crenshaw?"

"I should be going," Miss Crenshaw says emphatically, grabbing her coat and handbag.

"Yes, I am going to finish it, and then Miss Crenshaw and I are taking you home." He glances at Violet to see if this meets with her approval. "Of course," she murmures.

"Hey did you hear about these American, German, Japanese and Chinese businessmen who went to this fancy restaurant and when they gets there the ma-, mader-, the maître-d said, 'Hey, you can't come in here widout a Thai!'" His laugh is the guffaw of a drunk, his mouth open wide, his fat red tongue exposed. He grins, pleased with himself. "Thai! Get it? Like the Thai people from Thailand, that's a country down there somewhere close to India or New Zealand. That's a good one!"

Coop leaves his Pabst on the table, and presides over the evacuation of the town drunk from Bud's Tavern, and together he and Miss Crenshaw accompany him down Main Street to the Fremont Hotel, and get him up to his fourth floor room. Violet bid farewell on the second landing—"Good night, Coop! It was a delightful evening"—and turns into her room. Coop steps up the remaining two flights, retrieves a key from his suit pocket (Jules has given him a spare) and gets the man into his room and lays him out on his bed. "Thanks, Coop. I'm okay. You're a prince among princess—" The word catches him by surprise. "Princessess, no prin-*ces!*" He chuckles. "Princesses. That's a good one!"

"Night, Jules. I'm right across the hall," Coop says, and he shuts the door and returns to his room across the hall. The alcohol has done him in. He places the box with the crucifix in a cupboard. He'll think about a more permanent and suitable spot to display it tomorrow. He gets a fire going in his oil heater and then disrobes down to his Munsingwear and turns off the floor lamp. He sits down heavily on the bed in the dark.

Then—in a town in which nothing ever happens—something happens.

Chapter VI

COOP HEARS A RAPPING AT HIS window before he is able to define what the rapping is. He is in a groggy state. It could be he is dreaming. The rapping persists and then he is aware of shouting: "Hey! Hey there!"

At the same time he catches the scent of acidity, like rotting garbage. He rouses. His surroundings are indistinct and hazy. "Hey, Coop!" The voice is muffled and cloudy. He hesitates. Then he realizes that his room is full of smoke.

"What?" He props himself up on an elbow and looks toward the window.

"Coop, you gotta get outta there right away!" But Coop has already sat up, dropped his feet into his shoes, and grabbed a washcloth from the vanity basin. He knocks the ewer to the floor. "Criminey!" he mutters. He drops to his knees clad only in his Union suit which he bought just a week ago in Waterloo at Farley's because with winter receding Farley was getting rid of his Munsingwear overstock. Holding a damp rag over his mouth and nose, he crab-crawls across the planked floor to the double-hung window, catching a knee on a hooked rug en route. With the rear of his long johns untied, he looks like a white-tailed deer in a fog. He can hear sirens faintly. The volunteers are on the way.

Just then the window shatters and shards of glass fall tinkling to the floor in front of him like a sudden shower of hail. "Lord Almighty! What are you doing, Jules?"

"Coming to get you. Didn't know if you's up."

"I said 'what'?"

"I didn't hear you."

Grabbing the two brass handles at the base of the window, Coop lifts, and carefully hoists himself over the sill and onto the fire escape. Jules, in flannels, is waiting, hunching into the open window with a hand extended to help—assistance which is refused. "Come on, the whole place is going up in flames." Coop stands up slowly as though he might throw his back out of whack if he makes a sudden move. Jules' eyes are wide and questioning and his breath is redolent of last night's whiskey. The neon sign reading HOTEL is flickering madly, lighting up half of Jules's unshaven face like he's a clown in a carnival. Coop notices that his friend's nightshirt is buttoned neatly but one buttonhole off from top to bottom like a bad zipper. He turns. Not sure this rickety affair can hold us up, he thinks. They have four flights to descend.

By the time they hit ground, Bathington's No. 502 new Dodge Power Wagon has arrived, and another two are en route from Charles City, Chief Dixon says. A small crowd, mostly men, has gathered, although Fredrika Solvig has hiked the two blocks from her bungalow on Crescent Street to find out what the commotion is all about.

What she finds is the marshal's black and white with its red light whirling and firemen evacuating the residents, mostly elderly. They are taking a head count to determine if all twenty-seven souls are accounted for—including about a half-dozen men. When Coop steps on solid footing about half the permanent residents of the Fremont Hotel have been discovered and removed including Harriet Armistan who appears with Chauncey her cat.

Also rescued in the fire are Mrs. Charlotte Brunner —whose salvation is a particular blessing, says Millie later, because she is organizing the duck-picking bee in preparation for the Ladies Aid Annual Duck Dinner at Bathington Community Church this coming Wednesday evening; and Mrs. Clara Knauff who is suffering from a cold and doctoring with Musterole.

One by one, Coop notes, they appear through the oak doors of the doomed hotel, fragile waifs with their grey hair un-bunned and flowing on their shoulders. They skitter slowly in half steps across the street, delicate nightgowns flapping slightly in the night air. Defying this description is the sole occupant of the first floor suites who appears in coat and fur hat and who steps confidently into the street and disappears into the crowd. The others are assisted by gentle firemen who guide them down a bridge of stairs and escort them away from danger across Main Street where they are given blankets. They huddle nervously near the curb, a coven of crones, standing in pink bedroom slippers or similar footwear, waiting for further assistance and direction. Mary's Kitchen has opened, and some accept an invitation for free coffee and a roll.

They all make it out under their own power except for Widow Brown who is carried down two flights of stairs and out the doors by the strapping young Franzhiemer boy. Mrs. Clarabell Russell, a divorcee, who at 52 is the youngest of the group, wanted the Franzhiemer treatment herself. She opens her door in time to see Widow Brown hauled off and calls after Franzhiemer to come back for her, but he doesn't, and she has to make the trip down the stairs and out the doors under her own power, bosom heaving beneath a red silk peignoir, but not before she'd grabbed her jewelry box, and tossed on a string of pearls—a gift from her third husband. Unlike the others, her dusty blond hair is done up in 2-inch rollers; she had enough conduit on her head to meet the irrigation needs of all the farmers in Clearwater county.

What am I going to do now? Coop wonders.

He and Jules alone made a getaway by means of the fire escape. The interior stairwell is perfectly functional but he assumed that beyond his door lay nothing but gloom and billows of smoke. Now with a windy "whoop" the fire springs to life and flames can be seen coming from the third and fourth floor windows. The roof will soon cave, Coop is sure of it. Main Street glistens in an orange glow like a summer sunset. Coop feels a draft.

"You gonna close that rear window of yours?" Jules asks matter-of-factly. Coop grabs his flap and secures his modesty. "You're a bloody mess," he adds. "You should see a doctor." Coop now feels pain in his hands and knees. His long johns are stained red at the knees and his hands, especially his right hand, are dripping blood. Some of the blood drips onto the ground, creating crimson stains that seep into the snow and expand until frozen in a round crystalline shape.

"Yeah," he says. I should sit down, he thinks. Jules leads him next door to the steps of Rachel's Millinery Shop. He eases down slowly. "I should go to Millie's," he says suddenly. "What time is it anyway?"

"'Bout four." Jules sits down beside him and wraps his arms around himself, shivering.

"Four! Oh boy!"

Fire Engine One has disgorged all its hoses, and teams of firemen with topboots, swoop-winged helmets and heavy jackets are directing torrents of water into the hotel, some right through Coop's broken window on the fourth floor. Two red engines from Charles City have arrived and the street is glistening wet and littered with ropes, buckets, extinguishers, hooks, ladders, hoses, and shovels, hatchets and axes. Chief

Dixon holds a trumpet and is barking orders. The air smells like wet wood and campfire smoke.

Already the charred hotel foyer appears gutted and spectral. The structure, once the pride of Bathington, the architectural jewel of northeastern Iowa, will be a total loss, although its glory has long faded and its degradation is complete when the owners add the neon HOTEL sign in the early thirties, remodel the parlor and turn it into a coffee shop. In the intervening years the front porch has tilted and a pine-wood fire escape has been added. The small gardens in front and to the side are neglected and overrun by Canadian thistle, knapweed and cockleburs. The building has stood proud through more than fifty winter and summer storms but now is kneeling in its own ashes.

"Coop!" He looks up and sees someone indistinct but tall and angular hurrying toward him through the haze. The Reverend. He stands above the two men, his thin face, sharp features focused in concern. He sees the blood. "Coop, what happened?"

Coop lifts his hands and glances at them briefly and then sets them down awkwardly in his lap as though his arms are holding his hands as objects separate from himself. "I'm fine. Just some glass got in the way crawling out, I guess."

"Had to break the glass," Jules offers, looking up at the Reverend and drawing his flannelled sleeve across his mouth, "'cause I was going in to get him, you know, but he wuz up, crawlin' to the window. You shoulda seen him, a-crawlin' that way with his back door open. Wonder he don't have glass in his—"

"Right." Cushing waves Jules off and touches his finger to the bridge of his nose, pushing up his spectacles. "I'm going to get my car and take you down to Millie's and we can see what the damage is and get you to a doctor if necessary. You stay right here," and he runs off. "And get a blanket for him," he calls back to Jules.

# # #

When Coop and Jules arrive at Millie's house in the Reverend's Chevrolet the kitchen light is glowing like a lantern in a lighthouse. Cushing has called ahead to alert Millie of their imminent arrival. Coop sees her standing over the sink. The Reverend leads him by the elbow ignoring his feeble protests. The screen door slams behind Jules when they are all in the kitchen. Tippy is prancing and hopping around people, and scooting under the table and chairs. Millie wipes her hands on her gingham apron which is tied around her pajamas and house coat and steps quickly across the checkered linoleum floor to relieve Cushing of his duty and embraces Coop who says, "I'm fine, I'm fine." He sees that she's been crying.

"You have no idea if you're fine or not," she sniffles, releasing him slowly. "Sit down here, and let me take a look. Kick off your shoes. Coffee's perking. Would you like some?"

"I'd love some coffee, ma'am," Jules says brightly.

"Of course you would, Jules," Millie says. "Pull up to the table. I have a tea cake for you, too. Frankie made it special for you just last night, Coop, and Vic brushed on the butter and powdered it herself."

The examination then begins. Millie has no nurse's training but she is a mother and teacher and has examined more lacerations and abrasions than all the pediatricians in Clearwater County. Her hair is dark and straight falling almost to her shoulders and when she leans forward as she does now, she frequently gestures her hair back behind an ear in a quick unconscious motion. She assesses the situation quickly, appraising Coop's condition. Coop sits bolt upright in his chair with an afghan wrapped around him, one supplied by Solvig who returned to her house to get blankets for the exiles. Millie looks at his hands and sees immediately that no stitches will be required. The cuts had lacerated only the epidermis and drew blood but they were not deep. She'd need to pull some minute slivers of glass from some of the wounds.

She asks the Reverend to go to the washroom to retrieve a pair of tweezers and, while he is doing this, she produces some scissors, kneels in front of Coop and flicks a trailing end of the afghan away from his legs for a better view of his knees. "I'm going to make a cut up your long johns, Coop, because I don't want to push the material over your wounds, okay? Relax. I just need to take a look." She slides a scissor blade under the material. It feels cold to Coop. Then she snips up the side of his left leg to above the knee and then makes a lateral cut, and carefully peels the Munsingwear to the side.

"We'll just wash this out now," she says, fully in command of the theater of operations. Cushing reappears with the tweezers. "Reverend, perhaps you can get that basin over there, get some warm water, and I'll take those tweezers now." She takes Coop's left hand and begins the extraction. Coop winces but has to admit that this daughter-in-law of his sure knows what she is doing. Within minutes she's taken care of one hand, washed it, towel-dried it with firm pressure, and then repeated the procedure with the other hand and shifted her attention again to his knees. Washing and cleaning is all that is required. The fabric has provided some protection, keeping the glass from becoming imbedded too deeply in the flesh.

After cutting his long johns on the right leg and applying her ministrations there, she pronounces him ready to go. "Reverend, I put a pair of trousers in the washroom, as you probably noticed, and a shirt and socks and fresh briefs. Maybe you could help him get presentable—unless you want to rest Coop? I can get some of Johnny's pajamas and you can take the attic bed. It's real comfy—Tippy! Bring back that shoe!" Tippy has Coop's left shoe in her mouth and is making for the door. But at Millie's command, she stops. After a slight hesitation, she drops the shoe at the door. "Honest to God, that mutt ain't no use except for catching shoes and running off with them," she says to no one in particular.

Coop knows he can't sleep now. Probably later. "Reverend, I can do this on my own," he says, standing up. He pulls himself erect, his long johns in tatters at his knees and the afghan around his shoulders. He looks like a war refugee from a prison camp. He shuffles off to the washroom. Millie wipes her hands again on her apron. It is a nervous gesture. Cushing is watching her with transparent admiration. "Coffee, Reverend?" she suggests, turning to the stove. "Sit down, and rest, you've had quite a night. I want to hear what happened."

"You're a regular Florence Nightingale, Mrs. Cooper," Cushing says, taking the chair Coop had vacated. "You have a certain understated equanimity, or emotional equilibrium when working under stress."

Millie scoffs at this nonsense. "Not at all, just experience. Vic's always coming home with a gash on her knee or an abrasion on her arm or some such thing. You never know what with her." She brings the coffee pot to the table and fills Jules' and Cushing's cups and then one for herself. She sits down and brushes her hair back showing more of her face, and lifts the cup to her lips. "I hope it isn't too hot."

"Just right, Mrs. Cooper," Jules says, "and the tea cake too."

"Have another piece, Jules," she says. Then, turning to Cushing: "So tell me all about it. What on earth happened?"

"If I hadn't had to pee—use the bathroom—I might've slept through the whole thing," Jules declares. Millie and Cushing turn to Jules. He is talking into his plate, head down, and taking bites of tea cake when he can. Among Jules' qualities is an uncanny and sublime lack of self-consciousness. He continues his narration until he reaches the point where the two of them are resting on the stoop of the millinery shop. Cushing listens patiently through this rambling recapitulation of events and then says that Chief Dixon will not know the cause of the fire until an investigation has been completed, but it is likely due to a short circuit of some kind as it is well known that the wiring in that ancient Queen Anne is old and out of code, or perhaps combustibles were too close to a heat source. As for the residents, they are being taken to the school house, relatives are being notified, and he is sure that they'd all have a place to sleep by end of day. Jules isn't sure where he'd stay, but he'd heard that Mrs. Pettigrew has an empty room or two in her boarding house on account of a recent death.

"You'll stay right here with us and Coop for a day or two," Millie says, getting up from the table to get some cream from the icebox. "That will give us some time to think about the future and make some decisions. Coop can stay here as long as he likes."

"Oh, no, I couldn't do that, Mrs. Cooper," Jules says nervously. "That's just too much of a pother, you know."

"Sure you can, Jules," she says, closing the fridge door. She turns about and faces him, creamer in her hands. Looks him right in the eyes. "Sure, you can, Jules." She pauses. "But only three days. After that you'll be a pother!" They all laugh.

"Well, you are sure kind, Mrs. Cooper," says Jules. Then, "Can I have another piece of tea cake?"

The phone jangles twice. "Oh, that's us," Millie says. She jumps up to answer it. "It's for you, Reverend." Cushing sets his coffee cup carefully on the table, and strides to Millie to take the receiver from her. "This is Cushing," he says crisply. Silence ensues. Then he says, "Thanks, Chief. I appreciate the update."

He returns the receiver to its wall cradle thoughtfully and says to no one in particular: "Violet Crenshaw died in the fire."

Chapter VII

January, 1952
Chicago, Illinois

CARLO ROSSI STANDS MOTIONLESS IN HIS sleeveless white undershirt and briefs in front of a tiny sink with a rusty ring around the drain hole. Above the chipped porcelain basin is a small mirror mounted on the door of the medicine cabinet. Carlo tilts his head first one way, then another—better to see his handsome self. He leans into the mirror and brushes a hand across his chin and sighs. There is no reason for the sigh. He is neither happy nor sad, just indifferent, which, for him, is the way most days begin. He opens the medicine cabinet and withdraws his shaving mug with its small bar of shaving soap and an ivory-handled brush of silver-tipped badger hair. After wetting the brush with tap water, he agitates it upon the soap in the mug and soon has a rich lather which he applies liberally to his face including the mustache area and the chin and below and underneath the jaw line. He looks like a Santa Claus, his lips pink like rose petals. He retrieves a double-edge razor from the cabinet. At the bottom of the handle is a cap which turns. Carlo twists it for several revolutions causing the head of the razor to open fully. Removing the razor, he flicks it into a dust bin beneath the sink and selects a new one from a small package of blades and drops it into place and twists the cap on the handle in a counter-motion, tightening the blade in place. He leans forward and begins to scrape three days of heavy Italian beard off of his young face.

Clean shaven, he emerges from the bathroom and walks to the window of his two-room wallpapered flat above the elevated on Lake Street. He pulls the drapes aside and stares out across the dreary downtown Chicago metroscape. The morning sky is ominously gray. Below, cars and buses are grinding away at the winter snow, jostling for position in heavy traffic like logs pushing downstream through a forest of granite and glass. He nods.

Today I am f**k*ng going to rob a f**k*ng bank.

Watching languidly from a far corner of the room that's shrouded in a blue-white fog of cigarette smoke is another youth dressed in a chauffeur's uniform including a white shirt and narrow black tie. He holds a newsboy cap in one hand, and a Chesterfield in the other. His hair is brown and has been buzzed into a brush cut, the front waxed up so that it looked like the teeth of a wood saw. His ears stick out from a rounded, puckish face that still bear traces of acne. He puts the cigarette to his lips and takes a draw, exhales and waits.

Carlo turns from the window and goes to the armoire and grabs a white shirt with French cuffs and puts it on. "So you got any questions, Wason?" he asks casually.

"Nope." Carlo puts on a suit—a navy blue Brooks Brothers double-breasted with light pinstripes for which he'd paid $45 out of the "seed" money from their last job—"Cost of doing business," he likes to say.

They've gone over the details of this heist many times. They have visited the bank. They have studied the personnel of the bank. They'll do it on a Friday at noon in broad daylight, they decide, the busiest hour of the week for the bank. It will be their last score, Carlo says. Bank robbers who rob their first bank are successful 70% of the time, he claims. But the odds go down after that. You can't rob banks for a career and expect to stay out of jail. This will be their fourth. It has to be their f**k*ng last. The problem with bank robbers is they get greedy. They don't know when to stop and they can't resist the next big score. Carlo says he weren't interested in no big score, just a few small ones and then they are done. Today they are going after $4,500. Peanuts. It is hardly worth the time and expense of the feds to go after them. The idiot bankers? They'll write it off and consider it money well spent on how to tighten up security. Carlo argues that if he is caught he can reasonably say he was going to give them their money back. He was just teaching them a little lesson; it's not hard to relieve a bank of its assets, you know.

Moreover, he doesn't believe in using a gun. If caught, the penalty will be more severe. A well-planned bank robbery doesn't require a gun. The best jobs are those in which no one is even aware the bank has been robbed. Keep the human factor to a minimum he says.

He tucks a white handkerchief into the breast pocket, and jumps to the bathroom to take a final look at himself. One more thing. He grabs a bottle of Old Spice sitting on the toilet tank lid, shakes a few drops into his palm, rubs his hands together briefly and then slaps them to the sides of his freshly shaven face. Turning, he takes a deep breath and then says, "Let's go."

# # #

The job is a necessity (Carlo's word) because of an occurrence of the previous week which has upset the order of things. And things are always ordered in Carlo's life. He hates disorder more than a Greek philosopher. It grates on him, makes him irritable and he is feeling irritable now. It's the fruit of his upbringing. The sisters didn't abide any foolishness and allowed no untidiness whatsoever. The squat Sister Margarite with the chubby hands was seldom surprised when inspecting *his* dormitory room. Books on the shelf were arranged by height and weren't jammed to the back of the shelf but the spines sat evenly a half inch from the edge. Desk tops were clean, sharpened pencils were in a pencil box, with a rubber eraser. Three-holed lined paper in a stack and in its proper place. The bed made, with the cotton white sheet folded over the blanket and a pillow situated just so. Shirts in the wardrobe (he had three) were on hangers, shoes were under the bed, T-shirts and underwear folded and in the dresser drawers. Carlo's cosmos, as indeed the world of all the kids at St. Joseph's School for Orphans, had started in chaos, although not having a mother or a father when you're a kid in a home for kids without mothers and fathers was neither upsetting nor unusual. It was the world as he knew it and understood it. But he became aware of it soon enough, the nuns made sure of that, not because they were intentionally cruel but because there was no point in hiding the truth. These kids were abandoned and the orphanage existed not only to provide for body and soul, but to give the children a universe that somehow made sense, and Carlo had a temperament that aided in this education. He *naturally* understood the necessity and *value* of organization, that there was nothing more important than the ability to reason and get everything arranged properly. One must think ahead, like a chess player, must plan for eventualities, and above all not be excessive. *Modus omnibus in rebus*, said Sister Margarite. Moderation in all things. It is an adage by which, largely, Carlo is able to live.

He is a photographer by trade. The objects he sees through the lens of his Leica are girls. Naked girls. And he does this for Mr. Patrick "Lefty" Donovan, who publishes gentleman's magazines under different names, and distributes them across the country, trying to keep one step ahead of the authorities who are eager to confiscate his type of literature if it runs afoul of local obscenity laws—which it unfailingly does. He also employs Wason Jard as a printer. Donovan has called them to ask them to come over on Saturday to his office to talk. This is unusual. He doesn't give a reason, and Carlo thinks that when someone refuses to divulge purpose, the outcome cannot be pleasant. He paces and frets about this. Wason seems unconcerned, but nothing ever concerns Wason. This is perhaps due to Carlo's patronage. Carlo does everything, and Wason is happy with the arrangement and never needs to assert his own will in anything. He trusts Carlo. He's known Carlo since he was five. They met at the orphanage. They were like brothers. Although separated by five years, Carlo has defended the kid since the day he showed up. Carlo often wonders about this. Perhaps he has a blood brother somewhere out in the world living in a fancy house with beautiful parents, and a dog and a sister. Lordy, maybe he has a mother. He doesn't know. All he knows is that she left him on the church steps with a note pinned to his little coat. Doesn't matter, anyhow. It's stupid to think about it and a damn waste of time. But this business is no good. Donovan has something going, that's for sure.

Mr. Donovan's offices, if they can be called such, are in the grimy underbelly of Chicago's South Side, not far from Skid Row and under the shadow of the Pacific Garden Mission in a neighborhood populated by flophouses and derelict hotels. Wason loves to listen to the Saturday night dramatic radio program, *Unshackled,* that tells the story of bums shackled in sin who'd found Jesus at the Pacific Garden Mission and Jesus—the organ music swelled right here—had *unshackled* them and set them on the straight and sober road to salvation. The rents are cheap here, and the local constabulary is inclined not to bother them, and they get business done right under Jesus' nose without so much as a howdoyoudo.

They walk by the mission Saturday morning. Bums and tatterdemalions are milling about on the corner, some lazing against the rough red brick walls, while in the streets some guttersnipes are tossing a ball. A few of the unfortunates have cigarettes, others have coffee, and most are bundled up in layers of jackets and overcoats, wearing touks and gloves, like they are preparing for a trek to the Arctic Circle. Some offer Wason and Carlo a snaggle-toothed smile as they stride by; most have teeth missing, and the nicotine-stained teeth that are still in the mouth are yellow and encrusted with plaque. Their faces are tough as elephant skin, and their eyes deep in the sockets are numb and expressionless. The boys keep walking; they've been here before. Near the end of the block, just beyond the Hoyt Hotel, they come upon the offices of P. Donovan and Company and underneath this: Publishers.

The sidewalk here is pocked and still black with oil stains and even inside the building Carlo imagines he can still catch the scratchy scent of old gasoline. They push the door open and are inside a small anteroom. The inside door is locked. They push a buzzer. Soon a slot slides open and two thin eyes appear, after which the door is opened and they step inside. Now in a hallway, all doors to the right are locked. These lead to the print room and the studio. Mr. Donovan's office is in the rear.

The two thin eyes belonged to Wang Xiao Hua. Little Flower is Chinese. Xiao Hua is probably not her real name, but Wang possibly is, as sixty percent of the Chinese are surnamed Wang, Carlo thinks he'd read somewhere. Mr. Donovan calls her Alice, or sometimes *Xiao Jin Hua*, Little Golden Flower. She is skinny as the Chinese are, and about medium height which for a Chinese girl is tall. Her head is round and her face cherubic, with a button nose, and her skin white, not yellow—where did that myth about Orientals come from?—with lips painted vermillion, and a hint of orange on high Mongol cheekbones. She has luminous almond eyes that slope upward, blue mascara on the eyelids. Her eyebrows are dark and painted, and her face is expressionless like the head of a mannequin—a head that is topped by what appears to be, but isn't, a wig of coal black, straight hair that fits over her forehead in bangs, cuts around the face, and falls over her ears covering them and clinging evenly around her head in the most attractive way. Wisps of hair hang below her bangs like a waterfall over her eyes. She is wearing a flimsy chemise and sandals, and a pearl necklace. Her shoulders are bony, her knees knobby and her breasts small and pointy. She leads them down the hallway, sashaying in a lazy air of nonchalance. Maybe she doesn't know what's up. Why is she here anyway? Or maybe she shows up on Saturdays all the time?

The office used to be a mechanic's garage. It has been built out into a print shop, dark room, camera room, and photographer's studio with lights and props and backdrops like a blue sky and sand dunes and ocean, or a landscape with snow-capped mountains. A girl would sit demurely on her knees, with her rear back on her heels, and lounge as though on a yellow beach, or beneath a Matterhorn of a mountain. She'd wear nothing but a pair of red shorts and thrust her shoulders back, her bosoms out and arms straight down to each of her white, naked thighs and smile into the camera as pleasantly as can be.

"Boys," Mr. Donovan says, after he offers them a seat and a whiskey—it is only 11 a.m.—"I've got a proposition for you." He pauses, his mouth open, as though about to say something else, and then thinking better of it, he grabs the shot glass, whistles it down and smacks his narrow lips. Donovan is about fifty-five, thin as a Lincoln rail, but half the height of Lincoln. His face is gaunt as though the fat has been vacuumed out of it, revealing sharp facial bones and a pronounced ledge below the cavity in which are cunning dark eyes. His hair is receding and slicked back with the aid of a few dabs of pomade. His nose is prominent furthering the perception of Mr. Lefty Donovan as an Important Personage, a persona enhanced by a smartly cut dark vested suit, French cuffs with mother of pearl cufflinks. Over his lips is a pencil thin mustache, and his fingers are cigarette stained. Lately he's taken up using a cigarette holder. After seven years he thinks the cells in his hands will be replaced by new ones and the stains will be gone.

Donovan walks casually over to a file cabinet stuck in the corner of the office, and opens the top drawer and removes a file. He does so even though the contents of the file have nothing to do with what he is about to reveal; it is merely a rhetorical device, a prop, something to hold in his hands. He waves it around. "My operation here is getting too big," he remarks gravely. "And it's not cost effective for me to buy bigger and better equipment to handle the business, or to add employees, or even to retain central distribution here in this office—get what I mean?" He glances at Carlo.

Wason nods encouragingly. "No, I don't get what you mean," Carlo growls.

"Besides," Donovan continues, "it's too dangerous. If the cops or feds come knocking here and I have all my asses in one basket as it were, then I am in a f**k*ng sh*t-hole, I'll tell you what." Donovan paces the office waving the manila folder in his hand.

"What's in the folder?" Carlo demands.

"What's in this folder, you ask?" Donovan says. "Your future, that's what's in this goddern folder!" He explains how his plan will affect the destiny of the two young chaps before him. He proposes getting out of the business altogether—in a way, and let others do what he is doing. But with a difference. He, Donovan, will set several crews in business for themselves, but he will be paid a percentage of the profits, and these crews will have to follow his business plan. So the photography, printing and distribution will be moved out of Chicago to the west, to the south, and to the east, while all he'll do is read weekly financial reports, and review deposit slips. The advantage is that each crew has a profit incentive—the harder they work the more money they make. And they're free to take on other projects as a legitimate printing company or photography studio. "I want you to have some legit clients so you won't attract attention, you know, keep the nosy bastards from noticing anything else. So whaddya say, boys?" Donovan finishes with a flourish, his arms wide and palms open as though he'd just bestowed a blessing.

Carlo stands and walks away from Donovan and then turns, facing him. "So how much front money are we talking about?" Donovan motioned to Alice who produces a couple of contracts, and the four of them spend the next hour exploring the details of the proposed arrangement.

"We'll think about it," Carlo says brusquely, pushing out of the chair, signaling an end to the conversation. "Come on, Wason."

"What do you mean you will think about it?" Donovan yells. "What's to think about? What choice you have? You gonna find work here on the south side? You have some rich clients I don't know about? How long you survive without me, huh? Without this work, you'll be standing under that Jesus Saves sign with the rest of those goddern bums looking for a f**k*ng handout. Well, I'm telling ya, this is the only handout you're going to get that's gonna be worth anything and ya better take it, because I ain't making the offer again. I don't have time for it—got things to do, you know? And by the way, Alice is going with you guys."

"Alice?" Carlo's and Wason's heads swivel as though on one pivot to look at Alice who has taken a perch on the desk, her legs almost bare to the thighs. She is swinging one leg casually and filing her nails. "Her?" Carlo says, pointing.

"Is there another f**k*ng Alice in this here room?" Carlo and Wason are mute. "You, Carlo, are Photography. You, Wason, are Printing, and Alice is Accounting and Distribution. You're going to make a great team."

And that is how Carlo and Wason—and now Alice—come to this morning which they agree is an auspicious moment to rob a bank and augment the funds which have been advanced to them, via Alice, who alone has the account numbers. Funds will be available when Alice says they are available. *These* funds, however, will be available right now.

# # #

Nicholas Papadakis, 41, sits behind a mahogany desk upon which is only a writing pad, an ink and blotter set, a couple of manila folders and a trip-tych holding the photographs of his wife and two young daughters. The office is a corner suite with a private washroom, and bounded by two floor-to-ceiling windows. His desk is situated in front of the window, giving him a view to his left through another large plate glass window of Cook Street which passes the entrance to his place of employment, a branch of the Illinois State Bank. The wall to his right is lined with book-shelves and cabinets, and in the far wall are two doors, one to the wash-room, and one glass door which opens to the lobby. The space between these doors is barren except for a framed photograph of himself standing in front of the Parthenon. A large potted plant sits nearby. He is dressed in a conservative two-button navy blue wool suit. The white shirt he is wearing has been ironed only this morning by his wife who has also starched his collar and cuffs just the way he requires. The olive skin of his face glistens. Beads of perspiration have formed on his brow. He reaches for his handkerchief and mops his forehead.

"I apologize," he says, "but it seems a bit warm in here, don't you think Mrs. ... Mrs. ... What did you say your name was again?" He woke up this morning with a slight fever and the collywobbles but came to work anyway.

"Alice. Alice Wang," says the little Chinese lady seated across from him who has been shown to his office only five minutes earlier. "No, it not warm at all." He'd met her at the door, a delectable creature in a smart sky-blue blouse and virgin white skirt combination, the former ter-ribly tight and low cut, the latter scandalously short. "Please call me Alice, plain little old Alice," she says in a high squeaky voice, as though she is talking to a 3-year old.

"What's that?" Papadakis looks up. "Oh yes, of course. Alright, Alice." Papadakis looks straight into her limpid eyes so as to not look elsewhere.

"As I was saying, my husband die wecentree," Mrs. Wang says, beginning her story. "It was *so* sad you know. Unbe*wievabree* sad. He stop out on Highway 6, North Avenue, west of Chicago you know, pulled over on side of woad which he wanted to cwoss because he wanted to get one of those Polish hot dogs he liked so much I could never get him to eat Chinese food," she giggles nervously, "and he waiting for twaffic you know to wun across the woad standing there minding his own business and *evidentwee* there was this big 18-wheerer coming down the woad lost one of its tiweres those things are about five feet tall you know and poreeice say it come wroose but just keeps spinning down the woad and Warry pay no mind attention, why wuld he? You don't expect a goddern tiwere to come out of no where, strwike you down dead, but that's exactly what happened. Anyway, he didn't have no insurance, and the poor bastard didn't leave me anything and we riving in rittle apartment over on Harvard hoping buy place someday. And I wasn't working or anything. But I got job now serving drinks at big Wabash Bar downtown, so I got my eye on rittle cottage on the south side but need $3,000 ..."

Papadakis nods as she continues her story, but breaks his gaze to look toward Cook Street just as a black limousine pulls up to the front of the bank and double parks. The chauffeur gets out immediately, strides around the back of the vehicle and opens the rear passenger door. A young man who looks to be anywhere from 25 to 30 years old, attired in a dark double-breasted suit, and a black fedora steps out holding a black valise. He glances up at the bank, nods to his chauffeur and then steps briskly to the stairs at the entrance and disappears from view.

"... monthly payments you know would not be so hard to make with a 20-year mortgage—"

"Mrs. Wang—Alice—what I'd like you to do—" he pauses while he pulls open a large drawer on his right to retrieve some papers. He pushes his chair back, twists his body to use both hands to rifle through some folders before finding the form he wants. He turns to face Mrs. Wang again whose placid face and inquiring eyes are following everything he does and continues: —"is to take these forms—" he pushes them across the desk, "and complete—"

The door opens, and his secretary leans in. "Papa, there's a gentleman here to see you and he says it is most urgent, a Mr. Cutler Williams of Williams Enterprises and he said his business won't wait. He gave me his business card." She now enters the office, steps to his desk and hands Papadakis the card. It reads:

Mr. Cutler Williams, Esq.
WILLIAMS ENTERPRISES, LTD.
5684 Morgan Avenue,
Chicago 57, Illinois
Phone: **CA**lumet 5-6378

Papadakis bolts up immediately. "Mrs. Wang, please excuse me for a few moments. While I am gone, you can begin to fill out these forms and then we'll discuss your loan."

"Thank you, Mr. Papadakis," Alice says, "I'll work on these wight now, you go off now and have a good time!"

Papadakis hurries out the door. He sees Mr. Williams standing across the lobby which at noon is full of lunch time customers filling out withdrawal or deposit forms, or in lines at teller stations. Some are seated at desks with junior officers. He greets Mr. Williams and together they cross the marbled floor to a vacant office reserved for conferences and staff meetings. This room is not a corner office but has a similar window facing Cook Street, and the conference table in the room was rectangular mimicking the shape of the room itself. Williams enters the room first, and then Papadakis, who sits at an end chair and invites his guest to sit facing him. Williams instead walks around Papadakis and takes a seat with his back to the window. He sets down his valise chair-side, and crosses his legs and folds his hands on the table, after adjusting his cuffs.

"Well now, Mr. Williams," Papadakis begins, "what can I do for you?"

"That's very kind of you to ask, Mr. Papadakis," Carlo responds, "because here's the thing: I am going to rob your bank and you're gonna help me do it." At this news, Papadakis is completely bumfuzzled. His mouth drops in open surprise, like the tailgate of a dump truck—as though Cutler Williams has just declared that Greek baklava is a poor substitute for the superior Turkish variety. For the first time he really studies the man—as though he were conducting an internal audit for the FDIC. Williams is younger than he'd first thought but serious. He seems intelligent and his eyes under those thin brows never waver. He has a head of heavy Clark Gable hair, and a strong jaw. His wife would find Mr. Williams attractive, Papadakis thinks. Then he breaks into a nervous laugh.

"That's very amusing, Mr. Williams. I can assure you that our assets here at Illinois State Bank are perfectly safe and—"

Carlo raises his palm to bring Papadakis' reassurances to a halt. He says nothing, and Papadakis waits. One office over, Mrs. Wang observes through the plate glass window, one hand on a loan application, and the other fingering the little Smith & Wesson .38 in her handbag. Carlo opens his valise and withdraws a paper to which a cheque has been paper-clipped. He places it on the table and slides it toward the Senior Loan Officer. "I could sit here and yap at you and explain what's going down, but you being so nervous and all, you'd probably forget what the hell I said. So I've written it down all proper. I want this little note back in my possession but for right now, take a few moments to read it and I'll just sit here and wait for ya." He nudges the paper closer. "Come on, now, you take it. Read it. Take your time." Then, "Well, don't take your time, we're kind of in a rush, here."

Papadakis accepts the note and reads. He learns that Mr. Williams' associates are with his family at this very moment. However, his family is not aware of what is going on, and will not be harmed in any way as long as he follows directions explicitly. The names of his wife and girls are mentioned as is the location of his house on Courtney Street. Papadakis and Williams will go to the teller line and ask the girl at the end of the line, the one he hired last week, to get $4,500 out of her till and he's going to give her this check from Williams Enterprises in the same amount, and he's to tell her to hold onto the check and he will give her some assistance with the transaction momentarily. He is to keep his hands where Mr. Williams can see them at all times. He is not to call anyone—a guard, a teller, a colleague—by their name or it will be assumed he has betrayed their deal and Mr. Williams will walk out of the bank and unspeakable terror will be visited on his family. After they have the money, he will keep it and together they will walk out of the bank to Williams' car and they will have a nice conversation as they leave. All he has to do is follow his lead.

"So, you ready, Papa?" Papadakis looks glum. He is sweating now, as much from fear as he had from lust. He reaches for his hanky. "I'm ready," he says in a low voice. "I assume you're a man of your word."

"You can bank on it," Carlo says, standing. "Hey! A little joke! Come on. Let's go." He pats Papadakis on his shoulder.

It goes according to plan. Like a great chef, Carlo has gathered the ingredients, mixed, measured and molded—the right partner, the right victim, the right temperature. He throws in a little of the fear of God, a threat or two, an incentive and a dash of cojones. The soufflé comes out of the oven a work of art. Carlo notes two guards in the lobby, one near a bank of elevators, and the other sitting behind a small desk near the entrance. Both are armed. He cannot be certain that either guard has noticed him but it will not have mattered if they have. The transaction at the teller's window is smooth. Carlo thanks the girl—the name plate reads CARRIE—and with just a touch of his hand at Papadakis' elbow, steers him around to the door. The money is in a small business pouch.

"Your oldest little girl, Ellen, right?" Carlo asks as they move toward the doors.

"Ellen, yes."

"She's a bright one, I'll bet. Probably about five years old and in first grade next fall, right?"

"Kindergarten."

Carlo wants to keep him talking while they walk past the guard. "Tell me about her! What's she like? Shit! I bet she takes after her old man, eh?"

"Well …"

"Come on, you gotta be proud as punch of such a cute looking kid. Goddern! Takes after you, but looks like her mama, thank God, right?" He laughs and slaps Papadakis on the back.

They step quickly down the stairs of the bank built in a classical Greek style to the waiting limousine. A CITY OF CHICAGO patrol car has pulled up behind the limo and the cop is talking to the chauffeur. "Nice and easy, Papa," Carlo whispers as they approach. "Nice and easy now."

Wason sees them arrive and turns to the officer. "Here they are now, officer." Then to Carlo, "He doesn't want us double-parked Mr. Williams," he says.

"Apologies, officer," Carlo says in a louder voice. "We're on our way." To Papadakis, "Get in the car."

"But you said—"

Carlo looks him square in the eyes: "Trust me. Get in the car."

The officer returns to the patrol car, and Wason opens the rear door for Papadakis who crawls in and skootches over to make room for Carlo. Wason gets behind the wheel. "Down to the next block," Carlo says. They drive down one block and pull over. Wason lets the motor idle.

Carlo turns to Papadakis. "Give me the money." Papadakis hands him the pouch. Carlo removes the bills, and counts out $300. "Here," he says, proffering the money to Papadakis. "Take it."

Papadakis, wide-eyed and sweating, says nothing but shakes his head.

"Come on," Carlo says all friendly-like. "Consider it combat pay. Sh*t, it ain't your money" and he takes Papadakis' hand and places the money in it and folds his fingers around it. "But it is now. You just made yourself 300 bucks. Get outta here, and have a nice day. Go home to your wife and kids."

Papadakis gets out of the limo and shuts the door. The car speeds away. He stands at the curb for a minute watching it disappear. His shoulders are rounded and slumped. He reaches for his hanky and then turns back for the bank and Mrs. Wang. But she has already left, and is strutting down Cook Avenue in black three-inch heels.

Papadakis pockets the money.

# # #

They drive to Grand Central Station, picking up Alice along the way, and park the limo in a proximal alley off Harrison. Inside the car they get out of their duds and put on street clothes and bundle up the suit and uniform in a duffel bag. They glance up the alley both ways, and then up above them, checking the windows of the buildings lining the lane. They see no one.

Wason walks up the alley to dispose of their clothes in a trash bin. Carlo opens the trunk. Inside is Carlo's travel bag and a man, the chauffeur of the purloined limo. He is about 50 years old, slight of frame, bound and gagged, struggling like a cat in a bag, and trying to shout. "Looks like our friend has come to," he mutters. He removes the twine around his wrists, and Alice gets his feet undone. Together, they get the hapless fellow out of the trunk and stand him on his feet. Carlo leans into the trunk to retrieve his grip. "Get the other bags out from the back seat," he says to Alice. She turns to move to the side of the car and open the rear door, but as she does so, she glances back and sees that the freshly liberated limo driver has managed to grab a tire iron in the trunk and his arm is now in motion to bring the end of that instrument crashing upon Carlo's cranium. She bounds to the rear of the car, pivots and then executes a full revolution of her body bringing her right leg and high-heeled foot up, so that the power of the full body twist increases the force and effectiveness of the blow when her heel catches the driver in his mid-section and sends him staggering back. Before he realizes what has happened, Alice takes another half-step and delivers a karate chop to his neck. The tire iron clatters to the pavement making a ringing, clanging sound. He slumps to the ground, groaning. Alice steps back, and tugs her skirt down to its previous, already daring, position.

"That was a really stupid thing to do, you moron!" Carlo says, grabbing the fellow and hoisting him up. Wason has returned, hearing the commotion, and the two boys shove the moaning man into the driver's seat where he sits sideways with his feet out of the car and on the ground. They bind his feet again and his hands behind his back. Then they shove him into the car so that he is laying down, trussed up, on the seat. Carlo leans in through the window. "Listen to me," he says firmly. But the fellow is still moaning and crying. Carlo walks around the front of the limo to the passenger side, opens the door and bonks the guy on the head. "Hey! Hey! Stop whining and shut up for one goddurn minute. I don't know why I'm taking the trouble wit chou anyway." The man momentarily relaxes. "The rope's loose. You should be able to wiggle free in about ten minutes or less. Then you can take the gag out. Thanks for the use of your vehicle. Here's some money to cover your expenses." He puts $200 on the dashboard and places the keys to the limo on top of the money. "Gotta go now," he says cheerily. They grab the suitcases and then they are gone.

They go to the station to purchase tickets. As they walk to the platform, Alice stops to pull out her compact to apply a fresh coat of red to her pouty lips. Wason waits nearby with a newspaper.

"You were pretty good back there," Carlo says with a sideways glance.

"Umm." Wang Xiao Hua purses her lips and opens them again, making a slight smacking noise. Then she looks at him. He says: "Did you use that fake Chinese accent when you's talking to Papadakis?"

Alice giggles. "I couldn't help myself." They laugh uproariously.

They're standing at Car No. 4, about to step inside. Someone behind them speaks: "Mr. Carlo Rossi?"

The trio turns around. Facing them are two burly police officers. "Mr. Rossi, you are under arrest for suspicion of robbery at the Illinois State Bank. Please turn around with your hands behind your back."

The soufflé has just collapsed. The three are led away in handcuffs.

Chapter VIII

COOP IS DRESSED BUT HAS GIVEN up his attempt to don a bowtie. He can't manage the knot with his mangled hands. Millie has even laid out a belt for him. And his brown shoes and argyle socks. He keeps some of his things here, just for convenience, but he wouldn't live at Millie's although he spends a lot of time here. He likes his routine. He likes having his room in the hotel, listening to "Fibber Magee and Molly" and his other "operys" in the afternoon, taking care of his correspondence, getting out into the neighborhoods of Bathington to visit friends, returning to Millie's for supper, doing up the dishes again and perhaps watching TV. But when the girls get crabby, he heads home. *Millie's going to want me to move in now for sure.* He doesn't want to do that. Sometimes the girls are rambunctious. It isn't just the girls. He enjoys his liberty and values his privacy.

He bends his frame over the sink. He turns the cold water four-fingered porcelain faucet to the right, cups his hands under the flow and splashes some water on his face and rubs it around, and runs his palms lightly over his head. He peers into the mirror and wonders how he got so old so darn fast. He grabs a hand towel and dries off his face and noggin and hangs up the towel on his hook, *his* hook—for this was once his bathroom too. He and Antonia raised Johnny right here in this house. So he knows this bathroom. Why, he put in this very sink himself and Antonia hung the paper. Not this paper. Millie and Johnny redecorated. He sees a framed photo sitting on the window sill and picks it up. Millie and Johnny and the girls, then 13 and 3 years old. He is in uniform, Millie's arm tucked inside of his, all smiling at the camera. Before he left for Korea. Before he didn't come back.

# # #

Two days later, Jules Joyce, 72, goes to Mrs. Pettigrew's after all. His room has an external entrance via a flight of wooden steps flung up the side of the clapboard house to the second floor where a window has been turned into a door. She offers one meal a day, plus a room. Pettigrew, whose husband had been an attorney in town, hesitates, for a sense of propriety is important to her as it is to her vast circle of friends, and she is not keen to be embarrassed publicly by the behavior of her tenants. Jules is the most active of the Pettigrew coterie and one whose habits and general comportment is known occasionally to have been troublesome. These reservations notwithstanding, she decides Jules' presence will not interfere greatly with the tranquil aspect of the house.

Violet Crenshaw was a Roman Catholic, but only by marriage. Still, she rarely missed a week without attending mass. She was a Calvinist by birth, however, and thus her affliliation with Bathington Community Church seemed predestined. Her funeral is held in the Bathington Community Church where she'd been an active member of the Ladies Aid and served as the church secretary on a part time basis, her duties being limited to producing the Sunday worship bulletin and the monthly newsletter, the *Bathington Chimes*.

The closed-casket service is delayed until the following Friday to locate relatives, a task which is difficult owing to the fact that she apparently had none. Cushing thought he'd heard of a sister back east, and beyond that, nothing. The people of the village of Bathington are apparently all the family Violet Crenshaw had or desired. Carlton Cooper is one of the pallbearers, and the Reverend Archibald Cushing delivers an excellent sermon in Coop's judgment entitled, "The Master Is Come and Calleth For Thee." The congregation sings her favorite hymn, "In the Cross of Christ I Glory." She would not soon be forgotten. On that point, everyone seems to agree.

The marshal is involved in the death since it occurred in a fire of unknown origin, and the scuttlebutt according to Mrs. Mang is that Violet drugged up on sleeping pills on account of her insomnia and had not awakened. Mang's alternative report is that Crenshaw was drinking at Bud's the night of the fire and had to be helped back to her room on account of her being drunk as a skunk. She was dead in her bed. She was not discovered missing until a count revealed a discrepancy, and it was learned that although twenty-seven heads had been counted, that number included the guest on the first floor who was not a permanent resident of the hotel. It is only when Chief Dixon has the fire under control and is investigating the cause of the blaze that the body of Violet Crenshaw is discovered in her second floor corner room. The body is sent to Charles City for an autopsy and returned to Bathington, but it will be some time before the results are back.

# # #

Coop stays with Millie and the girls for over a week and except for sleeping in the house at night, the routine isn't much different than before the fire. He stays up late one night, the dishes done, and sits at the kitchen table with his writing notebook. Millie and the girls are in bed. He takes out his eyeglasses from its hard-shell case, and wraps the stems around his ears where the hair on his tonsured head meets them and adjusts the glasses on the lower end of the bridge of his nose just right. He withdraws his fountain pen from the breast pocket of his shirt, unscrews the cap and draws up a list of what perished in the blaze and what survived. At the age of 68, he is taking Inventory. He came into this world naked but at least was not then conscious of his nakedness. Now he is.

In the "Perished" column he begins with personal items: Two photograph albums, correspondence, diaries, a photo of his beloved Antonia at age 16 that had been in a walnut oval frame, a set of cufflinks given to him by the station agent in Cedar Rapids, Viewmaster reels of San Francisco, his Underwood portable typewriter, reams of loose leaf paper, onion skin and carbon paper, a shelf-full of books including several by Bess Streeter Aldrich (one of which was autographed) and Willa Cather. One King James Version of the Bible. Clothes: shoes, trousers, two winter suits, plus summer suits and shirts that were due to be de-mothballed soon, his winter topcoat, two umbrellas, two pair of gloves (one calfskin leather). Furniture and "household" items: one single brass bed, one bureau, a red end table, a drop-lid mahogany wood secretary desk, a stuffed chair and ottoman, two hooked rugs, his traveling grip and one long-handled cream spoon. Toiletries: two toothbrushes, a tube of Colgate, one Glasco Squat Eyewash Cup, one box Epson salts, Murine eyedrops, Norelco electric shaver, his Dopp-kit.

Crenshaw's crucifix has survived—miraculously. Both the cupboard and the box protected it somewhat. The box is severely damaged, but the cross itself suffers only slight charring at the base. Coop is glad.

In the "Survival" column he makes only one other entry: "Me."

He hears movement beyond the kitchen. Millie appears in a turquoise terrycloth bathrobe. "Couldn't sleep," she says. She pours some water in a teapot, sets it on the stove, joins Coop at the table and pulls out a chair. "How you doing?"

"Oh fine, fine," Coop says, closing his notebook. Millie glances at it. "Just taking inventory," he says, sighing.

"It's going to be okay," she says after they sit in silence for a while. "I can't imagine what it's like to lose all the stuff that has so much sentimental value."

Coop nods. "Well, I think you can imagine," he says.

"Yeah, well maybe."

"Funny I've been dreaming about Johnny lately. Don't know why except it's been two years now, I guess. You still have any problems like that?"

"Not too much anymore," she says in a low-timbered voice that suggests the opposite is true. "It's sort of become a chapter, well more than one I guess, of my life, but now that chapter's over and I'm in a whole different chapter, whole different book, actually—!" She laughs. "A whole different book!" She pushes away from the table and leaves for the dining room and returns with a tea cup. "You want some?"

"No, no, I'm fine," he says.

"You all healed up now?"

"Good as new," he says. "Better than new, thanks to you."

Millie sits down with her tea. They talk for another twenty minutes and then he leaves her for bed.

Rev. Cushing initiates an effort—Coops called it the "Save the Orphans Fund"—with the other churches of Bathington—the E&Rs, Lutherans, Catholics, Baptists and Apostolic Pentecostal church, or, in Jules' words: "Germans, Swedes, Irish, Southerners and holy rollers"—to assist those who suffered loss in the fire. He obtains a list of the erstwhile Fremont residents and arranges to have each one interviewed about their losses. Each church solicits donations in kind to be dropped off at the Bathington Community Church for distribution to the appropriate individuals. Coop reluctantly gives him his Inventory—although it was made before he knew that such a campaign was underway.

# # #

Mrs. Hazel Hemming *nee* Wilson is the redoubtable proprietor of a boarding house she runs on Main Street in a folk Victorian house built in 1895. The saffron-colored three-gabled, two-story house sits back from the street a good fifty yards fronted by a lawn on which are a maple and weeping willow. A side walk bordered by a low boxwood hedge on each side leads to the porch with spindled railings which wraps around the south and west aspect. The eaves are bracketed, and the shutters are forest green. It is the house into which she moved as a bride in 1912 after marrying Mr. Walter Hemming of Des Moines, fifteen years her senior, and an industrialist in the coal business (his father Horace had dug out all the coal that was to be found in Polk County). His siblings bought out his interest in the business, and he bought the Bathington State Bank and ran a few small side businesses out of his office in the BSB building. He met Miss Wilson at a Christmas party in Des Moines following a concert at Hoyt Sherman Place at which Miss Wilson, aspiring to opera, offered an inspired rendition of "Un bel di" from Puccini's *Madame Butterfly* and followed that with the saccharine "Star of the East" at the party itself. Three weeks later they married—he was established in a career, was heir to his father's coal money—opera be damned. They moved to Bathington to the house already under construction for his bride—whoever she might be. They raised three children, and then in 1935 he had a massive heart attack and was dead. She wore widow weeds for one month and then took stock. Except for Reginald who still worked at the bank, the children soon moved out, and the boarders moved in. Not that she needed the money, but the Great Depression had depleted her assets and moreover, she desired to keep her servants. A houseful of servants and boarders at the very least sated her thirst for a small kingdom of vassals and serfs.

She meets Rev. Cushing, whose hat is in hand, in the parlor where, after some polite talk in which he inquired about her health in a most general way, he broaches the topic of the town's new refugees. "I was thinking of Carlton Cooper," he suggests.

"I'll take Carlton," she says, coughing delicately. "Thirty-five a month, one meal."

"Capital!" Cushing replies, rising. "I will talk to him straightaway to see if this will be suitable."

"Suitable? Of course it will be suitable. Besides, I like Coop. He wears bowties."

Cushing conveys the news to Coop who accepts the offer. Mrs. Hemming's house is eminently suited to his disposition since it is quiet, refined and spacious. He thinks he might be happier there in the long term than he'd been at the Fremont. Cushing agrees. "It'll take some time to get together the necessaries," Coop says cheerfully, "but I suppose I don't need much to get along." So it is settled.

# # #

A week later and a week closer to Resurrection day, Violet Crenshaw scarcely cold in the ground, Coop is feeling like he's risen from the grave himself. When he heard the news of Crenshaw's death, he collapsed on his bed as though he had been run over by a Caterpillar—his insides seemed flat and steamrolled. His chest was constricted and somehow he thought he was struggling for his own life. Her death was more shocking than Antonia's because he expected *that* death. This one, no. Her death was a snatching, a grabbing. Antonia had been "called home." It was a slow and peaceful home-going. Both she and Coop had prepared and made arrangements, traveled through the transition together until one day she was gone. Violet's death, on the other hand, was an outright theft, a violent and sudden robbery depriving her friends and the Bathington community of a good, decent soul—and of those a town cannot have too many. Something was not right about this death. And strangely, Coop resented it … resented the brazen unfairness of it. To Cushing he said that it was "unseemly" that she, of all people, should have died. So he grieved deeply for her and had thought of her every day since the fire.

But now, on this spring afternoon, for the first time since she died, he feels a recovery coming on. He steps out on to the veranda of his new lodgings in the late afternoon to take a seat in a white wicker chair, part of a set which includes a loveseat and a couple of small tables. The temperature is 62°, unseasonably warm, but he still requires his worsted wool topcoat. He wraps a white silk scarf around his neck and, on his head, he sets his gray chapeau at a jaunty angle. It is his first such outing in the new year. It is time. Mrs. Hemming removed the slip covers only today. To celebrate he has his pipe, but better, a 1935 bottle of single malt scotch, given to him on V-Day and a luxury in which he indulges only on special occasions. The last time, he muses, must have been when Vic had her fourth birthday a couple of years ago after her daddy died. His pipe is a straight-stem cherry wood pipe handcrafted by Tom the Pipe Carver who had a narrow shop on Hubbard Street in Chicago just north of the Chicago River. "I got this pipe when Antonia and I were married and living in Chicago, which means," he says out loud, "that I've had this pipe for forty-three years." He places the scotch and a glass on an end table, and sits down heavily in the chair.

This is the life, he thinks. Material possessions mean nothing if your basic needs are taken care of—shelter, food and clothing—and if you have someone, even one person, who loves you. He has *three* people in his life who love him, Millie, Frankie and Vic, and a good number of people who, at the very least, have some degree of affection for him. He has enough. He cannot ask for more. And as for worldly goods, what he lost were only possessions and not many of those. He was surprised to discover how much he left in Millie's attic after his Antonia died. And now, thanks to the Save the Orphans Fund, he has the "necessaries" he needs. It's wise to live simply and quite simple to live wisely. It's not complicated. He had a car in the 1940s but decided he didn't need the old Pontiac and gave it to Millie when Johnny died. She prudently sold their new Ford and put the money in savings.

Coop retrieves a tin of Prince Albert from the pocket of his topcoat and begins to feed tobacco into the bowl, pausing to tamp it snuggly with the end of his pinky. Then he adds more and tamps again until the bowl is full. He lights the bowl with a stick match, enjoying the sound of the scratch and miniature explosion and the quick scent of phosphorus before the match ignites into a flame. He sits back for a moment. Then, turning, he picks up the scotch and pours a finger into the clear bottom. He holds the glass high to look at it through the amber light of the fading sun and enjoys its texture and viscosity. He sticks his nose in the glass and draws a breath. Then he sips and taps his lips together absorbing the warm feeling of the scotch passing across his tongue and down his throat. He takes a toke on his pipe. "This is the life," he says again out loud.

He looks past the veranda railing. The last snow patches have disappeared, receding into the soil like soapsuds left in the sink. Perhaps a freak snow will hit yet in April, but winter has vanished. Coop shivers in the cold. The air is fresh, the soil soft and moist. Hyacinths and daffodils have been up for some time, tulips are nosing up, as though the earth is shaking off its slumber, sloughing off its bedclothes and preparing to take a shower—showers which surely will come in this month.

He has not been sitting for five minutes reveling in his "this-is-the-life" perfect setting, when the veranda door opens and a woman steps out pausing to glance toward the south porch and the west. She is medium height and of erect bearing, standing in calf length high-heeled black leather boots which disappear under the hem of a double-breasted wool coat adorned with a coffee-colored mink fur collar around the neck. Her face is not round but pleasantly angular, and lean. Her skin is brown and hard, creased in places, suggesting that she has suffered more than her share of hardships in life or has spent a lot of time in the sun. Pulled over her head, hiding her hair and framing her face to create the effect of a cameo, is a large fox fur hat. Her eyes are the eyes of the canard, gray in the fading light and shifting quickly to survey the landscape. Her lips are painted red. On her arm is a soft leather bag.

This is not a woman, Coop thinks rakishly, *this is a goddess!* This is not a woman who can be pushed around. In just three seconds, he knows this lady is a *presence*, a woman of affairs and accustomed to certain ways of doing things. She might prove an interesting foil for Mrs. Hemming, he thinks. She will not play the vassal to Hemming's dowager queen. Coop assumes that if she intends to relax she'll choose the south, unoccupied, wing. Instead, she moves without hesitation to the settee where Coop has encamped and sits in the other available chair with the loveseat between him and her and directs her gaze across the pale lawn and to the sun low in the western sky.

Coop has seen her before. On the night of the fire, she was escorted from the Fremont wearing that fox fur hat. She is the first floor lodger.

Coop sits still. He exhales a cloud of pipe smoke and is slightly dismayed that it wafts in the direction of this woman. He tries turning his head to his right, expelling the smoke more forcibly, but nevertheless it lazes back past him and toward his porch companion like a leaf on a languorous stream. He tries waving the smoke away but he looks like he's a cop giving traffic directions. And he vainly imagines that he's doing all of this discretely and that the Stranger does not notice.

She seems not to notice, anyway. Coop watches, using his peripheral vision as much as possible so as not to appear prying. The lady digs into her handbag and produces a silver cigarette case. She snaps it open, and takes a cigarette with practiced ease and closes the case returning it to her bag. She pulls out an exquisite cigarette holder with a bone stem and six-sided silver end into which she pushes the cigarette. Her red lips part and she inserts the holder with its cigarette into her thin mouth and clamps it shut. In her right hand now is a diamond-encrusted platinum lighter, and quickly the cigarette is lit and she inhales deeply and then removes the holder with her left hand and holds it in the air dramatically. Her nostrils flare slightly as she releases the smoke explosively through her nose. It is an amazing performance. Coop is now staring unabashed.

"It's a gift from my husband," she says, waving the lighter slightly. "May he rest in peace."

"Ah," says Coop cautiously.

Suddenly the woman shifts her weight in the chair and turns to face Coop, extending her hand, saying in a raspy yet refined voice: "I'm sorry, how rude of me not to introduce myself. Hello, I am Mrs. Penelope Cuttingham of Chicago." She pronounces her name Cutting*hum*.

Coop stands immediately, thinking to play this game, takes his pipe in his left hand, advances quickly to Mrs. Penelope Cuttingham of Chicago. He stands stiffly at first, clicking his heels, and then taking her hand in his and bowing slightly, he says "Enchanté. And I am Mr. Carlton Cooper of Bathington at your service."

She looks at him in surprise and then smiles. "Ooh," she purrs. "A gentleman and a man of manners! Mr. Carlton Cooper, I like you already!" She takes a drag on her cigarette and exhales—slowly.

Chapter IX

Davenport, Iowa
April 8, 1952

WASONENSKAR JARDOKOLOKOWSKI SITS NERVOUSLY ON A bench in Stanley Park, not far from the Mississippi which is rising due to recent rains. It is cool even at two in the afternoon. The bench is dark green and the paint is peeling. It has a slat missing and it makes his bum sore if he sits too long in the same position. Still, he is not inclined to move, find another bench, sprawl on the patchy lawn of crabgrass, or lean against one of the many elms that populates the embankment of the river not far from the Cameroon Bridge. He is uncomfortable but too lazy to seek comfort. He puts his fingers to his mouth to position a sunflower seed between his incisors like a squirrel shelling an acorn. The pod cracks and Wasonenskar expectorates the chaff to the ground, while his teeth and tongue continue to worry a mouthful of seeds until the kernel of each one is extracted from the husk.

Presently he pauses long enough to get some more seeds. He fingers the rabbit's foot in the pocket of his jacket. He told Carlo that he was taking the day off, not that they were doing anything in Davenport except getting the press prepared for shipping to Bathington. But, although such a simple task can often be more complicated than it should be—and in their case it is—today Wasonenskar wanted to knock off and do nothing. And doing nothing in the park seems like the best thing. In fact doing nothing is what this insouciant youth does best. Wasonenskar saw these green commons once while riding past on a bus, so he hopped a bus and went back.

He is affected by seasonal changes. April is not his favorite month. And April 15 coming up soon is not his favorite day. He doesn't have any favorite days, although Christmas comes close. But April 15 is for him an ominous day. Abraham Lincoln died on this date. The Titanic sank on April 15 fifty years ago. April 15 is the anniversary of his father's death. He died after being trapped in a 60,000 bushel silo near DeKalb. He wasn't even a farmer; he was a florist. One day he visited a friend who showed him the new silo built by the cooperative. When he walked across a footbridge at the top, a section broke loose. He didn't fall too far, and it was certainly a soft landing, but he sank in the yellow grain like it was quicksand and that was that. That was April 15. And then his mother died only days later, hardly even time to sit *shiva*. She and her little boy went to the funeral and returned for the *seudal havra'ah*, the funeral meal. Neighbors in DeKalb brought food. His mother choked on a deviled egg and expired on the spot. After that, friends of the synagogue took him to St. Joseph's as there was no family to take him in, no Jewish orphanages. But the Reverend Mother, a remarkable woman who had read widely and was an admirer of the Mahatma, promised Wasonenskar's temporary guardians that she would make sure that the boy was raised Jewish. She wondered if Conservative was okay, or whether she needed to get him the full treatment. Conservative would be fine. So Wasonenskar was raised Jewish, although the Reverend Mother who made these arrangements died of natural causes, and her replacement was not so zealous and sometimes Wasonenskar had to attend Catholic masses. He became in practice, if not actual belief, a Catholic Jew, or he thought, a Jewish Catholic. In any case, he carries around more guilt than all the felons in the Cook County jail put together. He is the sorriest fella Carlo has ever met. He is always saying he is sorry for this, that or the other thing. And if he isn't observing Lent, he is doing Passover, and he traverses easily between Chanukah and Christmas. He is bi-religious, bilingual and bi-cultural and as such he approaches life with a certain lassitude and detachment. The nuns on good days described him as thoughtful and restrained; on bad days, which was most of the time, feckless, indolent and lethargic.

The Reverend Mother, in spite of her respect for religious, cultural and ethnic differences, shortened his name. The Jardokulokowskis were from Poland. Wasonenskar was born in Proznan, but in 1933 his parents, presciently aware of what was happening in Germany, were able to get themselves to Amsterdam with the help of friends and from there they immigrated to America when he was just a tot. When he arrived at St. Joseph's he could scarcely speak, and when he did, it was Polish. His ac-

cent is still noticeable, but not in an annoying way. The Mother, as Carlo
called her in those days, pronounced him Wason Jard and so it was.

The sunflower seeds are gone. He reaches for a cigarette and lights up.
The breeze along the river has picked up so he tightens the scarf around
his neck. He crosses his legs and slings an arm over the back of the bench
and gazes out across the waters to the hills of Illinois. He has never been
in Iowa before. Doesn't feel any different really. He doesn't mind being
stuck in Davenport, but it is driving Carlo nuts. The purchase of the
Johnson Power C-3 offset press has been completed for $933 which is a
good deal. Lefty saw an ad in the trades and began negotiations before
they left the Windy City, giving Alice $500 toward the purchase price. It is
now simply a matter of getting the press to Bathington. At first they decide to ship it by rail, but for what they are asking they think they should
try something else. They look into renting a truck, but can't find one, but
discover a 10-footer 1936 truck for sale for $235, so they buy it and figure
they'll drive the press to Bathington and sell the truck or keep it for future use.

So they have the truck. They have the press. But they are waiting for
an "all clear" from Alice—whom they don't have. "I've got to go back,"
she said almost as soon as they'd checked into their crummy hotel near
the river. She made a collect call to Lefty to tell him they arrived in Davenport, and he asked her to get on a Greyhound and come back. Something to do with contracts, or paperwork, she said. Wason didn't catch all
the details, but it didn't really bother him too much. Alice is a little high-
strung for his taste, but Carlo is irritated and has been in a bad mood ever
since. Her departure was almost 10 days ago. "She should be back by
now, and if she doesn't get back soon, I'm going after her, or I'm getting
out of here. This is a pile of crap!" While not as agitated as Carlo, Wason
doesn't want to be stuck in Davenport any more than Carlo.

They aren't. Alice arrives two days later via bus, and tells the boys they
are moving out. "When?" Carlo asks peevishly. They are sitting at the bar
in Mookey's Saloon located in a broken curb, broken glass, broken people district of Davenport. Alice is wearing lavender pants and a red
blouse, an outfit she bought at Marshall Fields. Patrons stare. Not many
Oriental women ... or any women ... in pants in these parts. Alice sits
between Carlo and Wason. The boys are drinking beers. Alice has a shot
of Jack. "Tomorrow," she says matter-of-factly. "Heading out tomorrow."

"And who are we hooking up with in Bathington?"

"Whaddya mean?"

"I meannnn," Carlo says, drawing out the words, "Who … is … we … meeting? Who's setting this up? What? We're just driving into town as fine as you please with a printing press, camera, lights and tripods and all this crap and we're not going to see nobody?"

"You worry too much," she says, throwing down the whiskey. She signals the bartender for another shot. "It's all arranged. We got a shop with plenty of room, a pretty good setup. I guarantee you'll be surprised. It's A OK!" Her black bangs bounce when she nods her head.

"And you made all the arrangements? Have you ever even been to this hick town?"

"Nope. We've been working with an agent Lefty has who's on the ground in Bathington as we speak."

"And who's that? And how do we meet him?"

"Cuttingham. Penelope Cuttingham. And we don't find her; she'll find us."

"Cuttingham?"

"Yes, Cuttingham. I believe you know her."

"Yeah, I know her … I knew her … been years. I used to see her at St. Joseph's. She'd come in for school plays, or visit with the Mother Superior. I think she gave money or something. What's she got to do with this?"

"Let's say she's connected, and she's the one who sprung us from jail and I'm not sure how, but for right now, we got a get out of jail free card, so we're going to take advantage of it. Maybe we'll get the whole story some day. Something's going on. But for now, we have our own job to do and that is to go out and make a f**k*ng mountain of money. But before we blow this town, there's one more thing we got to do."

"Yeah, what's that?"

"Did you bring that suit with you that you wore for that last job?"

"No, we disposed of it, remember?"

"Right. Then we'll go shopping for two suits, one for you and one for Wason."

"Why does Wason need a suit?" Carlo demands. "Why do I need a suit? We're not doing any more jobs."

"Well, you got one more job. Come Sunday, you're going to church, and you're gonna need suits."

Chapter X

"ACTUALLY, I AM NOT BEING COMPLETELY honest with you, Mr. Cooper." Mrs. Cuttingham takes a long drag on her cigarette, and blows the smoke forcefully into the cool evening air. Coop after introducing himself so smartly, has returned to the settee and relit his pipe as Cuttingham speaks. "I am afraid I have the advantage, because I know who you are. We've never met, of course, but I've been in church a few times—dressed down considerably—" She breaks off with a laugh. "And I have made some inquiries about you, and the church, and, again, in the spirit of complete transparency, I saw you leave for the veranda and made a point of coming out to visit for a few moments, if you have no objection."

Coop doesn't know whether he is more surprised or intrigued by this turn in the conversation. *But why should I be surprised?* His heart is full of mirth. *I DO have that certain* je ne sais quoi, n'est-ce pas? *You just never lose it. If you have it, you have it!* But, on the other hand he has absolutely no idea where this is headed, but is curious. "No objection from this quarter," he says generously. "Mind you, I reserve the right to raise an objection later, but please, continue."

Cuttingham smiles. "How very kind of you, Mr. Cooper." She pauses. "You wouldn't by chance be able to share any of that delightful scotch you have there, would you?"

"Of course," he replies, rising. "Let me run and get you a glass."

"Thank you so much." Off he goes. He is glad for the diversion for it gives him a chance to review this development in the conversation. But he has to confess as he returns with another glass that he is no closer to divining Cuttingham's possible agenda than he was before he left. He pours some scotch into the glass and offers it to her. She sips and smiles, and then launches: "I have a proposal that I think could be as beneficial to you as it would be to me. Actually, I don't have a stake in this, except I am interested in lending a helping hand, but you and the church would definitely be ..." She searches for the right word and finds one she doesn't use often, "... blessed." She glances at Coop who is observing with interest.

"Please go on," he urges.

"You've got a problem."

"Only one?" Coop retorts.

Cuttingham laughs. "It's about the secretary you're looking for," she explains. "My understanding of the situation is that you need, or Bathington Community Church needs, someone who can fulfill their printing needs. The most urgent of these needs is the weekly program, but the church also has a monthly newsletter, and I am sure there are other printing needs, are there not? Like posters or flyers, brochures that you might leave with newcomers at the church, business cards, reports—do you have an annual business meeting?"

"Oh, yes," Coop responded dryly. "It's a high point of the church year."

"And have you been producing any of these materials yourself, Mr. Cooper?" She notices Coop's surprised look, and adds, "Oh yes, I know you are the typist who does the program, but I also know you don't intend to stay in the job and that you were drafted as an emergency, stop-gap measure in light of Miss Crenshaw's imminent departure, although no one thought she'd depart in such a dreadful manner, God rest her soul. And therefore I am assuming that you are doing only what is absolutely essential, and the monthly newsletter, for example, was not published last month, and nothing in fact has been published except the program. Of course were these other things to be produced—programs, reports, agendas, posters—it would require more of your time or the future secretary's time, and that involves more expense."

"Well, you hit the nail right there, Mrs. Cuttingham. Fortunately, Miss Crenshaw was very smart about this, and quite skillful. She could do in one day what it takes me several days to accomplish, I'm afraid."

"Quite." They sit in silence for a few moments while they nurse their scotches and puff on their respective tobaccos of choice. Then she resumes. "What would you say if I told you I had three people coming to town who are interested in setting up a business and establishing themselves, who would be willing to take on this little weekly task of yours, and more, and do it for free?"

"Sounds too good to be true, Mrs. Cuttingham," he replies cautiously.

"These friends are young people, but responsible young people—which is so rare in this modern day and age don't you think?—and the arrangement could work like this: One of them, the young lady, is a typist. One young man is a printer, and one young man is a photographer. They want to set up a publishing and photography business and develop a client base throughout northeast Iowa. But they're short of ready cash, as young people often are, but they are not short on talent and ambition. I propose that the young lady be the church secretary, that is, do the actual work on the typewriter while the printer would print the programs and posters—whatever you'd need. They would also produce a church directory which is becoming quite fashionable these days, and the photographer could shoot the church families for free—if they wanted to buy some of his photos, that would be fine—and the photos would be published in a book along with names, addresses and phone numbers as a handy reference for the people of the congregation."

"For free?" Coop asks skeptically. He's waiting for the other shoe to drop and he's expecting it's going to be a size extra large.

"Well, yes, and no. Free, in the sense that the church would not pay them any form of monetary compensation. The compensation would take another form."

"And what, pray tell, would that be?"

"Mr. Cooper, they need space. At this stage, they can't really afford to pay rent on a building, and I've looked around Bathington and there's really not anything suitable." Coop remains silent. He is beginning to see where this is going. "My thought is that the church, in return for services rendered, would allow them the use of the walkout basement or ground floor on the west side that opens out onto the parking lot. They could then begin to establish themselves, while also satisfying the printing needs of the church. And, let me say, we're not talking about a program printed on a mimeograph machine that might have rips and tears and black smudges on the finished product—Oh, no offense, Mr. Cooper! I know how difficult the process is. But I mean to say that, if this arrangement goes through, the church would enjoy programs every week printed on an offset printer, looking very professional, very professional indeed. And likewise the *Bathington Chimes*, I believe you call it. These young people are top notch, I know you will be delighted."

"That basement is a mess," Coop warns. But he is thinking that the proposal has merit and he certainly cannot dismiss it out of hand.

"Yes, I know. I've taken the time to inspect it myself. These kids are very enterprising, and they will have it cleaned up in no time. And, the room is large enough to be able to subdivide with moveable partitions or even curtain off an area, or build out a room where the photographer could take his portraits of Rev. Cushing, the Session, and other officers or leaders of the church—I don't know what you call them, and indeed of all the church families. They would do all of this just to have a place to grow their business. They were thinking if they could do this for a year, they would then want, or, I don't know, expect, the church to review the arrangement, and they would likely want to perhaps make a monthly contribution in cash to the General Fund, or, perhaps after 12 months they will be ready to move out, and into another facility in town. What do you say?"

Coop isn't sure how often Cuttingham has been in a church. Bulletins are not usually called "programs," but he supposes it is just as good a word as any. "Bulletin" is not an apt word, either, really. Sounds like something coming over the teletype, or an announcement that might be read over the radio. "Program" is a word with more cachet, but he thinks the word implies a *performance* which doesn't really indicate what happens at a worship service. But, then, how else to describe the paper in one's hand that one uses during the service itself? It's usually called a "bulletin," or a "worship bulletin." No one calls it a "program" or "worship program." Perhaps he is reading too much into this. And even if Cuttingham isn't a churchgoer, what of it?

A train rumbles by in the distance, whistling past county roads as evening falls. "There goes the six o'clock Rocket," Coop says. "Better get down to Millie and the girl's for supper."

"Millie's your daughter?" Cuttingham asks.

"No, no, my daughter-in-law, raising the girls." Coop begins gathering his stuff, getting the shot glass and his pipe in one hand and the bottle of scotch in the other. He straightens up awaiting Cuttingham's next response, as he is sure it is coming.

"So, your son is not around?"

Coop pauses, and sighs. "No, he was killed in Korea a couple years ago, well, not quite two years ago. Gave his life for his country." Cuttingham is silent momentarily. Then: "Well, I'm always pushing into things where I have no business. Please accept my apologies, Mr. Cooper. It was insensitive of me to pry."

"Well, thank you, Mrs. Cuttingham. I appreciate that, I really do. But the truth is, it helps to face it, say it out loud. It sort of takes practice, you know. And I think I am getting the hang of it. Miss him terribly of course. But it's getting easier to talk about it. Johnny was a great young man, terrific father and husband, and he was killed in the war. Now Millie's doing a great job teaching, raising the girls, and I help where I can, and still have time to volunteer at the church to do the bulletins. But this proposal, Mrs. Cuttingham, sounds promising. Very promising indeed!"

# # #

Later that evening Coop returns to Frau Hemming's Haus, as he calls it, and places a call to the manse to apprise the Reverend as to this latest development, saying that it sounds promising. But would the Session agree to let this party of three set up a business in the church? Would they take the long view that they would be providing assistance to some enterprising young people but at the same time receiving from them valuable services? The basement room with its exterior door is unused anyway except as a gathering place for unwanted and unused materials, like old Christmas pageant sets, for example, or Vacation Bible School supplies. Cushing thinks that the Session would be favorably inclined. The walkout room is of no tangible benefit to the church or congregation.

The lynchpin of the entire arrangement, however, is the typist. *Have you interviewed her?* Cushing inquires. No. *Have you interviewed any of the others?* No. *Can she type?* Evidently she is an excellent typist but I will have no way of knowing until I have an opportunity to test her. *I say, what do you know of this Cuttingham woman?* Not much, not much at all. She's from Chicago. *How old is she?* Well, obviously, she didn't divulge that information, but I'm guessing about 55 give or take. *How does she get on, then? Support herself?* Don't know that either, but I have the impression that money is not a concern for her. Her husband has passed and he may have left enough for her to live comfortably. *And the others, what do you know about them?* Nothing except that one's a photographer and the other's a printer. *And they will provide all the materials, not expect us to buy paper, ink and supplies?* That's right. *And in return?* As I said, Reverend, they get the space rent free for at least a year. *How does Cuttingham know these kids?* I believe they're friends of a friend. I think there's been a connection for some time. *When do they want to start?* I think they're ready to go. Well, not actually to start the presses, but to get into the room, get it cleaned up. They need a definite word from us. *Well, we can't give them a definite word until you've interviewed the girl—how old is she?* In her 20s I think. *Married?* No. *Ummm, that could be a problem. Can't do anything until you've interviewed the girl, and I would like to meet her as well before any decision is made. And we need to meet the young men in question, size them up and all. And you'll collect letters of reference?* Yes, sir. *What about signage?* Signage? *Yeah, signage. Do they expect to put a business sign above the entrance or on an exterior surface by the door or, are they thinking they might erect a sign near the street at the edge of the parking lot? Really, I don't think the Session is going to go for any sign at all.* Don't know about that. I'll ask. *I think they will need to rely on word of mouth or advertisements in the* Beacon-Gazette. Well, I'll find out what they're thinking. *Jolly good! So what's the next step?* The next step is to see Mrs. Cuttingham and to report that the minister is on board, pending official interviews, and that the minister believes the Session will respond favorably, and that before the press and supplies can be moved into the building, he must first have an interview with Miss Alice, and that an interview must take place with the young men as well. If and when the young people want to come into town, that's their business, because until the interviews are completed, of course, there can be no definite answer. *Good, I think that sums up the situation nicely. So, your tenure as the most unlikely secretary in the almost 100-year history of Bathington Community Church may be coming to an end!* I certainly hope so. I certainly hope so!

Chapter XI

Good Friday,
April 11, 1952

Up at 6:15 a.m. WOI says 63°. Might have some rain
today. Met with a representative of the Social Security Administration who says that based on my earn-
ings at the hardware store after retiring from the
rr my monthly SS check could be raised to $20 from
its current $17.75. However, I also learned that the
Railroad Retirement Board has been in contact with
the SS board to see if I was drawing SS and how
much, and this may affect either my rr pension or ss
or both. But in any case, the SS guy said, I should
be getting a little raise.

Visits: Alma Hickle (complains of corns and con-
stipation), George Humphrey and Rose—who's getting
more senile by the HOUR! Today she attacked me with
a flyswatter. Better than the .22! George and I went
outside for a curbside visit. He's trying to find
some place to put her. Also Allison Huber, who gave
me an avocado. Uptown forenoon to check mail. None
for me.

Attended the ecumenical Good Friday service at the
Baptist church where the Reverend Hoyt Hood preached.
He also played a beautiful version of "God So Loved
the World" on his violin, and accompanied on the piano his 10-year-old son, Norman, a boy soprano--with
whom he seems quite close--as he sang "The Lord's
Prayer." Then went to church office to begin work on

bulletin. Word is that the new crew arrives town today or tomorrow. Not sure where they're staying.
Think they're supposed to be in church Sunday.
That's when we're going to try to have an emergency
meeting with the Session and interview them all at
once. Maybe I will meet with Miss Alice first, because if she doesn't work out, then the entire enterprise is a moot point.

# # #

Carlo Rossi has not been in a good mood since they got busted in Chicago just as they were about to catch a train. He is grateful, no question, to
be out of that sh*th*le but being in Davenport is not much of an im-
provement in his opinion. Then Alice abruptly leaves. Uncertainty as to
what is going to happen next. The sense that events are swirling around
them about which they know nothing. This is unsettling and cannot be
tolerated. Had he to do it over, he would say "No" to Donovan and go
his own way. Decisions now seem to flow through Alice and thus Carlo's
cosmos is subject to yet another outside force which he cannot entirely
control. She is telling him what he's going to wear, when he can and cannot smoke, when to piss and where to piss. And Cuttingham! What in
tarnation is she doing in Bathington? And why Bathington? Why this
town and not another town?

"Because we got this swell setup with the church, see?— "

"A CHURCH!?" They are all are sitting on wooden chairs at an old
plank kitchen table of widow Clayton's nineteenth-century farmhouse
three miles north of Bathington. They're having soup for lunch. The
floors are of unfinished wood, and except for the counter and cupboard
areas, the walls are of tongue-in-groove wainscoting covered with old
brown paint and, above this, wallpaper featuring waterfowl. Inset in a jog
in a wall is a corn cob and wood stove on which sits a water kettle. Nearby is a wood box. Above the sink are two small windows with frilly curtains drawn aside. Two doors provide entry and egress: one to the parlor
and the other to a covered porch and back door. "We don't pay rent and
we do a few jobs for them, and in the meantime we start building our
business," Cuttingham explains.

"Why don't we just set up in this farmhouse where we can operate quietly and do what we do?" Carlo protests.

"Because." Cuttingham sighs, like a mother with a complaining child.

"Because?"

"Because, how are you going to get an offset press in here? And a darkroom, sitting room with lights, cameras? And how can we ask people to come clear out here to have their portraits taken? Use your head, Carlo! Lefty doesn't want us running a business in a farmhouse like we're trying to hide or like we're doing anything illegal. He wants a legitimate publishing business. He wants to become the mogul of far-flung publishing enterprises that will someday include newspapers which will form public opinion, magazines that will have features from around the world, as well of course as satisfy the huge demand of the American male for smut. So we can't hide in a farmhouse. We will hide in plain view."

Everyone is silent. "Is the business model clear? Do we understand? So from today forward, we become upstanding, model citizens. Our experience in Bathington is a test. If we can do this, perhaps we can go on to better things. But when we leave this town, we shall leave this town as the honored business people we are, and they shall run us through town on a fire truck, sirens blazing, with banners across Main Street, GOOD LUCK CUTTINGHAM, WANG, ROSSI AND JARD! and they'll hold a banquet in the grange hall for us, and name a street after us or something. We will make our mark! They will know who we are!"

Chapter XII

Easter Sunday
April 13, 1952

CUTTINGHAM GETS TO CHURCH EARLY, BRINGING Alice with her. They are to interview with Coop before the worship service in the CHURCH OFFICE. Coop has set out some chairs. At precisely 9 a.m. Penelope Cuttingham comes through the door of the office and behind her the diminutive Xiao Hua *aka* Alice Wang. For a moment, she and Coop exchange a glance and hold it, and then she looks away.

That brief look is enough to bore a hole through Coop's male cranium. He is surprised and strangely excited. He has not actually heard Miss Alice's last name. What is her surname? An Oriental woman! How interesting. How ... how ... exotic. Oh, dear! Mrs. Broughton will have a conniption! This will cause a murmur. But what possible problem can it be? Well, she must speak English, of course; why would Mrs. Cuttingham suggest her as a typist? Certainly she's not a communist! But aren't all the Chinese communists? Does she have good grammar? Of course I can see her résumé and check her references and all will be revealed.

Coop unlatches the fox terrier gate in the office, allowing the ladies inner access and then he invites them to have a seat in front of the desk, just as he had some weeks ago when auditioning for the late Miss Crenshaw. But before they sit, Mrs. Cuttingham interjects.

"Mr. Cooper," she says unctuously, "allow me to introduce my young colleague, Miss Alice Wang." Miss Alice smiles—demurely, in a most winsome manner—batting her eyes once and looking down, and bowing slightly. She is wearing a pillbox hat with front netting, and a gray suit, very conservative style, and a high neck pale blue blouse with a gold necklace. On her hands are white gloves and on her right arm a small black purse. On her suit jacket is a small brooch with a floral design. Her glossy hair, midnight black, is perfectly straight and freshly banged, and frames her angelic face precisely, as though it had been snapped onto her head like a helmet; not a strand is out of place. Her mouth stays open partially when she isn't speaking, showing off pearly white teeth offset by ruby red lips freshly painted. "It's very nice to meet you, Mr. Cooper."

Coop smiles nervously. "I am very nice to meet you, too, Miss Wang." Cuttingham looks at him strangely. "Very pleased to meet you, Miss Wang," he corrects himself, and offers an awkward nod that's a couple inches short of a recognizable bow. Then, feigning a slight cough, he once again invites the two of them to have a seat, which they do and then he sits in his wooden, swivel desk chair and swings around to face them. He feels as though he is still babbling. He is not sure if he ever has actually sat down and had a conversation with an Oriental before. Of course he's been to Chinatown in Chicago and Los Angeles, and San Francisco, too, and has had occasion to converse with shopkeepers, waiters and the like. But this is different. There's not even a Chinese restaurant within sixty miles of Bathington! She looks to be about 25 years old, but that baby face! Not a wrinkle on her countenance, positively cherubic! And the way her hair surrounds her face! Oh how charming!

"Perhaps we could begin by having you tell us about yourself, or background, experience, and then I can explain more about what the church requires of the person sitting in this chair—the chair I've been sitting in—and that should tell you that the church won't be requiring much!" They titter appropriately at this little joke. Coop clears his throat. "Well, then, why don't you start, Miss Wang?"

"Of course," Miss Wang says, leaning forward. Her gloved hands are clasped and resting in her lap. "I was born in Suzhou, China, in the late twenties. My father was a Presbyterian pastor of a local church. Until then, there had been no problem in teaching Christianity and no hostility to missionaries who were in China. Sun Yat-Sen, the Father of China, is said to have been a Christian himself, you know. But he died in 1925 I think it was, and shortly after I was born, the political climate heated up. Soon the country was in civil war between Chiang Kai-shek's Koumintang and the rebels, Mao's Communists. And the rebels were no friends of Christians, that's for sure. It became very dangerous. I could tell you stories." Alice speaks earnestly and Coop listens enraptured.

"Please go on," he urges.

"Well, my parents believed it would be best to get out of the country, even though the KMT and the Communists had reached a sort of a truce in order to beat back the Japanese. That didn't work so well, but anyway, we left. It's a long story, but we landed in Chicago where we were befriended by some Oriental families here. I went to school and took Home Ec, Bookkeeping and Typing in high school, and then went to a business school for a two-year degree, and have been working part time for Donovan Publishing House in Chicago. It's hard to get work now. But when Mrs. Cuttingham told me about an opportunity to begin a new business which included the availability of some venture capital, I was intrigued, and when I learned that I could render some assistance to a small town church, I was even more pleased. It sort of brings me back to my roots— which is very important to me. So here I am."

"How very fascinating!" Coop says excitedly. "Did you know that our church here is actually a Presbyterian church? We call it the Bathington Community Church—"

"—am I interrupting anything here?" The speaker is Rev. Cushing, who at that moment pops into the office. He is dressed in a natty grey business suit and white shirt with French cuffs, red tie with faint diagonal stripes. His black shoes are shiny, and his face has a fresh scrubbed appearance. He is beaming. Coop makes introductions. Miss Alice lowers her eyes and her head, and Coop briefly gives Cushing an iteration of Miss Alice's birth and departure from China.

"I was just asking Miss Alice," he says to Cushing, who has pulled up a chair and joined the group, "whether she was aware that our church was a Presbyterian church."

"Oh, no," she murmurs. "I was not aware. This feels like coming home."

"Well it's been Presbyterian for about fifteen years," Cushing says, warming up. "Before that it was Methodist and before that Evangelical United Brethren. Don't know if that means anything to you. But at some point the UBies's were not evangelical anymore, definitely not united and there were more sistern than brethren, and there was a big hullabaloo, and finally a split and the only ones left standing were some Methodists and Presbyterians. And then the General Conference of the Methodist Church did something stupid which they do once every ten years or so, and I guess things really boiled and the Methodists decided they'd rather join the Presbyterians. Which is really strange. Pelagius becomes Augustine, Wesley becomes Calvin. Doesn't seem possible, does it? But anyway—I'm sorry to go on like this, but perhaps a little history helps you understand our local context—"

Alice nods, and Mrs. Cuttingham says, "How true."

"Anyway, it was at that time the congregation decided to change the name to Bathington Community Church for the sake of future continuity. Come back in ten years and we could be Congregationalists, although that's probably unlikely as I don't think people in these parts really want to be Unitarians, do they, Coop?"

"Quite right!" Coop affirmed.

"Well, carry on, then!" Cushing says smiling and looking at each of the three, all quite astonished with this impromptu review of Bathington ecclesiastical history. Coop resumes his role as the moderator of the interview and explains to Alice what her duties could entail, and also tells her a little about his job, about the stencils, the Gestetner mimeograph, the ink.

At this point, Alice interjects: "Of course we will not be using stencils and the Gestetner, Mr. Cooper, to produce the worship bulletin, the Bathington Community Church *Chimes* or Sunday school curricula. Our process is a completely offset printing process that involves the use of a camera, plates and an offset printer. And, I hope the congregation will be interested in having a church directory. We want to publish a book that will have the photos of every family in the congregation, along with their information, like mailing address and phone number and birth dates. I am sure that this will be much appreciated by church members, especially at Christmas when people will want to send out greeting cards."

"Oh yes, that would be most helpful," says Coop, concurring. "I sent out 235 Christmas cards last year, and having a directory such as Miss Alice describes would be a wonderful time saver." They continue to chat for a few minutes and then Coop inquires if Miss Alice might not sit at the typewriter and do a little typing. Give them a sample of her work. "Pica or Elite typeface?" she inquires. They actually have both. The Elite conveys a more professional appearance she advises. The typewriter at the desk has Elite keys. Coop gives up his chair and Miss Wang rises and glides around the desk to sit where he had sat, as he, in turn, maneuvers awkwardly to get out of her way, standing to the side, looking over her shoulder. She sits down in front of the black boxy Underwood and smoothes out her skirt and removes her white gloves setting them neatly on the desktop. "Coop, maybe she can work on those minutes from the last Deacon's meeting. I haven't gotten around to typing them up yet." Cushing points to some papers on the corner of the desk. They are handwritten notes. Alice positions them on a typing stand and places her tiny hands on the typewriter keys. Coop wonders if the stroke action will be too stiff for her. Miss Wang advances the carriage back and forth a couple of times, and does some fake typing with an empty carriage to get a feel for the keys. "Do you have some paper?" she asks.

"Oh, yes, yes!" Coop steps quickly to the desk, and leans forward and downward to pull open a bottom drawer, slightly embarrassed to be so close to Miss Wang's lap and legs. He catches a scent of her perfume. He thinks he might be blushing. He grabs some sheets and places them quickly on the desktop and steps back. Cushing and Cuttingham watch with amusement. Miss Alice inserts a sheet of paper, swivels her little Chinese head to look at the minutes on the stand and begins typing and does not stop until she's reached the end of the first page. She does not even glance back at the carriage to see when it is coming to the end of the line. She knows by instinct when the carriage needs to be returned. When she finishes, she grabs the paper and whirls it out of the typewriter with a flourish, swivels on the chair and gives it to Coop.

Coop gazes at it in admiration. "I'm sure there's a mistake here somewhere," he says. "But I'm not going to look for it."

"There isn't," Miss Wang declares, "although the escapement's not quite right, and the platen is pocked, so some letters will look darker than others. But not bad. Underwoods are sturdy machines. The Cadillacs of typewriters."

# # #

The interview goes well. Cushing is invigorated and beaming like someone with a hard-to-keep secret. He asks Miss Wang if she can stop by Monday for a second interview, provide references and get some more training with Mr. Cooper. He cannot tarry (his word) now because it is, after all, Easter Sunday, and he has much with which to attend. His far-flung flock is already arriving and today attendance will swell with the "E and C" folks.

The thirty minutes prior to the start of the worship service are always chaotic, and especially today. The Altar Guild is arriving. Mrs. Ferguson and Mrs. Gertie Johnson are arranging fifteen seven-inch lily plants and are in conference as to where to place them—whether to position them in a line on the platform, or clump them in groups near the pulpit and lectern and around the altar. Other members of the Guild are preparing the linens and paraments, setting out the Easter banners which hang on the wall behind the pulpit and on either side of the cross, one which reads "He Is Risen!" with a sun rising, and the other "I Am the Resurrection and the Life" with an empty tomb. Art Bandy has a six-foot step ladder and is arranging a white linen cloth to drape on the *patibula* of the cross.

Choir members are likewise arriving for their pre-service rehearsal in the Fellowship Hall with Director Byrd. Anita Lyons, the organist, and Clara Wild, the pianist, are working on their duet for the prelude, and Mrs. Wild in particular is making pains to ensure that the piano can be heard above the organ.

From these pre-service pastoral scenes of vibrant congregational life Cushing likes to flee. The best location for this retreat is, naturally, his office, although it is also the first place someone will look for him if he is needed. Generally, he has to admit, his congregation seems to understand intuitively the sacred nature of the Pastor's Study on a Sunday morning, and are too afraid to breach the barrier lest they find the Reverend on his knees in prayer, or doing something else equally righteous. This would be too much. So, gratefully, Cushing knows he is likely to be left alone. This is a good thing. He uses these moments to slow down his mind and re-center his thoughts on the cup he must drink, the cross he must bear. This is difficult for him to do because he is by nature an active, not a contemplative, personality. It is hard to clear his head. Out in the foyer he's just been told to announce that those leaving pie tins and casserole dishes after the duck-picking bee needed to pick them up in the kitchen; that the committee for the Mother-Daughter banquet would meet at the Manse this Wednesday. He also conferred with Wild, Lyons and Byrd to ensure that the prelude commenced precisely at 10:59.59 with the Processional Hymn immediately following. He doesn't believe one can ever be on time. It would be too much of a coincidence. On time would mean 11:00:00. That means there is only one second in which to be "on time." He believed in starting early, because if you didn't, you were starting late, and tardiness is the thief of time. Prelude music should begin at 10:55 a.m. Today, he will be processing with the choir and the acolytes as they like to "church it up" a little on Easter Sunday, as they do on every Sunday of Advent. If Wild and Lyons can get the Processional Hymn going on time, it will save him from lingering irritation during the service.

Organists are a breed apart. You can tell a piano player what to do. Even a choir director will listen to your ideas about possible and future anthem choices. You can reason with a schizophrenic in moments of lucidity, and generally people with a wide variety of neuroses will accept and seek treatment. You can work with bullies, thugs and miscreants, and make a deal with the devil. But organists cannot be told a blessed thing. One cannot reason with the organist. One cannot make deals. Bribery will not prevail nor flattery avail. The morals and spirituality of organists are pre-Christian, antediluvian and pagan. There was never a more obstinate personality of such intense egocentrism created than that of the church organist. They play what they prefer and show up at rehearsals according to their good pleasure. They play as loud as they please, and regard the non-musical world as a community of cretins. They are bilious, natural born complainers conceived under the twins signs of Melancholia and Hypochondria. Their complaints include paltry compensation, dead drawbars, sticky pedals, poor lighting and a general sense of congregational mistreatment. They believe their musical genius is unrecognized. They're never happy unless the minister is unhappy. The music budget is galling and appalling. They're congenitally obstructionist, money-grubbing, parsimonious extortionists who belong to a sort of musical Mafia. On some Sundays, Cushing would just as soon have a beggar grinding on a barrel organ, than the tendentious Mrs. Lyons hammering on her Hammond.

These tedious thoughts about punctuality and outrageous assertions regarding the moral proclivities and musical idiosyncrasies of church organists are typical of the cerebral clutter strewn across frontal cortex of the Reverend's mind prior to a Sunday morning worship service and of which he now tries to purge himself so that he might be filled with a fulsome sense of the gospel and feel quickened by the Holy Spirit. When he steps into the pulpit, he wants to feel holy, to feel energized, charged and powered up with white hot purity and the zeal of the Lord. Therefore, he hunkers down in an upholstered chair near a wall of theological tomes and opens his Bible, and fingers his notes. He doesn't feel "quickened" but it will come.

Today the title of his sermon is "When the Stone Was Rolled Away." He thought about using "Who Can Roll Away Your Stones?" But this makes him think of kidney stones. He isn't sure about the title anyway. There is a rap at the door. It is 10:51 a.m.

"Come in," Cushing calls out. Into his office comes the Nelson boy, an acquiescent, freckle-faced lad of about 11 years and dressed in the white robe of an acolyte. His straw-colored hair is combed, parted and gummed down neatly with his mother's spit, suggesting that the same is making him do this. "We can't find another wick for the lighters, Reverend," he says matter-of-factly. Here we go, thinks Cushing. He smiles. High church Sundays are targets for the most devilish and impish things to go wrong and this, he knows, is just the beginning. He sets down Barth's *Romans*, and leaving his Bible and notes on the desk, races out of the office to solve this emergency. By the time the brass lighters have been re-wicked, it is time to go. The prelude is beginning punctually and the twenty-two member choir attired in maroon robes and white satin stoles have been herded from the Fellowship Hall and corralled temporarily in the foyer where they are milling about, mooing and lowing thoughtlessly. Howard Byrd shushes them. Lyons and Wild finish their prelude, "Open the Gates of the Temple," and now there is silence. Only faint rustling is heard in the sanctuary. Latecomers shoulder through the choir in the foyer to get a seat inside. Ruddy-faced men in ill-fitting suits who yesterday were farmers are today unctuous ushers clutching worship bulletins with thick hands and fingers the size of sausages. They direct some of the tardants to the less desirable balcony seats where the pews are not padded. The organist begins the introduction to the processional hymn, "Christ the Lord is Risen Today." The congregation stands. They begin to sing. Byrd glances at Cushing who gives a faint nod. Byrd positions the two acolytes. They process first, their lighters lit. The choir moves forward after them single file through the sanctuary doors and down the center aisle which has a slight slope to it as in a theater.

The sopranos are clear of the sanctuary entrance and the altos beginning when Cushing realizes he doesn't have his King James. He flies out of the foyer, his black robes flapping like the wings of a raven, down a hallway to the study. He spies his Bible exactly where he knew it would be, checks to ensure his notes are tucked inside, and hies back. The basses have left and are halfway to the Resurrection. No matter. He takes a deep breath and steps inside the sanctuary. The congregation is on the fourth and final verse:

Soar we now where Christ has led, Alleluia!
Following our exalted Head, Alleluia!
Made like him, like him we rise, Alleluia!
Ours the cross, the grave, the skies. Alleluia!

Cushing is wearing his black robe with velvet panels and an ecru stole with a prominent Celtic cross embroidered in threads of auburn and jade. The congregation is singing lustily as Cushing passes through. The women are wearing Easter hats many of them purchased at Rachel's Millinery Shop—others, like Mrs. Broughton's big brim hat with lace and bow, came from such centers of *haute couture* as Osage and Mason City. Straw hats, pillbox, felt, velvet, crocheted, big brims with bows, jewels and feathers, hats of every shape, size and color—all are on display, many of them sit on the female cranium at a jaunty angle. Mrs. Constance Curian, an amateur hat arranger, wears a straw creation that features plastic fruit in a small heap and bounded by ripe yellow bananas. She is also the artist responsible for Mrs. Lindsay Bound's hat that resembles a cornucopia, and Mrs. Winifred Aker's hat that bears a marked similarity to a Greek salad. Mrs. Ellen Hostetler, a very tall woman, is wearing a big brim hat with a circumference so large that it provides more shade than an Indian Banyan tree for her diminutive husband, Fred, when they linger after church visiting on the sidewalk with friends. From the rear of the auditorium the congregation looks like it is bedecked in facsimiles of unidentified flying objects. Frankie and Vic have matching pink bonnets. The men and laddies are in suits. Rosy-cheeked popsys are beaming in chiffon frocks, pinafores and colorful taffeta dresses with rosette necklines. On their feet are black patent leather shoes with white anklets, and their heads are crowned with Easter bonnets of every color of the rainbow. And, although the temperature is mild, several women view Easter as the last opportunity to wear fur; there is more than one fox stole slung over the shoulders of the Bathington women in church this day, with the snout of the beady-eyed Reynard resting lightly on the matronly breast. Thus, the sacred auditorium is a polychromatous marvel of dead flora and fauna, fabrics, textiles and straw, arguably more spectacular than the Resurrection itself. Some children have their white Sunday School Bibles won for memorizing the books of the Bible.

Cushing pauses with his back to the people, faces the large cross before and above him on a white cracked-plastered wall, bows his head, and
then turns to the lectern on the people's right. He is astonished to see
that the Nelson boy is having trouble lighting the altar candles. Fortunately, Howard Byrd is rushing to his aid. *Is it too much to ask the Altar
Guild to pre-light the wicks?* By the time the choir is in the loft, the congregation is singing the last "Alleluia" and the Nelson boy has successfully set
the altar aflame. As the congregation yet stands, Cushing intones: "Let us
pray." There is coughing and a rustling as people bow their heads, hats
lower and nudge akimbo, and he offers the invocation following which the
congregation is seated. The worship service has begun.

The sanctuary is in the shape of a square. The chancel area cuts across
one corner, so that as Cushing looks out over an expectant audience he
sees people in two sections of walnut pews, sections that curve from one
side to the other with a center aisle separating the sections. The room has
a vaulted ceiling, and in the wall to his right is a huge stained glass window featuring a bigger-than-life image of the Good Shepherd with his
staff holding a lamb. Opposite this window on his left is a companion
work of stained glass, this of Jesus in the Garden of Gethsemane praying
as his disciples sleep in the background.

As the ushers are taking up the collection, which is bound to be one
of the largest of the year, the choir rises to present its anthem, "On This
Bright Easter Morn." Cushing uses the time to review the worship bulletin. Coop has outdone himself, he notes. We should just try to hire him
on a permanent basis. But the proposal of Miss Wang this morning is
interesting. It merits further attention. Tomorrow, we'll talk some more.
He surveys the congregation. Usually he knows where to look for people
because regulars plant themselves in the same pew Sunday after Sunday,
and on special occasions often come early knowing that the E and C in-
terlopers might arrive and sit in their spot. To his left on the "Jesus in
Gethsemane" or Gethsemane side, he sees, as he expects to see, Fredrika
Solvig; Charlotte Brunner, whose duck-picking bee had been a huge success; and Henry and Harriet Howe, the erstwhile Postmaster and his wife
and some unfamiliar faces as well. On the Good Shepherd side he notes
Mr. and Mrs. Jon Toews, Theodora Vogel, the Hansens, the Thurstons
(whose son and wife and children just about fill a pew), and Mrs. Broughton, who is staring at the Chinese woman seated across the aisle on the
Gethsemane side. Miss Wang is with two good looking young men, one

of whom holds up the offering plate momentarily while he fishes for some money. Behind them, he sees Coop sitting with Mrs. Cuttingham on one side and Millie on the other. Mrs. Cooper looks splendidly radiant, he thinks, in an attractive blue suit, white big brim hat with a pink ribbon around it, and white gloves. Beside her is Vic, who just got her hair banged, and Frankie, and! Naomi Shimel! He glances up. The balcony is full as well. Easter and Christmas Eve are two annual occasions when it can be reasonably asserted that perhaps eighty percent of the Bathington citizenry are in a house of worship. At this very moment, what with the Catholics, Lutherans, Pentecostals and Baptists, just about everyone is in church, and in point of fact, it must be rather embarrassing, he can only imagine, to be seen on the streets of Bathington at the 11 a.m. hour and not be in church today. This being a Christian nation and all, only the most irreligious, and fortunately, they are not many, have the courage to stay out of a church, and if they did, they stay in their homes and shutter the windows until about 1 p.m. The number of people in houses of worship right now, Cushing mused, probably outnumbers the official population of Bathington, given that these services attract people from outlying rural hamlets too small for a church, and farmers who often are in the fields on Sundays. But the farmers are not planting corn today. Watsons are not present as they go to a colored Baptist church in Charles City when they can find a ride. Easter is virtually a national holiday and the town celebrates it as such. It gladdens his heart to see so many people. He knows that their presence has nothing to do with him, *per se*, although granted, were he an *unpopular* minister whose sermons were dry, dull and lifeless, he could correctly surmise that the turnout might not be so big. This Sunday is about Jesus not about Cushing. He knows that, but like most preachers, he prides himself on his study of the homiletical craft and likes to think that of the tasks and responsibilities that befall a minister, the preaching office is the most important, even when, he admits, it isn't. He knows well that it is what a minister does among his parishioners from Monday to Saturday, visiting them in their homes, sharing a meal, stopping by the hospital—all of this is far more important. But preaching! No congregation wants a minister who is a poor preacher, a soporific sermonizer. The ability to deliver a well-crafted sermon that is exceptional not only in content but in delivery is deemed critical by every pastoral search committee that ever convened to find a minister. Cushing studied the principles of Ciceronian rhetoric, and earli-

er in his ministry, he spent time in front of the mirror practicing his elo-
cution. In the past, he often took time to virtually memorize his sermons
so that nothing important would be forgotten. In time, however, as his
confidence and skills increased, he simply studied hard, made a few notes
and delivered his sermon extemporaneously, knowing that a sermon that
is read is a sermon that is dead. Cushing in his preaching style is something of a maverick. He admires the way Bishop Fulton Sheen can stand
in front of an audience and just start speaking, and deliver a message of
such utter cogency and logical power, not to speak of spiritual insight,
that it is effortless to listen to him, and he himself has adopted the unusual technique of moving away from the pulpit and standing in the center
of the platform with only a card or two in his hand and delivering his
sermons. Initially, this caused a stir. Some congregants attributed the
change to the carnal influence of television and felt that the Reverend was
grandstanding. Imperceptibly, however, this attitude shifted as Cushing's
motives seemed above reproach. As for the preacher himself, he believes
that he is a better preacher for it, and the responses he's received from
his congregation seem to bear him out. Easter and Christmas, therefore,
are opportunities not only for the E-and-Cers to meet Jesus, but to meet
Cushing, and if they could be attracted to the one, they might be willing
to follow the Other and become faithful and regular adherents in the life
and ministry of the church. Such is his philosophy. This morning, however, he will stay behind the pulpit.

Carlo and Wason arrive at the church shortly after Alice's boffo performance in the church office and quickly connect with Mrs. Cuttingham,
who is in a conversation with Alice and a man they learn is Mr. Carlton
Cooper, an elder in the church, and the person currently typing up the
worship bulletin. Carlo is in a new suit. Wason is likewise splendidly attired in a suit accessorized by a white monogrammed handkerchief in his
suit coat pocket and a white carnation on his lapel. Cuttingham reminds
both of the boys of the meeting with the Session following the service,
and they assure her they are ready. Carlo has a portfolio of photographs,
and, fortunately, he is able to find a few photographs in which the wom-
en have their clothes on, and since he's done a fair number of weddings,
it is not too hard to cobble together a presentation that is gospel pure.

Carlo is surprised that he feels so comfortable in a church, a Protestant church at that. Father Mike never had too much nice to say about Protestants who were responsible for just about everything that was wrong with America, and who were in a perpetual state of searching for the truth and never arriving at it, all the while ignoring the Mother Church where alone, as with all mothers, the truth can be found. Growing up in Chicago under the beneficent reign of Cardinal Stritch he isn't sure if he really knows who Protestants are anyway. Just that there is a lot of them, and too many varieties to keep track of. As that thought skitters across his brain, he snaps his head up to take a closer look at the cleric now in the pulpit down front. Cushing! Damn! Isn't there a Cardinal by that name? Robed in black with a colorful stole, his presentation doesn't impart the sense of gravitas as did the Catholic, but this Cushing appears to be a sterner version of Stritch, the amiable prelate of Cook County, and of course, much younger.

Perhaps the stained glass windows help to sooth Carlo's jitters. How long has it been since I went to mass? he wonders. Some time. There are no saints here, no statuary of any kind. No crucifix. Actually there isn't much that makes this place feel like a church except the windows, the empty cross up front, the robed priest, that's about it. Otherwise it looks like a community theater or small concert room. There is a board on the wall off to the priest's right with the word HYMNS above a series of slotted rows into which some cardboard numbers have been inserted to identify the songs that are to be sung. The people sing in this church a lot better than at St. Joseph's, he allows. He's never understood group singing. Why would you do that? Still, when everyone rises to sing the processional hymn, he stands up and sings with everyone else after listening for the melody on the first verse. Wason isn't singing, but Wason can't sing. Wason can scarcely talk.

Carlo comes back to the priest. A baby is crying. The priest steps up to the pulpit and taps the square chrome microphone. It isn't working. For a few minutes nothing is heard except a fool kid hollering on account of his parents will not get him out of the church. That's another thing, Catholic churches are a little noisier. People are always getting up and moving around and at the high altar something is usually going on. Here everything is rather staid and quiet, and the baby bawling makes Carlo feel that perhaps there is some life in this church after all. The microphone issue is solved and now it appears that the priest is going to speak, and Carlo wants to hear what he has to say.

A couple of weeks ago I read an article in the Des Moines Register *that gave examples from history of things that so-called experts had said or believed that later turned out to be absolutely wrong.*

See! Now there you go. How can I not listen to this guy!

If you've had any experience with experts, you know what I mean. An expert is someone who has made all the mistakes that can possibly be made in a very narrow field. That was said by an expert—who ought to know. Based on that definition, I myself might be an expert! But let's look back for a moment in history. Many centuries ago, medieval alchemists believed that there was a secret formula which would change lead into gold. They'd noticed how some substances could get bigger, or expand, change their color, smell funny, and thought that there had to be a way to turn lead into gold. But they were wrong! This newspaper article also reminded me that experts used to think that heavier objects fall faster than lighter ones. Galileo proved them wrong in the 16th century. And here's another one. Less than a hundred years ago surgeons didn't think that washing their hands before operating or disinfecting a wound was important. They were wrong! And finally, a long time ago, the experts said that if we can put Jesus in the grave that'll be the end of it. Well, the experts were wrong. Very wrong!

Penelope Cuttingham shifts her gaze from the handsome Reverend to look down for a moment and then to her left, bringing into her field of vision Mr. Cooper's upper legs and lap, his hands folded and interlocked and resting easily there. His hands are youthful, well, not youthful, but they don't seem to be the hands of an old person. No brown spots and no flabby skin. His hands are thin, a little on the bony side; she can see the tendons that connect the wrist to the fingers and some arteries that bring a supply of blood to the fingers and veins that haul it back to the heart. His fingers are long and lean. She understands how he could be a good typist. She notes the French cuffs, the worsted wool material. This man is just an Iowa bumpkin but he has a sense of style. A railroad man with some culture. He knows a little French? How much? Where did he get it? He said he went to Doane for a year or two. She looks back at the preacher. I haven't sat next to a man since I had to take the EL last year, and goodness, I can't *remember* the last time I've sat next to a gentleman for this length of time or for *any* reason since I ... since I was in court sitting with my crook of a lawyer ... What a shyster! My! What would the Reverend and all these respectable people ... Mr. Cooper! ... think if they knew who I *really* am! She smiles ruefully. They'd be shocked! Simply shocked. She is relieved not to feel guilty sitting in this church, and is surprised that she doesn't. Usually the only time she attends church is on those rare occasions when she does feel guilty, or thoroughly depressed and at her wits end. And that isn't often. Now, she's in church but it is a calculated gesture and for that reason she knows the good Lord can't really give her credit. Perhaps in a Protestant church you never feel guilty. Maybe it's the naked cross up there. Just a plain, boxy cross. No crucified Jesus. No gory wound. No sticky bright, lipstick red blood painted on the body of Jesus, coming from the gash in his side. No crown of thorns clamped down on his head, blood trickling down the face. None of that. She could never really look at a crucifix for long. The one at St. Joseph's is made of wood and, the last time she was there, the crucifix had a crack in it that ran from the left thigh up through the right eye. The paint was peeling. She never felt good about herself at St. Joseph's, but here it seems much different. So much more positive and upbeat. Maybe I am just feeling better about getting out of the business. Been a long time coming and I never intended to get into that business anyway. So now here I am, getting out of one business and into another, out of the fire and into the frying pan! Maybe someday I can get out of the kitchen altogether. Cuttingham shifts her weight and her shoulder touches Mr. Cooper. She is aware of the contact, but shakes it off and listens.

> *Who were these experts back in Jerusalem who believed such an opinion on that first Easter Sunday? The chief priests? They believed it. The Pharisees? They believed it. Pontius Pilate? He believed it. The disciples? Yes, even they believed it. Most of them had returned to their homes and their former lives. But were they really experts? No. No. No and No. At least when it came to the resurrection they were completely ignorant.*

Millie Cooper knows all about experts. She learned real fast when Johnny was in the Army, because there is NO institution in the world with more experts than the Army. One thing about Army experts, they lie better than a Persian rug, and what's more, they swear it's the truth, and you're in no position to judge the difference. Jesus and Johnny in a grave, but Jesus got out. I wonder if Johnny is with Jesus now. I suppose he is. The experts are telling me he's with Jesus ... that there's a heaven ... that I will see both Johnny and Jesus someday. Well, I don't want to think about Johnny. I am glad I don't think about him so much anymore. It's hard to even picture him in my mind. Heery Park. He had Frankie on his shoulders. They ducked behind a tree and then leaned out the other side all grinning ... I guess I won't ever forget that image ... Cushing's a good preacher ... sometimes seems a little cold ... too smart or something ... proud of my girls ... and boy I've come a long way in the past two years ... Second Easter service. Couldn't hardly get to church after Johnny died, but I'm moving forward ... I don't know why Johnny was taken from us, but life has not been taken from me and I got two girls to raise and Coop to keep my eye on and what's this Cuttingham woman doing anyway? I don't think I care for her at all ... eyeliner, store-bought dresses, fur hats and boots! ... the lilies are lovely, but they sure smell ... Constance's hat is ridiculous—if she knew how she looked ... I'm glad Naomi came to church today, and I am glad Frankie is befriending her ... what a mature grownup thing to do ... some of the grownups in the town, well, they could take a lesson from Frankie. She said she'd go to Naomi's synagogue sometime, too, in Des Moines ... I hope the roast is done ...

   And to whom did Jesus appear on Easter Sunday morning? To non-experts, like the two Marys, for example. Read through the gospels and the women in the gospels are shadowy figures with rather small roles to play. But Jesus appears to them first. The experts, the people who should have known the truth, the disciples, they were gone. He did not appear to the very ones who were best equipped to understand what was going on. He appears to the Marys. That is, Jesus tends to appear to those who have faith. It is these women who first reported the news of the resurrection, and nineteen hundred years later, the same is very much true today. The resurrection is still being reported by people who do not pay attention to the experts, people whose faith is so strong that they've seen the evidence of the resurrection not only in their own lives, but in the lives of others. They are people who have even seen the resurrected Lord, catching a glimpse of the risen Jesus in the middle of human life. They have seen Jesus in their neighbors. They see Jesus in people whom experts would say are not our neighbors. Hear then the gospel: That when Jesus rose, he rose to appear not to a few select people of the same color of skin, status and station in life, but to the people of the world, a world he loved and for which he died.

Coop thinks it is an excellent sermon and a wonderful service. He is thrilled to see the church packed to the gills, even if it is a special occasion. He is happy to be sitting with Millie, her first Easter service since Johnny passed. She is such a blessing in his life. He feels Cuttingham, on his left, move about slightly, perhaps getting more comfortable. Their shoulders touch. He feels her body. But he doesn't move away. He's not sure whether Cuttingham is going to be a blessing. His thoughts turn to Crenshaw. He feels a genuine pang when he thinks of the pride Miss Crenshaw would have felt today—this first Sunday back in church since the fire. He stayed away on Palm Sunday even though he prepared the worship bulletin as usual. She has been gone not quite two weeks, and somehow he thinks of her absence as just temporary. She said she was going to Los Angeles, and Coop half expects to get a picture post card from her after her arrival. Rev. Cushing remembered Miss Crenshaw during the service, which was nice. But there'll be no resurrection for Crenshaw—at least not until Jesus comes—but perhaps there'll be a way to keep her memory alive.

Chapter XIII

THE MEETING WITH THE SESSION TAKES place following the
Easter service. It is not a convenient time and several of the members
wonder why the rush. Their wives complain that the ham is in the oven,
that the spuds will be overdone, or that Grandma won't last past two
o'clock before she'll need a nap, and that this uncle or that aunt will be at
each other's throat before the mashed potatoes are served. But Cushing is
reluctant to agree to a different time as he thinks that the Easter service is
close to a 100 percent guarantee that he'll have his flock in the fold at the
same time. If he lets them go without this meeting, well ... "All we like
sheep have gone astray and have turned every one to his own way ..."
Once they leave, who knows when he'll ever see them together again? So
they meet in the Fellowship Hall and most of the men have alerted the
womenfolk about it and they agreed to set the Easter dinner back and
won't start the ham or the roast until after church and woe-betide if the
meeting goes beyond the cooking time of an 8-pound Yorkshire ham!

Cuttingham does not attend as she and Coop feel that an entourage of
four is a little big. Three people entering into a relationship with the
church is a considerable number as it is and highly unusual. Moreover,
Cuttingham has absolute confidence in Miss Wang to amend any mis-
statements the boys might make, to fill in whatever gaps might be missing, to answer questions hitherto never asked, and so on. Her mind is not
entirely at ease, however, because it will not be Miss Wang who'll be doing the talking, but Carlo Rossi. It would never do for a woman to take
the lead in these negotiations and an Oriental woman at that; actually, it is
unthinkable. No, Carlo has to be the lead dog; he has to appear to be the
go-to man at all times. This suits Miss Wang just fine as she is culturally
attuned to the necessity of staying in the background, eyes down, gaze
averted. It does not come naturally to her, but she is aware of the role

and knows how to play it. As for Wason Jard, Cuttingham has no concerns. Wason says very little, and when he speaks, he speaks thoughtfully and sincerely and earnestly. Wason, she thinks, will make the best impression of the three.

Carlo believes it is important first to lay out their reasons for being in Bathington and then to present their credentials and demonstrate how the church will benefit. "No point trying to sell a pig in a poke," he says, chewing on a toothpick. They meet around three 8-foot folding tables pushed together so that the surface area of the tables is almost square. Carlo, Wason and Alice take seats at one end, while the board sits around the perimeter. Cushing gets the meeting going with some very brief remarks, and then turns it over to Carlo.

Rossi stands, and looks at the people around the table who are giving him the once over. It is an expectant moment like when a crowd gathers at the base of a building to see if the jumper on the tenth-story ledge is going to take the leap—or not. There is silence, a hush. Then Carlo begins to speak. "I want to thank you for—"

"Wait a minute," says a voice. It is Howard Byrd, the choir director who's also on the Session. "Aren't you forgetting something?" Carlo stops, appearing confused, and looks to one side, and then another, then at Cushing. Suddenly Alice stands up, steps to his side, and taps him lightly on his shoulder.

"I think Mr. Byrd—that's your name, right?" Byrd nods, surprised, and looks around at others approvingly. "I think Mr. Byrd is reminding us that before we go any further, we should have a word of prayer. If you gentlemen don't object, well, my daddy was a Presbyterian minister in China and I learned a few prayers at his knee and learned there's no point making plans if the good Lord isn't in on them." She pauses to let that soak in. There is a general murmur of approval. She says, "Alrighty then, let us pray." She clasps her hands, bows her head and forthwith uncorks for the first time in the entire Upper Midwest the opening prayer by a woman at a local Session meeting—ever. It is a long prayer. She prays for the president, though she knows full well that Iowa is not Truman country, and that it had been a long time since *anyone* had prayed for Truman. She prays for the boys in Korea, for those leading the fight against Communism, for good weather for the farmers, for the pastor and the Session, for parents and their children, for teachers doing such an important job teaching the little ones, and finally asks the Lord's blessing upon this little gathering. After this prayer, she could have asked the Session for cream cheese and they'd have given her as much as she wanted.

Carlo does admirably. He explains that the three of them want to start a business in their church, and they want to find some space rent free. He doesn't try to beat around this bush because it is a bush that can't be beaten. He explains their roles. He distributes photographs of his works, slinging them across the table. Alice wishes that he would've walked around the conference table and presented a photograph to each member in a more dignified manner, but Carlo prefers a more free-wheeling approach which suggests that they are creative, energetic, breezy people who will not be hard to get along with. Wason explains a little of the printing process. They provide samples of their work. Coop speaks of Alice's skills at the typewriter.

Carlo also explains, since they were, after all, Presbyterians, what is in it for the church: *free* secretarial help. *Free* worship bulletins on Sunday done by a professional printer. *Free* picture church directory. This causes a lot of comment. One 8 x 10 photograph *free* to every family who sits for a photo for the directory. If they want more, there would be a nominal charge of course. They need three rooms: one for the press and a small reception area, one which could be turned into a darkroom, and one which could be used as a sitting room. No, they can't take portraits in the Fellowship Hall and that room needs to be available at all times for the church's use. They need a studio room that would be private and accessible.

Fortunately, the layout of the basement floor of Bathington Community Church is ideal for their purposes. There is an outside entrance as the church is built on a inclined lot. Although one can enter the sanctuary at ground level, the street slopes and the parking area is at a lower elevation allowing for a basement and exterior access. It is perfect. Customers can come to the shop for business and all the shooting and printing and developing can be done on site as well.

Although the mood is favorable, one member wants to delay a vote on the proposal. But the general feeling is that no controversial issues have arisen that warrant a delay. Yes, a contract will need to be drawn up, but given the near unanimous acclaim that has met the proposal of these young people it is unlikely that there'll be a problem. They agree to the proposal in principle and allow the trio to begin setting up. Rossi, Jard and Wang are in!

# # #

After Rev. Cushing got Jesus all resurrected and after the last Alleluias have died down, and after a meeting that has gone one Yorkshire ham and a casserole too long, Cushing accepts an invitation to dinner with Millie and the girls, and of course, Carlton Cooper would be in attendance. Normally, Cushing doesn't care to go out for dinner following the church service because being with so many people, and Christians at that, leaves him enervated and wilted. He desires nothing more than to return to the Manse and flop down on his couch and turn on the radio and listen to a program, or put a record on the Victrola and listen to Bach, or Mozart. But today he thinks that being by himself might be more stressful and irritating than to be with others, and having dinner at Millie's will not at all be difficult. He feels at home there, enjoys the girls' company, and Millie's too, although she can get on his nerves the way she is always fidgeting around everywhere, doing something, and getting after Frankie about one thing or the other. She needs, in his opinion, to slow down and relax just a little. So there are five people around the Cooper table this Easter Sunday afternoon, participating in as rich an American tradition as the turkey at Thanksgiving. Everyone is tight in their homes today, even the Shimel's who actually rejoiced when Easter arrived, as the Christian Holy Week can be a harrowing experience for a Jewish minority in a Christian land. Holy Week is an annual event in which, if Christians had forgot about the role of some Jewish people in the death of Jesus, they now remember, and so Christians often put aside their Christian-ness— and Jews suffer as a result.

So the Easter dinner is a family affair. The girls are used to both their grandfather and the Reverend being around at a meal time. And it is quite common for Coop to be included in meals whenever and wherever the Reverend is invited. Most of Cushing's parishioners feel it an obligation to have the Reverend over for dinner at least once a year—it is only right, especially him being a bachelor and all. But they are nervous about entertaining the man of God alone and unprotected and thus, needing some sort of buffer, Coop often gets a dinner invitation as well. A woman cannot be invited for such a purpose, and when Coop receives a summons, he is under no illusion that his hosts are inviting him on his account, but rather to act as a shield, a distraction, so that the conversation will not be awkward, rough moments can be smoothed over, and to ensure that the Reverend won't scare the children.

Ordinarily, the Reverend is entertained in the sitting room by at least one member of the family, but in this case, when Coop trudges to the kitchen to help get the meal ready, Cushing joins the girls and helps out. Spuds are in a boiling pot ready for mashing. Millie gives this task to Cushing. The girls get the linens out and prepare to set the table. "Girls," Millie calls out, "don't forget the serviettes and serviette holders." She says this for Cushing's benefit who likes to imagine that he is in England dining on bangers and mash, not in Bathington eating pork. The ham roast is ready to eat. Coop slides it out of the oven and sets it on a trencher and keeps it stable as Millie bastes it with juices, and decorates it with some warm pineapple slices. It delivers a sweet and syrupy aroma throughout the house. Dinner rolls, broccoli, coleslaw and tea are on the table. Frankie makes a pitcher of tropical juice flavored with crystals from a paper pouch. To get this feast ready for consumption means creating havoc in the kitchen and leaving it in shambles while the meal is eaten. The kitchen can be cleaned up later which is also when Tippy will get the ham bone and leftovers.

Vic offers grace and the dining begins. Generally Frankie and Vic observe the "be seen and not heard" rule, but because it's just the Reverend—a frequent visitor—the rule is relaxed and everyone is at liberty to speak at will. But it is a freedom the girls exercise only occasionally as when, for example, Cushing asks Frankie about her paper—Coop had briefed him on some of the details.

"It's okay. I still got a lot of work to do on it yet," Frankie says, between mouthfuls and while paring away a strip of fat from the ham on her plate. "I'm kinda stuck right now with the books here in the library. I need to get to Des Moines sometime 'cause some of the books I need aren't in our library." Millie says she thinks that can be arranged because often she needs to go to the big city for important Avon meetings, and Coop suggests a trip to Chicago since he is thinking of going to the railroad fair. But that will not be for several weeks, if at all.

"Too bad about the Goodnow family," Millie says. "Would anyone like more potatoes?" She picks up the platter and starts it around again.

"The Goodnow family?" Cushing asks. "What about them?"

"Well, I don't know too much," Millie replies, "But I was talking to Harriet Cutler, you know, the marshal's wife, this morning after church and she said that Clare Goodnow, their 17-year-old daughter, was not in Boston on a student exchange program this year, but was there for personal reasons, if you get what I mean."

"Personal reasons?" the Reverend asks, looking up from his plate.

"Yes, *personal* reasons, the kind that may take about nine months to resolve, you know?" Millie waves her fork in his direction, raising her eyebrows and glancing knowingly toward Victoria.

"I know what personal reasons mean, Mother," Frankie says wearily.

"What are personal reasons?" Vic asks, finishing a sip of milk and putting down her glass. She has a big milk mustache that curls up in a grin above her mouth.

"Who told you this?" Cushing asks.

"Harriet Cutler. She said Hazel Goodnow had herself confided in her as she needed someone to talk to."

"I'm afraid I can't place the Goodnows," said Cushing matter-of-factly, diving back into the mashed potatoes. "Coop, do you know anything about this?"

"Yup," Coop replies with a small laugh. "I'll fill you in later."

While the women folk are cleaning up after dinner—Coop offers to do the dishes, but Millie refuses, saying she has two dishwashers. "Well at least save me the pots and pans," he says—he and Cushing repair to the front porch and sit in two Adirondack chairs and let their food digest and to enjoy a bowl or two. They light their pipes and gab. It is an opportunity to visit and unwind, which is an inexpressible joy for Cushing and a delight for Coop as well. They discuss crops, rain, the sermon, the service, but most of all the new people in town. When the conversation comes around to the Trio, their speech is expectant and hopeful. "Two guys and a doll," says Coop lazily.

"Umm, two guys and a doll, quite a doll." He puffs thoughtfully. "I guess if you include Cuttingham you have two guys and two dolls—"

"Guys and Dolls!" Coop says forcefully. They laugh.

"You know I saw that play on Broadway last year," Cushing says.

"No, I didn't know that."

"The songs were great and the choreography amazing. Bad guys and fast women! And good guys and good women. Interesting story. Gangsters and gamblers, you know …"

"Ummm…" They fall into silence until Cushing says suddenly: "Say, what about this Goodnow family?"

"Oh, nothing, really," Coop says, embarrassed. "Just a little tomfoolery on my part, I guess. I couldn't resist."

"What?

"Oh, well, the story about the Goodnows and their daughter? It is complete fiction. Folderol. No Goodnows. No daughter. No nothing. Every word of it a lie. I just wanted to see what would happen, what Mrs. Mang could do with a little gossip—even if it was fabricated."

Cushing roars with laughter. "Coop, I hope God has a sense of humor!"

"Well, I'm a goner if He doesn't."

And so they continue until dusk falls on Easter Sunday, and it reminds Coop of the evening two weeks ago when he headed for Bud's Tavern with Miss Crenshaw. How much has changed in just a fortnight. He didn't have anyone to take his place in the church office. Now he has not one, but three! He didn't know a Penelope Cuttingham, but now he does. Miss Crenshaw was alive, but now she's dead. He was bored—at the hotel; but now he's boarded—at Hemming's house.

Chapter XIV

THE MOST IMPORTANT THING IS TO remember people's name," Coop is saying to Miss Wang. "Of course this won't happen overnight ... perhaps you have a system that works for you. Actually when I am introduced to someone I simply focus very hard on the name and the face, and later I might make a note or two. I find that when I have forgotten a name it's simply because I wasn't paying attention, or didn't really care if I remembered the name or not. It's simple concentration, I think."

It is the Monday morning after the Resurrection. Miss Wang got herself to the church for an additional interview, more like training, with Coop and the Reverend who has not yet shown up. Coop scheduled this time in advance of the Reverend's usual appearance so that he could unload upon her some of his vast experience garnered over the past eight weeks as the typist of Bathington Community Church. Cushing never takes a day off per se. The custom among the Presbyterian ministers in the Midwest at least—who knows what the Methodists or Lutherans do?—is to take Mondays off. But Cushing, being a bachelor, finds that he does not need a set time for a break in the routine in order to be with family, for example. He prefers to work every day, if necessary, and if he needs or wants to take time off—to work in the garden at the Manse, or take in a round of golf up in Charles City, well, he feels completely at liberty to do so. He isn't punching a clock, and the congregation trusts him to give them full value. And whatever is rumored about Cushing, a reluctance to work is not a topic.

"Now some names are more important than others, that's true for sure. So, for example, if—I should say when—you meet Mrs. Broughton, the President of the Ladies Aid, you will want to remember her name. She'll be put out if you don't, and it wouldn't surprise me at all if she'd be

upset that you did not already know her name before being formally introduced. She sort of expects that her reputation goes before her." Coop
continues in this vein for some time, and he does not mind that it is *some
time* as it has been some time since he'd sat in such proximity to such a
delectable little flower as Miss Wang; he'd all but forgotten the sensation
such a felicitous moment can bring to any man, let alone a man of his ...
maturity. He is enchanted by everything Miss Wang does, the way she
toys with a strand of her hair as she listens; her manner of looking up and
into his eyes intently as though to assure him that she understands completely what he is saying; the way she toggles the foot of her leg which is
placed delicately over her knee. He knew Violet Crenshaw for years, but
had only recently *noticed* her and then only because an obligation had
thrown them together. There are, Crenshaw once told him, more than
eighty widows in town, and he is vain enough to think there isn't a one of
them who wouldn't consider him a good catch. But he admits, in a spate
of internal astonishment, that he knows more about Miss Wang after only
a few hours than he does of the entire widowdom of Bathington, a harem
of potential mates of which he's been aware for years—since Antonia
died. He sees and remembers details, like a white spot in the enamel of
one of her upper cuspeds, that she has no earlobes to speak of, that her
skin is white like alabaster, and her eyes curious, inscrutable and limitless
in their depth. She doesn't smile often, yet her countenance is never unpleasant. Rather, it is inquiring and inviting, accessible and measured. Her
hands are slight and delicate; he imagines them to be light and almost
weightless. He can see the faint blue of a vein beneath the skin.

"The membership is recorded in this black register," he says, reaching
across her to snatch a hardbound ledger on the desk. She leans back to
make way. He opens the folio and spreads it out before them. "You can
see here the name, date received, and manner received, such as 'Confession of Faith,' or 'Transfer,' and if a transfer, from what church, and
birthdays, baptismal date, marriage, and in some cases, deaths. This ledger
goes back to, let's see ..." Coop flips through the pages to the beginning
... "Ah yes, 1930, these would be all the members who were current at
that time, you see ... several pages ... and you can see a number have
passed away in the intervening years. Like this one: Tom Hollis ... well, it
doesn't matter."

Coop thinks he is flushed. He is now officially "carrying on" and he
needs to stop it. Besides, Reverend Cushing will be coming soon, and no

doubt wants to have a few words with Miss Wang himself. Coop is conscious that he is playing the old fool, but in his case there is no other fool to play and, besides, he rather likes it.

It is not absolutely essential that Miss Wang be made conversant with the polity of the Presbyterian church, nor of the various official boards and committees of the Bathington version of Calvinism, but Coop thinks it wouldn't hurt for Miss Wang to acquire as much background as possible so as to ease the delicate thing's transition into church life. But just then the Reverend pops into the office with such ferocity that it startles both Coop and Miss Wang and they jump from their huddled positions over the desk and look in amazement at the preacher who has crashed through the door announcing, "Cheerio, one and all! Christ is risen! What a glorious day! Do you not agree, Coop? Good morning, Miss Wang, splendid to see you once again." They both stand up. Coop's hand brushes hers, and he draws it quickly, perhaps furtively, away. Cushing appears not to notice. "Come now, are you quite done there you two? Follow me into the study and let's have a word, perhaps a spot of tea, what?"

Cushing swings merrily around on his heels and passes jauntily out the door and down the hall, leaving the church office door open behind him. Miss Wang and Coop stand at attention briefly after the whirlwind has vanished. "He talks funny," says Miss Wang, breaking her stance, and sitting down.

"Yes, he's a misbegotten Englishman, thinks the English are his kindred spirit. Studied there for a while, and I'm afraid it got in his blood, like a disease, you know." Coop does not sit down, but gathers a few papers and shuffles things around a bit awkwardly. He is slightly disappointed that the training with Miss Wang is over ... for now. No doubt she'll need considerable assistance, at least in the beginning. She could benefit from his tutelage.

"If it's in his blood, he should get a transfusion," Miss Wang deadpans.

"A transfusion!" Coop laughs a fake, hearty laugh and then stops, and moves to leave the room. He looks back. Yes, Miss Wang is following him ... her slight frame, wearing a beige skirt and a cotton sweater, a string of pearls at the neck, and black flat-soled pumps.

Cushing has a hot plate in his study, and by the time Coop and Miss Wang arrive, the water is boiling. Cushing has a tea caddy and a tin of cookies. He offers Miss Wang a choice, and she selects green tea, while Coop chooses a Lipton tea bag. Cushing taps Miss Wang's tea into a wire caged ball and lowers it into the hot water to let it steep for a while. Cushing's office is arranged with an ensemble in a corner opposite the desk. It consists of a loveseat and Cushing's wing-backed chair, the same one in which he sat some time ago when he posed some questions as to why an old man would even consider taking on a job. So now, Coop thought for a second that he'd sit in Cushing's chair, but of course he can't do that. "Oh, sorry … well, then … okay I'll just sit … here." Miss Wang is already on the loveseat. The hem of her skirt is almost to the top of her knee which—now visible—seems pale, bloodless and bony, with the skin drawn tight around the knuckle. "So any second thoughts, Miss Wang," asks Cushing in a gentle, fraternal manner.

"None whatsoever, Reverend." She clasps her hands on her lap and looks directly into his eyes. Cushing does not avert his and grabs her gaze and holds on. "Splendid! And no questions?" He takes a sip of his tea. Miss Wang does likewise and then answers. "Not right now. Mr. Carlton has told me more than I can possibly remember …"

"Well, actually …" Coop doesn't have the will to complete the objection to her misidentification.

"… and I am sure I will have questions in the days to come and knowing that you and Mr. Carlton—"

"Actually Carlton is his first name, Cooper is his surname," says Cushing quickly, hitching himself upright in his chair.

"Oh, dear," says Miss Wang, turning to face Coop. "I am so sorry!" She lays a hand on his arm, effectively setting it afire. "Please forgive me! See? If I can't remember or learn *your* name, however am I going to remember the names of people in the congregation?"

That question is never answered because at that moment there is a solid knock at the door. The trio look at each other, and then Cushing hollers, "*Entre vous!*" He is English first, French second and an American third. The door opens and in walks Marshal Cutler with a cowboy hat on his head and cowboy boots on his feet. He is followed by his deputy Jeff Scott, and a third officer whom Coop does not know. At this, Cushing, Coop and Wang rise in unison and wait. Coop and Cushing speak at once—

"Morning Jake, Jeff—" Cushing says, stepping forward, his hand outstretched.

"—Oh dear," says Coop. "Is Vickie in trouble again, Marshal?" The lawman laughs, removing his hat. "No, Coop, why would you say that?"

"Well, you impounded her bike, didn't you?"

"Oh, that! Well she was riding on the sidewalk again—I guess you know about that—so I took her bike, and Millie says she's saving her money to pay the fine and get it out of jail!" He chuckles. "Good kid, that Vic. A pistol."

"Oh, well, that's good then." Coop steps back slightly, a cue for Cushing or someone to take the lead.

"Actually we just come from Humphrey's place … old Rose was on the back porch with her shotgun picking off squirrels as they ran the telephone line." Cutler shook his head. "Poor George, don't know what he's going to do with that woman … Squirrels in no danger, mind you, but she's going to do some damage someday if he don't figure something out."

"She's loonier than a duck on dope," says the deputy, shifting on his feet uneasily.

Coop stiffens at this remark and says, "Well, she went after me with a flyswatter not long ago, but no one decides to be senile. This is no fault of her own, and I know George is trying to find some help—he's working on it."

Cushing interjects: "Okay, then! So what can I do for you, Marshal? Need a little prayer before arresting some speeders, eh?" The three lawmen laugh lightly and good naturedly and shift about restlessly. The marshal's doing the talking. He is a man who looks to be fiftyish—Coop knows him well, and guesses he can't be more than 55—with thinning hair and an expanding girth. His mid-section is so impressive that for it to be properly corseted requires a belt two inches wide and a large silver buckle which, Coop thought, made the marshal look as though he'd been strapped and saddled like an appaloosa. His belly hangs over his belt all but obscuring the buckle. He is not wearing a uniform *per se*, but a pair of Levi's and a plaid shirt with button-down pockets on the chest decorated with mother-of-pearl snaps and on one pocket is affixed his marshal badge. His eyes are small and peer out through fatty layers of flesh. He has a wide, bulbous, beer-drinker's nose. Covering his nostrils is a bushy mustache that drapes haphazardly around his mouth. He isn't wearing a gun. His deputy, Jeff Scott, is young and thin, a graduate of the Police Academy in Des Moines. He is in uniform, khaki pants, two-pocket button-down shirt to match and thin black tie and he has a revolver in a holster on a belt slung around his waist, a police hat on his head and sunglasses. He doesn't smile. And he takes a position at the door with his thumbs tucked at his hips behind his gun belt. The State Patrol fellow is also in full uniform, dark blues, with a black stripe running down the sides of the trousers, some silver bars on his lapels. He also is wearing a trooper's hat, round and flat-brimmed, and sunglasses. He is clean-shaven and serious.

"Well, first let me introduce a colleague, here—" motioning to the officer who is unknown to Coop and to Cushing. This is Sergeant Fowler, Fred Fowler, of the Iowa State Patrol out of Ames. Sergeant, this here is the best preacher this side of the Mississippi, Reverend Archibald Cushing—" The two men shake hands.

"Nice to meet you, Reverend."

"Likewise, I'm sure," and they both step back.

"And this here is Mr. Carlton Cooper, who was the station agent here in Bathington for years, but for the last three months or so has been the church secretary, right Coop?" More laughter. Coop steps forward to shake the trooper's hand.

Marshal Cutler continues, "But I am afraid the identity of this beautiful young lady is unknown to me." He turns to Cushing whose mouth has opened to make the introduction, but Miss Wang arises and steps smartly forward with her white delicate hand outstretched to the marshal, saying, "I am Miss Alice Wang, Marshal, the *new* church secretary." She shakes the deputy's hand and Sergeant Fowler's.

"The new church secretary!" the marshal booms. "Well, I'll be danged! Pardon, Reverend." Turning to Cushing, he says, "I don't see no ring on her finger. The rumor mill's going to be working overtime for sure now, you know."

"Absolutely," says Cushing. "There's no stopping a rumor, is there? We might as well get it started right here, right now!" They all laugh, including Miss Wang, Coop notes ruefully, disappointed that it has not occurred to the marshal or apparently to anyone else that he, Coop, one of the few true and unattached gentlemen of Bathington, might also be the object of such a rumor.

"Actually, Miss Wang, as much as I would like to detain you longer—maybe I will find a reason to arrest you and throw you into my jail! Ha!—I wonder if you could give us a moment or two? I have some matters that need discussing with Mr. Cooper and the Reverend."

"Not at all, Marshal. I have work to do in the office." She sashays to the door as the five men in the room follow her every sinewy undulation.

Then she turns and says, looking directly at Marshal Cutler: "And I'd be happy to be arrested and tossed in your jail any time, Marshal!" She closes the door while the uproar continues inside. "She's a saucy little thing, ain't she now?" says the marshal, grinning.

"Well, that little sauce better not be too spicy, or she'll be out of a job, soon!" Cushing says, chuckling.

"And then she come work for me, eh?"

"Oh, that would be hunky-dory. Let me tell you something, Marshal—not to be too cheeky about this. You hire her and put her in your office and one of three things will happen: First, Harriet will shoot you, or second, before the year is out, Miss Wang will be the marshal of this town, and or third, you'll be selling insurance in Osage and Bob's your uncle!" The pride of lions continue to roar and growl and paw around for a while, and then it is silent again.

"Well, Reverend, Coop, sit down. We'll stand, it's okay. We won't be too long." Cushing will not hear of it. He brings his desk chair around next to his wingback. Deputy Scott remains at the door at attention and with his thumbs in his belt, Coop and Cushing takes the loveseat while the officers of the law sit in the upholstered chairs. "So what's going on?" Cushing asks.

"It's about Violet Crenshaw," the marshal begins. "I got a call from Sergeant Fowler here, saying he was going to pay me a little visit, which he did, and now I am going to let him give you the details." He looks at Fowler and nods, and the sergeant begins to speak.

"I'm going to give you the short version, and then fill in some details. The short of it is that Violet Crenshaw did not die as a result of the fire. She was murdered."

To Coop and Cushing, these three words are like a bolt of lightning and a clap of thunder. The force of this unnatural occurrence sucks the air out of their lungs and drains the color from their faces—makes their heads ache from the pain of it. The word "murdered" passes their lips in a gasp as both a question and a statement. "Murdered!?"

Shocked, Coop sits in silence, but Cushing continues: "Who? How do you know? Why? Murdered? This is unbelievable! It can't be!"

"I know, it is unbelievable," Cutler says with a sigh. "We haven't had a murder since I've been marshal, and the last murder on the books was when Nellie Gorton put a shotgun blast through her daddy when he came after her in a drunken stupor … and that was self-defense … and that was before the war, back in '38 I believe. The things that went on in that house. Poor Nellie … guess she married a Mason City boy and they moved to Alaska and haven't been heard from since."

Fowler continues: "As you know, Violet had willed her body to science, the Medical Science department at the U of Iowa, but her body was so badly burned that the coroner only sent the cranium to the university—" No, Coop has not known this at all. This is extremely distasteful and shocking.

"So it was a headless corpse in the coffin at the funeral?" he asks.

Fowler nods. "When the docs got around to looking at it last week they noticed two clean holes, one near the right temple and the other in the back. Bullet holes. Our lab is doing some more tests right now, but we're pretty sure it was a .38 revolver. She was dead before the fire started, and the fire was no doubt started to cover up the murder. The fire chief and some arson experts from Des Moines are coming to town now to conduct a thorough investigation. But that hotel, what's left of it, is now a crime scene."

"The reason we're here," Cutler interjects, "well a couple reasons, obviously as her pastor you'd want to know, and I understand that you, Coop, knew her fairly well, we thought you should be the first to know. I don't know how or when this information is going to become general knowledge, but, for now, we'd like to keep it quiet so that we can work more efficiently. The State Police are going to handle the investigation, and that's also why we're here … to see if the Reverend might have some information that would cast some light on this mess …"

"Anything I can do, marshal, sergeant," Cushing mumbles. "Anything … but I don't know what I might be able to add …"

Fowler speaks, "I understand that apart from the murderer himself, that you, Mr. Cooper, were the last person to see her alive."

The question unleashes his mind and those particular neurons and synapses which connect the brain to the tongue, for the man had heretofore, well at least for the last few minutes, been dumbstruck. "It's just so amazing," he says flatly, staring at his hands gripping his knees.

"Yes, it is amazing, and it happened right under your nose, too!"

"Well that's true but how was I to know something like this was going to happen?"

"That doesn't even make sense because no one knows when something in the future is going to happen. We're only human after all."

"But on the other hand, when certain things happen, well, you *can* predict things, right? If it rains, we can predict the crops are going to grow. There! But I just didn't know. I mean, *murdered!* Miss Crenshaw, she could be cranky I guess at times, and she never won any beauty pageants, but being homely's no reason for someone to bump you off."

"Of course not! And besides Miss Crenshaw didn't have an enemy in the world."

"Although she did talk about the problems at the bank—"

"Coop! ... COOP!" Carlton turns his head in the direction of the voice. It is Cushing yelling at him.

"You're talking to yourself!" He lays a hand on Coop's shoulder and then looks up at the bemused officers and in an off-stage whisper says, "He does this sometimes." They nod. Coop looks at Cushing blankly, and then breaks into a relieved expression. "Oh, pardon me! I guess I got lost in my thoughts there for a moment. Millie calls it a 'reverie.' This is all such a surprise. What was your question, officer?" Fowler repeats his query to which Coop responds: "Yes, I suppose I was the last person to see Miss Crenshaw alive ... although how would I know? All I can tell you is that the last time I saw her was about 10 p.m. that Sunday night. I don't know if anyone saw her after that."

Deputy Scott had excused himself and returns with a glass of water. "Here," he says, "take a sip of water ... it will help you stay hydrated."

"Thank you, I think I will," Coop says gratefully. He grabs the glass and drinks about half its contents and hands it back to the deputy who then withdraws.

"You were at Bud's the night before the fire with Crenshaw, is that correct?" asks the marshal.

"Yes, that's right."

"And why ... what was the purpose? Just a social occasion? Were you ... close?"

"Uh, well, we were ... Close? Oh, no, not close. Friends to be sure. She was leaving in two days for California ..."

"Did she say *why* she was leaving? Didn't it seem sudden or strange for her to be leaving after living in Bathington for so long?"

"Well, I thought that too," Coop says, his voice quickening. "But you know a lot of people are going to California these days, and she said she didn't have any family, that it was time for a change, she was tired of the winters, and so on."

"Did anything unusual happen when you were at Bud's?"

"No, we just had a couple of beers and talked. She was congratulating me on an error-free bulletin ... we drank to her future ..."

"Nothing out of the ordinary?"

"No ... well ... she did seem to get impatient and eager to leave toward the end. She said she thought she saw someone she knew, but she didn't say anything more about it."

"Someone she knew? That's very important, don't you think, sergeant?"

"Yes, very. Did you see anyone there you didn't recognize?" asks Fowler, continuing the interrogation.

"It was crowded, even though it was a Sunday night ... there were any number of people there I couldn't put a name to."

"Can you retrace your steps? What time did you leave? Did you go directly back to the Fremont?"

Coop thinks for a moment, trying to recall those minutes. Actually, he's gone over it many times in his head. "Jules was there drinking at the bar. I was keeping my eye on him ..."

"Coop is Jules' guardian angel," Cushing interjects.

"Who's Jules?"

Cushing again: "He's—not to put a delicate face on it—the town drunk. A real nice guy when he's sober but when he's in his cups, well, he needs to be taken care of."

"Jules was drinking heavily, and I knew there'd be trouble ahead—"

"Would he get violent?" Fowler asks.

"Oh no, but when Jules is bladdered, especially if there is a crowd around—sometimes they'll egg him on—he'll start reciting dirty limericks ... for him that was the problem with booze—"

"What was the problem with booze?" Fowler asks, replacing his hat on his head and snapping his head at a slight angle, watching Coop.

"For Jules, the problem with booze," Coop answers, "is that it leads inevitably to poetry, and he'd start spouting a dirty limerick—"

"Jules doesn't sound like an Irish name," Fowler interrupts. "Was he—is he—Irish?"

"Oh yes, he's Irish through and through. Julian Jameson Joyce. *Erin go Braugh!* Sometimes you could hear him on the street! After a few beers he'd be giving you his lineage, claiming a direct affinity with James Joyce, and thus the poetry ... although Joyce didn't write no limericks ... I tried reading *Ulysses* once and I tell you anyone who says that he understands Joyce is lying through his teeth. That fellow—"

"Coop!" says Cushing sharply.

"Sorry ... Anyway, sometimes he'd propose to an unsuspecting female in the bar that he recite a poem for her edification—he'd actually used that word, edification—and she'd accept, sort of flattered, you know, because Jules had the air of a gentleman, a drunk gentleman to be sure, but a gentleman nonetheless, so he'd strike a pose, standing erect as a paragon of civic respectability with a Guinness in one hand and his hat in t'other and spurt out some filthy limerick to the startled woman—you know, a lot of women in town, or at least the ones who patronize Bud's regularly, know what to expect when Jules offers a poetic recitation and, believe me, some women actually *invite* him to tell them a dirty rhyme—but if the lady is unaware of this proclivity, you might say, sometimes she'd slap Jules, or her gentleman friend nearby would do it, and being unsteady on his feet, he'd land on the floor—well there'd be trouble. Lots of trouble, you know. And I could see that there was going to be trouble as there were people in the bar I didn't know, and alls I knew was that I needed to get him back to the Fremont, besides which if I didn't help him he wouldn't make it up the four flights of steps and I'd find him later passed out on the second floor landing. And then, too, Violet was getting antsy—"

"Antsy?"

"Yes, she was ready to leave—oh yes! Someone approached her thinking she was someone he knew from Chicago a long time ago. But she said he was mistaken, she had no recollection of him at all—"

"Someone recognized her?"

"Well, he *thought* he did."

"Did he refer to her by name?"

"Yes, but he had the name wrong. He didn't call her Violet, but someone else ... Eleanor, perhaps. ... I don't recall."

"Think, man! This could be important!"

"Well, I'm thinking. Perhaps it will come to me later."

Fowler is plainly exasperated. "For pity sake!"

"Shall I continue?"

"Please."

"So she and I escorted Jules out of the bar and shuffled him back to the Fremont, he was singing 'Molly Malone' at the top of his lungs, and when we got to Miss Crenshaw's floor, I said I could manage the last flight, so Violet left us and went to her room, and that's the last I saw of her."

"And Jules?"

"I got him in his room and put him to bed."

"So in your opinion he was in no shape to do violence to Miss Crenshaw?"

"Oh, Jules wouldn't do violence to anyone, drunk or sober."

# # #

Beyond the door to the Pastor's Study, Miss Alice Xiao Hua Wang, holding her pumps in one hand while she balances herself with the other, listens intently, her face pressed to the oak wood and her ear to the crack between the door and the casing. When the meeting breaks up, she steps away and pads quickly down the hallway to the Church Office before the officers, the Reverend and the railroad man appear.

Chapter XV

Thursday, May 15, 1952

Up at 6:35 a.m. it's getting lighter these days, and
I can only sleep in if I close the drapes, otherwise
I'm up by 5 or 5:30 a.m. Temperature at 6:45 a.m.
57° according to the radio, 55° according to thermometer. Saw a mouse in my room last night but he
disappeared under the bed somewhere. But didn't
sleep too much. Need a mousetrap and some cheese.
Went to Millie's for supper, then watched the girls
because Millie had some committee meeting at school.
Watched Eisenhower give a speech but the picture was
too grainy and too often got wavy lines making him
look like he was in a house of funny mirrors. Millie
said she's got to get the neighbor to go up on the
roof and adjust the antenna for her. Watched
"Groucho" and then back to Hemming's and listened to
"Mary Noble" and "Gildersleeve."
  Visits today: Back to the Humphrey's to see
George. Rose is better thanks to ample doses of laudanum so she's much calmer but still as batty as ever. She has a giant stuffed animal, a rabbit I
think, she calls "Jimmy Jesus" and now she communi-
cates exclusively to and through him. George has not
been able to get any help for her other than the
laudanum. I think--I hope--he's locked up the shotgun.
  The Crenshaw case continues to be the primary topic of conversation no matter where you go these days

in Bathington. And a television crew came up yesterday from Des Moines KUTV to shoot some background on
Bathington and interview a few of our citizens including yours truly, Reverend Cushing, Mrs. Broughton, et al. Jules tried to get on hoping to recite a
limerick but the reporter said he had enough interviews. Everyone has a theory including one that says
more than one party was involved. Some say I did it
to keep quiet a love affair. Oh, boy! Others say it
was Jules. Shimel is even under suspicion because he
was seen going to the hotel after our arrival from
Bud's with a package, and he admitted that it was to
see Violet, but she had called him and said she
needed the dress he was making for her asap as she
needed to leave first thing in the morning. Which
was strange because she had not said she was leaving
in the morning Monday, but on Tuesday. Shimel said
he called to ask if he could bring it over right
then as the dress was ready and so he did. She answered the door, did not let him in, paid, closed
the door and he left the hotel. I believe him of
course, although it was a surprise to me that Miss
Crenshaw had Shimel making her dresses. What's interesting is that the dress or swatches of it was
not found in the room after the fire. Why would the
murderer take a dress or steal a dress? Some say she
killed herself, which is ridiculous since no gun was
found at the scene. Then there's the bank. Rumors of
funny business and since Violet worked at the bank,
well, two plus two, and so on. And perhaps the most
persistent theory advanced is that the murder of Violet Crenshaw and the sudden appearance of the four
out-of-towners cannot be a mere coincidence. I have
been surprised at the number of people who do not
believe in coincidence. When you consider the thousands of small and large actions that flow through a
person's life in one day and so many more in a week,
what's surprising to me is that there aren't more

events coming together in a way that seems auspicious or suspicious. It's on this foundation--that
there are no coincidences--that fortune tellers make
a living. I just don't think that when stuff happens
it is by design, but rather that it is random, except of course for the fact that a lot that happens,
happens because we bring it upon ourselves. Cushing
would disagree with me and start talking about the
providence of God. I think the universe is so full
of words and actions floating around, there's bound
to be collisions for good or for ill. Anyway, a fair
number of people think that our out-of-town friends
are in some way or t'other connected to this nasty
business. The State Patrol still has the Fremont
boarded up as a crime scene and for a while had a
guard on an around-the-clock assignment. Now it's
simply boarded and locked up. In spite of all the
theories, I do not believe the marshal or the State
Patrol have any viable suspects yet.

Miss Wang is performing admirably and everyone
loves her. We do not see too much of Mr. Rossi and
Mr. Jard. They are either in the press room--that's
what they call it! Haha! Press room, or in the darkroom or Mr. Rossi is with a client or a church member taking their picture for the new picture directory. The Centennial Committee has contracted with
Mr. Rossi to take photographs of the Centennial
weekend.

Miss Wang (sometimes Mr. Rossi calls her something
else which sounds like Shaw Wah, I don't know what
that means, I should ask her about it someday) gave
me two letters of reference yesterday, one from the
Illinois State Bank of Chicago, Illinois, signed by
a Nikolas Papadakis, and the other from a Mr. Patrick Donovan of P. Donovan and Company, Publishers,
also with a Chicago address. Both letters were highly complimentary, and somehow unusual, different.
But I can't put my finger on it.

# # #

"Oops! The little guy's got his finger in his nose ... can't have that now can we?" Carlo reappears from beneath the camera canopy, holding a shutter switch in his hand flashing a phony smile at his clients. He is glad to be working ... shooting ... developing film and so on. He is dressed in light tan suit pants held up by suspenders, a white cotton shirt open at the neck. His clients are the Chapman family, mom and dad and 9-month-old baby. They are posing for their church directory photograph in the newly sanctified studio of what is now the Publications Ministry of Bathington Community Church. With the Session's permission they have completely remodeled the entire lower floor of the church with the exception of the Fellowship Hall that lies behind it, an arrangement which the Session enthusiastically supports since the remodel will not cost the church a dime but will be paid for by the "guys and dolls" as Cushing irreverently expresses it. The funds came from the front money from Donovan, although Carlo complained that they hadn't heard from Lefty since they got on the train. Alice said he went to Florida on business. The remodel is done quickly because local vendors put this job at the top of the queue when Carlo flashes cash at them. It is an arrangement convenient for them, the vendors, clients and congregation. Church members or customers can turn in to the lower parking lot, walk into the door that is now marked with a professional looking sign done by a sign maker in Charles City that reads: Publications Ministry. Carlo is not happy about the sign ... "How can a business that has a profit incentive be called a *ministry*, anyway?" he grumbled. He thinks that having no sign is better than this sign which will deter his "clients" from doing business with him. "Carlo," Cuttingham tells him, "the girls who come to see you will be coming by appointment, and all the others will understand." Alice reminds him that any enterprise that serves the needs of their fellow man can be called a ministry, and their business certainly caters to their fellow man, as it were, and definitely serves at least some of their most basic needs. She calls it the sanctification of the erotic, or erotic sanctification—the divinization of the human. "Where did you even learn words like that?" he grouses.

"My daddy was a preacher," she chirps.

"I thought you was lying about that."

"Oh, no. Some things you don't lie about." The offices of the Publications Ministry are busy as word gets out from the few brave souls who are among the first to patronize the Ministry and have their photo portraits taken free of charge! Their family portrait will be published in a small booklet with other church families, and they will be given one 8x10 "for free" and can buy additional copies in a variety of sizes if they so choose. Miss Wang's role is crucial because she sets up the appointments, and she keeps track of the church members who have come in for a sitting and those who have not. She doesn't hesitate in the slightest to contact those who have not yet made an appearance, because, after all, what they are offering is free. And the first members to sit for their portraits take along some other important news to their fellow congregants: no hard sell. Mr. Rossi and Miss Wang apply no pressure to buy additional portraits. Of course, they do give them a price list so that they can make an informed decision, but there is no sales pitch. It is a beguiling strategy that greatly impresses the penny-pinching, parsimonious denizens of northeast Iowa. There's no better way to get someone to buy your product than to say you're not interested in selling.

There is a terrific argument among the guys and dolls, however, in the immediate days following the shocking revelation—brought to them immediately by Alice—that a *murder* had been committed just a day or two after they had arrived in this sleepy little town out in the middle of nowheresville. At first, a strong sentiment is advanced that this is a coincidence that the townspeople will find hard to ignore. They will surely be regarded with suspicion, and the place will be lousy with coppers. For a while, they are inclined to take the money they have, find another location and start over. As the discussion advances, however, a new consensus emerges, counseling them to stay the course and see what happens. No virtue in deciding how the town is going to react before they've actually reacted. In the meantime, they'd go about their business and do business. To cut and run would only provoke deeper suspicion and in fact might be the very thing to cause the cops to look in their direction anyway. No, they could not do anything but plan to work and work the plan.

In their favor is the salutary presence of the two women. Were it Carlo Rossi and Wason Jard alone, things might have turned out differently. The two men alone would have engendered misgivings that now the women can allay. Without them, they may have been dogged with doubt, rumors and innuendo. The women are a moderating influence, and moreover, are a positive factor in gaining the acceptance of the local people. Cuttingham's natural urbanity and charm smooths many a ruffled feather, whereas Miss Wang is regarded as a delightful curiosity. Even the womenfolk of Bathington like them both—Cuttingham because she is not a serious threat for their husbands' affection due to her age, her good looks and apparent wealth notwithstanding, and Miss Wang because she is just so darn cute. Although the good people of Bathington are certainly no strangers to benign Midwestern racism, or even anti-Semitism, race in the case of Miss Alice Xiao Hua Wang seems to be a *positive* factor. Even Mrs. Broughton, although suspicious, understands that she is innately suspicious of *everyone*, and she admits to herself privately that she finds the little Chink appealing. There is no thought whatsoever of a link with the Communists. She is as American as all the Dagos, Krauts and Wops who seem to be pouring into the upper Midwest these days from the eastern seaboard. A part of the huddled masses and all that. Miss Wang is Chinese, but she speaks perfect English. She is a tiny thing, and smart, and beautiful. People vie to speak with her and to win her favor. And in her case, as in Cuttingham's, the Bathington wives are unconcerned about their husbands because it simply does not occur to them that their husbands might not only win her favor *but also win her favors*. Miss Wang is no comfort lady, and in any event, as everyone knew, there are no secrets in Bathington.

Miss Wang further defuses any possible criticisms by producing a worship bulletin that evokes positive gasps of admiration. The brochure looked splendidly professional. The paper stock is glossy and the type is set in Times New Roman font. The Prayer Requests are set apart in a sidebar with a picture of praying hands. The Weekly and Monthly Calendar of Events are bulleted in a box with curlicue corners. What is even more striking about the bulletin is not what is in it but what isn't: no smudges, no ink blots, no spidery lines across the page and no dropped words or misspellings. Gertie Johnson reads the bulletin three times, once out loud slowly, trying to find a miscue and comes up empty. After more than two weeks, it appears to most folks that Bathington Community Church is making out like a bandit on this arrangement with the young folks trying to establish a business. The professionalism exuded by what the Publication Ministry is producing gives the congregation a sense that their church is "going places" even if they cannot define clearly what place it is to which they are going. No matter. They were going—on the move!

As for the cadre from Chicago, the business model, as Cuttingham predicted, appears to be a success. It creates a lot of conversation and publicity for their enterprise. Most people think it very creative and novel of these kids to offer to do something *for free* (free printing, free labor, free directory, free bulletins and so on) and therefore they feel a curious obligation to give them a hand by throwing their business to them. Giving these kids their business makes them feel good about themselves, as though they are helping some unfortunate waifs get their start. It is all so *American.* God helps those who help themselves. If these children are willing to go to work, and can be so clever and creative, then it is their American—if not *Christian*—duty to lend whatever assistance they can to encourage them. Nothing unleashes the philanthropic impulse better than potential recipients who demonstrate that they are worthy of it. Soon restaurants, schools and business establishments begin to send their agents to the offices of the Publications Ministry of Bathington Community Church. The insurance agents and banks want calendars. Miss Wang shows them what they can do with photos of the American West, or the great cities of America, the mountains of Colorado, the cowboys of Wyoming. The auto repair shops, body shops and gas stations want calendars, too, and when they don't seem too excited with some of the photos Miss Wang shows them, she retrieves a *special catalog* from a drawer under the counter that features—for example—a tall flaxen-haired girl standing by a sweating golden stallion. She's all cocky-hipped with a lasso in one hand and in the other, a pistol, that greatest of all American phallic symbols, which she has raised to her mouth making like she's blowing away the smoke from the barrel. She is clad in rhinestone studded cowboy boots, denim short shorts, and a plaid shirt that is unbuttoned down to the low-slung belt of her skin-hugging pants, revealing all, including a delicate gold cross dangling from a necklace that is wedged deep between the colossal décolletage of the left and the right hemispheres of that gorgeous continent known as Miss Cheyenne Rodeo Queen of 1951.

# # #

The lives of Frances Katherine Cooper and her sister Victoria Ashley Cooper are largely unaltered by the violent death of Violet Crenshaw or the resultant uproar. This is certainly true of Vic, but less so of Frankie. Vic's behavior evinces no noticeable change in emotion or intensity, and

this is not surprising inasmuch as the Crenshaw woman was largely unknown to her. But even in the aftermath of her father's death in the rice
paddies of Korea, Vic's temperament was not in the slightest altered.
Death for her was *absence*. This was the palliative approach her mother
used and for Vic it was a wise tactic. When her mother explained that her
daddy died, it was no different than when she'd told her that her daddy
was going to Korea. When he got on the No. 64 at the Bathington depot,
he was gone. The last thing she remembered about her daddy was that he
was leaning out of the Pullman window waving his hat and yelling, "Bye
Vic! Bye Tiger!" Then he was gone. Absent. When her mother said he'd
died in the war, she was vaguely aware that her daddy's absence now was
permanent. But her daddy was not the only one who was permanently departed. Her grandpa and grandma had gone on a permanent leave of absence, as well as various aunties and uncles. So death had not inconven-
ienced Vic in any way, nor had her heart been seriously troubled.

It would be fair to say, however, that Frankie's mood darkened in the
month's following her father's death and the violent manner of Crenshaw's demise is an unpleasant tear at a suture that is still red, raw, swollen and unhealed. At the age of 13 when her father left, and 14 when he
died, Frankie's personality is already undergoing a seismic shift and can
do without the added blow of a death drama. She was a happy and laughing child; then, suddenly, not happy, not laughing. Some aspect of this
transformation was natural, that is to say, hormonal. But it intensified in
the months following her father's death. She now was moody and driven;
Millie called her "intense." Her manner became sharp and often com-
bative. She experienced death as *loss*. Her conceptual agility was impressive. She understood that her father possessed life but now he didn't; that
she'd once had two parents, now she had but one; that once upon a time
she had a father, now she didn't. Once she had a father's love, now she
didn't. Intuitively—she could not yet have expressed it this way—she felt
her life to be diminished. Her father's strength, his skill, his hands and
arms, his voice—gone! But this very diminishment caused her to re-
gather her resources; it steeled her resolve. If she was a determined child
before his death, now she is more so. If she had aimed high before, she
aims higher now.

Crenshaw's death, therefore, has been shocking for Frankie. It reminds her of the loss she's suffered. She becomes aware again of herself
in the drama/tragedy that is her life, and she feels anew the surge of en-

ergy that once pushed her to transcend that loss if not indeed to transform it into gain. It is this need to transcend and transform that gives birth to her creative force; it ignites a fire of sheer determination to complete the essay she proposes to enter in the contest. Shimel's forthright appraisal of her initial work caused her to fish for a new angle. Shimel said people like stories, but it would need to be a story that means something, she thinks. It must not be sappy or sentimental. To that end she begins to map a genealogy of the Bathington family and discovers to her surprise that such a tree-mapping has never been done. She thinks that providing a genealogical history of Bathington's forebears will be an interesting and useful appendix to the essay itself. Moreover, she believes that in every family tree there are bound to be some bad apples, and she is determined to find them. "If I could find a few bad apples," she confides to Naomi, "I just might be able to make a spicy little applesauce!"

"A saucy, spicy, juicy essay," Naomi says back. "That would be so swell."

"Yes!" Frankie says eagerly. "One that will taste really good to the judges."

"Well, it probably wasn't too smart buggering Mrs. Broughton like you did."

"Yeah, I know ... She wouldn't hold it against me, would she?"

"Yes ... she would."

Genealogical resources are meager in Bathington. She is able to construct a tree for the time period of the town history, some one hundred years and more, but the leads sputter out prior to 1850. She knows that she'll need to go to the city for further work, and her opportunity comes when Naomi announces that she is going to Des Moines on a certain Friday right after school to go to synagogue with her parents, and that they need to get to the city before dark. Frankie can come with them, and attend synagogue with her just as she had attended Easter service with her.

Naomi knows that she'll get no argument from Frankie about attending synagogue. Frankie is perceptive enough to know that the God of the Torah is also the God of the Gospels. But Frankie would not have had a problem attending a service at the Buddhist temple in Des Moines, either.

"Your parents won't mind me tagging along?" Frankie asks. They are at Naomi's house in her bedroom and are listening to some 45s.

"Of course not! They love you. They're thrilled that you're my friend, I mean they want me to have Jewish friends, you know, but where are you going to find a Jew in Bathington? That's why they try to get to synagogue in Des Moines so that I can meet some nice Jewish boys! But they love you. You're different, and they know it."

The trip occurs the first weekend in May—she cannot be gone over Mother's Day weekend—and following the service at the synagogue, the Shimel's take both her and Naomi to the Public Library, saying they would come back in about two hours. They are going to do some shopping. "Are they allowed to do that on the Sabbath?" Frankie asks. "Oh sure, my parents are observant, but not *that* observant, you know."

Frankie has some success at the library. She is beginning to broaden the trunk of the Bathington family and actually establish a root or two. She has many names, husbands, wives, sons and daughters, but she has not yet found a story, although she supposes that the migration could be a story in itself, but for even the Bathington diaspora to be interesting she needs a story within that story, and she isn't finding anything, not in old newspapers or birth records.

She locates a certain Goodman Bathington of the mid-1600s, not the first Bathington to arrive in America, but among the first. She learns that Goodman is a designation between Mister—which Thomas Bathington never was—and Farmer, which Thomas also never was. Goodman Bathington was in the prime of life when he joined the colonists at Massachusetts Bay. He had a good education in England but was by no means well-to-do when he settled on the west bank of the Saugus River about three miles from its mouth. From what she read, Frankie surmises that those early years were hard. But this is interesting: Bathington and the other early settlers got help from the red man who came to his aid, and he to theirs, on many an occasion. Bathington was an enterprising man and, in 1633, he built a bridge across the river and a weir for catching fish. He cured 150 barrels the first year of operation. He was, for a time, in partnership with a certain Mr. Leighton, carrying on a trade with the Barbados in which they exchanged cod fish for rum. They also kept a small store without paint or clapboards, the front adorned with odd signs reading "Corne Meale, Candells, Salt Fish, Tooles, Lowe Cloth, Pyke Staves, Hoope Poles and Cyder."

Although a God-fearing man, his active and energetic life brought him quite often into courts of law, often as defendant, but more often as plaintiff. Indeed at one time he had six suits in court simultaneously, all of which were decided in his favor. Frankie finds a note that the Massachusetts Court Records and the records of the town of Lynn are well-sprinkled with items about him.

And then, when she has her nose deep in a large dusty folio, Frankie finds what she is looking for. She comes across an Indian by the name of Sachem of Poquanum, who was also known as "Black Will."

Chapter XVI

BATHINGTON IS A TOWN OF SHOPKEEPERS and single proprie-
torships like Mary's Kitchen, although there is no actual "Mary" in Mary's
Kitchen these days as Mary Stananberger passed some time ago. It is a
curious feature of this town, Coop thinks, that so many, if not most, of
the business establishments are identified in two ways: by the owner's
name, and by the type of business. So you have Ted's Barber Shop, Harriet's Millinery Shop, Ray's Market, Bud's Tavern, Dick's Plumbing, Clayton's Department Store, Sid's Bar, Phoebe's Salon, Betty's Bookkeeping
Service, Cranston's Office Supply, Tom's Diner, Leo's Dry Cleaners,
Lucky's Gas Station, Gertie's Fabric Shop, Roger's Garage, Don's Auto-
motive Parts—well, the town is full of busy people transferring their
money from shop to shop in exchange for goods and services, sort of
economically incestuous, you might say. The town could issue their own
script and it'd all stay in town, or certainly Clearwater County. The corpo-
rate world has not reached Bathington, except for the Standard Oil station that Lucky Hollis runs. No car dealerships in town. For a new car,
you have to go to Charles City or beyond. You can get a Ford or Chevy
there. For a Pontiac you need to go to Mason City. And a foreign car?
Des Moines. There is a John Deere factory in Waterloo which employs
some Bathington men. Not much else. So Bathington is an enterprising
town of people who, if they aren't working for someone else, are working
for themselves, and since they are in business for themselves everyone
knows exactly what they are doing—their business signs tell all.

Coop and Jules have planned to meet uptown for lunch at Mary's
Kitchen, looking forward to the blue plate special. Coop notices that the
sign that extends out above the sidewalk is in need of re-painting; the
paint on some of the letters is peeling or fading. The K in Kitchen is virtually invisible, and the sign for all intents and purposes reads: Mary's
itchen. Coop isn't wearing his hat today. He is dressed in tan trousers,

brown shoes, brown belt which has a buckle that features a brass corn cob. His shirt is a long-sleeved blue cotton weave, and he has a bowtie made of tartan material. His watch is tucked in its pocket secured by a silver chain. He pauses at the door, looks up and down the street, but doesn't see Jules yet. It is 11:50 a.m. He opens the door. An OPEN sign hangs in the glass window of the door beneath a window shade. Inside, he quickly finds a booth, slides across the red plastic upholstery of the bench, and unfurls a copy of the *Bathington Gazette*. The waitress comes over.

"How ya doin', Mr. Cooper?" she asks, jawing on some gum.

"Oh just fine, Sally, thank you." Sally Hildebrand is a dusty blond whose hair is a jangle of curls which fall every which way. Her face is heavily made up, and her eyelashes seem to flutter nervously. She is wearing a yellow dress, with white trim at the collar, on the sleeves and around the hem. A series of dark yellow buttons run vertically from the neck to the hem as though the girl could unbutton the dress and step right out of it. The neckline is provocative, but not because the cut is particularly low and revealing but because her bosom is so abundant and begging for revelation. Around her waist is a small apron on which is a pocket with an order pad inside. Coop glances up from the newspaper, turning his head in her direction and his gaze hones naturally but quite unintentionally on Sally's large bosom area, as the waitress is standing close to the table. The buttons here seem to be doing a Herculean job keeping the material from bursting apart like the curtains opening at the beginning of Act I. Her dress seems to be pulled in two directions, scalloping the fabric along the vertical cut so that Coop sees in just a flash within her dress a glimpse of her undergarment. Coop quickly adjusts his line of sight and ratchets his eyes upward to catch Sally's face. She appears bemused: "Just a cup of coffee for now," he said. "Jules will be by soon." Sally stands there, looking at him, chewing her gum.

"You sure that's all you want?" she asks.

"What? Yes, for now. Probably get the blue plate when Jules gets here."

Sally slides into the booth and sits across from him and leans toward him. Her heavy breasts splay atop the table. "Mr. Cooper, you've heard about Clare Goodnow? What do you think she's going to do?"

"No, I haven't heard about any Clare Goodnow," Coop says, picking up his paper.

"Oh, yes, she's the 16-year-old kid who was sent back to New York cause she was in a family way, you know, and then she had triplets!"

"Oh, *that* Clare Goodnow."

"Can you believe it?"

"No, I can't believe it," Coop says, mildly irritated.

"Well, I wonder what she's going to do. Gertie Johnson said that there was some talk that she might just bring all three of them back to Bathington. Wouldn't that be grand? Do you know them Goodnows very well?"

"Actually, I've never met them."

"Neither have I," Sally gushes. She leans back against the stall. Coop stares into Sally's blue eyes seeing absolutely no depth there whatsoever, as deep as a blank sheet of paper.

But moments later, it is not Jules, but Sergeant Fowler and Marshal Cutler who show up at Mary's itchen. Sally jumps out of the booth, makes way for the officers and takes coffee orders from them and disappears. Fowler and Cutler sit down across from him.

"Any progress on the case?" Coop asks, putting down his paper.

"Well, perhaps not progress, but at least developments," the marshal says.

"What developments?"

Fowler speaks. "Well, here's the thing. How well did you know Crenshaw?"

"Like I told you, not that well, until recently when we were working more closely together at the church when she was leaving and I was learning the ropes at the office and all, but before that, I knew *of* her, but didn't really know her."

"You didn't know anything about her past, where she came from, her family, husband, children, nothing like that?"

"No, nothing. She's been in Bathington a long time, twenty-some years, I think, and I've never seen any family visiting or heard her speak of family, and she seemed to suggest when we were talking about her going out to California that she had no family ... she said the church was like her family. What's this all about anyway? "

"I'm not the detective on the case," Fowler says.

"Well, who is?"

"That would be Detective Crumbley and he's FBI out of Des Moines," says Fowler.

"FBI!" Coop exclaims. "Why is the FBI getting involved in a little murder in a little town like Bathington?"

"No murder is a little murder, Coop," says Marshal Cutler. "It's like this—"

Just then Sally arrives with three coffees and the conversation stops while the three men give the waitress their orders, two blue plates and a Reuben sandwich. Sergeant Fowler lowers his dark glasses better to see the menu and better to see Miss Sally. Fowler doesn't look any different on this day than he did the day after Easter when he was in Rev. Cushing's office announcing for the first time what had happened. Cutler's appearance is of the same sartorial genre as before; Coop is not sure that he's ever seen Cutler in a *uniform* as such. "Okay, as I was saying," Cutler says, after taking a sip of the coffee— "Sally, could we have some sugar over here, sugar? It's like this: It wasn't but a week after the fire that the Bathington State Bank got a letter from the Iowa State Banking Commission saying that some alleged irregularities about the banking practices here had come to their attention and they were sending an auditor up here to take a look, see what it was all about, see if there was anything to the allegations. And I don't know who alleged what, but an auditor was on the way. About the same time, we learn that Miss Crenshaw had been murdered and she worked at the bank and all, so we thought there might be a connection—"

"See, we think we know why Crenshaw decided to leave town so suddenly after all these years," Fowler says quietly, leaning forward.

"Why are you telling me all this stuff?" Coop asks.

"Aw for Pete's sake, Coop, we're just gabbing," Cutler interjects. "We're not saying nothing confidential or anything, nuthing that ain't gonna be in the papers anyway." He drinks some more coffee. "But we can shut up, if you prefer. I guess it can be painful talking about personal stuff, and all."

"No, no, just curious," Coop says, looking Cutler in the eyes and Fowler at his shades. Coop can see a little miniature version of himself in the reflection in Fowler's sunglasses. "Actually I am kind of honored that you would share some of this information, because I am certainly interested."

"Well as I was saying, we think we know why she was anxious to leave now. We learned shortly after the auditor appeared that the bank was setting up a process to fingerprint all of its employees. Evidently this is part of a statewide and nationwide initiative, to help solve bank robbery cases. Hoover's building this huge nationwide catalogue of fingerprints, 'cause a man's fingerprint is a unique bodily signature. We think that—for some reason—when Crenshaw heard that everyone was going to need to have their fingerprints taken, she decided to get out of town instead. It wasn't until after we learned that Crenshaw had been murdered that we put this hypothesis together. First, Crenshaw is working at a bank at which there are some irregularities; second, the bank announces a plan to fingerprint everyone; third, Crenshaw prepares to leave town. Fourth, Crenshaw is murdered. Somehow all of these events are related."

At this moment two things happen. Sally Hildebrand appears with three plates and distributes them accordingly, leaning wonderfully over the table to give Sergeant Fowler his dish thus obscuring for a moment like a total eclipse of the sun, Cutler's face from Coop's view. Coop thinks that Sally's very top button has surrendered in the battle to hold things together, for there seems to be, in his mind, more chestal area now in view.

Also appearing at this moment, or just as Sally leaves the table, is Mrs. Penelope Cuttingham who exclaims at the sudden and unexpected surprise of seeing Mr. Cooper. This is an artless subterfuge occasioned by her visit to the Publications Office only minutes earlier. She was looking for Mr. Cooper who was not at his room at Hemming's. She wanted to discuss with him some printing matters relative to the Centennial and also to ascertain whether he'd been hearing good things about the new team. The boys were in the darkroom. Miss Wang was at her desk behind the counter. She was working on names, addresses and phone numbers of all the members in the congregation. "Coop? He said he was meeting Mr. Joyce at Mary's at noon." Wang said. "Something like that." She flew out of the Publications Office like a hot wind, hoping she could alight upon Mssrs. Cooper and Joyce, persuading them to let her join them so she could get a sense of what they were thinking. So here she was now, at Coop's table, dressed in an attractive white dress with large blue polka dots, cinched at the waist by a wide red belt. She is wearing red heels, and has a small white handbag on her arm.

Coop is pleased to see her. Suddenly he realizes how tense he's become listening to Fowler and Cutler. "Hullo, Mrs. Cuttingham! Aren't you a picture! Would you like to join us?" he asks brightly.

"Are you sure I wouldn't be intruding?" Cuttingham purrs, even as she slides into the seat next to Coop, putting her left hand on Coop's thigh momentarily to steady herself and to give her leverage for a final nudge securing her place. "I know menfolk like to have their time to beat their chests and howl." Coop realizes that Cuttingham does not know these men nor they she, so he immediately makes introductions. "We were just discussing the Crenshaw case, and Sergeant Fowler here was explaining why he thinks, or Detective Crumbley of the F.B.I. thinks Miss Crenshaw was eager to leave town."

"Why! Are you a real sergeant?" Cuttingham asks, gushing. Suddenly, Coop realizes this is an act.

"Yes, I am, ma'am." Fowler says flatly, staring directly into Cuttingham's eyes. She doesn't flinch but says, "And why did Miss Crenshaw leave town?"

"She didn't. Someone made sure of that."

"Yes, of course, but she had *intended*, you said, to leave town, and why was that?"

"Did you know the deceased, ma'am?"

"I can't say that I ever had the pleasure. I arrived only a few days before the fire that claimed her life. In fact I was a guest in the Fremont the night of the fire and had to be rescued by some dear man from the fire department."

"Is that right?" Fowler asks.

"Yes, it is. Why? Is there a problem?"

"No, ma'am, we're just trying to discover all of the victim's known associates."

"Associates? Did she have *associates?*" Cuttingham looks in surprise to Cutler and then to Coop.

"That's what we're trying to find out," Fowler says.

"So," Cuttingham continues, "you were saying that you thought you knew why Miss Crenshaw *intended* to leave Bathington."

"Yes," said Fowler, "we now believe, to cut to the chase, that Miss Crenshaw was leaving town to avoid being fingerprinted."

"Fingerprinted!"

Suddenly, Sally is at the table again. "Would you like anything, ma'am?" she asks with her order pad positioned and her pencil poised. "A cup of coffee, black," Cuttingham says.

Marshal Cutler speaks: "Fowler ain't done yet. Tell them the good part."

"Since we have a bank involved, a murder, and a victim who was preparing to leave town, we had to follow procedures and this meant getting fingerprints. The problem was that the fire rendered it impossible to get fingerprints from the body, and the contents of the room were destroyed as well, but we visited the church office and we found something we were confident would confirm Miss Crenshaw's identity."

"And what was that?" Coop asks.

"The crucifix she gave you."

"The crucifix!" He never retrieved it from the office desk. "Surely my fingerprints are all over it."

"Yes, they are, Mr. Cooper. You're right about that."

"How did you get his fingerprints to compare to the unknown prints on the crucifix?" Cuttingham asks. Coop thinks that is a good question.

"We dusted the Gestetner."

"When was this?"

"When we first told you about the murder. We knew then that we were going to need your fingerprints."

"Wow, you guys are certainly thorough," Coop says in amazement. "But surely you've been spinning your wheels, although I guess solid detective work involves following as many leads as possible, eh?"

"Well here's the interesting part, Mr. Cooper and Mrs. Cuttingham, or the 'good' part as Cutler here puts it: Based on the prints we've recovered so far—and we're taking more to confirm this—we believe that Miss Violet Crenshaw was not Miss Crenshaw at all, but someone else."

"WHAT?" Coop spits out the interrogative so loudly that people at other tables turned to observe the disturbance.

"Quietly, people!" Fowler cautions. "Not what, but who?"

"Who?" whispers Cuttingham. "Who?" Coop echoes.

"Elizabeth Morley."

Cuttingham gasps, but Coop speaks immediately: "Elizabeth Morley? Who in tarnation is Elizabeth Morley?"

"She's the woman you knew as Violet Crenshaw and the FBI has been looking for her for 25 years in connection with a number of crimes committed in Chicago."

"Well, blow me down," Coop says, leaning back against the booth.

"Yeah, me, too," Marshal Cutler adds. "Who-da thought?" They all sip on their coffees, thinking.

"Wait!" Coop cries. "I remember now. That's the name this guy called Violet when we were at Bud's: Elizabeth Morley. He called her Lizzy!"

"Now we're getting somewhere," Fowler says, exhaling a lungful of air and leaning back against the booth. "Did he tell you *his* name? The guy that recognized her—what was his name?"

"Yes, yes, but I don't remember … John, perhaps. I remember it was a biblical name."

"Oh for pity sake."

"Why … would she change her name?" Coop muses.

"People have their reasons, and sometimes they're good reasons," Cuttingham says quietly.

"Or, most often, they're running from something or somebody. Hey, we had a case like this about fifteen years or so ago. Well not just like this, there was no murder or nuthin' but remember the Hitler family that lived out the other side of Osage? They got their name changed, went to court and everything, for obvious reasons. And Willie Sanders, a quiet little mousy guy—short guy no more than five five—lived out north of town, kept to himself, a bookkeeper, he changed his name to Joe Louis even though he weren't colored, Louis, you know the fighter? And darned if his personality didn't change! He was still this weasel of a man, but in his head he became a tough guy, assertive, firm, kinda arrogant really. Quit his job and became a Fuller Brush salesman, pretty good at it too. Don't know what happened to him."

"It's strange, that's for sure," Coop says. "I'd like to know *when* Violet changed her name … and *where* was she when she changed her name. If we knew the when and the where, we'd probably be able to guess the why."

"You could be right, Mr. Cooper," says Fowler in the clipped matter-of-fact tone of an accountant. "But clearly, we need to know more about Violet Crenshaw. She was hiding a secret, and that secret might be connected to her death."

"Yes, I suppose you're right," Cuttingham says, "the motive for murder could be connected or she may have been killed for reasons totally unrelated to her change in name. She's lived in Bathington … how long? Yes, yes, a long time. Plenty of time for a motive to be born … although I understand she didn't have an enemy in the world."

# # #

June 1, coming up soon, will mark the official beginning of the Centennial festivities which will culminate the second weekend of August, on the date Bathington was founded according to the incorporation papers. It is on this date that the men of the village are to begin growing facial hair, and come July 4th on the 176th birthday of the United States of America, any male appearing on the streets of Bathington without a beard will be thrown into the newly erected public "jail" in the city park. Offenders can be released by paying a hefty fine which will go to a charity. The Centennial committee has not yet determined the charity, but frontrunners include "Have a Cow," an organization that provides Iowa corn-fed beef to missions and soup kitchens throughout the state, and "Bread for Threads," a Des Moines outfit that raises money for clothes for needy children. Of course, the offending gentlemen will get a one week probationary pass to appear in Bathington again, at the end of which, lacking facial hair they could be re-incarcerated.

Shimel is busy during this period. He has orders for mid-19th century dresses and frontier wear, and has ordered more calico, chintz and what not. Most mothers are pedaling their Singers like there's no tomorrow, creating sundresses and bonnets for their girls, while the boys will be in high tops, short pants and suspenders. It is not critical that the garb reflect the fashion of one hundred years ago, only that one's apparel during the summer months be retrospective. Thus, Coop, who still has a couple pair of plus fours, will not hesitate to get them out of mothballs and the cedar chest, and dust off a newsboy cap and appear on the streets, even in church, thus attired.

Clarice Broughton has been unsuccessful in her attempt to remove Shimel from the centennial affairs. She had been wounded by Art Bandy's ill-advised bullying in a previous meeting, and it has cast Shimel in the role of a victim, and Shimel, being generally well-liked, and keeping to himself, well, it is a battle she doesn't want to fight. He probably is a Communist, but she is also willing to adopt the State Department's policy of "containment." As long as Shimel is working in his garage/shop, at least they know where he is. And it could be worse. He isn't a banker after all, or in journalism like all those Jew York Jews. Better for him to be sewing clothes with a needle, than sowing controversy with a pen. Truth is, she tells herself, I just don't like the man, and that's no reason to persecute him. In this she acts, she feels, according to the principles of her Christian faith, and she notes with satisfaction that she is growing as a Christian, capable as she is of modifying her views, and altering her position, without appearing to be weak and waffling. Her release of further antagonisms may also be due in part to her failure to secure the presence of Senator Joseph McCarthy of Wisconsin at the Centennial celebration in August. Further, she is not going to invite any of her "America for Americans" colleagues to the Centennial. And thus, Shimel will not be an embarrassment after all.

Still, although she is willing to release her antagonism toward the man on a personal level, should it become apparent that the man does indeed have ties to the Communist Party, then she will be forced to take action. She subscribes to the "love the sinner, hate the sin" philosophy of retributive justice. It is a point of view by which countless sinners have in the past thirty years or more been loved right up to their lynching. What Clarice Broughton identifies as "love" is not actually an emotion that connects her to the object of her love; it is rather indifference. If Broughton, who claims to love all people, can honestly acknowledge that she holds no personal animosity toward an individual, this she identifies as love, that is, the absence of hate. Thus she is indifferent as to the sinner, but passionate as to the sin—which, if identified by Clarice Broughton as a sin, is zealously prosecuted to the full extent of the law … and then some. Her indifference is so entrenched that it amounts to blindness. She does not see the criminal; she sees only the crime. She doesn't see people; she sees *behaviors*. And in this she is like most of her fellow citizens, for, in a changing world, how can one possibly *not* be indifferent to the vast multitudes of people that crowd the cities and highways of the land? And what basis of moral judgment is there but one's actions and behavior? Thus, not really knowing Shimel—she's had a few conversations with him—she has no other yardstick by which to measure the man except his behavior, and his behavior to this point suggests no reason he should be harassed. But this can change. And, she reflects, behavior is not the only factor: color and religion are others, not because any particular racial skin tone is preferred or not preferred or religion good or bad, but because it is simply a matter of observation. Coloreds have certain tendencies and it's silly to say otherwise, the same with the Mexicans, and it is certainly true of Jews. Who can deny it? So better to be forewarned than embarrassed. She'll lay off Shimel, but it will be a mistake if anyone, including Shimel, mistakes her generosity as weakness.

# # #

The typist, the photographer and the printer have to this point garnered little but the total approbation of the public and the congregation. Miss Wang's error-free worship bulletins came to an end when Gertie Johnson spotted the word "different" which was used adjectivally when it should have been used adverbially, and once the Prayer of Confession was omit-

ted, but not the Assurance of Pardon, and thus the Reverend was assur-
ing people of forgiven sins which they'd not been able to collectively confess. Things like that are more a source of amusement than irritation, and
Miss Wang is of such a nature as to receive their good-natured criticism
in the spirit it was intended. The *Bathington Chimes* came out the end of
May and was met with universal acclaim, with its abundant use of photos,
including one of Reverend Cushing preaching on Easter Sunday, a photo
of the sanctuary choir, and photos of Wang, Jard and Rossi, accompanied
by a brief description of their duties, as well as suggestions as to how the
congregation could utilize their talents. Actually, Miss Wang did not
spend too much time typing for Bathington Community Church. She
rendered the church a great service because the church office was open
every day, having been moved from its earlier location to the lower level
in the Publications Ministry office. The church phone had been installed
there, and a second line which the Ministry Team paid for was installed
for the printing operation.

The team is busy. Rossi is shooting every day. Church families occupied a good portion of his time early on, but by the end of May this has
slowed down. A cutoff date is established so that the church picture directory could be published. They have incorporated quietly as RJW Enterprises, Inc., and it is under this name that the company begins to increase their business, printing business cards, calendars, brochures, flyers,
agendas and more. The magazine that no one outside of RJW sees is *New
Girl*. It is now in production. Cuttingham, whose special talent is for finding special talent, keeps the girls coming, although the strategy is to shoot
as many and as often as possible, and then to quit when the pool of photographs is sufficiently deep so as to make possible a couple of issues …
at least.

Thus May is a busy month. Church families are setting up evening
appointments, and young women are coming and going. Even Marshal
Cutler notices. When he and Harriet had their portraits taken for the directory, on leaving the Publications Ministry office, they saw a winsome
blond come in and sit in the waiting area. Cutler remarks that Bathington
Community Church has the most beautiful membership of any church in
Bathington. But he's noticed how busy the office is on other occasions.

"Quality breeds quantity," purrs Miss Wang, when the marshal says
something about it one day after he stops by the office. Leaning over the
counter, she says, "When you do a job well, people come back and they

tell other people ..." She takes a deep breath. "Word of ... mouth." She locks her eyes on Cutler for seconds that seem hours. "Well, you're right there," he says, breaking the spell, laughing. "You're quite a doll, you know that?"

Still there are incidents that give pause. Coop arrives for a sitting for the picture directory one evening about 7 p.m. and Alice is nowhere to be found. Coop thinks she might be in the bathroom upstairs or perhaps she doesn't always come in evenings. He shuffles toward the studio. The door is closed. He doesn't see a light through the crack at the bottom of the door, so he grabs the handle and pushes it open. Carlo and a beautiful girl in a onepiece yellow bathing suit are talking in front of a beach scene and standing between two reflective umbrellas and in front of the camera. The room is otherwise dark. Carlo gives a yelp, and rushes toward Coop explaining that he needs to leave for the sake of the client's privacy of which they are always assured. He thought the door had been locked, but remembered that when Alice had left he had not locked it behind her. Coop expresses some curiosity as to the kind of work Mr. Rossi is doing behind closed doors, and in a house of God, no less. Carlo assures him most vigorously that everything is on the up and up, and that these photographs were on behalf of a detergent company—"All the major corporations, Mr. Cooper, in their advertising, understand that an ad with a pretty girl with great gams is going to attract attention, right? Dig? When you thumb through a mag, you notice the girls, right? That girl you saw was a product girl, a poster girl. The photos will show her holding a box of detergent—which is associated with the cool, pure water of the ocean, and the whiteness of the sand, and the beauty of the chick herself, you know what I mean? You dig, right?"

"Dig? No, I am not sure I dig."

"It's an expression. Never mind. Tell you what, you want to come back inside the studio and meet Miss ... um ... Smith? She's done a lot of work for quite a few advertising agencies."

Coop allows as that isn't necessary. He is beginning to feel overwhelmed by the intrusion of feminine personalities into his life in the past few months. He took the temporary job as the typist for the church because it filled a need and Coop enjoyed feeling useful, and then suddenly, or so it seemed, this bald old guy of 68 has more women in his life than Solomon in his heyday. What's going on? Mrs. Cuttingham, Violet Crenshaw, Alice Wang, Elizabeth Morley, Sally Hildebrand, Mrs. Hemming and now this Miss … Smith. It's not like they are in his life in any mean-ingful sense, especially Sally and certainly Miss Smith, but still, heretofore Sally hardly spoke to him, and he can't remember the last time he's seen a gorgeous representation of the female form in a bathing suit, and espe-cially one cut in the modern style. Such exposure to female pulchritude, and his proximity to Miss Wang—forget she is young enough to be his granddaughter—has aroused a memory of virility that has been becoming more faint by the year. Suddenly, he's feeling what it's like for a man to be around a woman again.

And speaking of Sally, Coop had seen her coming out of the offices of the Publication Ministry one afternoon, and he was quite confident that she was not on the membership rolls of the Bathington Community Church. He wonders if she'd been in a yellow bathing suit in Mr. Rossi's studio. And what would she be selling?

Millie has voiced some concerns as well. She and the girls went to the studio for their sitting. Mr. Rossi took great pains to get them situated just so. Vic insisted that the teddy bear be included as part of the family. So Millie was positioned on a stool, and standing behind her was Frankie, and in front of her, but beside her, was Vic on a smaller stool. What alerted Millie to danger was that Mr. Rossi appeared to be flirting with Frankie, and giving her undue attention. He was forever repositioning her, touching her shoulders, rushing in to adjust the tilt of her chin or the angle of her head. And, moreover, she was bothered somewhat by the interest Frankie, in turn, took in Carlo's photographic equipment, asking so many questions—my, she's such an intelligent and curious child—and Carlo's patience and eager willingness to explain the minutest details about F-stops, apertures, shutter speed, focal point, depth of field and so on. Later, Frankie said that Mr. Rossi, who is 24 years old (!), said she could stop by any time and watch a shoot, learn more about cameras and photography, and that he'd even be willing to shoot her for free!

"Well, I don't think that's a good idea," Coop says, his mind a blur of yellow, sun, sand and flesh.

"I totally agree," Millie says, "But you can't tell that child anything. It's like I'm the enemy."

"That won't last forever, Millie, believe me." But it will last for a while, he admits. Then, the predictable happens. Frankie goes to the stu-dio one evening, by herself, and sits in on a session. It is a shooting of one of the church families, the Calhouns, and she simply observes as he positions the family, entertains the children, sets the shutter speed, advances the film. Carlo invites her, when he is ready to shoot, to stand by him, to look in the viewfinder so she can see what he sees, to explain to her what he is doing. She finds it all very interesting, but her mother, when she tells her about it later, flips her wig. She believes that she had told Frankie that she was not to go to the studio. "You said no such thing," Frankie counters.

"Was the door shut?"

"Of course it was, but I wasn't alone with him, you know, the whole Calhoun family was there? And even if they weren't, what is the problem? We're in the church! Mr. Jard was in the darkroom and Miss Wang in the office working on the *Chimes* or something. Why are you having such a cow about this anyway? You can get on the horn and find out for yourself. Basically you don't trust me." Oh for Pete's sake! There's the trust thing again. A mother can't try to provide some protection and guidelines for her daughters without them making the situation into a "trust" thing.

"Yes, Frankie, I trust you, I trust that you always want the right thing and will always *intend* to do the right thing. But I have enough experience to know that sometimes, when through no fault of your own, you're in some situations, you are not able to do the right thing or make the smart choice no matter how pure your original intentions. I am sure this is all okay. But he's 24, I know nothing about him, do you? And you're 16, and it's not a proper thing for a young lady to be alone, unchaperoned, with a gentleman—and I pray he is—like that."

"It's about my dam, isn't it," Frankie says. Millie throws up her hands and leaves the room, shaking her head.

One more thing that counters the generally positive attitude that RJW Enterprises is receiving is that none of the photos, that is, the 8x10s have yet been printed. No one has seen the results of the sittings and, although people have not paid a sitting fee, they are anxious to get their free photo as promised, but so far, none has arrived or been distributed.

Chapter XVII

THIS YEAR FRANKIE AND NAOMI ARE going to the high school Spring Formal. Last year their parents wouldn't allow them and as sophomores they couldn't go unless invited by a junior or senior boy. Both girls had been asked by upperclassmen to attend with them, but, alas! it wasn't to be and there was weeping and wailing of biblical proportions in both households. Charges of inequity, gross dereliction of duty, bad parenting, negligence, cruelty, hatred and stupidity skittered like bats in the dark melancholy belfry of those spring nights a year ago and were linked as well to other earthly woes such as poverty, illiteracy and disease. But now, both Millie and the Shimels know they can't say "No" yet again and in truth they both feel that the girls are ready; after all, it is a high school event and their peers will be attending. Refusing to allow them to go is out of the question. The lads who coveted the girls' companionship last year were this year no longer interested and, for several weeks leading up to the gala, the girls were not confident that *anyone* was going to ask them. They feared that their moment of opportunity to be introduced into high society—even if the *high* of high society is high *school* society—had fluttered away like a feather in the wind. Thanks to their parents they had become pariahs in their own parish. The lack of suitors led them to realize that they were without doubt destined to a life of spinsterhood as aging, corseted aunties, wearing drab chintz and black, sturdy shoes and their hair done up in a bun. Naomi had no siblings. She couldn't be an auntie. "You can be auntie to Victoria's children," cries Frankie one day when the two of them are mixing the oleo in Shimel's kitchen. "She'll probably have a dozen of them, more than enough to share!" They then considered that they might become nuns—"We could be sisters!"—but on account of Presbyterians don't have nuns, and Judaism doesn't have nuns either since having a Jewish mother is enough to keep one feeling guilty for most of your life anyway, they'd need to abandon the idea or become Catholics.

Joel Shimel, however, wisely proceeds with the fabrication of the formals the two debutantes will be wearing, the girls' despair notwithstanding. "Faith," he says, as conversant with the New Testament as with the Torah, "is the fabric of things hoped for, the thread of things not seen." So he goads and prods, cajoles and advises the girls to make decisions as to the material and style of the formals they will wear. Frankie, after consulting with her mother and Rev. Cushing, who at Millie's invitation is visiting at this critical moment to offer his opinion on some drawings rendered by elementary school children in the Centennial Logo Contest—"I do like this one of the tall man with the beaver top hat that looks a 1 and the zeros filled in with the faces of an old woman and a young woman ..."—has chosen a sleeveless gown of purple georgette which she'll wear with long white gloves (she's already stretched and ironed them) and a string of her grandmother's pearls. Naomi picks out a design without soliciting suggestions from either of her parents that is a sleeveless, strapless, daring number of lemon chiffon which would contrast stunningly, she thought, with her flawless, dark olive skin. But of course, they sniff into their tissues, it has been a total waste of their time and energy, since no one is going to ask them to be their dates for what is not only the most important evening of the year, but verily, their entire lives. This mood notwithstanding, Mr. Shimel continues sewing—against all odds.

The apparent reluctance of the local young men to consider Frankie and Naomi as suitable or desirable companions for the Spring Formal is in part due to their emergence not only as weird eggheads but as rather outspoken ones at that, with opinions on subjects that are generally thought to be matters for men. "Boys don't like smart girls," Naomi observes.

"No, I think it's that *smart* boys don't like smart girls," complains Frankie. "So whoever *does* ask us out are likely to be as dumb as posts. Smart boys want dumb girls, Nomes, 'cause they think they're sluts. That's probably how that Clare Goodnow girl got knocked up—a dumb girl with a smart boy."

"Shut up, Frankie," says Naomi. "You're making me depressed ... who's Clare Goodnow?"

Neither of the girls is enrolled in a Home Ec class, both of the girls aspire to a university education, both of the girls are supporting Harry

Truman over either Taft or Eisenhower, both think that the Korean conflict was a travesty, and Naomi's affiliation with Jewry left her without many, if any, male admirers.

But these same qualities, plus the fact that they are both attractive, especially Naomi with her Mediterranean complexion, dark hair, and deep set eyes, also produce a few secret admirers. These young men know that the girls come as a set. They both need to be invited; one will not go without the other, and it will be a double date. The local swains who will ask them out will need, therefore, to be friends themselves for the evening to be successful. And they will also need to be fellows who can withstand some ribbing from their peers, especially the hoods, when it becomes public knowledge that they have asked two gals to the dance who are known to be somewhat difficult, and also females with whom there is no chance that they'll get even to first base, let alone around *all* the bases. The best they can hope for is that they'll be in the batter's box, and that the girls would be pitching ... something ... anything ... easy to hit.

Stepping up to the plate are juniors Seth Hardison and Randy Moulton. The boys are taller than their dates, which is good, and, while no one will mistake them for James Dean or Rock Hudson, they aren't unattractive either. As 17 year olds, they still bear traces of acne on the cheeks and oily foreheads and they have the social sophistication of squirrels. But they are boys. The girls accept with alacrity. "Randy is even half Jewish," Naomi crows. "His grandmother on his father's side married a Jew."

"So his grandfather is a Jew."

"No, that man is not his real grandfather. His real grandfather caught the flu and died. And his grandmother married this other guy who was Jewish."

"He's not *half* Jewish, Nomes, and really not even Jewish, unless you can be Jewish by marriage three generations removed or something. Now, if his grandmother had married a colored, he wouldn't be colored, would he? 'Cause he wouldn't have any colored blood in him, or if she'd married an Indian he wouldn't be Indian, would he? Jesus wasn't a Gentile was he, even though he had Gentile blood in him through Ruth? He was still Jewish, right? So this guy's not Jewish just because his grandmother's second husband was Jewish."

"Stop it! You're confusing me," Naomi counters. "It's *something*, anyway." But Frankie thinks then of Black Will ... the Indian of yore who had dealings with *her* ancestors. She just isn't quite sure what those dealings are yet. She has discovered that, in 1630, Goodman Bathington purchased Nahant, that long, narrow peninsula extending into Massachusetts Bay from the town of Lynn. But years later there'd been some trouble with this purchase, and the difficulty arose because of two considerations: the seller and the price. The seller was Black Will, the Indian Sachem of Nahant, Poquanum. The price was a suit of clothes and a broken Jew's harp—an excellent bargain since the purchase consisted of five hundred acres. For twenty-seven years, Bathington enjoyed undisputed possession of this property. He fenced it, he grazed his cattle there, cut wood, cleared land, and gathered sap from the trees to use in making tar.

But in the year 1657, the town of Lynn divided Nahant into parcels of land to be distributed among the town freeholders. Bathington was furious! He filed suit to prevent the seizure of his property. Although he presented witnesses to verify his claims, the court decided that a suit of clothes was not a proper payment and that Black Will's mark on the deed was of no validity, so the case went against him.

More than twenty years later, Bathington's son, Nathaniel, sued to recover Nahant. Although the law prohibiting the purchase of land from Indians without public permission was not in effect until after his father purchased Nahant, the suit was decided against him. Another twenty years still later, Goodman Bathington's two daughters, Mary and Frances, brought suit on behalf of their father's claim. Once more, the effort was in vain.

Frankie can't shake the conviction that there is more to the story; she just doesn't know what it is. She needs more information on Black Will.

\# \# \#

Although the Spring Formal doesn't officially get underway until 8 p.m., in both the Shimel and Cooper households, and doubtless scores of others in Clearwater County, the Spring Formal is a day-long event that is rife with preparations, doubts and uncertainties, assignments and errands, questions, adjustments and arrangements. Victoria observes the goings-on in subdued silence, wandering about the house like a shadow, mostly watching her big sister practice walking around in high heels of purple patent leather, lurching and stumbling back and forth across the bedroom floor with all the grace of a new born colt on roller skates. Millie spends the day crying. "How can you see what you're doing, Mother?" Frankie complains when Millie is helping with her makeup. Preparing this filly for the formal is no small task. It involves hose and garters, a special brassiere, a petticoat, blush, mascara, eyeliner, false eyelashes (about which Millie knew nothing), curlers and pins, and the added challenge of disguising two pimples near the right temple which have quite inconveniently made an appearance that very morning. Then she gets a snag and a run in her hose. "There's a run in my nylons, Mother!" And Millie runs for the nail polish to apply it to the affected area. "It's on the thigh, Frankie," her mother says. Her eyes are red and swollen. "No one's going to see it anyway." Frankie is not consoled. "Are the seams straight?" she asks, twisting to see herself half-dressed in front of the mirror. "No one is going to see much of the seams," her mother adds assuredly.

The gentlemen appear at 7:30 p.m. on the dot. The Hardison boy is driving. The Hardison and Moulton families discussed what vehicle was going to be used for the occasion. The Moultons have a 1949 two-tone Ford, but Randy backed it into a mailbox and the left tail light is broken, whereas the Hardisons have a 1951 Chevrolet automatic with power steering and an AM/FM radio, chrome dash and carpeting in the front and back. Seth will drive, pick up Randy, go to West Bath for Naomi, and then be at Cooper's by 7:30 p.m. So here they are, the three of them, on a front porch with peeling white paint surrounded by hedges, standing before a holey screen door which is slightly ajar. Seth pulls a hand out of his trousers, extends an index finger on which the nail has been chewed down to the nubbin and depresses the white hard rubber button of the doorbell. Tippy immediately starts barking, a high-pitching yelping phrased in six or seven staccato bursts, one after another. "They're here," Vickie screams, turning in Rev. Cushing's direction, who looks up startled. He is lurking by the sideboard and fiddling with a Brownie box camera. He is a chaperone and by rights should be at the school already. But, he sensed that Millie needed moral support. The least he can do is to show up, offer a shoulder, and take a few snapshots if possible. Vic runs from the window, clatters toward the stairs, and hollers up to the second story. "They're hereeeee!"

"I heard you!" comes a muffled shout from above. Frankie and her mother are huddled in Millie's bedroom in a last minute consultation. "Remember you're a good Christian girl," Millie says, dabbing at her eyes with a pink, wet handkerchief on which are embroidered lavender forget-me-nots, her voice quavering. But she is quietly weeping less for the daughter stepping out with the young man waiting on the landing below than she is for the mother whose daughter is walking through that door. Any mother, of course, has every reason, yea, a right and responsibility to be weeping at such a moment as this. For when the girl walks through that bedroom door, approaches the stairs at the bottom of which far below is a young man, why, that girl has stepped through the Portal of Childhood and Innocence and is now negotiating the Stairs of Responsibility, Decision-Making and Choices, away from all parental restraints. It's a defining moment, a tear in the fabric of the universe that changes everything, that will from that moment on create an alteration in the relationship between the mother and the daughter. A mother at such a time as this *must* wail, for the daughter who passes through that door is, in some respect at least, never coming back. And therein lies the conflated and irrational knowledge that slices like a double-edged rapier through the heart of every mother, to wit, that the daughter who leaves is never coming back, and further that it would be a disaster if she did. A mother is slain either way. It is the way of the world. Daughters leave their mothers. Millie's head feels heavy and her heart wet and soft with all this thinking.

"Are you sure I look okay, Mother?"

"Oh, yes, dear! You look absolutely splendid! Stop frowning! It doesn't become you! You'll be the belle of the ball, I know it!"

"And you stop bawling, Mother! It doesn't become you." She pauses to look at her mother. She is sitting on the bed, shoulders stooped, hands in her lap grasping her hankie. She notices the faint blue veins on the back of her mother's delicate hand; the lines webbing out from her wrist to her fingers, scarcely beneath the surface of the skin, looking like aerial photographs she'd seen in Geography of the Mississippi delta. How odd, she thinks, that she should remember such a thing right now. Frankie approaches and leans over, steadying herself with a light hand on her mother's shoulder and kisses her on her forehead. "I'll be back by midnight," she whispers. Then she clomps to the door as though she's a 5-year-old playing dressup, grasps the brazen knob, pulls it open and teeters through it as Frances Katherine Cooper, woman.

# # #

Coop, attired in a dark blue suit, his favorite Arrow shirt and a bowtie, opens the door gravely like a butler at Balmoral, and invites the threesome to step inside. "Wait here for just a few moments," he says bowing slightly. "Her ladyship will be down momentarily." They enter and Coop closes the door behind them. "In due course," he adds. The boys stand awkwardly with their weight first on one foot, then the other. Their arms seem to hang down to their knees like chimpanzees. As with all teenaged boys, they have no idea what to do with their hands while standing, when idle with nothing to do or to say. Alternately, the hands are clasped in front covering the fig leaf area; or they are hanging loosely at the side; or clasped behind; or folded across the chest; or in the pockets. No single stance lasts more than a few seconds before a different pose is adopted. Naomi has no such problem. She wears white gloves and simply, and quite naturally, places her right hand in the open palm of her left hand and holds them loosely at her waist. Just like that. The suits the boys wear are ill-fitting. Seth Hardison's navy blue suit is too short in the sleeves (it is a hand-me-down from an older brother), the Windsor knot of his blue tie is too big, and the trousers come down to his ankles revealing white socks. His hair, blond, is slickered back with handfuls of Brylcreem and his face is scrubbed raw. Randy Moulton is wearing a brown tweed suit, white shirt with a yellow tie. His red hair is buzzed, brushed and waxed. Only Naomi, dazzling in her lemon chiffon gown that looks like it has been drenched in the sun, is poised and relaxed, chatting with the boys while they wait for Frankie. Her laughter is light, and she tosses her head back slightly when amused, and her teeth shine like they've been irradiated by the Atomic Energy Commission.

Coop breaks the ice. "And who may I ask, will be driving tonight?"

"That would be me, sir." The Hardison boy raises his hand, giving it a little wave, flashes a quick smile which then vanishes and his face returns to its former torpid and vacant aspect.

"Excellent. And you are?"

"Seth Hardison, sir!"

"And are you with Miss Shimel tonight or Miss Cooper?"

"Oh, Miss Cooper, sir!"

"Wonderful!" Coop says fulsomely. "Now, could I see your driver's license, please?"

"Excuse me?"

"Your driver's license. You do have a driver's license, don't you?"

"Oh yes sir, I have it right here." Cushing watches with amusement from a spot deeper in the parlor. He observes that the three teenagers actually seem relieved to be a part of this interrogation as it interrupts the tedium of standing about with nothing to do or to say. Hardison reaches into his rear trouser pocket and retrieves a leather wallet, flips it open, produces his license and gives it to Coop who goes through the motions of examining it carefully.

"Your daddy has about 700 acres out on Powler Road, doesn't he, Mr. Hardison?" asks Coop, handing the license back to the kid.

"Yes, sir, that's right, sir."

"What's he got in there, anyway? Mostly corn, I suppose."

"That's right, corn, but some soybeans, wheat and alfalfa."

"Looks like rain. Your windshield wipers in good working order?"

"Oh, yes sir. Absolutely sir."

"I suppose you've been driving tractor and a pickup since you were big enough to see over the steering wheel, right sonny?" Coop gives the lad a light slap on the back.

"Oh, that's right, sir. Since I was knee-high to a grasshopper I guess." Just then they hear a door open on the floor above them which is followed by approaching footsteps. Frankie floats into view, light and ethereal like a gossamer butterfly, preparing now to descend and alight on her admirers one and all. Naomi squeals with delight and claps her hands. "Oh you look so *bee-u-ti-ful*," she exclaims. An angel, Coop thought; it was so clear. They say that in a plane crash or a car crash your whole life passes by an instant, an atom of time. Well this, Coop thought, is another such moment. Seeing her at the top of the stairs, something explodes in his brain like a Sylvania flashbulb in Rev. Cushing's camera. Everything, instantly, has been stripped away—the quarreling, arguments, adolescent angst, the homework, growing up, visits to the doctors, consultations with teachers, walks in the park—it is all gone, and now here is the essence of who this person-in-the-making really is: an eager, delightful and happy child, whose moral and experiential slate is as clean as Millie's blackboard on a Monday morning, a child whose life lies before her as infinite as the rolling corn fields of Iowa. She is so beautiful, and so happy! He watches as she clasps the banister with one gloved hand, and holds a hand purse in the other and begins her descent, like an angel down Jacob's ladder. With each step she takes there is a rustle of gown and petticoat, like the rustle of wings. She looks marvelous in her gown, and the pearls.

Frankie is pleased. She sees the faces of the people waiting below: Randy Moulton standing behind Naomi, Rev. Cushing off to the side with Vickie, Pops who is positively glowing, and Seth, her escort on this Evening for the Ages. Their eyes are fixed on her; she holds their gaze. She smiles when she sees Tippy at the foot of the stairs, looking at her with a sloppy grin, tail a wagging blur. But she cannot see that on the third riser from the top, a carpet tack in the runner has wormed up out of the wood, rising a quarter of an inch or so, or that the head of the nail is a mere eighth of an inch wide, and she doesn't know that if she steps square on that tack with her heel which measures at least a quarter, perhaps a third of an inch square she might simply jam the tack back into its place in the wood. But as it is, she comes down on the tack off center and the tendons in her young ankle, unaccustomed as they are to reacting quickly in a very new type of emergency, fail to tighten and tense and strengthen her joint in the very moment it is required that they do so, so that instead, the ankle collapses in a horrifying flash causing Frankie's hand with the hand purse to fly upward, her left leg to lose its footing and kick out, sending her purple shoe whizzing through the air like a Lockheed missile, while her right knee with its offending ankle below buckles and pushes forward. She loses her grip on the banister and thus begins her tumble down the stairs, her georgette gown flaring like a parachute.

Coop, Cushing, Randy and Naomi see it all happen and freeze momentarily like they've been turned into stone. There they stand, their mouths agape, powerless to do anything. But not Tippy. When Frankie's shoe sails over the bannister, the dog is off in a flash and snatches it on one bounce. And not Seth. The glissade has no sooner commenced than he bounds two stairs at a time to get to her side whereupon he grasps firmly at a baluster with one hand and with the other catches her on the fly about the waist, thereby breaking her fall. She comes to rest about two-thirds of the way down. Her gown flutters to a respectable position; Seth smoothes it out some. Perhaps the run in her nylons had been visible after all.

Unfrozen, the rest of the onlookers now rush to her aid—assistance which is both unnecessary and unwanted. Frankie does not cry out. She winces in pain. "Dadgumit," she grunts through clenched teeth. "This is so punk." Coop, Cushing, Naomi, Randy and Vic jostle to get near her. Millie, upon hearing the uproar, has by now likewise rushed to her side, descending from the bedroom and is perched on a riser above her daughter.

"Are you alright?" says one.

"Does it hurt?" says another.

"Can you walk?" asks yet another.

"Where's my shoe?" Frankie cries.

"Her shoe!" Millie shouts.

"Tippy's got it!" Vickie yells.

"Make sure the kitchen door's closed. Don't let her get out of the house, Vickie!" Millie shouts. "Do it now."

Vickie succeeds in wrestling her sister's shoe from Tippy. And further, it is determined, most important, that the gown has sustained no injuries in the tumble. Therefore the evening's mission will not need to be aborted. Frankie's ankle, however, has experienced severe trauma, and it is painful to walk on. "If the ankle were broken," Coop advises, "you would not be able to walk on it at all." Frankie, completely mortified that this has happened with everyone watching—it is a nightmare!—now just wants to get the hell out of there. Someone suggests a crutch. Coop offers her great-granddaddy's cane. He is joking. She finds that if she takes Seth's arm—as it might be appropriate to do anyway, given the nature of the evening—she can hop, skip and jump, perhaps even mimic a walk, and thereby make it through the evening. She and Naomi embrace as sisters.

All of this does nothing to stem the waterworks coming from Millie's eyes, all the more reason for Frankie to get out of the house, the sooner the better. They pose quickly for Rev. Cushing who wants two shots, one of just the four kids, and one with Coop, Millie and Victoria in it as well. And then, to Frankie's complete exasperation, Cushing, who didn't use the camera often, has trouble removing the spent bulb, inserting the second flashbulb and twisting it into position. When picture-taking is done, Randy and Naomi exit the house, Seth and the cripple follow. It has started to sprinkle. "Do you want an umbrella, Frankie?" Millie calls out. Frankie ignores her. The Chevrolet is parked in front of the house on the street. Randy and Naomi crawl in the back seat. Coop notices that he opens the door and holds it as Naomi gets in. Seth likewise, out of necessity, given Frankie's infirmity, as much as courtesy. Then both boys circle the automobile and get in themselves. They wave at the clutch they are leaving behind now huddled in the cool evening air on the porch: Coop, with Victoria in front of him, his hands on her shoulders; and Millie, clad in a housedress and an apron upon which are printed the words, "Lord, Bless This Mess" and which has a pocket for her moist hankies, and Rev.

Cushing behind her, his hands likewise resting lightly on Millie's shoulders—providing comfort in her time of need. Millie raises her hand with the hankie and gives it a wave.

Seth inserts the key into the ignition. He looks over at Frankie who is sitting by the window, her gown filling the passenger side almost obscuring her vision. He motions with his head. Frankie is puzzled. "Slide over," he says. "You're my date. For tonight, you're my girlfriend, and dates and girlfriends sit here, not there."

"Oh, sorry," she says meekly, surprised that Hardison can make a cogent argument and at the same time embarrassed that she is so obviously ill-acquainted with dating etiquette. She shoots a glance of the two in the back seat. Good Lord! Naomi is snuggled up to Randy and, if she gets any closer to him, he'll have to make a proposal of marriage right then and there.

# # #

"Isn't this grand!" exclaims Naomi as they walk—with the exception of Frankie who limps—into the gymnasium of Bathington Senior High School. Tonight, however, it is no gymnasium. Tonight it is the darkened and softly lit Kasbah of the Sultanate of Arabia. The theme of the Spring Formal this year is "Arabian Nights," a theme that was chosen after first considering Hawaiian Breezes, Arctic Snow, Caribbean Carousel, Urban Utopia and Mediterranean Melody.

They are late but not excessively so. The underclassmen have decorated the gym with the help of the boys in shop class, turning it from an arena of sporting activities to a carpeted and pillowed, softly lit and colonnaded cantina of exotic foreign delights. The art department has painted murals on the west wall on which is a desert scene with a caravan of camels traversing it laden with spices, scented oils, cashmere, nuts and jewels. The effect is that as Frankie sat on the east side under Bedouin canvases or danced under a tent-like canopy, she could look as though from the "inside" of the Kasbah out upon the desert, where could be seen a far flung oasis ringed with date palm trees.

There is plenty of room for dancing, of course, and even now, the Kasbah is a miasma of whirling young dervishes bedecked and begowned in flowing silks, and scarves, cotton and chiffon, taffeta and georgette. Earrings sparkle as the twirling globes of light above catch the cut and the jangle; the lithesome bodies they adorned gyrate to the tunes of Bobby Hightower and the Belltones, a small band that has been hired all the way from Dubuque. "Maybe we could find a place to sit down for a moment," Frankie says groaning lightly. She is leaning on Seth, who for his part does not mind tending to her needs, holding her in his arms, steadying her as she walks up the steps, guiding her by the hand, helping her to find her seat. "Sure, Frankie," he says brightly. "Let's go over here—" and he points to a row of folding chairs along a wall. "Or would you rather recline on this carpet and lean up against some pillows?" Frankie wants the dark brown folding chair on the back of which was stenciled the letters Property of BHS. "Can I get you something to drink?" Frankie nods. "Don't you go anywhere now, okay?" Seth shakes his finger at her in jest and laughs. Frankie smiles wanly. She appreciates his attention and realizes he is being an awfully good sport about everything. She needs to change her attitude. If she is going to be glum and moody and dumpy all evening, she might as well go home. But if not, then, why, she should grin and bear it and let it rip as best she can. She owes it to herself and she owes it to Seth. So she waits and looks out over the sea of undulating classmates. She registers surprise or pleasure or simple acknowledgement as she sees various friends and the dates they are with. The "cheerleaders" are dancing with the jocks. Nomes and Randy are doing the jitterbug now. She's so funny. She sees Rev. Cushing standing in a far corner on the other side of the dance floor speaking with some of the high school faculty chaperones. What's with him and Mother? she thinks. Then—

"Oh hi, Frankie! Seth told me you'd sprained your ankle. That's so bad, are you okay?"

"Hey Frankie! I'm so glad you're here and with SETH! [squealing]. He's so good-looking and tall ... and good-looking!"

"Oh Frankie, you poor, poor dear [this is Mrs. Severs, the Geometry teacher speaking], and in such pain! There, there ... I can only imagine how cast down you must be in your spirit. But I'm sure you will have a good time anyway!"

In turn, friends and teachers stop by to say hello. "Where's Seth," she wonders. "What can possibly be keeping him?" Seth is not derelict in his duties, but is similarly detained by friends and well-wishers as he journeys from Frankie to the punch table, and while at the table, and en route back to his date in the brown folding chair.

"Hi baby doll, what's going on?" Frankie looks up.

"Oh, Rondo, it's you." She is referring to Ronnie Harmon. "So good not to see you. Good-bye."

"Hey, doll, is that any way to talk to a friend? Come on!" Rondo steps back, spreading his arms, his palms open toward Frankie, in an Italian-esque gesture of disbelief. He is about six foot, slender in build, angular face, and dark hair that has been greased and slicked into a ducktail. Hanging over his forehead and dipping past his right eyebrow is yet another ducktail, or duck-curl. He's wearing a dark narrow suit, white shirt, and a thin black tie secured with a tie clasp. Frankie sees the bulge in his left breast pocket. He has a pack of cigarettes there for sure. He is masticating a wad of gum with more enthusiasm than a Hereford chewing cud on a dairy farm. His right leg is set slightly ahead of the left, and it is moving, tapping, as though keeping a beat, but it was not the music of Bobby Hightower he is hearing.

"Amscray, Ron-dumb," Frankie says, looking away. Just then Seth appears with two tumblers of tropical punch.

"Oh hi, Ron," he says nervously. He gives a glass to Frankie, and then turns to face Rondo as though to get his permission to take a seat himself.

"Is this squirrel your date, tonight, doll?"

"Yes, this squirrel is her date, Rondo, that's right," Seth says tersely. "Now, please move on."

"Seth, just sit down and don't talk to him," Frankie says with a whine in her voice.

"Just having a friendly conversation is all," Rondo says. "Catch you later, gator." He cocks his finger at her and fires. Then he swaggers away.

"If you do, I'll need a tetanus shot," Frankie calls after him.

They sip on their punch. "Can we go outside for some fresh air?" Frankie asks presently.

"It's raining cats and dogs, Frankie," Seth says apologetically.

"Oh." They sit in silence. Then at Frankie's suggestion they take to the dance floor. The Belltones are doing "My Baby's Going to Miss Me Tonight." Frankie says, "You dance, and I will pretend to dance, okay?" Seth nods. It is hard to hear above the music. And so they dance. Frankie finds that if she hops and moves on her good foot, with just quick, slight pressure on the bad one, she can move pretty well, and in fact, the more she dances, the more she feels as though she is creating an entirely new dancing style. Doing the "Frankie," they'll call it someday, a dance that requires a lot of hopping and dipping to the side, circular motions, revolutionary in its own way. Seth plays along and even tries to mimic what Frankie is doing. And when Naomi and Randy swing close, they, too, began to mimic "the Frankie," and before long, as her friends brush by her, as the story of her mishap spreads, and seeing her courage on the dance floor, they too ape Frankie's movements. For a while, it appears that all the dancers on the floor are cripples.

Chapter XVIII

THE PRECIPITATION WHICH HAD BEEN FALLING according
to Seth's account like cats and dogs is now nothing but a low mist interrupted by an occasional sputter of hard rain. But the northern Iowa night
is still shuttered by clouds and County Road 119 is dark. The moon is
hidden and a night sky that usually is rich with stars is a formless slate of
black. Shuffling up a gravel road which rises and falls gently with the rolling fields of corn is Naomi Shimel and clutching her side her best chum,
Frankie Cooper. The road stretches before them only vaguely defined
and disappears into the darkness perhaps a couple hundred yards down.
The budding cottonwoods that line the road in spots are dark skeletal
specters stretching bony limbs above the lane. Bushes and hedges grow
from the ditch—shadowy barriers behind which lurks who knows what.
But the girls are not frightened; they are furious.

"Boy oh boy, if they think they can get away with this," Naomi
seethes, running a cold hand across her brow to mop away the moisture.
Her hair is wet and stringy and her undergarments are soaked and cling to
her body, sometimes chaffing the skin.

"Oh, they'll get away with it alright," Frankie counters. "Nothing will
happen, you wait and see." Their progress is slow as the gravel makes it
difficult for Frankie to secure a good footing without pain. Her steps are
tentative since she's barefoot. Both are carrying their shoes, Naomi in her
right hand and Frankie in her left. They try to stay to ruts in the road
where the gravel has been splayed away, leaving dirt which is now mud,
sometimes so soft they can feel it squish up between their toes. Frankie's
left arm is draped about Naomi's left shoulder and Naomi has her right
arm about Frankie's waist. They look like they're auditioning for a three-
legged race at the county fair.

"Wrong, sister!" Naomi cries. "They will *not* get away with this! Not by a long chalk! Something will happen. I'll see to that for darn sure."

"My mother is going to freak."

"Oh my gosh, she'll go nuts. She probably already is. *My* mother on the other hand will sit in silence and wring her hands … like she's sitting shiva or something."

"What time is it anyway?"

"Probably midnight, which means we're officially missing."

"What do you think they're doing?" Frankie asks.

"Well your mother is probably calling my parents, or maybe my parents have already called her. Then they've probably called the Hardisons and Moultons, and so it's been established that no one knows where we are." They pause for a moment to take a breather. Their gowns are soaked and hanging from their limbs like fresh laundry on a clothes line. Their hair is wet and straight. They are shivering and cling to each other.

Frankie says, "Mom will probably call Rev. Cushing, or maybe the marshal."

"She won't call the marshal, not yet, because the marshal wouldn't do anything anyway. Just some kids who are late home from the prom he'll say." They start walking again.

"Where are we going?"

"Maybe a car will come by and we can get some help," Naomi suggests.

"We've been walking for a half hour at least. If I thought a car would come by I'd just stop walking and wait."

"Maybe we should. Maybe we should just hole up under a tree until the light of day, and get help then."

"No, we have to try. Mom will be going nuts."

"Do you have any idea where we are?"

"North of town I think."

"Do you see that light?" Naomi asks.

"What light?"

"That light." They peer forward into the night. A yellow, blurry dot, a pinhead of light in the blackness, flickers ahead and off to the right.

"Maybe it's a farmhouse," Frankie says hopefully. "Let's go see."

"Or maybe it's the hideout of an ax-murderer and we're jumping from the frying pan into the fire," Naomi says, shuddering suddenly as though she really believes what she is saying.

"Stop it!

They press on down the road, the halt and the lame, for Naomi, too, is feeling the cuts and lacerations on the heels and toes of both her feet, despite their attempt to stay in the mud. "Maybe you should go on ahead," Frankie says wearily, "and get to the farmhouse and bring help back for me … might be faster."

Naomi considers this for a moment and then says, "No, we don't know who or what's at this house. Going alone I put myself at risk and you too. It's always best in an emergency to stick together."

So they walk—stuck together—side by side until presently they reach a lane leading to a rangy house shrouded by trees. A mailbox sits atop a pillar of welded and rigid chains, but bears no name or address. A light shines in a window. They move toward it. The house is two stories and fronted by a wraparound veranda, but inasmuch as the light is coming from the kitchen, they approach the house via the side porch, and limp up the stairs. They hear voices inside. Naomi raps strongly on the windowpane of the door. The voices cease. They hear footsteps. A light goes on in what appears to be the entryway or a back pantry. The door opens slightly at first, and then completely.

A young man stands before them, peering at them as though he is having trouble seeing who is there. He's in slippers, striped pajama bottoms and an oversized flannel shirt. "Hey, what's going on?" he asks, grouching at them. "What are you doing out here this time of night?— What time is it anyway?"

Frankie's mouth drops open, but Naomi begins speaking immediately—and loudly. "It's about two in the morning. It's been raining cats and dogs, but my friend here and I are from the Salvation Army to collect umbrellas for the needy! What do you think we're doing out here, you TWIT! Could we please come inside?"

"Naomi! Hush!" Frankie admonishes. "Mr. Rossi, Mr. Rossi, it's me, Frankie Cooper. You took my photo for the church directory, remember? I am sure I am totally unrecognizable what with this rain and all and this disaster, but we need to use the phone and maybe just rest a bit."

A girl with black hair appears behind Carlo. "Get them inside, Carlo, and close the damn door." Then turning back to the kitchen, "Wason, get those photos rounded up and off the table, we got company." The girls hear a sudden clattering and a furious shuffling of papers and chairs scrapping the floor as though they're being moved around. They step into the entry way. The girl shoulders her way past Carlo to help them. She's wearing slippers and what Frankie believes to be an immodest, if not colorful, silk chemise decorated with lotus blossoms and plum trees. "Hi girls, I'm Alice Wang, the new church typist. I remember you Frankie. Come in, come in. What on earth happened?"

They are shown into the kitchen which has a wood plank floor, a wood-burning stove as well as a small electric hot plate set up on the counter which runs along the wall. A window is above a porcelain sink which is piled high with dirty dishes.

They sit down around the table. "Can I get you some tea, girls?" Alice asks, smiling pleasantly. "And you need to get out of those clothes. Have some tea first, and then I will take you upstairs to get you into some warm duds."

"I need to call my mother," Frankie says. "I know she's worried sick."

Alice glances at the others and then back at the girls. "The phones are out, I'm afraid, with the storm. But I'll tell you what, we'll get you warmed up a little, some warm clothes and then I'll drive you into town and return you to your parents. That sound okay?"

"Oh, that would be splendid, Miss Wang!" Frankie says effusively. "Thank you ever so much."

"Alice, I could take them in," Carlo offers. "You shouldn't be out in the middle of the night."

Alice looks at him sharply. "Surely you don't mean that I can't take care of myself?"

"No, no, just …"

"I think it would be better if the girls arrived at their homes in the middle of the night escorted by me than by a young man their parents don't really know, don't you agree?"

"Well—"

"Do you have a tea preference?" Alice asks cheerily. The girls reply that they do not, so Alice gets a pot of water going on the hot plate, and then sits down at the table.

"What in heaven's name is going on?" The voice comes from the hallway, and soon a woman appears in an elegant house robe. Her hair is brushed—whatever emergency she believed was in progress in the kitchen could wait while her appearance was revised in the boudoir so as to be presentable.

"Frankie, Naomi, this is Mrs. Penelope Cuttingham, our den mother, as we like to call her," Alice says smiling. "Come on in, Penny, and pull up a chair. We're about to hear a story."

Cuttingham clucks a bit, and draws herself into the room in a sweeping sort of way and floats into an available chair. "Well, I am all ears," she says, examining the two waifs who have appeared out of nowhere. Turning to Wason, she says, "I assume you were able to get all of your work tucked away before our guests arrived—leaving work lying around can be so distracting."

"Oh, yes, ma'am," Wason averred. "All tucked away."

"Wonderful. I do so like a tidy kitchen," she says, noting the dirty dishes in the sink. Just then the whistle on the kettle begins to sing and Wason jumps up to take it off the hot plate, and moments later Naomi and Frankie are sipping hot Earl Grey which immediately revives their spirits.

"Well go on, Frankie—or Naomi," Alice urges. "Tell us what happened."

Frankie draws another sip of tea and then, with a look at Naomi who nods encouragement, begins: "It was about 11 o'clock. We were at the Spring Formal, at the high school. I was tired and my ankle was throbbing—"

"What happened to your ankle?" Carlo asks.

"Let her tell the story, Carlo!" Alice hisses. Carlo glares at Alice and gestures with his open palms as though to say "What?"

"No, that's a fair question. I'm pretty clumsy and fell down a flight of stairs just before the Formal—well, half a flight of stairs. My prom date, Seth Hardison, caught me half way down. But my ankle was twisted. Anyway, I went to the Formal and danced like a spastic, but had a good time, but at eleven o'clock I felt it was time to go. It was pouring outside, so Seth and Randy said they'd bring the car around the front entrance and for us to watch and make a dash for it. So we saw the car, and then we ran or hopped as fast as we could and reached the car. Naomi flew in the back and I got in front, slammed the door and we took off. When I turned to say something to Seth, it wasn't Seth driving, but Rondo! I screamed and at the same time Naomi started yelling. She was in the back with a yuck named Lester. She punching him like blazes till he got her hands and sort of subdued her—"

"The snake—"

"Honestly, I think she broke his nose, because he had blood on his face. I still didn't understand what was going on. I think Nomes understood right away. Rondo and Lester wanted to make out with us. They peeled out of town, there was no chance of opening the car door and running although I thought about it. I asked about Seth and Randy but Rondo just laughed. I thought we might be headed for Hadley pond where I know—not from personal experience—that a lot of couples go to make out and stuff. But we kept driving it seemed like forever. Finally, we pulled off the road, sort of a wide spot, backed up and Rondo turned off the lights, but kept the motor running and the heater on. We just sat there."

"Did he try anything?" Carlo asks.

"At first it was just a lot of talk and drinking. They had some beers. I'm sure they'd had a few before we even took off from the school. I'm not sure what was going on in the back seat. Rondo was talking about me giving him a fair shake, and why can't I be nice, and be like other girls, and I was too stuck up, and he slid over to be closer to me and then he had his hands all over me in places where they weren't supposed to be, and that's when I started pummeling him with my fists. Naomi landed a jab right on Lester's mouth, opened a cut on his lip I guess, cause there was more blood on his face, and then there was more tussling and that distracted Rondo and that's when we thought it would be a good idea to try to get out of the car—which we did. Up to that point I thought it was futile to try to escape because with my ankle I could not possibly get away from them. But when it got nasty, we thought we had to get out of the car anyway so as to at least make it more difficult for them. I was sure they'd come after us, but it was raining, and I think they thought it was a lost cause and that they might be in enough trouble as it is, because Rondo put the car in gear, pulled out and slowed down as he drove by us. He rolled down the window and shouted dirty things at us and laughed and then they sped away and honked the horn a couple of times, and there we were. They just left us there, the jerks! Didn't have any idea where we were, so we started walking until we saw the light in your kitchen window. I don't know what you were working on so late, but I am sure glad you were. Thank you so much for the tea."

"Rondo and Lester, eh?" Alice says, musing. "I wonder what they're going to do with the car?"

"And what about Seth and Randy? Oh, this is such a mess! And mom! We need to get home as soon as possible."

"Right you are," says Alice, resolutely. "Drink up, and let's get you upstairs into some clean dry clothes and then we're off."

Chapter XIX

MILLIE IS SITTING IN A COLONIAL rocker in the parlor with stitching in her lap, but she's not stitching, she's itching—itching to know where Frankie is and why that girl's not home. The room is dim, but for the lamp on the stand by her rocker, giving a somber yellow hue. A light from the far kitchen provides some ambient illumination. Tippy is curled up on the hooked rug in front of the sink. She glances toward the grandfather clock standing in a shadowy corner across the room, the clock that fifteen minutes ago had announced the midnight hour. The only sounds in the house are the ticking of the clock, Tippy's wheezing in the kitchen, and Millie's sniffling in the parlor. *What are those kids up to?* That Frankie or Naomi could be engaging in any activity that ran contrary to their upbringing was not possible, emotions and the "damn dam" as Frankie put it, notwithstanding. Frankie has her morals, and by "her morals" Millie means not only Frankie's morals, but *her* morals and the code of morality with which she'd been brought up both in the home and the church. That they are not home, that they are late, cannot be because Frankie is doing anything she shouldn't be doing.

But she is less sure about the young men with whom Frankie and Naomi are spending the evening. She knows very little about them, really. What does she know? They seem to come from good homes. Their parents aren't Presbyterians, but she can't hold that against them, not in this matter anyway. And she heard that Mr. Hardison is a Lodge member and spends a lot of time playing cards. She thinks they're Catholic—and that would be an *impossible* divide were marriage being considered, for there are three groups of people in the world Millie can scarcely abide and they are Catholics, Democrats and Southerners—but this is the Spring Formal, a silly little dance. But still … She picks up her stitching, a little cross-stitching piece she's making, a set of kitchen towels with a flower and robin in the corner, something she'll give as a Christmas present to someone … she hasn't decided yet. In a far corner of her mind, she thinks the Reverend might appreciate them, but she isn't sure.

The clock chimes the half hour, and now Millie's emotional state is moving from anxious fretfulness to full blown anxiety. She becomes aware that her breath is short, she feels an empty pain in her chest, and a tightening in her abdomen. She removes her eyeglasses, puts her embroidery on the stand beside the rocker and pushing herself up, stands erect, and smoothes the front of her house dress. She glances out the window and notices that water is still running down the pane. She hears a faint whirring of the wind. The porch light is on. She walks to the kitchen to get a glass of water. Perhaps in this dark and foul weather the car's run off the road, or maybe Frankie's ankle has completely incapacitated her in some way. Truth is she cannot think of any plausible reason why her daughter has not walked in the door. The formal was chaperoned. It was held in town at the school gymnasium. The young men they're with are from respectable families. Their car is a new car and mechanically sound. Seth demonstrated that he would take care of Frankie and be gentle with her in her hobbling condition. So why aren't they home? She stands at the kitchen counter leaning on it with one hand, and in the other hand holds the glass of water to her mouth, but she's not drinking, she's thinking, trying to grasp the situation from every angle. Yet her thoughts are not coming together. They're bouncing around in her brain like ping pong balls ricocheting in a playroom. It's half past midnight. Frankie should be home. She feels forlorn and forsaken. Clearly something—she doesn't know what—has not gone according to plan. So why hasn't she called? Frankie is always so thoughtful that way. Maybe Naomi has cajoled her into doing something or going somewhere against Frankie's better judgment—except Frankie is not one to be persuaded to do anything that's against her better judgment. Oh, dear! What has gone wrong? What can I do? What *should* I do? Perhaps I should call the Shimels. Or the Hardisons. Or Coop? No, I can't involve him at this hour and besides what could he do? Maybe I should call Marshal Cutler, but he couldn't do anything either. It's the Formal. Kids get home late. That's it! I am no doubt not the only parent tonight wondering where their kids are!

What distresses her more is the realization that she's powerless to do anything. And what can one do when power has been stripped away but sit and wait? To be powerless requires patience, an infinite supply of patience—the ability to trust that those who do have the power to intervene, to create change, to save the day will somehow do so. In some people, powerlessness evokes rage. In others, resignation. It is toward this latter mood that Millie gravitates. Whatever situation Frankie is in, she'll have to handle it herself for the time being. Her mother is not able to leap to the rescue. Well, I could get in the car and drive over to the school … but what if Frankie comes home in the meantime? And I can't leave Victoria alone in the house. I could leave a note. No, I can't leave. Well, if they're not home by one o'clock I am calling *somebody*.

She phones the Shimels and learns that Naomi has not returned home. Mr. Shimel is calm, but there's an edge in his voice. Millie asks him to call the Hardisons and to ring her back, and says that in the meantime she's calling Coop and the Reverend. She replaces the receiver in the cradle and realizes that her hands are shaking. She picks it up again: "Holly, this is Millie Cooper. Can you get Coop for me? Thanks." The phone rings six times before he picks up.

"Coop, the girls are not home yet and it's one in the morning! I'm frantic." There's silence on the other end. "Coop!?"

"I'm here, still waking up. The girls are not home?" His voice is low and gravelly.

"No! They should have been back over an hour ago!"

"Well, they're big girls, Millie, I'm sure they'll arrive shortly."

"That's what I've been saying to myself for an hour, Coop, but they're not here! I'm going to call Cushing and ask him to come over and to pick you up on the way. Will you come over? I need some help to sort this out, to see what we can do! I'm just afraid something dreadful has happened!"

"Of course, tell him I'll be waiting down front. And Millie—"

"Yes?"

"Nothing dreadful has happened. Hang tight."

She dials Cushing and apologetically entreats him to make a nocturnal pastoral call and to pick Coop up on his way. He readily agrees. She calls Coop back to confirm. Twenty-five minutes later both gentlemen are in her parlor seated on either side of her on the divan. The Reverend had jumped into some dark green corduroy slacks, pulled on a white T-shirt and over that a lightweight, loose-fitting V-necked sweater. Coop had also dressed quickly, jumping into the previous days' clothes like a fireman on the way to an inferno—and that is precisely what he finds at 149

Maple Street—a conflagration of hysteria: Millie is a bundle of combustible emotions, crying inconsolably, heaving great sobs into her hankie, her slight body shaking with each convulsion. Shimel has called to say that the Hardisons report that Seth has not returned from the Formal, and that they have not heard from him.

The Reverend, feeling a bit out of his milieu, speaks at last: "Millie, I think that the marshal needs to be informed about this. It's two-fifteen in the morning. He may not be able to do anything quite yet, or perhaps he can send out a car to patrol some of the county roads. And I think I should get in the car and swing by the high school just for another look. It would be a place to start. What do you think?"

Millie sniffs and looks up at him wearily. "You shouldn't go out in this rain … I don't know. Yes, we should probably call Cutler. Oh where are those kids!"—She returns to her hankie. Cushing catches Coop's attention and gives him a pained expression of helplessness. This woman cannot be comforted. But both men know that when a *child* is involved, there is no comfort for a mother. There are no words, no wisdom, no explanation that can sop up the pain, sorrow, fear and sense of dread. By now, Millie feels completely hollow, emotionally eviscerated, and numb. She's lost the ability to reason and process what's going on around her. This the Reverend knows and understands. She made the right decision to call him and her father-in-law. Cushing leans toward Millie and puts his arm around her and squeezes, pulling her slightly toward him, and then releases her and stands. "Do you want anything from the kitchen, dear?"

Millie looks up, her eyes flushed and questioning. Cushing reddens and coughs, covering his mouth quickly with his hand and then sputters: "Um—Mrs. Cooper, Millie, while I'm up, can I get you anything?"

"There's a glass of water on the counter, you could bring that, thank you."

At that moment, however, they hear a car door slam, and then another door. Millie and Coop leap off the sofa and stampede for the parlor door with Cushing behind them. Millie flings it open in time to catch Frankie limping up the walk to the porch, leaning on Miss Alice Wang, the church typist, of all people!

"Frankie! Frankie!"

"Mom!" Millie is down the porch steps before the girls are halfway to the house and has Frankie in her arms. "Oh, Frankie my dear, are you okay?" she cries, running her hand across her daughter's brow and pushing aside her hair to see her better. "Where have you been? Oh, you can tell me later! Let's get you inside! Oh, I am so glad you're home safe and sound!" To these words Cushing and Coop are likewise adding expressions of happiness and joy and slowly the party moves up the porch stairs and into the parlor where Frankie and her mother head for the couch. Tippy has awakened and is yapping greetings. "Hush Tippy!" Millie cries, "You'll wake Victoria!" The Reverend offers Frankie some tea or water, but she doesn't want any, having had some already with Alice.

"I'm so tired, Mom," Frankie says, leaning on her mother's shoulder. "And so glad to be home." And then, all is explained, an explanation that is met with indignant interjections ("Why those hooligans!" or "I've got a mind to …" or "Whatever were they thinking that they could …?" or "This is what happens when you don't have a good Christian upbringing" or "There's going to be hell to pay …") and woeful cries of dismay and alarm. When the story is recounted, questions answered, and when they are all assured that Naomi is safe in her own home, Millie stands and approaches Alice who is still standing by the door. "Oh, my dear, how can I thank you or repay you for providing refuge and help for my Frankie? Thank you so much! I will never forget this!"

Alice, embarrassed, and deflecting the sentiment, says, "It was nothing but what anyone would do, Mrs. Cooper."

Coop and Cushing had approached Alice as well. "Nonsense," says Cushing. "You've been an angel. Are you going to be safe getting back to your house?"

"Oh, yes, no problem."

Cushing is thoughtful. "You know, we still don't know what's become of Seth and Randy. We should still probably call the marshal if the Hardisons or Moultons have not already done so."

"I think I might have a lead on the boys. Give me an hour. Would you like me to call you at, say 3:30 a.m., Reverend?"

"Oh, my dear," says Millie, alarmed. "It's the middle of the night. It's far too late for you to be out and about, alone, a woman, in the night like this. You need to drive back to your house, Miss Wang."

"No, I'll be fine. Reverend, where can I reach you?"

"Reverend, I couldn't ask you to stay any longer—"

"Oh, Mrs. Cooper, I doubt that you can sleep right now, and I can be useful getting a pot of tea going, and we can visit for another hour. I know you are worried about those boys, as you have been about your own daughter. Let's see what Miss Wang comes up with. I've learned that

Miss Wang is quite resourceful. So, Miss Wang, you call me right here, one way or another at 3:30 a.m. If you are not at home by that time, there's a new telephone cabin on Main street—as you probably know."

"Alright, then," says Alice, nodding slightly, "I'll be in touch." She turns to leave, when Coop says, "And if you don't mind, Miss Wang, perhaps you could drop me off at Hemming's place. I'm going to call it a night. Plenty of excitement for me!"

Both Millie and the Reverend seem to cough or speak at once. "Oh, Coop, you're leaving? Now?— " Millie catches his eye and nods slightly toward the Reverend. Frankie looks up, confused. Coop understands, but he says, "You two will be just fine." Turning to his granddaughter, he adds, "Frankie, I'm designating you the chaperone. Make sure they be- have." The Reverend and Millie redden and both have the same coughing sensation.

Frankie says, hobbling up from the sofa, "I'm not chaperoning any- thing or anybody, I'm going to bed. I'm pooped." She wobbles over to the stairs, and turns to face her mother who's watching her, the Reverend behind her, likewise staring: "Mom?" Frankie motions for her mother to come closer.

"Yes, dear?"

Frankie says, *sotto voce*: "Just remember the damn dam thing we were talking about, okay?"

"Frances Katherine!" But Frankie is already hopping up the stairs. There is a smile on her face.

# # #

After dropping Coop off at Hemming's, Alice turns her Chevy onto Main Street. The heater isn't working in the car, but her wool sweater keeps the chill off, and the way her blood's boiling, her body temperature does not concern her. She hikes her skirt up a bit to operate the gas pedal and clutch better. Her purse lies on the seat beside her and with the fingers of her left hand gripping the thin white, plastic steering wheel that's ribbed like a pie crust, she uses her other hand to fumble around in her bag. She extracts a pack of Chesterfields ("That's right, Mr. and Mrs. America! Nine out of ten doctors recommend Chesterfields!") and knocks the box against the steering wheel and nudges a cigarette into view. Holding the box to her mouth, she gums the cigarette free, throws the box back in her bag and pushes the lighter in the dashboard. Seconds later she lights up, and then slowly exhales a long stream of smoke. She takes another drag. The girls had given her a description of the Hardison car during their recital of events at the farmhouse. And on their way through town, she thought she'd spotted the '51 Chevy parked in front of Bud's. She decides to investigate. The car is still there, so she slides the car into a parking slot beside it and turns off the motor. *I wish I wasn't wearing this damn skirt.*

She gets out of the car and approaches the tavern. Bud's has two windows facing the street. In one is a bright neon sign that says PABST Blue Ribbon, and in the other, Schlitz. The door is solid but for a diamond-shaped window about eye level. Alice peers through it; only a handful of drinkers left. She opens the door and walks in. A few heads look up. A couple is seated at a small table nearby. He's probably divorced, and she's an old maid girlfriend. He just has that divorced look about him— uncared for appearance, hollow expression, laconic demeanor, and wary eyes. A couple of older guys are at the bar. They glance at her briefly and then turn back to their beers. In the back of the bar, two young fellows are playing pool. A jukebox is on the north wall, and she hears Danny Ferris singing, "It took you a long time to leave me." Behind the bar, there's a large mirror and rows of liquor bottles on either side. On the wall is an illuminated sign that shows an upright happy bear against the background of a forest with a river running through it and snow-capped mountains and blue sky in the distance. The bear is holding a can of beer: "Hamm's, the beer from sky-blue waters." On the other side of the mirror is a clock. It reads 2:40.

She takes a seat on a bar stool and motions to the bartender, an older man in his fifties. He approaches and she says, "How late you open anyway?"

"Well, we're supposed to close at 2 a.m. but if we got customers, we stay open a while longer."

"I'm from out-of-state and where we come from there's closing time and an age limit for drinking. Little Rondo and Lester back there certainly aren't legal, are they?"

The bartender steps back in surprise and peers cautiously at Alice and says, "Say, you aren't the law, are you?" Alice smiles. The bartender has just confirmed the identity of the boys in the back.

"Nah, nothing like that," she replies, laughing quickly. She slides a twenty dollar bill across the counter. "Those boys back there?"

"Yeah, what about them?"

"They need to be taught a lesson about manners. I'm going to be having a conversation with them. Do they have a tab running?"

"Yeah."

"Will this cover it?"

"Let me check." The bartender turns around to face the Hamms bear from sky blue waters where on the counter are his tab sheets. While he's doing this, one of the two men at the bar, this one to her right, drops off his perch and ambles unsteadily toward her, a distance of five or six stools. He climbs up on a stool leaving one stool between them. He's smiling at Alice, but then turns to his drink. "Hey, whersh my drink?" He sees it at the end of the bar whereupon, he gets off his recently acquired perch and says to Alice, "My memory's not what it used to be." He wanders back to get it.

The bartender turns back with an answer to Alice's query. "Yes, that will cover it and then some."

"Fine," Alice says. "So I'm going back there to have this little conversation and there could be a little disturbance. It won't be much, but I'd appreciate it if you just stayed away and let the situation be resolved. Here's another twenty in case a cue stick gets broken or something."

"Lady, I don't want there to be any trouble—"

"There won't be, well maybe a little. Trust me, it will be fine," she says in her most reassuring voice. "You stay there, now okay? You got a ring side seat, and I am much obliged. Remember, I will positively not need your help, in spite of what you see, unless I shout 'Help!' In that case you can help. But otherwise, stay put, okay?"

Obliged? They may talk that way in Kansas or Wyoming, but does anyone around here say obliged? But the bartender says, "Yes, ma'am. Stay here unless you say 'help'."

At that moment, the lush who'd forgotten his drink reappears. Alice is off her stool, and he has not yet ascended his new position. He reaches out to Alice and touches her on her shoulder. She turns slowly to look at him. His face is round and puffy, and his nose, red-veined and knobby. His eyes seem to be popping out of their sockets. Thin white hair lies askew on his head and flows over his brow and to the tops of his eyes which are blue. His eyebrows are bushy and still have color. His mouth is open, and he has a look of eagerness about him.

"Lady," he says, standing erect with effort, and with one hand placed on his breast as though he were about sing the national anthem, "I consider myself something of a poet, and wonder if you'd do me the honor, ma'am, of allowing me here to recite for your edification a filthy, dirty, most foul little limerick—"

"You must be Jules," Alice says, amused.

"Jules!" the bartender exclaims, "Sit down and don't bother the lady."

"Jules, I'd be happy to be entertained. Hit me, baby!"

Jules smiles and looks at the bartender with a "See there" sort of glance, and turns back to Alice. Taking a deep breath, he begins. "Thank you, Miss Chinese mamasan! So here's your po-em:

There once was a lass from Nantucket
Who preferred to piss in a bucket.
But when she waggled her ass
O'er a wee bit of grass,
Bucket or not, she'd piss and say "fuck it!"

At the conclusion of this recitation, Jules waits expectantly. "Why, thank you, Mr. Joyce, that was quite remarkable ... quite disgusting, but remarkable!" Alice says, bemused.

"Why, thank you, ma'am! Yous are too kind."

Turning to the barkeep, she says, "Get this man another drink, and put it on my tab!" To Jules, she says, "Now you sit down and stay there, okay?"

"Yes, ma'am, and thank you, ma'am. A fine lassie you are now—small little knockers, but a fine-looking ass—lass, you."

Alice looks at the bartender who shrugs. Alice walks away and toward the pool table. One fellow is leaning over to take a shot, waggling the cue stick between fingers poised on the felt, a sure sign a shot is imminent. The game is evidently a new one for about a dozen balls are still scattered about the green surface of the table. A rectangular lamp hangs low over the table. On the wall is a rack of cue sticks. A couple of resin blocks litter a small table where there's also a ball rack.

"Hey boys, I need to talk to you." she says, taking a position opposite the shot-taker and dropping low so that her face is not obscured by the pool lamp. Her black hair hangs forward as she leans slightly over the playing surface, her hands on the table rim, her butt out, and legs slightly apart. The other lad is to her right. He's holding a cue stick in one hand and a cigarette in the other. The player glances up and sees Alice and then slowly relaxes his grip on the cue stick, removes it from the table and stands upright, cue stick in hand with the butt end on the floor.

"Who are you?" he snarls.

"Who's asking?" she says evenly, straightening up and walking into view. She locks her eyes on his.

"Rondo."

"And who's this little lapdog?" She does not take her eyes off Rondo, emphasizing the lapdog's insignificance.

"Hey!" and the lapdog moves toward her, scowling.

Alice holds out her arm straight, hand up, toward him as a signal for him to stop his advance. She says to Rondo. "Tell me where's Seth and Randy, and I'll walk out of here. Or, of course, you can do this the hard way."

"What? What you talkin' 'bout, girl? I don't know *nuthin'* about Seth and Randy. Now, scram bitch, I got a game to play here." Rondo resumes his position to take a shot.

Alice removes a cue stick from the rack and waves it over the table and then drops it to the flat surface and rakes all the balls to one end where they clatter and knock about. Rondo reacts angrily and races around the table to accost her. "What the hell do you think you're doing?"

"I asked a simple question. I want an answer. But if you're a poor listener or a slow learner, I can repeat the question. Would you like me to repeat the question, dick wad?" These words are spoken sweetly and with the utmost sincerity.

Rondo grabs Alice by her shoulders and pushes her violently to the wall near the cue rack. Lester has now come closer to her right. His hands are balled into fists. His feet apart. Rondo has Alice's shoulders pinned to the wall. His face comes close to hers. She can smell the Brylcreem in his greasy hair. He's dressed in dark slacks, and a white shirt. No tie. His shirt is open from the neck four buttons. She sees he has no chest hair. She glances at Lester. He hasn't moved. He's snarling and talking at her in sentences that include a number of dirty words.

Rondo addresses her: "See around here *I* ask the questions. I don't *answer* questions, and I don't answer no *stupid* questions from a pukey Jap twat like you, you clear on that, sweetheart?"

Alice looks directly into Rondo's eyes and says softly, "You want to see my twat, Rondo?"

This question stops him cold. He glances around. The couple at the table have stopped their conversation. Jules is likewise trying to focus on

what's happening on the far side of the pool table. The bartender is wondering if he should intervene. "Do you, Rondo?" she asks again. He nods.

"So you *do* answer questions. That's a good start." Instantly Rondo
moves his left hand to her throat, keeping her pinned to the wall. He
pulls his right fist back as though to deliver a punch. He cocks his head
and glares at the girl in his grasp.

"Easy, big guy … I need to lift up my skirt … so you can see *everything,*
Rondo." His fist still hovers, for the moment stayed. Alice's hands drop
to the fabric of her skirt and she gathers the material and slowly lifts her
skirt above her knees and higher and higher—to mid thigh. Rondo lowers
his eyes, mesmerized, leering at her knees and the creamy flesh of her
upper legs. Her pale skin is so smooth and flawless, so—

Suddenly, Alice jams her right knee with enormous force between
Rondo's legs catching him squarely in the groin. Instantly he releases his
grip around her neck. He doubles over. From his mouth comes a guttural
gasp and an inarticulate sound that's not a scream so much as it is a curse.
Lester immediately leaps at her, but she raises her right elbow so that her
arm is across her face and parallel with the floor, and cocking it, whams it
into Lester's face, sending him sprawling to the floor like a rag doll. Then,
she uses her right knee once again—like a ballerina on the La Scala stage,
her arms are up for balance, parallel to the floor, her fingers splayed, her
straight black hair swirls as her head comes around, her left foot arched
in the ballerina's *pied*—as she pushes off to catch a bent-over Rondo under his chin with her right knee, lifting him semi-erect, whereupon she
grasps him and tosses him upon the pool table. They are a couple in this
performance dance, and Rondo plays his part perfectly. His torso is on
the table, and his legs are hanging limply over the edge. She spreads his
legs and stands between them, and grabs his privates through the soft
fabric of his dress slacks and squeezes. He howls in pain. The scene is
over. Curtain down.

The couple at the far table begin to applaud. Jules turns wide-eyed to
the bartender and says, "Methinks I got meself another limerick!"

"Now I would like to know what you did with Seth and Randy, you
F**KIN' little asshole," Alice says. "Spit it out. Time's a wasting." She
gives his nether region another squeeze and twist. Lester's groaning and
still on the floor. He props himself on an elbow and passes a hand across
his face and sees blood. "The bitch broke my nose! What's with these
bitches hitting my face all night. Jesus Christ!"

"Rondo! Where's Seth and Randy?"

Rondo is still howling. Alice relaxes her grip. "Seth and Randy, Rondo, or you're going to be in a world of hurt."

"They're at ..." He groans in pain.

"Where, Rondo?"

Lester speaks: "They're at the school. We locked them up in the equipment shed on the far side of the football field."

"Sounds like a confession to me," Alice says. "Did you hear that, barkeep?"

"Yes, I did," he says loudly.

"I heer'd something, too," Jules says.

"Let's go, boys." Alice lifts Rondo off the table, and helps him stand up. "Come on, Lester, you feel better now, right? No point keeping a secret like that. Let's go. You're driving."

"Can I go to the bathroom and clean up? My face hurts."

"No, but I'll get you a towel." She looks at the bartender. The couple near the door have stood up and come closer to the action. Their presence further discourages Rondo from any further resistance. "Come on Lester, you first, let's go." They begin to walk past the bar toward the door, Lester first, followed by Rondo and Alice. The bartender throws Lester a bar towel.

They walk outside. "Lester, you drive. Rondo and I are going to be in the backseat making out." She laughs at her joke.

In the back seat of the car, Rondo glares at her sullenly. "This is not over," he hisses.

"What are you, anyway, a masochist Rondo? Geez! And by the by, I'm Chinese. If you ever call me a Jap again I'll beat the shit out of you! Now shut up!"

Minutes later they arrive at the high school and drive to a gravel parking lot on the far side of the football field. Alice sees a small hut which sits under telephone pole on which there's a street light. Lester cuts the engine. "Give me the keys," Alice says. Lester reaches over the seat and hands her the car keys. "Now get out, both of you."

They all pile out of the car, and now Alice can hear Seth and Randy yelling. The sound of a car pulling up in the gravel has animated their spirits. "Hey, somebody! We're in here! Get us out of here!"

"Get the keys to the lock, Rondo." The equipment shed sits on four concrete posts sunk in the ground. Rondo squats down near the door and retrieves a key from an unseen nail under the floorboards.

"How come you know where the key is?" Alice asks.

"I used to be team manager," Rondo mumbles.

"Unlock the door." Rondo unlocks the door, removes the lock from the hasp, and pulls the door of the shed open. Seth Hardison and Randy Moulton tumble out, and blink in the sudden light. Then they see their erstwhile adversaries, and Alice—a woman they've never seen in their lives.

"Who are you?" Seth asks.

"Your guardian angel," she says. "You know Rondo here and Lester."

"You weasels!" Seth shouts. "What did you do to Frankie and Naomi?"

"We'll get to that later, Seth. Don't worry about it for now. Here's your car, and the keys. Before you go, you want to give these guys a punch in the nose?"

Seth and Randy look at each other, then shake their heads. "Not worth the trouble," Randy says. They get in the car and speed away.

The three are standing alone now on the football field, illuminated in part by the street light. "Okay boys, I guess we walk back to Main Street."

"What for?" Lester asks.

"Well, that's where my car is, don't know where yours is, and besides, I got to drop you off at the jail. Might need to make a call, wake somebody up. But that's the plan. Let's go."

Lester says, "Jail!?"

"Sure, jail," Alice says, looking at him like he's stupid. "You didn't think you could pull a stunt like this and not pay for it, did you? Really? If you did, you're a lot dumber than I thought. You gotta pay the piper, boys."

Lester persists, "This was just a little harmless fun—"

"No, Lester the molester, it was not fun. It was not fun for Seth and Randy, it was not fun for Frankie and Naomi who had to walk miles at midnight on a gravel road not knowing where they were, and it was not fun for you to be pawing all over them. It was not fun, Lester. How about if I kick your ass, Lester? Would that be fun?" Alice walks close to him so that her face is close to his, but she has to tilt her head up to look into his eyes. She pokes a finger in his chest. "I have a problem with guys who treat women like you do, Lester. You need to learn some manners, both of you. And I'm going to be watching you two. And if I ever see you disrespecting a woman, or hear about you disrespecting a woman,

I'm gonna find you, I will hunt down your asses and you'll wish you'd never been born. Am I making myself clear to you, Lester?"

"You know, Lester, I thinks we need to take another look at this here situation," Rondo says, stepping toward the two of them. "You put me in a lot of pain, doll. And I don't appreciate that. That was a real cute stunt with the dress and all. But I'm feeling better now. And you fooled me once, but that's not going to happen again. And you know what? I really would like to see your oriental pussy. You see, Lester, I'm thinking that we might still use this equipment shed to our advantage. What we got here is a fine little piece of ass. It's the two of us versus the one of her."

"Versus—very good, Rondo. Nice touch!"

"Okay, bitch, you know what? You have this ability more than any girl I know to make me really angry, you know that? Lester, tell this bitch what happens when I get angry."

Lester says, shaking his head, "Well it's not purdy, that's for sure."

"Lester, you go for her feet, and I'll tackle her to the ground, we'll tie her up with some rope from the equipment shed and take her in there, and let the fun and games begin."

"So are you going to get the rope from the shed *now*, or are you going to wait until you have me tackled and subdued on the ground?"

Rondo hesitates. "Now, Lester—"

"You answered another question! Very good, Rondo. And you said that around here you didn't answer questions. We're making progress!"

"SHUT UP, BITCH!" To Lester, Rondo says, "Get some rope, Lester, we're going to take care of this bitch once and for all."

"You're going to kill me? And why not? No one would *ever* suspect the two of you, after I just walked your asses out of Bud's."

"Lester, get the rope." Lester has backed away from Alice and from Rondo.

"I think I'm going home, Rondo. I've had enough for one night."

Alice says, "Good decision, Lester, except for the going home part. Just go over there and SIT DOWN on the 50 yard line for a few minutes, while I clean up this mess. Rondo evidently enjoys having his nuts crushed. Okay, will you do that?" Lester nods, and backs up, and walks to the 50-yard line and sits down.

"You sissy," Rondo sneers at him. He now stalks Alice, watching her intently, noticing her hands. Alice kicks off her pumps. She can feel the soft grass beneath her feet. Rondo does not know that Alice intends to do nothing, and that she herself can do nothing offensively until Rondo attacks. And he does. His right arm pulls back and lashes forward with a fist at the front, but Alice deftly steps aside letting the fist whiz by her while at the same time grabbing his arm in a forward motion, and then throwing all her weight into her movement, carries and twists his arm around him, twirling and flipping him like a fried egg over on his backside to the ground. Sunnyside up. Whereupon she places her bare left foot at his throat. Lester laughs out loud.

"So what's it going to be, big boy?" she asks. Rondo groans.

Just then, they hear the sound of a car, two cars actually. They pull into the parking lot. It's the marshal and his deputy. Alice removes her foot from Rondo's neck. Marshal Cutler and his deputy approach.

"Ah, Miss Wang," says Cutler. "You said you wouldn't mind being hauled off to my jail, right? Am I taking you to jail tonight?"

"Darn right, this bitch beat the crap out of both of us here. She's a crazy woman," Rondo shouts.

"Marshal, I think if you talk to the Hardisons and Moultons and to Frankie Cooper and Naomi Shimel, you'll be able to draw up a list of charges that will keep these boys in a jail cell for some time. Lester is a good kid in bad company, but he was part of it."

"Okay, Miss Wang. I'm sure I'm going to want to talk to you later. The bartender called—"

"I assumed he would—"

"And he says you handled yourself pretty well back there."

"Nothing really—"

"She's a crazy woman! You need to lock her up for assault!"

The deputy approaches Lester and puts him in cuffs. The marshal now goes to Rondo who is in a sitting position on the ground. "Rondo, you're telling me that this little Asian petunia beat you up? That's the story you're going with? This is a small town, Rondo, and that's going to make for a really juicy story! People will be laughing so hard, why, you just might have to leave town to avoid the embarrassment! Hey, that might not be a bad idea, eh Rondo? I mean, after spending some time in county lockup of course. Come on, Rondo, get up, let's go."

# # #

The deputy gives Alice a ride back to Bud's. She gets in her Chevy and sits quietly for a moment. She fumbles in her purse looking for cigarettes. Her hand passes over the cold steel of a snub-nosed revolver. She thinks suddenly of loan officer Papadakis and the bank job she pulled with Carlo and Wason. *Geez, Alice, you oughta take your own advice.* Then she retrieves a cigarette and lights up. She starts the car. She glances at the dashboard clock. It reads 3:25. She backs up and pulls out onto a deserted Main Street. The PABST and Schlitz signs in Bud's windows are dark. She drives north a block and suddenly pulls over. She gets out, and steps inside a Midwestern Bell telephone cabin, and dials the phone, holding the receiver in one hand, dialing with the other, and balancing the cigarette between her lips. She finishes dialing, and takes the cigarette with her right hand. On the other end, the phone is ringing. Someone picks up.

"Rev. Cushing? Hi, this is Alice …"

Chapter XX

Monday, June 9, 1952

Up at 6:45 a.m. cool 65°. WOI in des moines says
67°. Could be a warm one today. Slept in my new blue
percale sheets for the first time. Soft as silk.
Wash day, but Vickie and I had to make a trip uptown
for some Vaseline to grease the washing machine
mechanism. Frankie and I did breakfast dishes between "tubs." Got the washing done and clothes on
the line by 11:30 a.m. Thought we were going to can
some plums given to Millie by the Eschenhauwers and
some peaches, but decided to wait a couple of days--
tomorrow I am headed for Iowa City--and take care of
it on Wednesday, might get 15 quarts with some pulp
left over for butter.

The wait was dictated by Millie's needing to get
three weeks of Avon orders delivered for which she
got $40, $16 of which she gets to keep for herself.
So Vickie and I decided to do some calling while
Frankie busied herself with her essay preparatory to
our visit to the university tomorrow. Our first stop
was at Mrs. Fredrika Solvig's to deliver some socks
to be darned and some additional mending. Weren't
there too long. Mrs. Solvig gave Vic a Colorado
peach which she ate en route to our next stop, Mrs.
Lumm's. But the peach was so juicy her face and
hands were a mess, requiring a clean up job with my
handkerchief--as I knew it would.

The flies seem particularly pestiferous this season.

At Mrs. Lumm's we found a sack of newspapers crammed between the screen and shed door. Vic thought we should at least knock, so she did, but no results.

Next, to Mrs. Hattie Dent, wheelchair bound. I stayed on the sidewalk while Vic ran to the door to knock to see if she was home. That Vic is a card, little ragamuffin, dirty blond hair, cut straight, tied back behind her ears with a red cotton band, dressed in hand-me-downs—striped T-shirt, and denim pants, white socks and Keds. The Keds are new, well, they were new for her, but now her toes are poking through holes at the front. Guess Hattie saw her coming 'cause she had the door open before she got there. We had a short but good visit--when Vic's with me I generally can't stay too long at any one place as the child gets fidgety. But as we were leaving and stepping through the door frame, Vic tugged at me to whisper something, and said to me, "I want to ask a question." I said that was okay, for her to ask away. She said to Mrs. Dent, "How did you lose your leg!" Oh my! I started to offer apologies, but Mrs. Dent waved it off with a smile and explained, starting with her stepping on a rusty nail with her diabetic infected right foot which resulted in the amputation of the leg just above her knee. That satisfied Vic, and we left and returned back to Millie's via Mary's where I treated Vic and myself to apple pie a-la-mode.

At the house I was surprised to find the aforementioned canning operation in full swing. When it was done, Millie had 16, not 15 quarts of plums, as well as a few jars of crab apple (Whitney) pickles.

Millie told me that she'd heard from the Deputy Sheriff that Rondo and Lester had been arraigned and released on a $100 bail bond, and a trial was set for the fall, at which time she thought they'd be sent to a juvenile facility somewhere. No one's seen

hide nor tail of those boys since their midnight ca-
per a few weekends ago.

   Pooped. Went back to my room at Hemming's. Listened to the "Railroad Hour," and I think now that
I'll eat a sandwich and take the last of four sulfas
I've had today. Got my new electric fan going. It's
a bit stuffy in here, my heart's aggravating me, and
I need some good rest preparatory to my travels tomorrow with Frankie.

Chapter XXI

Tuesday, June 10, 1952

COOP AND FRANKIE PULL OUT OF Bathington at 7 a.m. after wolfing down a breakfast of corn flakes and a slice of toast with a dab of boysenberry jam. Millie packs a lunch for them consisting of egg salad sandwiches, an apple, and two peanut butter cookies. Frankie's dressed in a blue poodle skirt which she made herself, white cotton blouse with a reverse collar, white socks and oxblood saddle shoes. Her hair is pulled back into a ponytail, with a blue scarf tied around it at the base. She's wearing makeup and has applied a light shade of red lipstick. Coop is in a seersucker suit, a thin blue cotton shirt with matching bowtie. He's wearing suspenders and has a straw hat in hand. His suit jacket he places on the back seat of the 1946 Pontiac, while Frankie's notebooks and the lunch go in the trunk. The Pontiac which Coop gave to Millie after Johnny died is washed spic-and-span, the whitewalls gleaming, and Vic has polished up the chrome bumpers and front grille for a quarter. Coop has checked the oil, radiator and tire pressure. Everything is a-okay.

They ease out onto No. 150 and head south through the flood plain of Clearwater County, past fields of corn, sorghum and milo. The sun is well above the eastern horizon and partly obscured by clouds. It is more than 100 miles to Iowa City, and Coop figures to average 45 miles per hour, which should put them into the city by 9:30 a.m. or so. Frankie has a handbag in her lap, and she pulls out a small notebook and retrieves a pencil so as to note the out-of-state license plates, and the counties indicated on the Iowa plates they see. Clearwater County plates are designated by the number 12 which is followed by a dash and additional numbers. As expected, they see Blackhawk County plates (7), Benton (6), Iowa (48) and Johnson (52), as these are the counties through which they are traveling. But Frankie spots an additional 17 counties, although not one of the counties most fun to spot — the four counties of the four corners of the state, Lyon (NW), Allamakee (NE), Lee (SE) or Fremont (SW). Yet, on the trip she'd taken to Des Moines with Naomi and her parents when she attended the synagogue, she'd seen cars from all four of those counties!

Coop's noticed a change in his attitude toward Frankie since her ordeal the night of the Spring Formal. It's an adjustment in his thinking that probably had been already underway, but now, as he shoots a sideways glance at her in the car, he's aware of the shift. She is now in his eyes closer to her future adult life than she is to her past kid life as a child. He wonders if this makes sense. She's more adult now than kid. Why and how has this happened? It cannot simply be the dramatic experience she had when Rondo and Lester abducted her and Naomi and held them against their will and attempted to take liberties. Yet, that was a large part of it. She'd responded to that situation in a very adult way, and she seems to hold less animosity toward her mother than before. Not that she agrees with her mother all the time, but the disagreement is less acidic, and much more bland and casual. Life-and-death emergencies rarely appear as they did a year ago and prior when she was in Junior High—when such crises were common. Coop is surprised to be reflecting about this at all, but decides he likes Frankie now as a young adult, emerging—albeit unsteady and uncertain—from the cocoon of childhood into a new atmosphere of maturity.

"What exactly are you hoping to find in Iowa City?" Coop asks, breaking a period of silence between them. They've just crossed the Clearwater River for the last time and are leaving the flood plain and traversing the gently sloping terrain of Blackhawk County.

"Oh, I don't know," says Frankie, staring straight ahead.

"Well, you must have some idea," says Coop.

"I know," she says, "I know in *general* what I'm looking for, but not specifically. It could be important, it could be nothing. I don't really want to say for sure, because it could sound silly—or far-fetched."

"Um …" Coop lets that go for a minute or so. He steers the Pontiac around a possum carcass, maneuvering right and riding the curb slightly. A couple of magpies flap away. Then, "Yeah, you don't want to end up looking silly or anything."

"I have to get this thing finished. It's due by June 16, so whatever happens here, I have to wrap it up if I'm going to submit it for the contest."

"What do you mean, 'if'?"

Frankie shifts suddenly to face him, "Pops, I don't want to turn in something I can't believe in, or that's ... that's not *important*." She turns to face the highway. "It's a waste of time."

"Ah, well, there's some wisdom in that approach, I guess. Although, I have found—take this from an old geezer—that sometimes it's hard to know whether something's a waste of time or not, whether it was worth the effort, whether it was useful to anyone or for anything, cause only time reveals that kind of thing." He takes his eyes off the road and looks at her. She's looking at him. "Sometimes I thought I was wasting my time, but later I understood that the experience I gained 'wasting my time' was really helpful."

She shoots back: "Like when?"

Coop laughs and looks her way briefly, shakes his finger at her: "I just knew you were going to ask that, little girl!"

Frankie laughs. The feeling between the two of them is warm. Coop responds: "Well, of course the obvious answer is one's education. Plenty of times when I thought the stuff they wanted me to learn would never be useful, and I guess some of it wasn't. But a lot of it was. But for example when I was little and living in Ashland, Nebraska, my mother, your great-grandmother, made me learn how to do some of the cooking— which I thought was a girl's job. And then, Coxey's Army came through town on their way to Washington D.C. and mother was ill and she told me to start making corn chowder, and I made corn chowder all day long and took it down to those folks camping out in the town square. I still can make great chowder!"

"Yes, you can, Pops!"

"And—here's another thing: Mother made me take piano lessons. Once again, I sort of had the idea that this was something girls did. My teacher was a short little lady by the name of Mrs. Sorenson. She had the shortest hands and tiniest fingers you ever did see. But my oh my! She could run her right hand up and down the keyboard doing arpeggios and the like with her eyes closed. It was amazing. And she was tough. I took piano lessons from the time I was 7 to 17. I thought Mrs. Sorenson would die and I could stop but she kept on living—I think just to make sure I was practicing. Anyway, one day a few years later, a new organist came to the Congregational church to play its pipe organ, and she was a soloist, too. And to hear her sing was like listening to the voice of an angel. And it wasn't long before I was accompanying her on the piano when she sang in church. I had never thought of becoming a Congregationalist—far cry from being a Presbyterian, they're much too free-wheeling and liberal—but I didn't care. And that woman was your grandmother. So I didn't think learning to play the piano would do me any good, but it sure did, and in more ways than just helping me meet your grandmother, too."

"I remember her. How old was I when she died?"

"Oh, about 6 or 7 I think." They drove on in silence as though this burst of information and reminiscence had triggered new thoughts that needed private processing.

"I miss dad," Frankie said presently.

"Of course you do," Coop said. "I sure do too. He was my son, you understand that, right?"

"Yes, I understand, but ..."

"But what?"

"It just seems so pointless. He dies halfway around the world—for what? I guess I don't understand too much. Seems like it was pretty senseless."

"Umm ..." Silence. Then, "I've had those same thoughts, but then I figure there are some questions, or some answers, I guess, I just have to leave with God, and while I am inclined to agree that his *death* was a waste and unnecessary—Well, I can't even know *that*—but I know his *life* was not a waste, because he meant so much to so many people and because he left the world two wonderful little girls who in turn are going to turn the world upside down!"

"Let's change the subject."

"Okay, but before we do I just want to say that I see a lot of your mom in you, but there's a lot of your dad in you too—his passion and persistence, for example. When he sunk his teeth into something, he was like Tippy with a shoe: he wouldn't let go. It was more than stubbornness. He had an ability to learn what was worth hanging on to and what wasn't. I guess that's the difference between stubbornness and persistence. When you're stubborn, you want your own way, right or wrong; when you're persistent, you want what's right, not what's wrong." They continue on in silence, until Frankie speaks again:

"So what are *you* hoping to accomplish today?"

"I also knew you were going to ask that question."

"You know a lot, don't you?"

"Not really, just a few things."

"So?"

"Well, I'm going over to the university hospital and medical school and visit their lab or morgue and see if I can trace down the skull that was sent to them after Miss Crenshaw died."

"You mean you want to see Miss Crenshaw's head?"

"Yes, if you put it that way."

"Why?"

"Because since she died, so many new developments have occurred, like the theory that she was murdered, that she isn't who she said she was. It all seems a little confused and I just want the head poohbah there to explain a few things to satisfy my own curiosity."

"Head poohbah. That's funny. The poohbah of heads, the guy in charge of the heads."

"I didn't mean it that way. The person in charge of the department."

"I know, Pops. Sounds macabre to me."

"Well, sounds that way to me too."

# # #

They reach Iowa City about 9:15 a.m. and drive to the campus, crossing the Iowa River, and past the Pentacrest, down Washington to the new library building. Coop parks the car, and reaches into the back seat to retrieve his suit jacket, which he then puts on. The straw hat falls on his head at the right angle to shade from the morning sun. Frankie has collected her notebooks and papers from the trunk. They cross the street. "You nervous, sweetie?" Coop asks.

"A little," she says, "but nothing I can't deal with."

They climb lightly up the wide steps of the library to the main entrance and pass through revolving doors. In the lobby they look up to high ceilings, and beyond the reception desk are acres of stacks. Nearby are large glass exhibit boxes featuring new books, or antique artifacts relating to Iowa's history. To the right is a reference room where the card catalogs are housed, and to the left a study area with varnished maple desks and chairs. They approach a matronly reference librarian whose hair is teased high and into which thicket a pencil has been thrust just above the temples of her horn-rimmed glasses. Frankie and Coop stand before her and she peers at the pair over her spectacles. Frankie gives her a letter, a letter which the librarian herself had written in response to a request from the librarian of the Bathington Library asking that the university extend, as a courtesy, visiting privileges in the archives and genealogical section to a young woman working on a research paper. The reply in which this courtesy was granted would be itself the authorization to allow Frankie access. The librarian opens the letter and peruses it briefly, and then returns it to Frankie. "We've been expecting you," she says, smiling. "You know this building has only been open about six months so you might find things a bit discombobulated, but if you have any questions whatsoever, you just ask and we'll get you some help." She gets up from her desk and walks around to greet them.

She speaks to Coop: "Will you be with the young lady?" The short answer is "No," but Coop and Frankie confer briefly discussing how many hours Frankie will need to accomplish her work, impressing upon her that she is to stay within the walls of the library at all times, asking if she has a lunch with her, and establishing that Coop will return sometime between noon and 12:30. Those details confirmed, Coop leaves her, pauses at the revolving door and sees a young man escorting her to an elevator. Frankie turns and waves. He leaves.

At 12:40 p.m. he returns. In a coincidence, the same parking space is available. Coop strides briskly across Washington, takes the steps of the library quickly and pushes through the revolving door. Frankie is looking at one of the exhibits. But she sees him as he enters and quickly moves to greet him. Coop thinks she looks like a college student. He feels a sense of pride.

They walk out together. Frankie puts her notebooks and papers in the trunk as before, and Coop removes his suit jacket and places it on the back seat and crawls in behind the wheel. They both slam their respective doors at the same time. Coop puts the key in the ignition but doesn't start the car. Instead, he turns to Frankie and says: "And what did you find out?"

"I found out ... you won't believe this ..."

"Try me."

"... that we're part Indian!" she exclaims, positively beaming.

"Indian? What do you mean!"

"Indian! The Red Man. Injun. We're part Injun. It means that you and I have a great-great-great-great-I don't know how many greats—grandmother who was a Pocumtuk Indian woman!"

"Frankie, that's amazing!" He starts the engine.

"I know! I can't believe it! I am so excited. I can't wait to tell Naomi. I can't wait to finish this essay." She rolls down the window of the Pontiac and thrusts her elbow across the window frame. She looks at Coop: "So what did *you* learn today?"

They're driving down Washington Street. Frankie is watching him. Coop looks at her briefly and then back to the street. "I learned today that Violet Crenshaw is still alive!"

Chapter XXII

THE TRIP BACK TO BATHINGTON FLIES by as such travels do when filled with conversation. The startling news produced by both Coop and his granddaughter is so amazing that in the ensuing chatter, the distraction causes them to miss more than one turn on their way out of Iowa City. Still, the journey seems as though minutes. Coop, naturally, is eager to hear how Frankie has established that Pocumtuk blood is running through their veins. Having eaten Millie's egg salad sandwiches en route, they now decide to stop at a Chicken in the Rough joint on the edge of town. They order a basket of fried chicken to split between them. It comes with shoestring potatoes, hot biscuits and honey.

"Okay, kiddo, give me the run down," Coop says. Frankie's got a Royal Crown cola and Coop's drinking Dad's. "Shoot," he says.

"I don't know where to start," Frankie says, glancing up at him over her soda. Her eyes sparkle, her face is flushed.

"At the beginning."

"At the beginning is our first ancestor in America, Thomas Bathington, known as Goodman Bathington, which is better than Farmer, not as good as Master. But Goodman Bathington is a go-getter from what I could read—"

"How could you read that stuff?"

"Oh, it wasn't too hard, Pops. We had a unit in American Literature on colonial English. Nouns are usually capitalized, and an 's' can look like an 'f' and a 'y' sometimes replaces 'th' and there are some superscript problems, and spelling isn't as standardized as it is today—they'd sometimes spell the same word differently in the same document; they'd spell it as it sounded, so it could be confusing, but it wasn't too bad, really. I just had to read more slowly, like word for word. But that also helped me

remember what I read ... Anyway, Goodman Bathington had three children, Nathanial, Mary and Frances—"

"Frances?!"

"Yes, Frances! Isn't that neato? Nathanial was born 1632, Mary 1643,
and Frances 1646. Goodman Bathington's wife was a Rebecca Hemsley.
In 1630, Bathington buys this land, a huge parcel of land, like a peninsula
on Massachusetts Bay, called Nahant from a Pocumtuk Indian whose real
name was Sachem, but who was known as Black Will. I don't know why
they called him that. But twenty-seven years later, the town of Lynn takes
it—the land—away from Bathington because they don't believe that it
was a valid sale—even though when Bathington bought the land there
were no laws saying you couldn't buy land from Indians without permission. That law was passed later. Course, Bathington was mad, and went to
court and lost, and forty-seven years after the 1630 sale, the son Nathanial went to court and lost, and sixty-seven years after the 1630 sale, and
long after Bathington was dead, the daughters went to court to get the
land back, and they lost, and that was that.

"I kept thinking I didn't have the whole story about the land sale.
Then I happened to notice the publication notice for the marriage between Thomas Bathington and Rebecca Hemsley, and saw that they were
married in 1640. I just about had a cow. This was so kickaroonie. I was
shocked, and thought there must be some mistake."

"Why? What is the problem?" Coop finds this story fascinating, and
loves to hear Frances tell it.

"It doesn't explain Nathanial."

"What'ya mean?"

"Nathanial was born in 1632."

"Ahhh ... yes, I see what you're getting at. Go on." The waitress arrives with a basket of fried chicken, and they each lay out a paper napkin before them and grab some shoestring potatoes, a piece of chicken and a biscuit.

"Well, back to Black Will. Bathington had had some dealings with him
before. Black Will had assisted, I guess you could say, befriended, Bathington when Bathington was trying to get a salt works set up. Here, let
me read what I copied, and I'll read it as it sounds so you can get an
idea." Frankie wipes her fingers on a napkin, opens her notebook and
flips through some pages. "Whenever you hear the word 'ye' it means
'the,' so here goes: 'There hath been for some days an uproar about ye
destruction of ye salt works. Deeming yet that salt might be made to ad-

vantage here, not onlie—only is spelled o-n-l-i-e—to meet our own needs, but also of a surplus to supply others at a profit to ourselves and cheape to them, we went about setting up near ye foote of ye hill yet overlooks ye beach, a kettle or two and ye needed pans. Ye works went bravelie on. But on ye six days morning, it was found yet during ye night some Indjans as they say, came down and pitched ye kettles into ye sea and destroyed ye pans. But I am persuaded yet not Indjans but devils did ye dirty worke yet it is onlie another attempt of Satan to drive God and his people hence. But we will not goe, salt or no salt.'

"Black Will helped settle the Indians down so that Bathington could build his salt works. Black Will, on the other hand, wanted more of the rum Bathington was importing from Bermuda. And Black Will had something Bathington wanted, wanted real bad. Know what it was?"

"No, what?"

"Not what, who. He had a daughter."

"Bathington wanted Black Will's daughter?"

"That's right."

"Why?"

"To marry her. He needed a wife, and more importantly, he needed children. He's living in a wilderness, a new land that's just waiting to be developed and exploited and it's too much work to do by himself."

"But why marry an Indian? I didn't think back in those days that sort of thing was allowed. I think there are still laws in this country about interracial marriages. What's the fancy word for them laws?"

"Anti-miscegenation laws, and those laws are still in place in all but ten states, Iowa being one of the ten states that repealed their miscegenation laws sometime back in the 1800s. But anyway, as I was saying before I was so rudely interrupted—" Frankie reaches across the space between her and her grandfather and hits him playfully on his arm. "Just kidding, Pops."

"I know."

"As I was saying, he needed a wife."

"May I interrupt?"

"Yes, you may."

"Why not marry a white woman?"

"Good question, and there's a simple answer. There were very few white women available. If you're going to colonize an untamed wilderness and you have to send people across three thousand miles of ocean to do it, and you have limited space on ships, do you send men or women? You send men, very few women. When the pilgrims landed at Plymouth in 1620, of the one hundred or so passengers, only twenty-eight were women. So there weren't very many women. So that's why in 1622, I think, a special boatload of about one hundred and fifty 'pure and spotless'—that's what the document says—'pure and spotless' women were sent to the colonies. And these women were auctioned off for eighty pounds of tobacco, or something similar. And another reason women were scarce is because a lot of them died in childbirth. So anyway, to answer your question, Bathington wanted Black Will's daughter—her name was Shaningo, meaning 'beautiful one.' It was all a bit irregular, he probably had to get permission from someone—the mayor, or the minister, or the governor, I don't know. And he talks Black Will into thinking that he's doing him a favor by taking his daughter off his hands and he wants Nahant as the dowry. So Black Will gives him all this land, but to make it 'legal' the selling price is a suit of clothes and a Jew's harp. That's why later, twenty-seven years later, the town of Lynn annexed Nahant, saying that it wasn't really a sale, not for a suit of clothes and a Jew's harp and the seller was an Indian after all."

"So Thomas Bathington marries Shaningo," Coop says, summarizing, "and then two years later she gives birth to Nathanial?"

"That's right."

"So what happens to Shaningo? Because doesn't Bathington marry this Rachel person later—"

"Not Rachel, *Rebecca*. Rebecca Hemsley. Yes, he does. Shaningo dies in 1636 in childbirth, and the child, Jesse Bathington dies as well. So when a new boatload of 'pure and spotless' women arrive in 1639, Goodman Bathington and his 7-year old son Nathanial, are there to meet it, and he gets Rebecca Hemsley of Yorkshire for four cases of Bermuda rum."

"So we are descendants of Shaningo, the Pocumtuk squaw of Goodman Bathington?"

"Yup, but you shouldn't say 'squaw.' She was his wife."

"That's something, alright." He looks at her. "You're something, you know that? This is going to knock their socks off."

"Well, don't say anything, not even to mom. I want it to be a total, absolute surprise. I'll probably tell Nomes, but that's it, so if word gets around I'll know the rat is either you or her."

"Lips are sealed, kiddo." They ask for the bill, and Coop pays. It comes to $1.71 total. Coop leaves two dollars on the table and they exit Chicken in the Rough and head up the highway. But not for long. They need to get gas. He sees a Standard Oil gas station and turns in. "We got to stop here for some gas and a bathroom break, okay?" He pulls up to a tall red pump with a glass canister and gets out, and notes the price: 21 cents a gallon. A youth in oily overalls approaches him. A grease rag is stuffed into his back pocket. The patch on his overalls bears his name, "Roy."

"Fill it up, mister?"

"Yes, please."

"Regular?"

"Yes, thanks."

"Check the oil?"

"No need, it's fine, thank you." Frankie has already departed for the Ladies' Room. Coop visits the Men's Room and then thinks to go inside the small office to put a dime in the peanut vending machine. As he's fumbling around in his suit pocket for change, he takes in the interior of the office. A "Travel Information Center" stand is set up in the corner featuring photos of scenic spots, and stacks of maps in assorted slots, mostly maps of Nebraska, Minnesota, Missouri, Kansas, Wisconsin and Illinois. A bubble gum dispenser stands beside the peanut dispenser. On the wall is a phone—not a dial phone, however. A John Deere calendar featuring a pretty girl and a huge harvester. A poster for Quaker Oil, also featuring a pretty girl holding a can of Quaker State oil, and she's not wearing much of anything except a smile. The can of oil and the way her arms are positioned conceal the details. Coop looks away quickly, lest Frankie pop in. But then he looks again. He believes he recognizes the face. He steps closer. The face, and thus the body, belongs to Sally Hildebrand, the waitress at Mary's Kitchen! He looks at the fine print. The poster is the work of Donovan Publishing Company, Chicago, Illinois. That name sets off a reaction in Coop's head, but he's not sure why.

Just then Roy appears in the office. "Gas comes to a dollar forty-two, sir." Coop reaches into hip pocket and pulls out his wallet which has a small coin purse as well as a slot for folding money. He pulls out a dollar, and two quarters. "Here, keep the change."

"Thank you, sir!"

Coop and Frankie reboard and pull out into traffic on to No. 150 North. They travel in silence for a few minutes until Frankie says, "Whatcha thinking?"

"Oh, nothing, I don't know."

"You saw the poster of Sally Hildebrand, huh? With those big tatas, she's quite a looker, huh Pops?"

"Frances Katherine!"

"What? What did I say? You sound like my mother."

"I'm not your mother, I'm your grandfather, which you should keep in mind."

"What are you talking about? How could I forget that? What's the matter with you?"

Silence. "Just a minute, I got to pass this tractor." He waits for his opportunity and then guns it, and propels the Pontiac around the tractor and back safely into his lane. They pass a billboard of three women bearing food, the larger figure has a platter with a large turkey and fixings on it. The words read: "Make your simple meals taste better: BUD-WEISER." Another one features a huge hand holding a car. The words read: "For a big lift, get a TEXACO checkup."

"I guess it's going to be hard to eat at Mary's again, that's for sure," Coop says.

"Mary's? Because of Sally?" Coop nods.

"Oh, she's not there anymore."

"Where'd she go?" Coop asks.

"She left for Sioux City a few days ago, what I heard."

"How come?"

"Don't know. Don't know. But she's gone. Are you sorry? Wanted one more look? She's too young for you anyway, Pops!"

"Frances—" They look at each other and laugh.

"I could probably get that poster for you Pops—"

"Stop!"

"Okay, sorry." Silence. "So now it's your turn. Tell me about Violet Crenshaw."

"Um. Okay." Silence. "I don't know where to start."

"At the beginning," Frankie suggests.

"Right. You're not going to believe this."

"Try me."

"Well, I got over to the Medical Sciences building and at first had a hard time finding where I needed to be, but that's neither here nor there. I ended up in the basement, an interior room with no windows, and bare bulbs for lighting. Quite cold, actually, almost damp. I met a doctor who also has a degree in anthropology, which means—"

"I know what it means, Pops—"

"Okay, sorry. So I ask to see the skull of one Violet Crenshaw. Of course he wants to know my interest in the case and I explain, mostly personal, you know. So he looks around. But they don't catalog skulls by name, only by date and place of origin, that is, the date the skull arrived in the lab and the location from whence it came. Finally, we found a box that was labeled 'BATHINGTON, APRIL 23, 1952.' Well, that had to be it, as there were no other BATHINGTON boxes anywhere. So he opens it, and I admit I was a little nervous about this and wondered how I'd feel to see the skull of a person I had known for so many years and with whom I had recently had some long conversations, you know. And there it was. Laying there all by itself, with just a half sheet of lined paper with some typed notes. He let me hold it for a moment. I saw the hole in the back, sort of on the side, but toward the back that he says is consistent with a bullet hole. Something pierced the skull at that point with tremendous force, couldn't be anything but a bullet as there was no shattering or fracturing of the adjacent bones and all. Also saw the bullet hole near the temple. He asked again if this was a friend and I went on to explain, mentioning her name, and he says 'Her name was Violet? Your friend was a woman?' And I says, 'Yes, Violet Crenshaw.' And he says, "This is not the skull of a woman. This cannot be the skull of your friend Violet.' And I say, 'It has to be.' And he says, 'Well, it isn't. This is a male skull." He went on to explain in technical language why the skull I was holding was the skull of a man, not a woman. Stuff about the size of the cranium, sloping forehead, protruding brow, square chin, and so on. Here—" Coop fingers a sheet of folded paper he's stuffed into his shirt pocket and pulls it out and hands it to Frances. "—read some of these terms."

Frances takes the note paper and unfolds it. "Zygomatic bone, the superciliary arch, external occipital protuberance, mastoid processes, eye orbits."

"All of which," Coop continues, "prove beyond any doubt that the skull delivered to the university is not the skull of Violet Crenshaw."

"Which means that she's still alive!"

"That's a reasonable conclusion, I'd say."

"Why didn't the anthropologist guy send the marshal a report about the skull?"

"I asked him the same question. I says, 'Didn't your report to the marshal include the probable gender of the skull?' And he says, 'What report? They didn't ask me to send them a report. They just sent me this skull because they saw a hole in the cranium and wanted to know if it was a bullet hole, a possible cause of death. So I answered that question, yes, but it wasn't a formal report. I just said that the probable cause of victim's death was a gunshot to the left occipital lobe of the cranium.' And I says, 'So there was nothing in their request to you, or your response to them that indicated the gender of this person?' And he says, 'Nope, I guess not.' And I says, 'Seems like some communication is missing here, don't you think?' and he says, 'Yeah, I guess so.' Well, I guess so. Doesn't seem too professional to me that neither the detectives nor the doctors have procedures for keeping each other fully informed at every step of the way in their investigations. I get better reports from my mechanic when I take the car in for an oil change. The anti-freeze needs to be changed, the fan belt's frayed, spark plugs are old, and so on."

"So what do we do now?"

"We?"

"Well, you know. What happens next?"

"First, I'm going to talk to Reverend Cushing because he was present when we first got the news that Crenshaw was murdered. See what he thinks. But I think we need to dig up the casket and let the anthropologists take a look at the skeleton to determine whether the bones in that casket are the bones of a male or the bones of a female. And if they're the bones of a man, then who is this man? And where is Crenshaw? And why was the man shot? And why has Crenshaw disappeared?"

"Wow, this is exciting."

"And disturbing."

"Can I listen to the radio?"

"Why?"

"Why else? To listen to some music!"

"What music?"

"Frank Sinatra."

"You like Frank Sinatra?"

"Everyone likes Frank Sinatra, Pops."

"Not me. Hard to beat Nelson Eddy or the Glen Miller Band."

"You're old, Pops."

Chapter XXIII

BY THE TIME COOP AND FRANKIE arrive back at Bathington in the late afternoon, Coop is feeling old. He accepts Frankie's invitation to stay at the house and take a nap if need be and stay for supper. They eat together a nice meal of fried chicken, rutabagas, potato salad and pineapple upside down cake, and milk and tea. Neither Frankie nor Coop breathe a word about their respective discoveries. This makes Millie irritable, but Coop mollifies her somewhat by saying that he'd prefer to talk about it later when they can be alone.

But later, feigning weariness, he heads for Hemming's for the night. It's a cool evening and he has half a mind to start his fire, but decides against it. He begins a series of domestic chores which include applying a Lysol wash to the slop pail, shaving, giving his teeth a good scouring, cutting his toenails, and collecting dirty clothes to take to Lillie Schott who has advertised for washings. He also takes out his winter suits—finally!— and brushes and airs them out and puts them back in his closet with moth balls and preventative.

What's left of the evening is spent cogitating in his chair with his pipe in hand regarding the new situation in which he finds himself.

"I probably should call Marshal Cutler and tell him what I found out today and he can then call whomever he deems best, like Fowler or the FBI guy in Des Moines. I wonder if they even are working on this case anymore."

"Might be better, though, to talk to Cushing just to get his perspective, because I might not be thinking straight."

"I can't sit on this information, though; I'm not sure it's even legal to know something about a matter like this and withhold it from the police."

"But they might be really angry that I found this out because we all know this is something that the police and the detectives and the FBI shoulda known a long time ago. A long time ago."

Coop puffs on his pipe in silence, and then pours himself a finger of scotch. He muses, but quietly now. He thinks he likes this detecting business. It feels good to have discovered something important, something that matters. What he cannot answer is *why* it feels so good. Then he remembers that there are other matters that yet await his attention. As he sinks lower into his upholstered chair in the semi-darkness of his room, pipe smoke curling into the air in front of his face, his mind wanders to the smiling face of Sally and her silken skin which extolled the velvety viscosity of Quaker State Motor Oil. He wonders if he'd ever be able to grasp a can of Quaker State and gurgle it into the oil pan of Millie's Pontiac again without thinking about the virtues of Sally Ann Hildebrand. He's shocked to feel a slight stirring in his loins. Then he remembers something. He sets down the scotch and goes to his secretary, and fumbles at a small drawer and retrieves a paper. Then he returns to his chair and re-lights his pipe. He unfolds the paper. It is a letter, a letter of reference that Alice Wang gave him. He skims it quickly and studies the signature: Mr. James "Lefty" Donovan, Donovan Publishing House, Chicago, Illinois! The same company that printed Sally's Quaker State poster! Now how did Sally get hooked up with an outfit in *Chicago*? And how does Alice Wang know Lefty Donovan? What did she do for him? And why did she leave Chicago? Unless ...

He rereads the letter. It's a standard letter of reference. Nothing special, or exceptional. Except ... He lays down his pipe and grasps the letter with both hands, and brings it closer to his eyes, tilting both the paper and his head so as to make better use of the lamp light behind his chair. Yes! There it is: "If we here at Donovan Printing Company can help you further in any way, please let me know by letter or a phone call." Etc. Etc. "Cordially yours," Etc. etc. The C's and the W's are faint and uneven. The typewriter used to type this letter has a problem with the C's and W's sticking. The typewriter is the church's Underwood! Miss Crenshaw had warned him about this, and he'd never had the problem corrected. This letter was typed in the church office! Turning to his left, he now holds the letter up to the light to examine the watermark. "I'll bet dollars to donuts that this is the same stock I will find at the office tomorrow when I call on Cushing!"

# # #

Cushing and Coop meet in the Reverend's church study at 10 a.m. the following morning. It is a double pipe consultation, each of the gentlemen puffing through a conversation the theme of which is the news of Violet Crenshaw's unexpected resurrection. Cushing had been reading an article about the forthcoming publication of the Revised Standard Version of the Old Testament, written by scholar F.F. Bruce, who recommended it, in spite of its controversial rendering of Isaiah 7:14. But the textual squabbling over a Hebrew word is nothing compared to the news that Violet Crenshaw, at whose funeral he himself had officiated only months earlier, is very possibly—if not probably—alive at this very moment. She is somewhere, but where? And if Crenshaw isn't in the casket who is?

"The casket has to come up," he says, crossing his legs, and leaning back in his chair. He is attired as a proper vicar, clergy collar and all. Black shoes and socks. Coop is wearing a suit, a light-weight blue cotton weave, cream-colored shirt, bowtie of yellow and brown, and brown shoes, argyle socks. His straw hat is on the hat rack. Nearby, an electric fan circulates the air. They sit beside a window in wing-backed chairs facing each other, a small chess table between them as Cushing likes to keep a game going, and often plays against himself.

They agree that the authorities must be notified, and Cushing says that he himself will call Marshal Cutler who can then take it from there. "Cutler and the laddie from Des Moines are going to be gobsmacked over this one, I can promise you!" Cushing says, "This is going to take the investigation right back to square one, and now they're really going to want to know who Violet Crenshaw is or who Elizabeth Morley was. Because that knowledge is the key to finding her, if she is ever to be found." He gestures with the stem end of his pipe.

"So how's everything going with the Publications Ministry downstairs?" Coop asks, trying not to show more than a merely casual interest.

"Well, smashing, I'd say, don't you?"

"Don't really know. The *Chimes* looks great. The Sunday bulletin is very professional looking—could never do on a Gestetner what they do with that offset printer, and Alice is a whiz on the typewriter, and sharp as a tack—"

"—and she's picked up some other skills along the way in her young life," Cushing says thoughtfully, looking out the window to the neighbor's yard where Ola Jorgenson was pruning her rose bushes. "Marshal says that according to the bartender the way she dealt with those wankers that night in the bar was nothing short of spectacular. She knew what she was doing. She'd been trained, somehow, somewhere, that was clear beyond a shadow of a doubt. Rondo was way out of his league, and didn't know it."

"Yeah, she's very interesting, very indebted to her for what she did for the girls. But I think there's probably a lot we don't know about her ... but glad to know that the Publication Ministry is going okay ... looks like a good deal for everyone."

"I did ask her about the bar scene, because the barkeep said she used some language that was, shall we say, very colorful in the extreme. Which gave pause, as you can imagine. It was certainly not language you'd expect to come out of the mouth of a woman, let alone a Christian woman."

"What did she say?" Coop asks.

"Oh, she was quite straightforward about it all, quite!" Cushing says, laughing. "She admitted it completely. She said something about desperate situations calling for desperate measures, and that the art of communication is knowing what words to use for maximum effect. She said what needed to be said, and the barkeep agreed."

Two days later, Friday, June 13, Cushing's office is once again the scene of a meeting, only this time it is a full house. Present are Cushing and Coop, the marshal, Sergeant Fowler, and Special Agent Crumbley, FBI, up from Des Moines. Fowler is wearing his reflective sunglasses again and is trying hard to maintain an emotion-neutral face. Crumbley, whom neither Coop nor Cushing have met, is about 55 years old, short and slightly stooped—although that may be an optical illusion as he's carrying forward a generous paunch which hangs over a belt, and his dress shirt at the very point where it's tucked into his trousers has split below the shirt button revealing a small triangle of white, hairy flesh about which Crumbley is evidently unaware as he makes no attempt to tidy up. The brown suit he's wearing appears to have been slept in. He has a cough. His fingers are stained of nicotine, and his teeth are yellow. But he's clearly the lead dog right now. And he's in a snarly mood.

The meeting begins with Coop's recitation of the events of Monday, followed by an intense period of questioning. Coop remains unmoved and unperturbed. He knows what he knows and no more. "What I'm telling you is secondhand information," he says matter-of-factly. "You need to talk to the anthropologist at the University of Iowa," he says, looking around at everyone.

"Thank you, Mr. Cooper, for telling us how to do our jobs," Crumbley growls.

"Oh, not at all," Coop replies coolly. "I am not only *telling* you about your job—in fact, I was *doing* your job on Tuesday when I was at the U of I in the morgue of the Medical Science building. You should send me a paycheck. Make it out for $12 plus expenses." He smiles.

"Very funny."

"Okay gentlemen," Cushing says, intervening before there's bloodletting. "Why don't we talk about the next step?"

"So now the good Reverend is telling me how to do my job!" Crumbley grumbles. "Who's next?"

The casket that was buried with what was thought to be the remains of Violet Crenshaw will be dug up, they agree, and sent to the U of Iowa and this time the FBI will ask for a full report and ask for an expeditious autopsy. "I want to know whether the head and body match, whether he was a Negro, Injun, chink or white man. His height and weight. Blood type. I want to know if he smoked Chesterfields or Camels, whether he drove a Ford or a Chevy. Whether he was a Republican or Democrat, Catholic or Protestant, I want to know every goddern thing there is to know about this goddern sonofabitch. And you can tell *that* to that goddern anthropologist in Iowa City—maybe *that's* communication he'll understand. The goddern moron."

Fowler eases up to Chrumley and whispers something in his ear. Chrumley coughs. "Excuse me there, Reverend. Forgot my place. Beg pardon."

The study door opens and Miss Wang leans forward, with her hand still on the door knob. "Marshal, can I speak with you for a moment? Sorry to interrupt." Marshal Cutler looks at the others and shrugs and then follows her into the hallway. Miss Wang closes the door behind her. Moments later, the marshal reappears. "Deputy, Coop, you need to come with me. Rose's pulled out her twenty-two and shot Tippy in the street. We better get over there."

The afternoon air is still and hot when Coop, the marshal and Deputy Scott arrive on the scene. A small group of bystanders is huddled on the street, and Coop can hear Vickie screaming and sobbing. They jump out of the patrol car and Cutler shouts, "Where's Rose?"

"She's in the house, Marshal."

Cutler, Coop and Deputy Scott push through the people. "Let me through, people," Cutler shouts. They part to let the trio by and they see Tippy prone on the road, blood staining the gravel from a wound in the side. Her mouth is open and her tongue is flopped out, his eyes rolled up. Vickie is on her knees crying inconsolably. "Coop, take care of her, will you?" Coop is already at her side. He puts his arms around her and gently lifts her to her feet. But she doesn't want to leave. He hefts her up and into his arms, but she's kicking and screaming. Someone tries to soothe her and calm her down. "What'd she do to anybody?" she cries. "What she do to anybody? She's just a dog! She's just Tippy. TIPPY! TIPPY! I want my dog!" Coop carries her away.

"Can someone please tell me what happened here?" Cutler asks grimly.

"I think Tippy grabbed one of Mrs. Humphrey's slippers off the porch," says a lady in the crowd. "I was out watering my flowerbeds when I heard her come out of the house yelling at Tippy to bring her slipper back. But Tippy just sauntered down the street with her slipper like never-you-mind and that's when she shot her."

"I thought George took care of that shotgun," says the marshal.

"This weren't no shotgun," says one. "It looked like a twenty-two. Tippy here weren't shot with no shotgun."

"Where's the slipper?"

"Mrs. Humphrey got it."

"She shot the dog, and then walked down here, took the slipper and went back to the house?"

"Yessiree, Marshal."

"Alright then," the marshal says. "Criminey! Scotty, get someone to help you get Tippy off to the side of the road, and I'll call the pound and have them come over. Is she still alive?"

"Yeah, I think she's breathing."

"Christ!" Cutler stares at the dog. "Okay, get her off the road, and we'll get her to the pound. They're going to have to put her down, looks like … Now I got to deal with Rose. Gonna take her to the pound, too!" He turns away and heads for the house, and tramps up the porch steps where Mr. Humphrey meets him. "She's locked herself in the upstairs bathroom, Marshal."

The funeral is held early the next morning, Saturday. Frankie, Nomes and Tink dug a grave out behind the car shed under the shade of an elm tree. It's cool and the grass is still wet with dew. Tippy is wrapped up in an old bed sheet, hidden from view. The ends are secured with twine. Present at the ceremony are Coop, Millie, Frankie, Nomes, Tink, Cushing and Jules. And Vickie. She's wearing brown hush puppies, with yellow socks, and a plain house dress. Cushing is dressed in a black suit, and wears a clergy stole. He has a Bible in his hand. He is solemn.

"God gives to us many blessings," he begins. "The sun, the moon, mountains, lakes and rivers, trees and flowers, and the animals of His creation. Our pets are gifts we enjoy because they live their lives so true to their created purpose. Tippy was a joyful and happy little dog who brought so much happiness into our lives … with her boundless energy, her playful barking, her wagging tail. She was a dog and lived her life fully as a dog and blessed us every day simply by being a dog. She will be missed and always in our thoughts. Tippy will not be forgotten. God will not forget Tippy. Jesus said once, "Are not five sparrows sold for two pennies? Yet not one of them is forgotten by God." If God does not forget the sparrow that falls, neither will God forget Tippy, who was created by God. Amen. Now Mr. Joyce has a poem to recite."

Jules steps forward, removing a straw hat which he holds to his chest. He's dressed smartly for the occasion in a light tan seersucker suit and white shirt that has not seen an iron, and a wide red tie that flaps slightly in the morning breeze. He pauses to clear his throat.

There once was a dog named Tippy,
Whose bark always sounded like "Yippee!"
She'd take your shoe,
And say, "Yoo-hoo"
For she was kind, happy and zippy—our Tippy.

Jules steps back. Vickie sobs, clutching her mother who is also in tears. "Thank you, Mr. Joyce," says the Reverend. The girls lift the dog and lay her in the shallow grave as all observe. Then they prepare to spade the dirt into the opening.

"Wait!" Vickie cries. She hops on one foot, and removes one of her brown shoes. She tosses it into the grave.

"Vickie—" Her mother begins to remonstrate, but Coop, standing beside her, restrains her with a hand on her arm. And then, Tippy is buried. Vickie has also prepared a cross made out of two tree sticks fastened with string. With Frankie's help, she plants it in the grave mound under the elm tree. The group stands in silence for a few moments until the Reverend says, "Amen" again, signaling the end to the observance. They leave the spot, except for Vickie, and return to the kitchen for a special breakfast of sausage, eggs and hash browns.

# # #

Except for her appearance at Tippy's funeral, Frankie seems to disappear for days. She's in her upstairs bedroom, or she's at Naomi's, or she's at the library. Her deadline for delivery of the essay is Monday morning, June 16, 10 a.m. Of central importance to Frankie is not the body of the essay—she has plenty of content and a pretty good idea as to how to arrange it—but the introduction, particularly the first sentence, and the conclusion. And then there is the title, the most frustrating assignment of all. She is ambivalent about her strategy. Should she build the story brick by brick, paragraph by paragraph until the surprising news is sprung on her readers near the end, or, should she announce the central theme, including her startling revelation about Shaningo, at the beginning, and develop her theme around this news and why it is important for us today? She is leaning toward the latter scheme. "You may not know this, but this great town of ours was founded by someone who was, in part, a member of the Pocumtuk Indian tribe of Colonial America." She is not yet happy about this sentence, and erases and scratches and fusses with her No. 2 pencil for some time. Subsequent revisions yield: "It has been said that our country is like a great melting pot into which many hundreds of nationalities have been poured and mixed and that the result is what we call an American—someone who believes in the ideals of freedom and equality under the law for all." That seems better, but still she fusses. She doesn't like the idea of a melting pot because the metaphor implies that all these nationalities lose their individual cultural characteristics, and she knows from experience that the Swedes of Minnesota and the Germans of northern Iowa still retain many of their ethnic characteristics in their food, clothing, language and customs. America is more like a salad bowl than a melting pot, she tells Nomes.

She settles on: "My name is Frances Katherine Cooper, and my great-great-great-great-grandfather was Adonijah Bathington, one of the Bathingtons who founded this great town of ours. He was the last of the Bathingtons, dying in the town he loved in 1865, only thirteen years after the town was born. Adonijah Bathington was an Iowan. He was an American. And he was also part Pocumtuk Indian—as I am today, his blood descendant."

The title also takes some time to settle into place. "Bathington: A Backward Look" by Frances Katherine Cooper. "The Bathington Bombshell—" No, that doesn't work. She fiddles with something more sophisticated: "A Retrospective Examination of the Cultural Origins of Bathington, Iowa." Then she remembers Joel Shimel's criticism and abandons that idea. The inspiration for her final choice comes to her during a sleepless night. She would call this: "I Am Bathington. I Am America!" Rather than tie the title to the introduction of the body of the essay, the connection would become clear in the conclusion where she would personify the population past and present of Bathington by saying something like: "I am the Negroes who camped along the Clearwater fleeing from slavery and en route to freedom. I am Bathington. I am America." Her fingers fly over the keys. In two hours she is done. She is satisfied.

# # #

On Sunday morning, Coop stays in his room at Hemming's, hiding like a groundhog from his shadow, deciding not to go to church. He fears the word about Violet Crenshaw has leaked out. The marshal is known to have loose lips. He's not in the mood to answer questions. Millie attends, however, and at lunch at her place following the service, she says that Reverend Cushing said nothing about it. "I mean, what could he say, Coop? 'Rejoice, she who was dead is now alive?' No one knows. It's such an awful mess. Someone died, we don't know who, but now it looks like Violet is not the victim. Do you think she killed a man, Coop? How dreadful! Perfectly dreadful!"

Millie has roast chicken with raisin dressing, mashed potatoes and gravy, a salad, cherry-pie *a la* mode. The pie is Vickie's favorite and she hopes it will cheer her up. It's just the three of them, Coop and Millie and Vickie, as Frankie is spending the day at Naomi's. "And Frankie has been a zombie for the last five days, hardly sleeps, I hardly see that child at all. Do you think she's going to win the contest, Coop?"

"Millie, in all honesty, I wouldn't be a bit surprised," Coop says, stabbing another piece of chicken. "Course, it partly depends on the quality of the other submissions, but I think Frankie's is going to be hard to beat. You wait. You can be mighty proud of that girl."

They eat in silence. Coop is aware that Tippy's not scratching around, and yipping at this or that. "Well I am proud of that girl, Coop, you know that ... she's worked so hard on this ... I wish I knew what the secrecy was all about ..."

"You will, Millie, you will. Patience. Just trust the girl, she's doing something important—as important as *anything* she's ever done in her life. This could be ..." He takes some more mashed potatoes ... "a sort of, well, a turning point, a place in the road where you catch sight of something and you know where you want to go, like coming up on the crest of the hill, and suddenly you see hills and valleys and a future you had no idea was there. I kinda think Frankie's on that crest right now, or at least something like it."

"Well, have some more chicken, there'll be plenty left over for her and Naomi tonight."

"Oh, they'll be here tonight?"

"And Reverend Cushing, too—"

"—Reverend Cushing? Ah—"

"—He leaves tomorrow for Spirit Lake Bible Camp and has some flannel graphs, he's speaking you know both to the children and in the evening revival service—"

"—Oh, he's very good at revival—"

"And he's got some papers and ideas he wants to talk over, you know, get a reaction to ..."

"Great idea," Coop says, nodding his head, not looking at her. He knows Millie feels awkward about this. "Great idea."

"Anyway, everyone's coming over for popcorn and milk and then Naomi is to spend the night and together they'll go to the newspaper office in the morning to deliver the essay—and then it'll be over, thank the Lord!"

"Oh boy, popcorn and milk! Am I invited?"

Vickie pipes up suddenly: "Of course you are, Pops, wouldn't be POP-corn and milk without you, huh? Get it?"

Coop leans over and plants a kiss on her cheek.

# # #

Frankie spends Sunday afternoon at the Shimels'. There are two reasons for this. First, she has her penultimate draft in her hand, final corrections made and penciled in. All that remains is a final typing with a sheet of carbon paper and onion skin. The final, presentation copy, she would type at Shimel's out of the prying gaze of her mother and the annoying presence of her little sister. Second, before the final transcription, she wants Mr. Shimel to read the paper, having decided that she is willing to listen to his comments, and possibly even to act upon them. This is the mark of a good writer, she knows, that is, to be able to take criticism without making it personal. Every published author, after all, has an editor.

Shimel is working in his garage/shop. Mrs. Clarice Broughton has not moved him out yet and Sunday is not a holy day for him. She, Naomi and Tink come in. Shimel is bent over a sewing machine. He's working on a pilgrim outfit for the Centennial. He looks up and sees the girls, and pushes back from the machine on a chair that has wheels. "Hey! The three most beautiful girls in Clearwater County! Come on in!"

Mr. Shimel seems friendlier than Frankie remembers him, although she's seen him many times since the day he first looked at her paper. Frankie gets to the point. "Mr. Shimel, if you have time, could you read this one more time? I am going to type it up today as a final draft unless I get additional comments from you. This is due tomorrow. I want you to be honest in your opinion. It's only 2,500 words so, it won't take too long to read, I don't think." She steps forward and extends her typed, double-spaced, seven page essay toward Shimel. He takes it. "Sure, I'll take a look. Give me 15 minutes." He wheels around and puts the papers on the sewing machine desk and begins to tidy up his work space. He turns. The girls are still standing in place like stone pillars in the desert. "Ladies—" He waves his hands at them to indicate they're not wanted. "You can leave now. Go on. Come back in about 20 minutes."

Shimel doesn't have much to say about the essay, except that he thought it was very good and had an excellent chance at winning. Frankie thinks this is high praise. It is also her signal to stop fiddling with the essay, to type it up and wash her hands of it. Shimel spots a few typos, a split infinitive, and a modifier that is misplaced, and for those grammatical catches Frankie is very grateful.

Frankie types. She's been tested at 60 words per minute, but today she is typing more cautiously. They are in Naomi's bedroom which is rather messy. The bed is not made. A pillow is on the floor as are some 45s. The only furniture is the bed, a floor lamp, a nightstand with lamp, a dresser with four drawers and a small desk and chair. On the desk is a menorah from Bethlehem. On the walls are pennants from the University of Iowa, and some framed photographs of distant relatives. The Ten Commandments are posted on the back side of her bedroom door. Her bed is littered with a menagerie of stuffed animals. "If I win, I'm going to give you $5, Nomes." Naomi is the proofreader and, if there's a mistake, she has her ink eraser ready and the correction will either be typed or, more likely, made by hand with black ink.

"Where's the other $45 going?" she asks.

"College fund, probably. Into savings, that's for sure. There's nothing I really want, right now anyway."

That night, they are over at Millie Cooper's and Naomi is staying with Frankie, and they have popcorn and milk, a Sunday night tradition in the Cooper household. Cushing arrives, looking thin, reserved and flustered. Coop is there, too, as usual. Frankie's essay is inserted into a manila envelope placed on the dining room table for safe keeping, to grab and deliver the next day. The carbon copy is paper-clipped and taken to Frankie's room upstairs and placed in a desk drawer. The girls go to bed, Naomi and Frankie sharing a bed and Vickie to her own bed, a brass single bed in the attic. Coop reads a Hans Christian Andersen story to Vic, "The Princess and the Pea," and she occasionally takes a turn reading, too. While this is going on Millie and Cushing sit on the porch, and listen for the 9 p.m. Rocket; Coop joins them for a while in a conversation which ranges over the remarkable events of the week past. After some time, Coop calls it a night and walks back to Hemming's and Cushing and Millie repair to the dining room table to look at the Reverend's flannel graphs and sermon notes.

Coop thinks that he has a full and rich life.

Chapter XXIV

THE NEXT MORNING DAWNS BRIGHT AND cool. Dew covers the west lawn like a glass-beaded lace coverlet. Robins bob about on the lawn, and mourning doves sit on the phone lines cooing. Millie is up first in faded pajamas and a housecoat and slippers, padding about the house gathering laundry for the Monday morning wash. Light streams through the east dining room windows revealing dust suspended in air and windows which need to be washed. Millie mentally adds this to her list of chores. When she hears the girls stirring, she begins a breakfast of French toast with blueberry syrup. The oleo is not mixed. Vickie will need to do this first thing, she notes.

Vickie appears next in bare feet, a small version of farmer's overalls and no shirt and is immediately conscripted for oleo duty; she's mixing with a wooden spoon when Frankie and Naomi shuffle into the kitchen and plop themselves down at the kitchen table. They're in panties and over-sized T-shirts. Millie sets the table with three green Melmac dinner plates with matching tumblers for milk or juice, silverware, the syrup and napkins. Since they have a guest, she's willing to serve the children today rather than require that they do some of the work themselves. A platter of steaming French toast sprinkled with cinnamon is placed in the center of the table.

"Naomi, we usually say a grace before our meals," Millie said, standing near the table. "Is that okay with you?" This is not the gospel truth, especially as it pertains to breakfast, but whenever a guest is present, it seems like the right thing to do.

"Oh sure, Mrs. Cooper," Naomi says brightly, "We do too."

"Okay then." Turning to Vickie, "I think it's your turn, isn't it."

Vickie predictably protests, but says the grace. They start eating. Frankie has a few mouthfuls and then leaves to go to the bathroom. She enters the dining room and then hollers: "Mom, where's my essay?"

Millie hears this and stops in her tracks. "It should be right there, honey."

"It's not."

With these words a fracas of epic proportions begins to develop. Neither the composition nor the manila envelope in which it had been inserted is on the dining room table where Frankie distinctly remembers placing it for quick retrieval in the morning. Frankie becomes increasingly agitated while both Naomi and Millie try to offer words of encouragement such as "I'm sure it's around here somewhere" or "It didn't just walk out of here like it had feet."

As the essay is due at 10 a.m. and inasmuch as it is now just past 8 a.m. the panic in Frankie's voice is unmistakable and soon accusations are flying. Millie suggests that perhaps Coop took it home accidentally, but she has a growing fear that what she suspects really happened, did in fact happen.

She runs to the wall phone, gives it a crank and puts the receiver to her ear. "Helen, will you please get me Coop over at Hemming's?" She waits. "Coop? Did you take Frankie's essay home with you last night by mistake?" It is established that he did not.

"Helen, could you please put me through to Reverend Cushing? Thank you." But Cushing doesn't answer. "I'm afraid Reverend Cushing is on his way to Spirit Lake," she says, turning to the girls. Then she explains what she fears. That last night they'd spread out Cushing's flannel graphs and sermon notes, and when he'd left, he gathered everything including Frankie's manuscript, and put them in his briefcase or cardboard box for transport to Spirit Lake. "I think your essay is on its way to Bible Camp," she cries. Apparently the essay *did* walk off like it had feet— Reverend Cushing's feet.

"Mother! How could you let this happen?" Frankie wails. Millie feels worse than Frankie because she suspects that in her distracted state last night, she failed to safeguard the essay as she should have, and oh! What are they going to do now?

Frankie has a carbon copy of the essay, but she cannot turn in a carbon copy. There are 90 minutes left before the deadline. Frankie cannot re-type the essay in the allotted time, and it's a moot point as she has no typewriter and no paper.

The phone jangles with two quick rings, their party-line. It's Coop inquiring as to the outcome of the search for the missing essay. Millie explains the situation. Coop asks her to hang up, and that he will call back in a couple of minutes.

The phone rings again. It's Coop. Millie holds the receiver to her ear and waves at the girls to shush them. "It's Pops," she hisses. She listens carefully punctuating her attention with a few "uh-huhs" and then hangs up. Turning to the girls, she says as though out of breath: "Pops says that you should get over to the church as soon as possible. Alice will type up the paper, but you need to get crackin'."

Frankie intuitively knows that this is her only prayer. She and Naomi race up the stairs and change clothes in a flash and return within minutes fully clothed. Frankie's clutching the manuscript. "I'm going to ride my bicycle," she says. "Vic, can Nomes use yours?"

"Yeah, but I put baseball cards in the spokes."

"Let me take you in the car," Millie says, imploring, seeking an opportunity to atone.

"I want to do this myself, and not depend on anyone else," Frankie says curtly. "It's enough that I have to depend now on Alice to save six months of work."

Turning to Vic, Millie says, "So that's where my clothes pins are going, eh? Isn't there some other way to use baseball cards on spokes? For goodness sakes!"

"Nope," says Vic.

The girls, now fully clothed, feet clad in white socks and saddle shoes, hop on the bicycles and pedal off in a fury, their skirts billowing in the wake like sails at a regatta. The carbon copy essay is in Frankie's basket attached to the handlebars. They arrive at the church and Coop is already there. He knows that Alice can type 80 wpm with occasional gusts of up to 100 wpm. Alice has been briefed. The Underwood is ready. Alice has replaced the ribbon with a brand new one. The print will be dark and professional. She has also selected several types of paper to use: a common white 20 wt., a stationery vellum, and an elegant parchment letter stock. Frankie chooses the latter. Coop inspects the watermarks of each. Alice goes to her desk. "Can I have the copy?" she asks. Frankie hands the onion skin sheets to her which Alice inspects. "They're not too fuzzy," she notes approvingly. She inserts a sheet of the parchment stock into the carriage, centers the carriage, types the title and the by-line and swoops the carriage to her right and begins to type lickety split—clickety-clackety-clackety—like nobody's business. Frankie hoovers behind her.

Alice stops typing, her fingers at rest on the keys. "What's the matter?" Frankie cries, alarmed.

"Are you going to stand there the whole time?" Alice asks, looking up and over her shoulder.

"I don't know."

"No, you're not," Alice says. "You're both going to go outside and not come back in until I say so. If I have a question, I will let you know. Now scram." They do as they are told. While Alice is setting fire to the Underwood keyboard, Coop calls the newspaper office. He explains what is going on. Mr. Hughes, the editor expresses his sympathy but says he cannot fudge the time. Coop asks what time his clock reads. Coop compares it to the office clock in the office of the Publications Ministry. "Good," he says. "Our clock is five minutes fast. We'll have it there, don't you worry."

"I'm not worried," he says.

At 9:45 a.m. Frankie and Nomes are flying on their bicycles to the newspaper office, baseball cards rat-a-tat-tating like a pretend motorcycle, and they deliver the manuscript with three minutes to spare.

They walk out of the office slowly, suddenly very tired and hungry.

"I will never trust mom and Reverend Cushing again," Frankie says.

Nomes laughs.

# # #

While Frankie's masterpiece is being turned in, Crenshaw's casket is dug up. Marshal Cutler has enlisted the services of Norvel Nygren and his backhoe. Cutler has the requisite papers authorizing the exhumation and Nygren has a couple of indolent helpers with him dressed in Levi's and white sleeveless undershirts. They're wearing baseball caps and smoking Chesterfields, waiting to be told what to do. Sergeant Fowler is also present to supervise this untimely and unexpected resurrection of a body hitherto presumed to be that of Violet Crenshaw. He says he wants to make sure that Nygren digs up the right grave. "All we need right now," he said to FBI Special Agent Crumbley in Des Moines, "is for those yokels to dig up the wrong goddern grave, and they're likely to do it, too, for damn sure." Now, he turns to the marshal: "You sure this is Cren-shaw's grave?" He's in a surly mood.

"It better be," says Cutler. "Wouldn't that be a hoot?" He points at the polished red granite marker. "Headstone says right there, VIOLET CRENSHAW, eighteen ninety-nine to nineteen fifty-two. Here lies Cren-shaw, it's sad, but no fibbin', she sat at a desk for an honest day's libbin; she could type like the devil, I'm speaking on the level, but in the end she ran out of ribbon."

"Criminy! Who wrote that?" Fowler asks disbelieving.

"Says right here in small letters, Jules—Jules Jameson Joyce."

"Well, that's a bit odd, don't you think?" Fowler says. Turning, he hollers at Nygren: "Okay, let's get it done." A hearse has driven up from Iowa City and the casket is to be officially in the care of Wilson and Sons Mortuary, but Fowler is going to escort the hearse directly to the University of Iowa and stay with the casket until it is in the Medical Science building and he intends to be present when the casket is opened.

It took Nygren and the boys about an hour to exhume the casket and then they are gone. Before leaving, Fowler in his State Patrol car and the hearse stops at Mary's Kitchen for the blue plate special. But they learn that Sally Ann Hildebrand is no longer working at Mary's Kitchen.

# # #

The next day Coop is settled into the rattan settee on the veranda of Hemming's boarding house. The day has been warm and slightly humid. Even now, in the late afternoon, Coop feels moisture on the back of his neck. He wore his straw hat all day to protect his dome from the sun. He can't remember a time when he didn't need to keep something on his head when in the sun. Once, at Millie's, he sat on the lawn reading, and not having a hat at hand, he'd fashioned a paper sack and fit it over his head. But now, on the veranda, the hat is unnecessary. Cicadas are buzz-ing like band saws. An odd fly or two are performing aerobatic exercises nearby, occasionally alighting on his legs or arms. He has a tumbler of scotch already poured, and his pipe and pouch are lying on the side table ready for his pleasure at the right time. Also on the table, adorned with one of Mrs. Hemming's doilies, is the bottle of Glenfiddich, another glass and an ashtray. He is wearing his blue seersucker suit, but has discarded the jacket. In spite of the warmth, his dress shirt is a loose-fitting long-sleeved white cotton shirt with French cuffs. He has never liked short-sleeved dress shirts. His trousers are held up by red braces with genuine brown leather fasteners and a red plaid bowtie is at his collar. And here he is, waiting.

The object of his waitature soon appears. A small truck rattles and rolls to the front of Hemming's where the lawn and street gravel meet. The arrival is announced by one of the town's homeless curs a-yaffing and running after it. Coop sees Carlo at the wheel and gives him a friend-ly wave. Carlo waves back. Out of the passenger side steps Mrs. Penelope Cuttingham. She slams the door, as slamming is the only effective way to secure the door of this rattle-trap of a vehicle. The dog marks the rear tire. Cuttingham gives Carlo a nod, and Carlo and the truck sputter off and around the corner with the dog giving chase.

Mrs. Cuttingham walks up the long narrow and sunken cement path to Hemming's, and even in white heels, she strides with grace and finesse. She's wearing a yellow print sundress that has a haphazard pattern of squares all over, a dress that's cinched at the waist with a wide white belt and a gold buckle. She's carrying a white leather purse, and wearing white gloves. A light necklace with a cross is around her neck. Earrings, red lipstick and a sun hat complete the picture. Coop thinks it very attractive, and stands to greet her as she ascends the three steps painted in gray to the veranda itself. He greets her warmly, and to his surprise, she plants a light kiss on his cheek. They sit down together on the settee. Cuttingham pulls out a tissue from her bag and turns to Coop:

"Here," she says, solicitously, leaning in to him, one hand on his leg for support and the other at his cheek. "Let me get that smudge off your face—" she dabs at his cheek before he has time to protest. "Don't want neighbors talking, do we?"

"Which could have been forestalled had you resisted the temptation in the first place, is that not so, Mrs. Cuttingham?" He says this playfully.

"That's no fun," she replied. She removes her hand from his leg. "And you know that you are a temptation I simply *cannot* resist." He laughs at this, and they settle into an easy banter about the day, the weather, the corn, the church and why she is dressed to the nines. "Not at all," she protests. "Evening draws nigh, and I have a date with a gen-tleman, *the* gentleman of Bathington."

"You're not referring to me?"

"Yes, you."

"Well, it's not a date."

"You invited me, did you not?"

"That I did, ma'am."

"And you set a time, did you not?"

"Yes, I did."

"And you implied that libations would be available, correct?"

"Correct again."

"You see?"

"Yes, I see. I guess this is a date, then." He coughs nervously. "I haven't had a date since 1903." They have a good laugh.

Coop and Cuttingham had first met on this porch less than three months prior when Cuttingham was a temporary resident following the fire. But since then they'd often meet on this porch, smoke together, drink scotch, and listen for the nine o'clock Rocket to go speeding by in the distance, train whistle wailing and then waning. Today, however, it is not so late in the day, although the time is about six o'clock.

Coop stands to pour Cuttingham some scotch. He then re-seats himself and reaches for his pipe. Cuttingham suddenly goes for her purse. "Wait," she exclaims. "I have something I think you might like." She retrieves a six-inch cigar with a 5-centimeter ring and gives it to him. "I have a cutter," she says. "Do you like it? It's a Cuban."

Coop is surprised by this gesture and pleased. "I haven't smoked a cigar since 1922 when I was in Tijuana. Thank you so much, Mrs. Cuttingham!"

"If I wanted to impress you, I'd tell you that Hemmingway himself gave me that little stogie when we had drinks together at a little cabaña called La Rosarita in Havana five years ago."

"Really! Is that true?"

"Absolutely ... not!" They laugh loudly and it trails away like fading thunder. Cuttingham snuggles in to Coop a little. Her hand is on his leg again. "Mr. Cooper, I do believe that we should be on a first name basis, don't you agree—at least when we're alone and in private?"

"Well, yes, except we're never alone. Mrs. Hemming is lurking somewhere," Coop says nervously.

"Coop, call me Penelope, please. Or better, call me Penny, okay?"

"Penny, huh? Well, I guess I could do that."

"Wonderful!" Penny now produces her silver cigarette case and a cigarette, her cigarette holder, and the diamond-encrusted fancy lighter, and lights up. It's a ritual to which Coop is accustomed. Coop likewise lights up after snipping the end of the cigar, and, borrowing Penny's lighter, applies the flame to the edge of the cigar and then to the end and endeavors to get an even light, and soon a nice ring of ash develops. He sips on the scotch. It warms his throat.

Coop has not invited Penny for a tete-a-tete just to pass the time of day, or to in any way, shape or form, give attention to Mrs. Cuttingham that could be misconstrued, although in the dark hours of some recent nights he has admitted in oral conversations with himself that Mrs. Cuttingham was not unattractive and was in many respects a desirable woman. Today, however, he wants to broach a subject about which he is having increasing misgivings. And the subject is Miss Alice Wang.

"Why, Coop, what's the matter with Alice?"

Coop then goes into a litany of details. He begins with his observation of an unusual number of young women who visit the Publications Ministry. He tells her of the time he accidentally walked in on a photo shoot to discover a waif in a yellow bathing suit that was quite risqué posing with a box of detergent. He mentions Miss Wang's language in the encounter with Rondo and Lester at Bud's Tavern, according to the bartender, and of the way in which she manhandled those hoodlums. Of her work in the office and on behalf of the church he had no quarrel, and he was enormously—*enormously*—grateful for the times in which she'd come to the aid of his family, most notably when she had escorted Frankie and Naomi home the night of the formal, and for her role, however questionable, in the apprehension of those boys and the discovery of the whereabouts of Seth and Randy. She had, only yesterday, rendered invaluable—*invaluable*—assistance to Frankie in re-typing her essay and had refused to be compensated for her efforts. All of this was admirable, Coop confesses. But he has misgivings. He tells Penny of the poster he saw of Sally Ann Hildebrand in a gas station en route to Bathington from Iowa City. She was virtually naked, only two cans of Quaker State motor oil providing any sense of modesty whatsoever. He noticed that the poster was printed by the Donovan Publishing House of Chicago, Illinois, and that it was this very company that had provided a reference for Miss Wang. But the reference letter itself is a forgery. The watermark on the paper proves the stock came from the Publications Ministry office and the typography of the letter proved that it had been typed on the church Underwood. Of that there is no doubt.

"So, I don't know what to make of Miss Wang," he says, concluding. "I like her. I like her very much. But we also have the reputation of the church to consider, not to speak of possible issues of legality. And it doesn't help that the congregation never sees any of you—well, *you* get to church occasionally—never sees Carlo, Wason and Alice in church, so I fear a divide is developing ... people don't know who the kids are, haven't been able to develop a relationship with them. There's no basis for goodwill, and so if something should happen, God forbid, the outcome could be dire. But back to Alice, I'm telling you this because you know her better than I, the four of you board together, and I really need to be reassured that everything's on the up and up, and, quite frankly, I don't think it's on the up and up—more like the down and down."

Cuttingham is silent. She's on her second cigarette. Coop flicks his cigar ash into the ashtray.

"Is anything of what Miss Wang told us in her interview even true?" he asks. He settles back in the settee. He's done talking. He puts the cigar in his mouth and takes a puff, and removes it again. Cuttingham leans into his shoulder, pats Coop's left leg again and then lets it rest there. They do not look at each other. They gaze across the lawn toward the street. She begins:

"What she said in the interview was true—in broad strokes. Let me tell you about Wang Xiao Hua. Little Flower. She was born in China, in Suzhou as she said. Her father was a Presbyterian pastor, converted at a young age in Ningbo by Hudson Taylor himself. Xiao Hua's mother was his second wife. The first had died in childbirth and the baby stillborn. So he was older than many fathers, maybe in his early forties. When civil strife embroiled the country, they fled further inland to a small village called Miaosheo. There they lived with two Presbyterian missionaries, Richard and Alice Manley. Later, when Xiao Hua needed a Christian name, she took Alice in respect for Mrs. Manley. Her father helped Rev. Manley with his work. But a contingent of the Red Army soldiers marched through their valley, and Christians, foreign Christians, were rounded up and killed, under suspicion because they were *laowei*, foreigners, westerners. In 1936, Xiao Hua was 8 years old. The Communists came and grabbed Rev. and Mrs. Manley who refused to leave the village even though they'd been warned that the Communists were coming. They dragged them out into the street and demanded all the money they had. They said they were going to hold them for ransom, and they were

to write a letter to the China Inland Mission saying that they'd be execut-
ed if the Mission didn't give them $20,000. This was a common practice,
holding foreigners for ransom. The Communists needed money. But in
this case, nothing could come of it, and the Communists needed to keep
moving. They made Richard and Alice kneel in the village square for a
public execution. Xiao Hua's father stepped out of the crowd, and asked
the soldiers why it was necessary to kill these people who had done so
much good for the Chinese people, 'our brothers and sisters,' he said.
The captain or leader angrily asked if he, Xiao Hua's father, was willing to
give his life for these foreigners. Xiao Hua saw soldiers hack her father to
pieces. They then beheaded Richard in front of his wife's eyes, then slit
her throat and left her to bleed out and die. After they left, the villagers
took their bodies and gave them a burial.

"Anyway, you can only imagine what this does to a child. Xiao Hua
was taken by a Buddhist monk who was en route to the Shaolin Monas-
tery and Temple faraway to the north. She stayed with the monks for a
number of years. She made a connection with a local missionary there
and between the monks and the missionaries she got an education, for
she was a very bright child, and she also learned Kung Fu by letting the
young monks in training practice and fight with her. She'd often pick
fights with them." Penny chuckles and takes a long draw on her cigarette.

"Oh, she became their equal in every way and she received training
from the Shaolin masters themselves—unheard of that a girl would get
such attention. Well, later, she left Shaolin and she joined forces with the
Nationalists, or Chiang Kai-shek's Kuomintang army and fought with the
KMT until about 1946. Her martial arts training continued there, and she
became a crack shot as well. You should see what she can do with a pistol. She can shoot the eyes out of a gnat, swear to God. But when she
saw an opportunity, she fled to Hong Kong. She boarded a freighter,
landed in San Diego and made her way to Chicago as the Manley's had
been from Chicago. She got a job at Donovan's as a copy editor, and
that's where I met her because I hired her. I ran the office at that time.
And I sort of took her under my wing, became a surrogate mom for her,
although she had long been on her own.

"And you know what else? She's a good kid. Her moral universe looks
a little different than ours. Her language can be coarse. She doesn't feel
bound by our cultural mores and what we'd call conventional manners.
She's a survivor and she's experienced more of life, a hard life, than we

ever will, the Depression notwithstanding. But her sense of decency and fair play is rock solid. She'd probably never describe herself as a Christian, although her early religious training was in the Christian faith. But she's more Christian than most Christians. You don't need to worry about Miss Wang."

"But why forge a letter?" Coop asks, still uneasy about all this business. His tone was subdued and thoughtful.

"Because it was expedient," Penny says. "She and her boss—the big boss—didn't always get along. Sometimes she has a hard time getting along. She goes along to get along, but she has limits. And she's never had to have letters of reference before. It's not like she has a portfolio or *curriculum vitae*. She knew her own value and she knows who she is, and so she saw no harm in writing the letter. It's not right, but sometimes she uses dubious means to achieve a higher good."

"Ummm … So now, the Publications Ministry is doing essentially the same work as the Donovan Publishing Company of Chicago?"

"Well, sort of."

"Penny! We can't have half-naked girls having their photographs taken in the basement of a church! A house of God! That should be self-evident! Who knows about this besides me?"

"Coop!" Penny turns to him now and looks at him. "You better flick that ash." Coop takes care of the ash. "Coop, no one knows except you."

"You know this has to come to an end, Penny."

"I know."

"When?"

"I don't know."

"I think by September 1."

"That's pretty quick."

"I think you'll be lucky to keep this under wraps that long, and Lord knows this needs to be kept under wraps—the more wraps the better."

"You'll keep our secret?" She snuggles closer. Her hands slides slightly up on his leg.

"Yes, for now."

"Will you do me a favor?"

"What?"

"Look at me." Coop looks at her. "I know you value discretion. You're completely capable of keeping your thoughts to yourself. But, if you decide you can't keep the secret any longer, please let me know first, will you?"

"Yes, Penny." He sighs. "I guess I can do that."

"You're a good boy." She kisses him on the lips.

# # #

That night Coops is still drinking scotch. He's sitting in his soft chair a-cogitating and conversing. His angina is acting up and he's sure his blood pressure is off the charts. Kissing a woman for the first time in years will do that to an old codger he surmises. He's mildly surprised at himself, because he didn't just *receive* a kiss, he returned it as well. He smiles. He didn't know he had it in him. He thinks of himself as a piece of fruit—dried and wrinkled on the vine, still hanging on until the day he'll drop to the soil and be one with the earth. Dust to dust. But so much lately has been happening. His lecherous thoughts about a lithe-some Chinese girl young enough to be his granddaughter. The half-naked Sally Ann Hildebrand and her enormous bosom. Penny's hand caressing his leg and setting fire to his loins. Her lips upon his, flesh upon flesh. He's 68 years old, for God's sake. He's a widower. He's lost a wife, and a son in a senseless war, and now in many ways alone, no longer a father, no longer a husband, and now all … this! Old men arriving at his station in life are supposed to be gentlemen, cultural eunuchs, devoid of passion, assumed to have outgrown the desires of the flesh, to have come to some crazy state of pseudo-sanctification, sexless beings whose only contribu-tion to society is to reminiscence about the past, to offer advice and wis-dom which is routinely rejected in any case. Old men like him, well, we're not blind now, are we? Temptation is no respecter of age, is it? The same blood runs through the veins of an old man as runs through a youth of 19, right? Penny! Yes, there's an attraction, but it's not love, for Pete's sake. What is it, then? Actually, he feels something more akin to love for Violet, who was—is—perhaps not as attractive, no, glamorous, as Penny. With Violet he felt a connection on a deeper level … but Antonia! In a vague way, he feels he's been unfaithful, that the kiss he returned tonight was a sort of betrayal. She was his wife, she was the woman for him. There were no others before her, nor since. So what is this foolishness he's feeling? Where are these thoughts coming from? What does he want or expect? Will he marry again? Unthinkable! And why is he even think-ing about it? He's not lonely. He has a family. His life is rich and full. Ah! *What am I doing? What am I going to do about Penny? And about Violet?* He recalls the time he spent with her before she died, or he thought she'd died. How welcoming she was, teaching him how to use the Gestetner. How nervous he'd been just having a formal interview with her. Seeing her at her desk with the sign that said CHURCH SECRETARY. Waiting for her to get off the phone, wondering—

—The phone! The phone! He remembers now that Miss Crenshaw was speaking on the phone! What did she say? "Got to go now, Penny!" Penny! She was talking to Penny! Could it be? Penny Cuttingham and Violet Crenshaw? Penny *knows* Violet! She knows Violet! But how? How can this be?

Chapter XXV

BATHINGTON IN THE SUMMER SEEMS TO shrivel under the sun like a 2-week-old birthday balloon. The breeze is warm and the slightest wind kicks up a dust devil on the gravel roads. Lawns grow brown unless sprinkled copiously, but few want to use their well water for lawn coverage as the aquifer shrinks as well. People walk slower and talk slower. Summer's a quiet time in town. The cats aren't stalking the birds, and the dogs aren't chasing the cats. Cars pass through town unmolested by canines who consider it not even worth their while to bark and howl. Shopkeepers open up an hour later in the morning but stay open until 10 p.m. The old folks sit on their verandas conversing, reading the Waterloo *Courier* or the *Bathington Gazette*, or if unusually energetic, congregate in the shade of an awning or on the shadowy side of the street, sitting on steps or flower boxes, and thereby pass the time of day. Radios can be heard carrying a baseball game, or a speech by the Illinois senator who wants the Democratic nomination even though Bathingtonites, as a rule, are "I Like Ike" people—except for Joel and Ruth Shimel and other suspected Communist sympathizers. Bob Watson is shoeing horses for a few days on the southwest corner of the town plaza and that is always interesting. Sometimes Tink lends a hand. Threshers rattle through town with their machines headed for wheat fields where farmers are still getting their hay in with horses.

In truth, most of the activity in Clearwater County is in the land beyond the cottages and back yards of town. There, farmers are toiling under straw hats on green, red or gray tractors, mostly John Deeres and Fords, tending to corn, soybeans and alfalfa; or they're moving pipe, milking cows or feeding cattle.

Bathington in late June and July gradually flattens, like a tire with a slow hissing leak. The town clunks along as best it can.

Except for the children. There's not a kid in town who doesn't dance around a lawn sprinkler at some point during the day. Nor do they lack the energy to be flying down the streets on their Schwinn bicycles. Much of Vic's life in the summer is spent on the sidewalk where she might be playing jacks, hopscotch, frying ants with a well-trained magnifying glass or roller skating if she hasn't lost her skate key. Lately, she's taken to playing cowboys and Indians with Davy Denton on account of the new cap gun he has, and he lets her shoot it if she provides the caps. Or, she may be selling lemonade in Pixie cups for five cents a pop with her best chum Missy Chambers. Some days are good, others not so good. The girls get in on a couple of Threshing Days wherein they ask for and receive exclusive rights to peddle their special blend of lemonade to the hordes of people who gather to get the shocks in and the oats threshed. It's a rough and tumble summer, and it is not unusual for children to return home in the evening with all manner of scrapes and lacerations which are doctored with maternal kisses and a liberal application of Mercurochrome. Sometimes Vic and her grandpa Coop go to the fishing hole trying to coax some crappies onto their line, but even they are usually too tired to bite, disdaining the fermented mixture she's concocted for bait by letting chopped up bluegills decompose in a glass jar out on the back porch in the sun. Then, too, the fishing hole is also the swimming hole, and the pond is so churned up, the fish are no doubt scared out of their wits. That's what Vic says. The only animal species that are truly flourishing are mosquitos, moths and flies. Coop figures he's replacing his fly paper now at least once a week.

Centennial activities are scheduled to begin in July, but now in late June not even the anticipation of future festivities enliven the general sense of malaise that is typical of these hot June days. Fortunately, into this ennui comes at regular intervals some harmless chit-chat which, if salted with certain—often salacious—details, evolves to idle gossip and then, if substantiated by a sufficient number of plausible falsities, can be certified as a bona fide rumor from whence it is but a short distance to gospel truth. On these matters Mabel Mang is the most knowledgeable and it is from Mabel that news of the Goodnow's situation continues to titillate. Although few Bathingtonites can remember personally meeting the Goodnows, they can sympathize with their shame and embarrassment, what with a daughter in a family way and all, and now the additional news that the father is said to be that hood, Rondo Harmon, who is known to have ruined several of Clearwater County's young women. Frankie Cooper had been lucky to have squirmed out of his reach, that's for sure. Look what happened to Clare Goodnow.

Mrs. Mang's bag of rumors is full of such morsels. The most recent tidbit concerns the report of the University of Iowa Medical Center on the body that had been delivered to it from the Bathington cemetery. The body was headless, as expected, and also as expected, it was not the torso of a woman. It was rather the corpse of a male between 40 and 55 years of age, about 5'7" in height. This information by itself, like the sudden appearance of maggots on a carcass, spawned numerous speculations— quite without the help of Mrs. Mang. Who was this man, and what was he doing in Miss Crenshaw's room the night of the fire? Who was the agent of his demise and why was he demisified anyway? The conventional wisdom tittle-tattled from veranda to veranda and clothes line to clothes line on the subject of a motive for murder was that it probably involved money and/or immorality. Where is the money? Whose money is it? How much money are we talking about? And did Miss Crenshaw and this man have a relationship? If so, what was the nature of it? If Miss Crenshaw did not put a bullet into this man's skull, then who did? Only three other people had any contact with Miss Crenshaw that night, Mr. Carlton Cooper, Mr. Joel Shimel and Mr. Jules Jameson Joyce. Mr. Cooper wouldn't hurt a June bug—although Mrs. Mang cautions against making judgments about strong, silent types. "They're like boilers. They stand up well under pressure, but at some point, if there's no relief valve, they blow like Old Faithful." And, as Mrs. Mang points out, as far as she knows, Mr. Cooper has had no relief valve since Mrs. Cooper died in 1943. Mr. Shimel had no known motive to kill and had a reason for being at the hotel. As for Mr. Joyce, on the night in question, he was completely knackered and not capable of putting a gun to his *own* head let alone to someone else's. No, the killer is Miss Violet Crenshaw, alright, the erstwhile typist of Bathington Community Church. Of this, Mrs. Mang is certain, however: Mr. Cooper knows more than he is letting on. "That," she says, "you can take to the bank." People nod somberly.

Mrs. Mang is one of three women who play a role in the events of the summer of 1952 in Bathington, Iowa. Her role is that of the off-stage harpy, whispering lines or even suggesting scenes to actors and improvisational players upon the stage. Not that Mrs. Mang always exerts much influence about town. Usually she's considered a meddler and a nosy parker and abided with in the same way a person might suffer the mischief of a cocker spaniel. In a small town, a person's influence ebbs and flows, depending upon the season and the position of the moon. When conditions are right, people are eager to acquaint themselves with Mrs. Mang's intelligence, but otherwise they leave her alone.

But Mrs. Cuttingham is the second of the three women who factor into the events of this summer, a season that now has lolled from the sultry days of June to the equally torrid days of July. The farmhouse sits unnoticed under shade trees back from the road, almost hidden by road hedges, a dirty white structure with peeling paint and nails extruding from the clapboard siding. But it is at this cottage not too long after her conversation with Coop that Penelope Cuttingham convenes an informal meeting at the farmhouse to explain to her colleagues why they need to get religion and need to do it fast. "A little church-going never hurt anybody," she says when Carlo and Wason protest. Their conversation takes place while watching television, during commercials and between shows. They're watching "What's My Line?" on NBC and "Groucho." Cuttingham is hemming some sash curtains for the parlor. Carlo and Wason are drinking beers. No one knows where Alice is.

"Religion isn't exactly good for business," Carlo grouses.

Cuttingham shoots right back: "Not true, kiddo. Religion is darn *good* for business. You better believe it! Ever hear of a millionaire who wasn't religious? They're praying all the way to the bank. They're in church every darn Sunday. And every dollar they deposit is a dollar from heaven! Businessmen consider themselves the chosen people. How would you like to be doing business in the Soviet Union right now, or in Mao's China? Atheism and business don't mix. What do you think drives capitalism anyway? It's religion and the Protestant work ethic, that's what. That's the one thing Marx and Engels didn't understand. Religion is not the opiate of the people—it's the very blood of the people. Trust me, going to church will not hurt us one bit, and will probably increase business—"

"Yeah, but *our* business—" Wason says.

"Hold on a sec," Cuttingham says. "Listen to this." The jackpot question on "Groucho" is: "In case of the passing on of the President and the Vice President of the United States, who will fill the vacancy?" The pot is $2,500 and the couple answers "The Secretary of State."

"They're wrong. It's the Speaker of the House." She is right and the conversation strays when Wason wonders who fills the office of the Vice

President. Then Cuttingham returns to the matter of getting the old time gospel religion. "Yes, *our* business," she says. "There's no better customer for our product than a man afflicted by a religion that suppresses and condemns the very instincts that makes him a man and makes him human."

"Aw, you're crazy," Carlo scoffs. "My going to church is not going to help him."

"We're going to church," Cuttingham says firmly.

It can be truthfully said that religion has been very good for their business. The Publications Ministry has produced a very well received church photo directory that is the envy of ministers from Mason City to Cedar Rapids. It's a three-ring 5x7 notebook with half sheet pages three-hole punched. Each page features one family. On the upper portion of the page—a slick glossy white sheet—is a photo of the family. Underneath the photo is information such as the telephone number and street address. Below this information is a brief summary of the family provided by the participants themselves, telling about their family history or their hobbies and interests, where the husband works and what organizations the Mrs. belongs to. Since the pages were loose leaf, new pages could be added, and Alice had suggested to Rev. Cushing that a quarterly update would probably be sufficient to handle changes. At the front of the notebook is a photo of the church, and a page for the pastor with a photo of Cushing and a welcome note. Other pages include photos of the Session, the Sunday School Superintendent, and Sunday School teachers, the choir director and organist. All very tastefully done. Cushing knows of no other church that has such a notebook.

The success of the notebook has promoted good will, and Wason and Carlo are able to photograph and publish their magazines, distributing them to all of north central and northeast Iowa, and the money has been good. Cuttingham advises them that they might need to be out of the church building by September 1. If so, they'd have to find a new studio and workroom, and the farmhouse is not suitable because it will require too much money to renovate, and they'd have to buy the place in any case as they were presently renting. There will be changes coming, and they will need to be prepared for them.

The third woman who alters events during the summer of 1952 is Mrs. Clarice Broughton. She has revised her view of the danger posed by Joel Shimel to the American way of life, and insists that the laws with respect to permits and ordinances be observed. She marches Marshal

Cutler to Shimel's garage and shuts down the shop. This action encour-
ages other acts of hostility including the painting of a swastika on the side
of the shop and a cross burning—unheard of in recent years—on Watson's front yard. Mrs. Mang believes that Broughton has enlisted the help
of a Klan chapter out of Clinton to the east, for it was known that she
had traveled there one weekend not long ago for nigger night. Mang
thinks that Broughton is working with Bandy and the bank to buy up the
land cheap from Dog Bone Alley south to Crane Lane along the river and
sell it to a developer who will put in a Sears Roebuck, and new movie
theatre and a restaurant. Most of the town folk decry these actions and
privately agree that Broughton is throwing her weight around too much,
but the law is the law and there is nothing they can do. Shimel says that a
bad law is no law at all and that citizens have a duty to resist it. This
speculative interpretation of the Constitution of the United States of
America is met with skepticism by most town folk, their sympathy notwithstanding. Mrs. Shimel, whom no one ever sees, takes in more ironing
and mending, and fortunately, the Kaden Canning Factory opens and
both Naomi and her father get hired on, and as the beans, peas and tomatoes are coming in pretty good, the factory whistle usually blows about 7
a.m. giving them an hour to get to work for the 8 a.m. shift. Corn is starting, too. In the meantime, Frankie and Naomi are conspiring to contact a
Jewish lawyer in Chicago who might be willing to work *pro bono* to over-
turn on some legal technicality the town laws with respect to the licensing issue.

Most of the Bathington kids 16 and over, including Frankie, work at
the factory which is in West Bath on account of the railroad being there.
Frankie's job is to take dehusked cobs off the conveyor belt and put them
on a track on which the cobs would run through a machine that removed
the kernels. Damaged cobs are tossed in a bin and later turned into feed,
and wormy or dirty cobs go through another wash cycle. Sometimes, she
has to sweep up the floor and shovel corn bits into a wheelbarrow and
hose down the concrete floor. When her shift is over, she usually is covered in little bits of corn which dry on the skin of her arms, neck and face
as well as her clothing. Naomi works on a bean line and drops one piece
of pork into cans of beans as they move past her on the belt. She is to put
only one piece in per can, or the beans don't cook right — or so her su-
pervisor tells her. The work is tedious and exhausting, but it pays 75 cents
an hour which Frankie thinks is good money. Usually Frankie rides her
Schwinn over to Shimel's and changes into a set of work clothes which

consist of a white T-shirt and overalls. When she and Naomi return after their shift, they shed their clothes, clean up, and Mrs. Shimel launders their work duds, and has them ready for the next day.

One day in mid-July the girls return from the factory, change clothes at Shimel's, listen to a few records in Naomi's bedroom on her portable record player. They're drinking Coca-colas and lounging on the bed, or sometimes on large pillows on the floor, just loafing mostly and gabbing about friends, parents, school, teachers and the classes they will be taking next fall—and where they want to go to college. They both agree that they wish they could skip their senior year and go directly to college right now. "It's going to be so boring," Naomi says, "Cept for trig, and Mr. Jansen gives pop quizzes."

Frankie says that she's not concerned about her classes or teachers except it will be challenging to be in Mrs. Gosling's class as she has a big wart under her left eye. "I can't look at her without looking at that wart! It's so gross! I don't know why she doesn't have it removed."

"Maybe it's because that's the way she sees herself," Naomi says. "Wasn't there someone famous who told his portrait painter he wanted an authentic likeness, warts and all?"

"I don't see how removing a wart changes who you are," Frankie says. "Actually, it's inconsiderate in a way, don't you think? Making other people stare at it all the time."

"Maybe she doesn't care. It's just her external appearance and she's comfortable with who she is on the inside. Shoot, she's probably very courageous, leaving it there, sort of defiant, like, 'Hey I've got this big ugly wart, are you a big enough person to like me as I am or are you shallow and superficial?'"

Frankie jumps up to change the 45 on the player. "I'm not superficial. Heck, Nomes, if you took that argument to the extreme, we'd all run around naked. Can you imagine Mrs. Gosling naked? And besides she wears lipstick. She puts on makeup. She alters her appearance every day."

"Well, running around naked—that's a matter of modesty," Naomi counters. "There's a difference between being modest and wearing makeup. But I see your point. If she tries to improve her appearance by putting on lipstick and rouge, then I guess there's no reason not to remove the wart—unless she thinks it's a pleasing feature of her face."

Frankie drops a Sinatra record on the player. "Ugh! If I had a wart I would get rid of it, that's for sure." They listen to Sinatra for a few moments. Then, "Mr. Kendall, you know the Latin teacher, he was explaining the root of the word cosmetics, from the Greek word cosmos, and the Greeks were fanatics because of Plato about an orderly cosmos or world, everything in its place and a place for everything and all that. Cosmetics, he said, are used by women to help make everything seem right, or in its place. Like our face is a mini-world or cosmos and every day we try to get our faces arranged properly. And I am just saying that having to listen to Mrs. Gosling is a tad difficult because her cosmos is definitely weirdo."

"Yeah ... I guess it's like that great Italian philosopher Carlo Rossi said to me, 'A girl like you needs to accentuate her positive features.'" She laughs.

"Carlo? When did he say that to you? Why?" Frankie sounds shocked.

"Oh, he took my picture."

"He took your picture! You didn't tell me."

"I know, I'm sorry."

"Well, tell me."

Naomi is silent, but smiling. "You have to keep this a secret, pinky-swear, so help you God, Frankie."

"I swear. Wait, why am I swearing?"

"Because he took pictures of me with only a bathing suit on!"

Frankie gasps, and puts her hand to her mouth. "Nomes!" She drops to the floor on her hands and knees and gets her face directly in front of Naomi. "Holy crapola! Oh my gosh, Nomes, are you for real?"

"For real!"

"Why? Why would you do that?"

"Why not, Frankie? He paid me 50 bucks. Now I'm a professional model! Said it was a photo shoot like Hollywood models. Well, I didn't believe all that spiel, I knew that was a bunch of hooey. But fifty bucks is fifty bucks and we kinda need the money, thanks to old lady Broughton, the witch."

"Do your parents know?"

"Are you kidding? My dad would shoot me. Frankie, you can't tell a soul."

"Well, what if someone recognizes you? Will anyone actually see these photos, or just Carlo? What's Carlo going to do with them, like drool over them in his bedroom or something? Are you really only in a bathing suit? Is it really skimpy?"

"Skimpy is a relative term. My dad will consider it to be skimpy. I suppose it could end up in a men's magazine, that's what Carlo says. Nudie magazines. Even though I am not naked, far from it. Girlie magazines, like the ones soldiers look at when they're in Korea or someplace—"

"My dad would never have looked at—"

"I know, I know, but your dad was married ... I don't know Frankie, and no one will ever recognize me cause I had on this big floppy beach hat, my hair was tucked back, and I had on big sun glasses and held a fan over the lower part of my face. So I'm sitting there, you can't even see my face, but my bosoms—and I have big tatas, Frankie—they're right out there as perky as can be—safely in my bathing suit of course!"

"So Carlo saw you in your bathing suit, Nomes?"

"He had to, silly, to take the picture."

"And Wason will see you half-naked 'cause he has to print the photos, right?"

"I guess."

"So this little secret is a secret *you* know, *I* know, *Carlo* knows, and *Wason* knows. And probably *Alice* knows ... doesn't sound like much of a secret."

"Oh yes, they're very, very discreet, Carlo said. Not a word."

"Where did he take these, these, these—photos?"

"At the church in the basement studio."

"Really! Wow—does Cushing know that Carlo did this? No, of course not. Wow, wow, wow, Nomes, this is amazing. Will you ever see them? The photos, I mean?"

"I doubt it. And it would be too dangerous to have them around here. Mom's too nosy."

"You'd be in so much trouble."

"And the thing is—this is what I've been asking myself, about the ethics and morality of it all—what is the harm? What is the moral error? And I can't come up with a good answer. Like I was thinking, God made the human body, so our bodies are a good thing, right? So why this puritanical revulsion about the body? Well, there you go, the Puritans, that's where this came from. Why, during the renaissance famous painters were painting naked women all the time, and if we could walk through the Louvre in Paris—Oh, I would like to do that some day, wouldn't you Frankie, we must do it together sometime—if we went to a museum, even in Chicago, or Des Moines, we could look at paintings of naked fat women all the time and no one would give a tinker's dam about it. So I'm thinking, what's the fuss about?"

"Yeah, it's just that, we're—real people, right now, not four hundred years ago."

"Are you upset, Frankie?"

"No, no, Nomes, of course not. You're my best friend—my only friend. You just always amaze me. Actually, I'm proud of you, Nomes. You inspire me! It's just …"

"So what's the matter?"

"Carlo wants to take my picture."

# # #

It's about 4 p.m. and Frankie's walking down the dirt lane where the Shimel's live to the intersection that connects with a gravel road. She's walking, not riding her bicycle as the day before she picked up a cockle-bur that pierced her back tire like it was a balloon and the tire's still at Augie's gas station. She's in a sky-blue sun dress, white socks and Keds. A blue head band pulls her hair back and behind her ears. She walks with her head slightly bowed, her arms sometimes swinging. This street takes her past old Howard Griffth's house where he died in his sleep last year and no one knew it for about six weeks because rumor had it he'd gone to California to visit a daughter, but he didn't have a daughter, and some girls collecting for Demolay had noticed a smell. She sloughs along, kick-ing up a pebble or two, noticing that the canvas fabric of her Keds on the right foot was beginning to fray right at the big toe. The road leads past the railroad depot where her grandpa had been station agent for so many years and where her daddy had been born upstairs in that corner room. No train on the track right now, but a few automobiles are parked near-by, and the U.S. Mail truck is waiting for the afternoon CN&W coming through from Mason en route to Shell Rock and Waterloo. The sun is still high in the west even though the station clock says it is about 4 p.m. which is later than Frankie had anticipated. She'd promised her mother she'd help her get supper ready preparatory to them hosting a meeting of the centennial publicity committee. The air feels warm and still. Micro-scopic beads of sweat form on Frankie's cheekbones below her eyes. Frankie continues walking. A solitary fly makes the journey with her, buzzing in random elliptical orbits around her head and upper body. She swats at it occasionally, absentmindedly. She hits a paved county road which runs east and west and will take her across the river which separates West Bath from Bathington via Sully's Bridge named after the eponymous mayor who served Bathington at the end of the last century. The bridge is more than fifty years old and sits on two massive piers of granite, and features a camelback truss of wrought iron steel and the flooring of the bridge, even in 1952, is still of heavy wood planking. A pedestrian walkway runs on the south side of the bridge and at the center the height of the bridge above the water is 25-30 feet, but at flood stage has been as little as six feet. Frankie steps onto the bridge now and suddenly becomes aware of all the mental activity whirring in her brain in the ten minutes since she's left Naomi's bedroom. She's been thinking about Naomi and Carlo, about the morality of her sitting for a "photo shoot." Is it possible for something that sounds reasonable to be wrong? Is it okay to do anything you please as long as there's a rationale for doing it? Maybe what makes something right or wrong is whether that something harms someone else, or benefits someone else. So, maybe Nomes is in the clear. Frankie wonders what it is like to be poor like the Shimels and what it must feel like to have that poverty thrust on them by someone like Broughton and her pals. That would make her so mad. It does make her mad. Mrs. Broughton must be taking too much laudanum these days. Thinking about Broughton slings her mind around to her essay now in the hands of the committee and she wonders if Broughton has read it.

At the center of the bridge, she stops and leans against the bridge railing, and raises herself up on tiptoe, and peers over the edge resting on her elbows. She looks down to the water below. She focuses on one spot and then tries to follow the flow of the water downstream. Then she spots a leaf borne along by the current. She follows it as it darts and bobs like a steel bearing in a pinball machine, down the river and out of sight. She looks for trolls. She spots where she used to see them long ago. She'd cross the river after visiting her grandpa and grandma at the depot, and lean through the railings at this very spot and crane her head to see the trolls about which she'd read in second grade in the story of Billy Goat Gruff. But the first time she did this—looking for the trolls—it was winter, and she lost her cap into the water. It floated away. And her daddy bought her two more caps because of the cold, but she lost those too, and her daddy was so mad that he didn't buy her any more caps.

She resumes her walk across Sully's Bridge. She crosses the road that winds along the river on its east side. Berman's Drug Store is on the corner. The paved county road here moves eastward through the town, but the pavement turns into red bricks and on each side are bungalows, sidewalks, mature elms shading the street from the summer sun. On a whim, she drops into the drug store. The door with a large glass window is open, stopped by a brass spittoon, but there's a screen door. A little bell above the door announces her arrival. As she steps inside, she feels a rush of moving air and it cools her face. The store has three ceiling fans, and all three are whirring. She's in the mood for something sweet and she has a quarter in a pocket slit into her dress. She fingers some jawbreakers, inspects the suckers and a pack of five tiny wax bottles, each a different color filled with flavored syrup. She considers a small bag of jelly beans, but then decides upon a grape popsicle and a pack of Blackjack. "Afternoon, Mr. Berman," she says warmly to the white-haired and mustachioed man behind the soda fountain who's wearing a white lab coat. The logo beneath the breast pocket reads in red letters with a blue outline: "Johnson & Johnson."

"Hello, Miss Cooper," Berman says kindly. He cocks his head at an angle. "Been working hard, eh?"

"Not too bad, Mr. Berman, just the cannery, you know." She places the popsicle and pack of Blackjack on the glass-topped counter by the register. "Just this, thank you." She gives him the quarter, gets a nickel in change. "Say hello for me to Mrs. Berman," she says, turning to leave. She makes her way back to the entrance in the corner of the store, pausing at the magazine rack by the door. *Popular Mechanics*, *Field & Stream*, *Life*, *Time*, the *Saturday Evening Post* with a Rockwell cover. Up high on the top rack she spies *Gent* and *Men's Digest*. She begins to reach for *Gent*, but pauses in mid-reach fearful that Mr. Berman may be watching. She leaves the store.

She withdraws the double-stick popsicle from its paper pouch and gently snaps it in half and starts sucking. She likes to bite off a chunk in her mouth and then suck out all the juice, and then chew what's left, or let it melt in the heat of her mouth. She knows it will give her a purple tongue, but she doesn't care. She continues her walk down the brick-paved road on the south sidewalk. Old man Keeler is standing on his walkway below the porch dressed in striped pajamas that show beneath a cotton housecoat cinched around his waist. He's wearing slippers. He's leaning forward on a cane, his eyes vacant, staring directly at her, his mouth slightly agape, his face unshaven. "Good afternoon, Mr. Keeler," says Frankie, sweetly. Keeler hasn't said a word for over a year, not since he'd had his stroke. Frankie walks by. Across the street, she sees Mrs. Torgeson on her knees deadheading some marigolds in a flower bed that borders the shrubbery in front of their veranda. "Look out, Frankie!" She turns and sees Charlie Jensen coming up the walk on his bicycle with his orange canvas newspaper bag tied to the handlebars. He has three of four customers on this block. He flings the *Des Moines Register* to their doors, arching the folded paper so that it lands on the porch with a slap and slides right to the door. He never stops; he seldom misses. She passes a Bell service truck, and sees a workman on Palmer's roof, no doubt installing the line for the new dial telephones.

She reaches the city park, and sees the new bandstand on the north side and ambles now across the grass in its direction. It's a semi-circular structure, with the straight side backed up to the street, and the curved side opening up to the park. In a few weeks, the park will be filled with hundreds of folks from all over northeastern Iowa, maybe a couple thousand people. It will be so grand! There'll be bunting decorating the bandstand, and the flag will be flying and the high school band playing peppy songs. It will be the biggest and proudest day in Bathington's history, of that there's no doubt. Frankie mounts the steps, and upon reaching the top, spies a couple of wooden folding chairs and sits down. She begins sucking on the second half of her popsicle. She tosses the stick from the first into a trash receptacle in a dark corner of the platform. She looks out from where she's sitting past the new hardwood railing and balusters. Looks like they still await a good shellacking. The railing extends around the opening under the shell of the bandstand. Sprinklers are shooting water over a parched section of the park. Far away on the southwest corner she sees Watson shoeing a horse. A horse trailer is parked nearby where a couple of chestnut nags are standing, nuzzling tufts of grass occasionally. Behind her, a work crew is tearing up a chunk of the pavement to repair something, perhaps a water main. They have a jackhammer going and Frankie can hardly think. The park is not too busy. A quartet of old men are playing horseshoes. Some kids on the seesaw, more on the swings and slide. She takes another chunk of popsicle into her mouth, and then stands and moves toward the railing. She imagines she is making her speech, reading her essay at the centennial celebration in the park.

She says softly, lolling around the last bit of popsicle with her tongue: "Ladies and gentlemen, today—" She gestures with her hands as though to welcome or embrace her audience, the half-eaten—the bottom half of the popsicle as a sort of religious censer. "This wonderful town we call Bathington, founded one hundred years ago today, was given its name by our ancestors, some of whom had an illustrious, a very illustrious history." She chuckles. She now speaks louder as though to compete with the rat-a-tatting clatter of the road crew. "An illustrious history, or a history of lust, you might say!" She smiles and laughs at her joke.

But her amusement is broken by a sense of something—someone—watching. Her mind knows she is being observed before her eyes can verify the sensation. She turns and sees standing at the base of the steps to the bandstand with his hands on the handrails, Mr. Rondo Harmon. He's dressed as he always is: blue jeans and a T-shirt—no cigarettes rolled in the sleeve—but the shoes are different. Like Frankie, he, too, works at the cannery, and he's wearing a pair of boots.

Frankie freezes for a moment. Then she says angrily: "Stay there, Rondo!"

Rondo places his right foot on the first step.

"Don't, Rondo!"

"Frankie! Why are you always so mad at me anyway?" His face is lean and intense. Frankie notices that he appears to be growing a beard, perhaps for the Centennial.

"I'm not *always* mad at you, Rondo, only when I see you!" She doesn't take her eyes off of him, but her mind is assessing the situation. The design of the bandstand includes two sets of stairs on either side of platform. Rondo appears to be ascending one, so her escape must naturally be via the steps on the opposite side. But to make a dash for those stairs now would be premature as Rondo would merely swing around the base of the bandstand to meet her at the bottom of the opposite steps when she arrived. No, she must wait for him to commit to *this* flight of stairs—perhaps four or five steps, and then she can take flight.

"You just stay there, Rondo. I'm going home now, okay?"

"Frankie, relax, I don't want to hurt you. Honestly, come on now, listen to me—" His tone is not menacing, but it's unsettling. He's now on the first step and slowly ascending to the second, and his left foot is now above the third. "—I need to talk to you, and tell you something and then I will leave you alone … come on!"

"That's far enough, Rondo," Frankie yells. She hopes someone will see what's happening. Maybe she should just start yelling, that would scare him off. But she doesn't want someone to come rushing to save her. She can deal with this herself, at least now she can at 4 or 5 p.m. in the afternoon, whatever it is. She's watching him, though. He's at the third step, still shooting off his mouth.

"Didn't the judge say you couldn't come near me?"

"Yes, I know, but this is a coincidence and I thought you'd like to hear what I have to say, is all. Why do you have to be so dad-blame stubborn all the time?" He's on the fourth step now. Frankie figures that's good enough. She throws her popsicle at him and makes for the far stairs, and leaps down the stairs hitting only three risers and is off like the wind, running fast, knees churning high, across the damp fescue with Rondo now in pursuit. Why is he chasing me? What's he going to do in broad daylight? It doesn't make sense! He's stupid. She throws a glance backwards. His head is down and his brow is pushed forward. He's fast, even in those work boots, and darn, he's in good shape. His arms are churning, propelling him forward. His fists are clenched. Frankie, too, lowers her head and leans into her stride and feels light on her feet. She thinks she has about a 25-foot lead on him. She approaches the horseshoe players and veers around one of the pits and heads straightaway for the street beyond, but as she makes a cut, her right foot slips on the grass and soon she's a-tumble on the ground, sprawled like a rag doll. She comes to a half sitting position and sees Rondo making for her at full speed. At this point, Frankie knows that he'll be upon her in seconds kissing her, or pawing at her, or something. She isn't quite sure what. But she is suddenly unafraid, thinking that at least the horseshoe players will quickly come to her rescue and as embarrassing and inconvenient as it will be, it will be over. But Rondo, not taking the path Frankie had taken, careens straight for the fallen girl, a trajectory which takes him through the horseshoe course and as he passes between the two sets of players, a shoe in flight catches him square in the crown, and drops him to the ground like a coon shot out of a tree. He lies still.

# # #

Rondo lives. He's taken to the hospital in Charles City. Frankie has to answer a few questions from Marshal Cutler. "That boy has porridge for brains," he says, shaking his head.

"Why don't some *nice* boys come calling for you, Frankie?" Millie asks a few days later when they are eating at the supper table. "What is it about you that keeps someone like Rondo sniffing around?"

"What do you mean, Mom?" Frankie asks testily. "This isn't my fault!"

"Why hasn't Seth called? He's a nice young man."

"After what happened, I don't blame him," Frankie says. "I'm too much trouble."

"No, you're not at all," Millie says, lifting a fork with potatoes to her mouth.

"Anyway, someone else has called me," Frankie says.

"Frankie's got a boyfriend," Vic sings.

"Shut-up, Vic!"

"Who? Who has called you?"

"Carlo."

"Carlo?" Coop asks. "Carlo Rossi?" Frankie nods. Her mouth is full of food.

"I should say NOT!" Millie exclaims. "We've already had this conversation. Oh, he's much too old for you,"

"It's not like that, Mom," Frankie says, wiping her mouth with a napkin. "He just wants to take my picture." She's baiting her mother and wants to see what her reaction will be. But it's not her mother who reacts; it's her grandfather.

"Absolutely not," he says, his jaw set. He does not look at Frankie.

"Wow, that was a quick decision," Frankie says smiling. "What's the big deal?"

"No big deal," Coop says, "It's just not proper for a young lady to be alone in a studio with a man, unchaperoned and all."

"Then you come with me, Pops."

"Well, Pops is right, sweetie," Millie says.

"I don't really care much for what's considered proper, you know," Frankie says.

"I know that," says Coop. "That's why God gives children parents and grandparents and you have one of each. So, good. It's settled."

"Pops, come on! You know that nothing is ever really settled!"

Chapter XXVI

ABOUT A WEEK AFTER RONDO HARMAN was felled by a horse-shoe in the park, word comes to Millie via Marshal Cutler that Harmon wants to speak to her and to Frankie. The marshal says that Harmon understands that they will not want to meet with him alone, which is why the marshal and Deputy Scott will be present at the meeting. Would she object to a visit at 149 Maple?

Millie, Frankie and Coop all object to the venue, and Frankie has no interest in listening to anything Rondo has to say. Coop suggests that the parley be held in the Reverend's study, with his permission, and the Reverend could also be present. Cutler agrees that the pastor's study is neutral ground and doesn't think Mr. Harmon will have a problem with it. They set a time for the next day at 10 a.m. in the morning.

At the appointed hour, Reverend Cushing's office is full of people. Millie and Coop are present as is the Reverend. Frankie has arrived with her entourage. The entourage, consisting of Naomi and Tink, was Naomi's idea, an epiphany that lit up like a Fourth of July rocket the moment Frankie told her what was going to happen. "Frankie! Let me come with you!" she cries.

"Let you?" Frankie exclaims. "That's a super idea!" Of course, Tink wants to tag along. So it is settled. Millie's first instincts are to oppose the arrangement, thinking it best to keep this in the family so far as possible, but Coop's eye language when she glances at him for confirmation indicates that he supports the proposal, and she decides to go along.

Millie and Coop have dressed for the occasion, which is to say that Millie is wearing an ensemble that's between her everyday housedress and her Sunday clothes: a white patterned skirt, a smart chartreuse blouse, and a thin brown belt about the waist. No necklace, no earrings and no bracelet. On her wrist is a delicate gold wristwatch, a gift from Johnny on their tenth wedding anniversary in 1944. Coop is wearing a light tan suit, white shirt, brown bowtie, and has his straw hat in hand.

Frankie, Nomes and Tink have not dressed up for the occasion. They expect the cannery whistle to blow at about noon today and will need to be on the line by 1 p.m. They're wearing overalls and T-shirts. Frankie's hair is pulled back and held in place by a yellow ribbon.

Reverend Cushing, in a light grey suit and maroon tie, is arranging chairs when Marshal Cutler, Deputy Scott and Mr. Harmon appear at the door. Cushing invites them in and to take a seat. Scott elects to stand by the door with his thumb tucked under his belt per usual. He's worrying a toothpick in his mouth per usual. Rondo takes a seat on a folding chair near the door which is positioned in a way that he's facing the rest of the group who are doing their best not to look at him.

But Frankie is not afraid to look at her erstwhile tormentor. She knows that Harmon is also waiting for the noon cannery whistle. So he's dressed for work, wearing Levi's and a white T-shirt. What *is* shocking about Rondo's appearance, however, is not the jeans, the T-shirt, or even the fact that he's not carrying cigs in a rolled up sleeve, or that the Brylcreem ducktails are missing today. Mr. Rondo Harmon is toting a big, black Scofield Bible!

Cutler clears his throat, thumbs his cowboy hat a bit further off his head and leans forward in his chair. "Well, ladies and gents, let's get this going. This little confab is Mr. Harmon's ide-er, not mine. So I guess now we'll start by letting him say his piece, and then that's all that needs to happen. So Rondo, you wanted a chance to say something, so here ya are now." Cutler sits back smiling as though he knows what's coming and nods to Rondo who begins to speak. He straightens up in his chair, bends forward abjectly. His voice is quiet and his head is bowed. His talk begins as though he's addressing his work boots.

"First off, I want to thank—"

"Rondo!" Cutler interjects. "For criminey out loud, sit up and speak up and look at us when you're speaking. You mumbling like that, especially when you're talkin' to the floor, can't hear a dang thing you're sayin'. Could you hear what he said, Mrs. Cooper?"

Millie's startled. She says, "Well, it was a little difficult ..." Marshal Cutler glares at Rondo, who nods. He looks up at the clutch of people in the office. Reverend Cushing is standing behind his desk in a corner by the bookshelves. Frankie, Nomes and Tink are squeezed into the love seat, and Millie and Coop have the wing-backed chairs.

"Sorry," Rondo says. "First off I want to thank you for coming. You certainly could have refused, but thanks. What I want to tell you about is something that happened to me, but to first say that I am very sorry for the trouble I have caused you all, and especially you Miss Cooper, and you, too, Miss Shimel. What I did—and many things I have done—were wrong, and I apologize for them from the bottom of my heart, and I hope you will find some way, some day, to forgive me."

As he says these words, Frankie and Nomes shift about slightly in the loveseat, as though they're suddenly uncomfortable. In the back of her head Frankie's not sure what she expected Rondo was going to say, but she realizes now that she didn't expect that it was going to sound like this. Tink doesn't move a muscle. She has not been in such a meeting as this in her life! Her eyes are wide and white and she's sitting bolt upright like she's strapped to a steel truss.

"I suppose this is hard for you to believe, and I don't blame you, but I am very sorry, and I know there's nothing I can do to make it up to you … at least I don't *think* there's anything I can do … if there is, please let me, know—"

"You could start by disappearing—" Frankie snaps.

"—MISS Cooper! That's not helpful," Marshal Cutler roars. "You agreed to hear him out, so hear him out now." Millie is so glad he says this, because Frankie would just resent her if she'd been the one to say it.

"No, I understand, Miss Cooper, and actually I *am* going to disappear, I mean, you will not see me in a personal way anymore. I'm still working at the cannery, you know, but I will stay away after today, I promise you all that. This is something I can do, so yes, thank you. But I also wanted to tell you that the Rondo Harmon who did these things in the past is not the Rondo Harmon sitting here today in this here room. In fact, there is no Rondo anymore, it's *Ronald*, I want to go by my given name from here on, Ronald Harmon. Rondo is gone, dead and buried. Finished. I am done with him. The reason for this change is that about a month ago I found Jesus at a—"

"I didn't know—"

"FRANKIE!" Millie exclaims, exasperated.

"—Jesus at a revival tent meeting in Charles City. The preacher, he was from some place in Tennessee and he played the guitar and his wife

sang with him and he preached and told the story of his life, his life of sin
and rebellion and how he'd given his heart to Jesus and got saved and all.
I was at the meeting with some friends and thought I could stir up some
mischief, but I started to get interested, listening to the music which—I
can't explain it—just reached into my soul and grabbed me, and it was
like the preacher was preaching right to me, like there was no one else in
that big tent but me, so when he gave the invitation and altar call, I got
up off the bench where I was sitting and I marched right down the sawdust trail to the front, got on my knees and asked Jesus into my heart and
to forgive me all my sins, every last one of them, and to wash my robes
white in the blood of the Lamb, and to make me a new creation in Christ
and to write my name down in the Lamb's Book of Life and give me
eternal life. And Miss Cooper, Mrs. Cooper, and Mr. Cooper, when I did
that, when I prayed the sinner's prayer, 'God, be merciful to me a sinner,'
you can't imagine the feeling, the relief I felt, it was like I was carrying a
hundurd pound load of corn on my back and it was just lifted off, like I
could stand straight in my soul for the first time in my life. It was truly
amazing. I felt like a new person, and I guess I was, I *am*, a new person in
Jesus. Pastor says I was born again. So Rondo is dead and gone, crucified
with Christ. But Ronald Harmon, a sinner saved by grace, lives. I rose out
of the waters of baptism a new man. I was baptized last week by Rev.
Barnes of the Baptist church where I's attending now, baptized in the
Clearwater itself. And I am quite happy and I feel God has a purpose for
my life. But Pastor Barnes said that one of the things I had to do—well,
he said I had to give up my cigarette habit as it was a bad testimony to
unbelievers because if your testimony is that Jesus has freed you from sin,
but the cigarette habit still has a grip on you, well it don't quite make
sense does it? So I gave up cigarettes and I gave up drink, too. But Pastor
Barnes also said that I needed to take an inventory of my life to see if
there was anybody I needed to apologize to—and that's why I am here.
No other reason, but to say I am sorry and that I apologize. That's what I
wanted to say to you the other day, Miss Cooper, but you started running,
and I should not have run after you, and then it was like God just got a
hold of me and sent that horseshoe a-flying, as though to say, 'You're
going about this the wrong way, my son!' I sure was, I see that now. ...
So I guess that's it. God bless you all and thank you for listening to me."

　　Millie gets her handkerchief out about mid-way through this oration
and has been dabbing her eyes for some time. "Oh, Mr. Harmon—

RONALD!" She titters nervously. "That was so touching and well put. God bless you, too. We wish you the best—don't we, girls?" She looks to the trio sitting on the couch.

"A leopard can't change his spots," Frankie says with finality.

"The proof is in the pudding," Nomes says.

Ronald nods, saying nothing. Then he rises, Bible in hand, and turns to leave. Marshal Cutler rises as well, and says, "That's it then, I guess, folks. We'll be going now."

Chapter XXVII

July 20, 1952, Sunday

... Today was the official beginning of the unoffi-
cial centennial celebration. The beginning of the
pre-centennial as it were. The adult male inhabit-
ants of the town are on notice that they have less
than three weeks to grow a beard or risk arrest and
jail time in the city park, or pay a fine to avoid
it. I'll probably get the prize for Most Futile Attempt. The day was marked by two significant events,
namely the "Old Timers Picnic" and the "Parade of
Fashions" held on the stage south of the school
house. The former item occurred at the city park after the 11 a.m. church services were over. About 150
persons 75 years or older—no one was verifying ages—
who were early residents of Bathington registered
for the picnic which was catered by a consortium of
Ladies Aid groups from Bathington's five churches. A
number of "younger" persons, like me, also attended.

The Parade of Fashions was an evening event that
featured more than eighty costumes from years gone
by. Millie, Frankie and Vic modeled some of the outfits, Naomi, too. Mr. Shimel found time to repair
and alter some of the dresses, gratis. Mrs. Otto
Wilkens took a prize for the oldest costume, wearing
a dress 125-years old belonging to her great-great
grandmother, Abigail Hicks who was well known in the
early days as a true western heroine. It was said
she could talk Injun and shoot a rifle equal to any

man, and legend has it that she could shoot a rifle
ball between the lids of a deer's eye on the run.
She didn't like to wear dresses. It's a wonder this
one survived!

The fashion show notwithstanding, Millie is still
busy with dresses for Sunbonnet Sues so that she,
Frankie and Vic will have something to wear during
the centennial itself, August 7-10.

Alice's fingers are being worked to the bone and
the Publication Ministry can scarcely have time for
any other business these days than church and the
centennial—at least I pray not. Alice has been typing up the "Bathington Centennial Pageant" program,
publicity releases for all the newspapers within a
120-mile radius of the town, doing the Sunday worship bulletin per usual, and has the Centennial program to prepare as well, plus raffle tickets, certificates of recognition and appreciation and more.
And Mr. Rossi likewise as the Official Photographer
of the Centennial has been a busy lad, covering the
two events mentioned above, and has been taking head
shots of various VIPs, and of all the committees--
for the history book, and it has been a grueling experience. Just getting everyone scheduled and in one
place is a task. And if Alice is busy and Mr. Rossi
is busy this can only mean one thing for Mr. Jard,
i.e. he is equally busy printing the programs Alice
has typed or the photographs that Rossi has taken.
This knowledge makes me feel better, puts me at ease
in my uneasiness. I will be glad, glad, glad when
they are safely out of the church ...

Cuttingham, the boys and Alice all in church today... Special music by the Bathington Cornet Band
who will perform during the Centennial, too ...

July 27, 1952, Sunday
No sign of Ronald Harmon since his born again profession a week or so ago ... Dinner at Millie's. I

peeled the spuds in the morning before church. Millie used the Mirror-magic for the potatoes, and we
had chicken, mashed potatoes, pears, cucumbers, jelly, strawberries, and cream and cookies ...

Tonight the pageant practices began in earnest.
The entire cast met for the first time, rather than
rehearsing in small ensemble sections. There also
will be rehearsals this week Tuesday and Thursday,
the same the following week. My attendance as well
as Millie's will be required as I am playing a role
in the courthouse scene following the Indian Massacre of 1854 as Judge Aaron Kleinschmidt, and Millie
is playing a "guest" in the "When Great-Grandmother
Entertained" scene. Cushing is typecast as an itinerant preacher. The rehearsals the week after this
will be dress rehearsals. We will be giving two per-
formances, Thursday, August 7, and Saturday August 9.

August 3, 1952, Sunday
Church today was packed, as this is Centennial Sunday, the beginning of Centennial week. Next Sunday
is bound to be well-attended as well. This service
is of particular interest to Millie and Frankie because Editor Hughes of the <u>Bathington Gazette</u> was on
the program to announce the winner of the essay contest. More on that in a moment. Attendance was
helped no doubt by beautiful weather, and even some
of the farmers found time to get off their tractors
and come to church for an hour or two. Many of the
women folk and a few of the old-timers dressed up in
period costuming and Rev. Cushing himself had a
black, vested suit and stood outside the church
greeting people wearing the broad-brimmed black hat
of the itinerant preacher. And to make the effect
even better he'd borrowed Harvey Schmadeke's old
mare and rode the old girl from the farm, all the
way into town, about two miles all told, sitting
tall and erect in the saddle and a big Bible under

his arm, reins in the other hand. He clopped right
up to the church and dismounted, tied up the mare to
a hand-rail and greeted people coming in.

Millie and the girls were attired in farm dresses
and bonnets. Looked as charming as could be. Beings
as how I was the lector for the service, I processed
with Cushing and took a seat on the platform on the
Good Shepherd side of the sanctuary and had a good
view of the audience. My reading was from Paul's
first epistle to the Corinthians the part about our
bodies being the temples of the Holy Spirit. Fortunately I did not have to navigate through any begats
and begots or Hittites or Jebusites as I did last
time I read. But speaking of bodies as temples of
the Holy Spirit, during the singing of the first
hymn three late-comers arrived, a trio of young wom-
en who inhabited temples, yea, cathedrals, if I may
say so in the privacy of this diary, of such beauty
and anatomical proportion as any religious or bodily
edifice my eyes have had the privilege of resting
upon. I thought them to be triplets as they appeared
identical in appearance and dress. Their hair was
platinum blond, their skin as smooth as silk--
wearing more face powder than a Chinese opera singer. They wore white, high-collared blouses, open at
the front to reveal a necklace of pearls—no doubt
fakes, but the effect was stunning and around the
collar a light blue silk scarf which matched the
tight, form-fitting blue skirts—short skirts I might
add, coming to the knee and when they did sit down,
the hems were across the top of the knees, the knees
completely exposed, and they were sitting in the
front pew! As the pews were plum full, they had no
choice but to proceed to the very first pew and
there they stood while the congregation was singing
"This is my Father's world, and to my listening
ears ..." I considered stepping down off the platform to give them a hymnal while we were singing,

but Ted Klinetob beat me to it. Their attire was a
stark contrast to the old-fashioned getups everyone
else was wearing. There was nothing old-fashioned
about these girls. Later I learned that these were
the Emerson Sisters, an act out of Davenport, and
their names were Echo, Eos and Eudora--their father
was a professor of Classics at DeKalb University.
Anyway, one curious thing was that during the service, they would cross and uncross their legs--in
unison, like chorus girls. I don't know how they
communicated with each other, but they must have had
a system, because it could not have been coinci-
dental and they did this perhaps three times while
Cushing was preaching on our bodies being temples of
the Holy Spirit. I'm not sure how much of Cushing's
sermon anyone heard, at least anyone seated on the
Good Shepherd side of the church and within three
pews of these sisters. They were quite a distraction
and perhaps that is the effect they intended. You
know how show business people can be.

I saw them later talking to Mrs. Cuttingham and
Mr. Rossi and I knew then that the Emerson Sisters
were in town for more than just singing at the Centennial ...

Cushing, meanwhile, is preaching on the First Corinthians text, and it's becoming a hellfire and
brimstone sermon in the old-fashioned revivalist
style, which he thought wouldn't hurt. He was doing
it up pretty good too, while I noticed the Emerson
Sisters putting on their churchly airs here in the
sanctuary and knew that it wouldn't be long before
they were taking off those same airs and a lot more
in the basement below! They crossed their legs. ...

... Oh, I forgot to mention the essay contest.
During announcements and after the offering, Rev.
Cushing gave the pulpit to Editor Hughes who made a
little speech about the fine work of the contestants
who numbered 21, and explained the purpose of the

contest and the rules, and then announced that the
Second Honorable Mention went to Roy Larson, a junior at Charles City High School; First Honorable
Mention went to Sonja Jorgenson of Bathington, a
senior. And First Place, with the $50 prize and pub-
lication in the newspaper went to, yes, Frances
Katherine Cooper, a junior at Bathington High
School. I heard Frankie squeal and the congregation
broke into applause and all three young people were
invited forward to the platform where Editor Hughes
with Rev. Cushing assisting, delivered congratulations and certificates and cheques for $50, $25, and
$10. Frankie will also be asked to read a condensed
version of her essay at the Saturday afternoon con-
vocation in City Park, at which time she will be
able to meet Senator Charles who will be making a
speech.

August 4, 1952, Monday
The City Park is ready for the 5,000-8,000 visitors
Bathington is expecting this coming weekend. Grand-
stands finished and freshly painted, flower beds
planted with a variety of new annuals including pe-
tunias and marigolds. The Centennial Jail has been
erected and will officially open Thursday morning.
All fines will be donated to charity ...

I had a talk with Cuttingham and begged her to get
the gang out of there as soon as the Centennial is
over if not before. She pointed out some of the
problems with that proposal, viz., all the work they
are doing for the Centennial gratis, she reminded
me. She had a point there. Still it's hard for me to
condone the desecration of holy ground in order to
save a few bucks. But now it's out of my hands. I
thought the least I could do is to try to make sure
that whatever business was being conducted in the
final days of operation were at least confined to
church or centennial business ...

August 5, 1952, Tuesday
All the booths and tables seem to be up in City Park
for vendors, antiques and games of chance. Street
decorations are up thanks to the work of the Decorations committee headed by Martin Becker ... Pageant
dress rehearsal in the evening.

August 6, 1952, Wednesday
I am at Hemming's in my room. It is about 11 p.m.
and I am a complete wreck. Never in my life have I
felt so low and in so much despair as now. I got
home about an hour ago. I am ruined, this is so bad,
am at wit's end, and don't know what to do. I got
home, turned the fan on low to get a breeze going,
it's so hot and sultry up here, turned on the Victrola and listened to Puccini. Poured myself a whiskey and lit my pipe and plopped myself in the chair
and have been thinking and worrying ever since.

   Mrs. Cuttingham's revelation has left me completely whomperjawed.

   I wish I had never applied for the job of temporary typist. I did that only because I thought I
could help out, but since that day my life has been
filled with little but surprise after surprise, and
now, having failed to take decisive action and after
four months of poor decision-making, the pot has
come to a boil and my goose is cooked.

   I suppose I should get some perspective on this
whole disaster and project this experience out fifty
or seventy-five years from now when I am long dead
and gone, and imagine my grand-children or great-
grandchildren reading this sorry report, and whereas
I am anguished, they will no doubt be amused for
there is much in the events of this evening that the
mere passerby might find titillating, but for me as
one of the primary actors in this farce, it is now
anything but amusing and I face a very real chance
of being publicly humiliated and mortified. If Anto-

nia was here ... well, if Antonia was here there's a lot of foolishness I would have avoided.

I need to stop this sniveling and just get the facts down on paper, although God knows why. I need some clarity of mind, and reviewing the events of the evening might help, to wit:

Mrs. Blanche Evans, the pageant director, had called me wanting me to get the pageant programs and bring them over to the school house. I asked her if I couldn't do this tomorrow, but no, she wanted them tonight on account of some volunteers needed to stick some inserts into the programs and with the Centennial kickoff being tomorrow they'd be too busy. And I said you know I don't got no car, and she said yes she knew but could I be a dear and use Millie's and get the programs. It was really important.

So I got Millie to let me use her car--she'd just got back from Avoning--and went down to the church and the Publications Ministry around back and pulled into the parking area. The place looked deserted. It was about 6 p.m. I guess. The sun was already down behind the pines behind the lot. Maybe it was 6:30 p.m. Doesn't matter. I got out of the car, tried the door. It was locked, so I used my key to get in, and walked around the counter to the store room in the back, opened the door and flipped the switch and the bulb blew. It startled me, but I stepped out of the room, now in the area behind the counter intending to turn left down the short hallway to go into the studio so that I could access the janitor's closet inside to get a spare bulb. But first I needed a key as I knew the studio door would be locked so I fumbled around under the counter and found the extra key Alice keeps hidden there. Then, down the hallway to the studio, inserted the key, and then I thought I heard music. I paused, turned the key and pushed and walked into the studio.

I was surprised, shocked actually, for many reasons. I felt visually and aurally assaulted. I was
surprised to hear music and I was surprised that the
lights were on, in fact the photo lighting was on,
and I was even more surprised to see Mr. Rossi in
the room, but was absolutely nonplussed to see the
Emerson Sisters on the "beach." They were getting a
suntan. Well, actually the three of them were sort
of kneeling, if I can explain this right, their
bums--their naked bums I might add--on the heels of
their feet, their backs erect, and Eos the third one
was rubbing oil, probably suntan lotion, onto the
back of Eudora who in turn was rubbing oil on Echo.
They were wearing nothing but ribbons in their hair
and their backs were almost directly to the camera
so the front was not in view but their faces were
turned to the camera, but it was clear they were
dressed in nothing but their birthday suits.

So I took in all of this in seconds and, at the
same time, Mr. Rossi whirled around when he heard
the door open, and we both started talking about the
same time. I rushed forward toward the beach and Mr.
Rossi who had moved away from his camera. In hindsight I should have just skedaddled because I saw
stuff I should not have seen. One's nakedness is
something one should keep to one's self, but that
clearly was not the philosophy operating here. Hey,
says Rossi. And I think I said something like what
are you guys doing? You can't be doing this I said.
This has got to stop now I says. And I heard Mr.
Rossi trying to calm me down as though I was a child
who simply needed to be placated and then I'd go
away. Calm down, he says.

Calm down? I says. How can I calm down with this—
this, all of this? The Emerson Sisters were still on
the beach and I addressed them saying I'm sorry ladies but this is not the time nor the place and
you're going to need to leave. And to get some

clothes on. And I shouldn't have said all that because then the ladies turned and STOOD UP—oh, this
was too much—and started giggling and came over to
me jiggling, and I think Echo was on my right and
Eos and Eudora on my left. I was wearing a short
sleeve dress shirt, bowtie, slacks, my usual attire
for a hot summer day, and I could feel their skin on
my skin and I mention that only because that was an
experience I'd not experienced for many years and it
was happening right there and Mr. Rossi was a witness to it all. The girls are jabbering at me to let
them finish this shoot, and Mr. Rossi is yelling at
them to get back on the beach, and Echo and Eos on
my left and right have me by the arm. I am trying to
wrestle—gently—free while at the same time speak my
mind—my purpose was to shut this operation down then
and there. This had to stop. But the girls were pawing at me, and cooing and wooing, one had her arm
around my waist, and in the struggle my arms were
around their waists, and Eos was at my cheek to
plant a kiss and while Echo had squirreled around in
my grasp so that she was facing away from me and
whereas my arm had been around her back, it was now
around her chest and I realized I now had a handful
of bosom in my grasp. It was at this moment—as
though a flashbulb went off--this moment when Eos
had her lips to my cheek and when my hands were fon-
dling bosoms and bums that I heard an awful shriek—
a screech actually, like the deep-throated cry of a
peacock--and I looked up monkey-eyed--I think we all
did--and there filling the door frame to the studio
with her considerable and formidable bulk was the
be-feathered and red-faced Mrs. Clarice Broughton--

Chapter XXVIII

COOP HERE IS UNABLE TO GO on. He will not touch the typewriter again for several weeks but the scene he was describing does in fact continue to roll. Mrs. Broughton steps into the studio and bellows, "What is the meaning of this!?"

"You can't come in here!" shouts Carlo, jumping like he'd just stepped on a carpet tack. He moves toward her, his arm extended as though to usher her out by her elbow. Turning to the Emerson Sisters he says, "Leave Coop alone and get into some clothes." Mrs. Broughton shrugs his hand away and moves toward a table on which are some copies of *Gals & Dolls*. "That looks a lot like Sally Hildebrand, to me," she says contemptuously. She flips through the magazine. "If I look a little harder, am I likely to find anyone else I know? The Ladies Aid?" She pauses at one photo. "Who's this?" she asks abruptly folding the magazine and holding up a page. "The big hat, sunglasses and fan don't fool me, not for a minute. I know this person. I've seen her somewhere."

"I do not divulge the names of our models and clients," Carlo replies coolly, retreating to his camera. "Now, please will you please get the f**k out so that we can finish up our work here?"

"Mr. Cooper," Broughton bellows. She slings the magazine down on the table. "Can you explain to me exactly what is the nature of the work to which Mr. RRRRossi here alludes?" She rolls the R on Rossi.

Coop is sitting lugubriously on the beach, groaning, his head in his hands.

"This is an outrage," Broughton continues, now on a rampage, stomping about the room, pausing in front of Coop and at times shaking a fleshy ring-bedecked finger in the face of Mr. Rossi. "There are obscenity laws in this state, and this is taking place not only in my *town*, and not only on the *centennial* of the founding of our beloved town—indignities enough—but is being produced, spawned, from the womb of the church. I will not have it. I will *not* have it! Out there—" She waves a hand wildly to indicate "out there"—"the church is trying to feed the poor and clothe the children, while in here, we're feeding the rich and disrobing the children! Where do you find these trollops anyway, these ill-begotten wenches who live in such a moral vacuum as to be so easily talked out of their garments, and in what house of ill repute or irreligion were you raised, Mr. Rossi, that you could come into a religious sanctuary without moral hesitation, without fear of divine rrrretribution and participate in these depravities? It defies an answer! Why, it's beyond belief! I doubt that *anyone*, without evidence, would believe this tale were I to tell it. If I hadn't seen it with my own eyes, even *I* wouldn't believe it, and I am by nature a suspicious person. This is just the sort of thing that I would be inclined to believe, except this—no, I could not even believe this! And unfortunately the evidence is of such an immoral character and of such a lurid and degenerate nature that I could scarcely bring myself to show it to anyone—but yes, it will be told, and you can be sure that federal authorities in Des Moines will be interested in what is going on here, you can be sure of that—"

"Why Mrs. Broughton, I can't be sure of that at all, I'm afraid." Coop, still sitting on the beach has been staring at his feet in utter despair. It is not the despair of grief, deep and steady, like when Antonia passed; it is suppressed panic, like staring into the fangs of a snarling German shepherd when you're trying to burgle a house. But at the sound of *this* voice, he looks up. It is Mrs. Cuttingham! She looks sharp. Her face, tan from the summer sun, is set off by the highlights of her hair, brushed back, revealing pearl earrings. Her dress is a svelte, tight one piece that comes smartly to the knees and hugs her figure perfectly, leaving no doubt as to her gender or her grace. A woman and a lady! The outfit is cream-colored with broad, dark blue panels that curve around from top to the hem in an S-fashion. A red belt finishes the effect as does the red handbag she's carrying. At the appearance of Mrs. Cuttingham, Coop feels a sense of relief in his soul like he's been lowered into a bathtub of ice water, although he has no reason to feel such relief. Truth is, there is little that Broughton has said in her self-righteous monologue with which he has disagreed. What now can Cuttingham do except to cut her losses and get out? It is quite likely that Cuttingham knows this. She understands that when you don't have a hand you fold and leave the table. And her philosophy is—and she'd explained this to Coop on other occasions—that everyone at least once, and usually more than once, in their lives comes to that time when you got to get up from the table and leave, taking with you what you got before you lose it all, and then get in a fresh game at some other time. Coop is quite sure that Cuttingham will cut her losses, but she is going to leave the table with as much as she can get. Coop has no energy to even get up to acknowledge her arrival. So it is Cuttingham who first addresses Coop.

"Mr. Cooper, you're looking so, so ... baleful tonight," she says cheerfully. "What's the matter?"

Coop smiles wanly and waves his hand at the Emerson Sisters who have now returned to the beach with clothes on.

"I can tell you what ails Mr. Cooper," says Mrs. Broughton sternly. "He has a bad case of buyer's remorse. Or perhaps it a sudden attack of a *rrrrighteous* conscience. I suppose there are other possibilities as well."

Cuttingham turns from Cooper to Mrs. Broughton. "You go ahead and call the feds in Des Moines and let me know when they get here and when you're done with them, because then I'd like to have a little chat with them."

"About what?" Rossi now edges in from the shadows for a better listen.

"Before I get to that, may I ask who was it that signed the lease papers authorizing my friends here to work at the Publications Ministry?"

"What are you talking about?"

"Not a hard question, Mrs. Broughton. You're the head of the Session. Who signed the papers?"

"I did, of course, but—"

"And who signed the papers bringing the Publications Ministry into being."

"I did. This is—"

"So if I understand this right, you're going to call the feds and tell them this cockamamie tale, and expect them to come up here on a wild goose chase to investigate a claim for which you know there will by then be no evidence whatsoever—against an organization you yourself approved, condoned, and enthusiastically supported! Doesn't make a whole lot of sense, does it?"

"You wouldn't lie to a federal investigation," Broughton sneers. "You'd be setting yourself up for criminal charges for obstructing justice, or confabulating a story or some such thing. I am sure my lawyer will think of something."

"Of course, I'd lie," Cuttingham laughs. It's a mocking laugh deliberately offered for effect. "My sense of morality has several layers. I'll feed a stray cat back to health, give clothing to an orphanage and throw a saw-buck into the offering plate but assisting the federal government of the United States of America in their phony prosecution of Bible Belt morali-ty laws is not high on my list."

Mrs. Broughton is silent. Then she steps closer to Cuttingham, not far from Coop. His head is still bowed and now as he stares morosely ahead, he sees but two pairs of feet and legs. One set is thin and toned, and bal-anced in shiny red heels. The other pair of legs is lumpy and the feet are pushed into black granny shoes that are a size too small, so that the flesh looks like bread dough overflowing a pan. The shoes are facing each oth-er. Coop imagines that the shoes are talking to each other. The black granny shoes say: "Well, you're probably right. People like you of selec-tive moral ideals are people with no morals at all. Morality is not some-thing you choose, you know. Religious values are not something for which you shop at the department store. Ethics and morals are not plates or entrées at a cafeteria and you get to pick and choose what you like and what you don't like." Now the granny shoes begin to move. In a shrill, stage voice, and prancing around like a show horse mare, Broughton con-tinues: "I'll have the tenderloin instead of the meatloaf, the broccoli in-stead of the beans, the crème brulee instead of the pudding. I'll take a little lie today instead of a little honesty, a little malice instead of modesty, with a side dish of vulgarity, and for dessert a trollop and a tart. Perhaps on the *morrow* I'll partake of some faith, hope and charity and some good, old-fashioned decency." She modulates now to her own voice and the black shoes return to face the red shiny ones: "Well, none of that for me. Oh, no. I *stand* for something. I make things *happen.* You ... you are just a *happening.*" Coop imagines her wrist flapping dismissively. "Yes, yes, *you* may lie when it's convenient, and *you* would probably lie even to a G-man, but Mr. Cooper here will not. *He* saw what was going on tonight. He knows what is going on and—"

"—Excuse me, if I may, Mrs. Broughton," says the shiny red shoes sharply. They take a step toward her. "It will not be necessary to test the integrity of Mr. Cooper in this matter, and you are quite right about him, there's probably not a more noble soul in the town of Bathington or Clearwater County than Mr. Cooper. I quite agree. But you, Mrs. Brough-ton are full of claptrap, if I may say so—and believe me, other words comes to mind—a hypocrite. One of those Pharisaical snipes, what did Jesus say about them? I've listened to a sermon or two, you know. That they're like the tombs of Jerusalem that look so pretty on the outside but inside they reek of dead men's bones. You're a big bag of bones, Broughton, and you stink. You think we don't know—that the whole town doesn't know—what you did to Joel Shimel and his family? That we don't know how you threw your weight around to get his business closed? How you *falsified* documents to justify your actions? You make me sick, you Pharisaical, hypocritical, self-*rrrr*ighteous Hotentot." She mimicks Broughton rolling R technique. Coop looks up now to see Cuttingham pushing in to Broughton. She sticks a finger in her face. She's clasping her red handbag with the other. Broughton leans back in alarm, grimacing. "Now, see here—" she sputters.

"No, you see here," Cuttingham says firmly. "I've learned a few things in the school of hard knocks, and one tried and true rule is that those who think the world's painted in only two colors, Black and White, and those who think there are only two directions, Left and Right, and that there are only two values, Good and Bad, who talk the loudest about Right and Wrong—well they're seldom right and they're usually wrong, and they're always as phony as a three dollar bill. You're phony baloney, Broughton." She turns around quickly and dashes over to Cooper, who's still sitting on the beach, but listening raptly, head up. Mr. Rossi has joined him, but he appears to show little interest. Cuttingham puts her hand on Coop's shoulder and looks back to Broughton who's half hidden in the shadows created by the arc of the photo lighting. "What Cooper here has is integrity. What he doesn't have is sanctimony. He has morals, but he's no moralist. That's the difference, an irony, really, don't you think, between him and you." Cuttingham drops her hand from his shoulder and leaves him and begins to move again toward Broughton. "You are morally corrupt but think you're such a saint; whereas Coop— look at him—is morally pure, but thinks he's such a sinner."

"What I think is that I've heard quite enough," says Mrs. Broughton, making a show of leaving.

"Actually, you haven't heard anything of what I came here to say," Cuttingham says, moving toward the door to cut off her retreat. "I came here looking for you. Embezzlement, misapplication of funds, making false statements to a bank in order to obtain a loan, bank bribery, and false entries in bank books."

Broughton is short of breath, and a hand goes to her upper chest. "Why, whatever are you talking about?"

"You know exactly what I'm talking about, sweetie."

"I absolutely do not, and … and—" Broughton's voice catches, "even if I did, how would you know about such things?"

Rossi has stopped fiddling with the camera and equipment. Echo, Eudora and Eos are huddled on the beach, fully clothed. Next to them is Coop, whose hands are now in his lap and his back is erect and head held high. Suddenly, he believeth his redemption draweth nigh.

Cuttingham opens her red handbag and withdraws a black wallet. With one hand she flips it open and shows it to Broughton, as though presenting her credentials. "What does it say, Broughton?"

The old lady, flushed and nervous, peers at the wallet. Then, she withdraws suddenly as though she'd peered into a ViewMaster and seen a naughty picture. "FBI?" she exclaims in shock.

Coop and the Emerson Sisters leap to their feet like they'd been bitten by fire ants. "FBI?" they sing out in unison.

"I was going to arrest you, Broughton," she says, returning the wallet to the purse and withdrawing a pair of shiny handcuffs from her bag, "but instead—"

"Arrrrrrest me?" Broughton sputters. "You can't arrest me!"

"Yes, I can," Cuttingham says evenly, knowing that the momentum has turned her way. She puts the handcuffs back in her handbag, but withdraws a handkerchief. She dabs at her brow. "But instead, as I was saying, I changed my mind and decided that I would give you a courtesy call, sort of a warning, to advise you that there is an arrest warrant for you, but I do not need to be the arresting agent. And I expect that you will extend a similar courtesy to Mr. Rossi and his co-workers as well."

"You were going to arrest *me*, a God-fearing, law-abiding citizen, and yet allow these delinquents here to continue to traffic in immorality—"

"Broughton! You're not law-abiding and you obviously don't fear God. I suspect God fears you. Don't push me, or I'll just march you out of here now. Mr. Rossi and his work is none of your concern. This is a separate investigation that goes far beyond Bathington. Sometimes law enforcement agencies need to use—how should I put it—unconventional means to hook the big fish, you know? So my advice to you is to scram, and keep your big mouth shut, 'cause if you breathe a word of this, I will hunt you down like a dog and haul you away. You understand my meaning?"

Broughton says nothing but, instead, turns to the door, takes a last look at Cuttingham and the others—Coop, the Emerson Sisters and Rossi huddled around her—and then leaves, closing the door behind her.

Chapter XXIX

WHEN BROUGHTON LEAVES, THE STUDIO IS quiet like the silence after a thunderstorm. Then Cuttingham throws her red handbag on the small table atop the offending magazines and turns to face the group. She tells the sisters to gather their things and to head for Duluth on the evening train. "Carlo, darling, go back to the farmhouse; we'll have a sit down later in the evening. I'm going to chat with Mr. Cooper here, then I will join you."

Within ten minutes they are gone, and Mrs. Cuttingham and Mr. Cooper are alone on the beach. They say nothing for a few minutes. It's the type of interlude during which each party is mulling the choice of words to use to broach a subject they feel to be awkward. "Don't say anything, Coop," Cuttingham murmurs with a sigh. "I need a drink. Let's go to Bud's." Coop stands up, and offers Cuttingham a hand. She's up suddenly with his help but stumbles into his arms and stays there. "Oh, Coop, what a mess!"

They drive to Bud's Tavern in Cuttingham's car. Coop is nervous. It's twilight now. The western sky is patterned with gauzy, flat and layered clouds of yellow, gray and purple. Coop orders a Hamm's, Cuttingham a scotch. Then she pulls out her cigarette case and extracts a smoke. Coop is alarmed. "You're not going to smoke that, are you?"

Cuttingham's penciled eyebrows arch in surprise. "What the hell do you think I'm going to do with it, then?"

Coop whispers, "Well, you just don't see women in these parts smoking in public, you know, least-wise not women who care about their reputation."

"There you go, Coop," she says, laughing. Her lighter clicks, and a flame appears. She lights the cigarette and takes a drag and expels the smoke like it's the exhaust from a steam engine. "I don't care."

"Oh, alright."

"Do you care?"

"Oh, no, it's fine, it's fine." There's a hint of pique in his voice.

"But you care about what others might think of me, don't you? That's really sweet."

"Well …"

"Aren't you supposed to be rehearsing for the pageant right now?" she asks kindly, changing the subject.

"Mmm." Coop drinks his beer. "I'm a judge in the Clearwater County court scene, but after tonight, well, I'd be no good to the theater!" He takes another swallow. "I don't know what's going on, Mrs. Cuttingham. A few months ago my life was such a mundane, non-descript, you could say *boring*, life—well, not really boring, I was happy, you know, but my life was just *uneventful*, and I was quite happy with it, but the day you came into town, the same day as the fire, the same day as Violet dies, or *apparently* dies, Elizabeth Morley, whatever her name is—well, since then it's all been so different." They sit in silence. Coop drinks, Cuttingham nurses the scotch. They are not looking at each other. Coop has his hands around the beer mug and is staring past it at the wooden table top. It's full of names and declarations of love etched into the surface by a pen knife. Cuttingham is limp-wristing her cigarette, and now when she exhales the smoke it is slow, and relaxed.

They're sitting at a corner table far from the bar. A small window above them has a neon beer sign in it which casts a blue glow over the couple below. "It actually started the day I applied for the typist's job," Coop continues, "which is the same day I started keeping a diary. You know, Mrs. Cuttingham, it's as though, until then, there wasn't really much to record in a diary—a *diary*!? What do I want with a *diary*? Nothing happens! What do I write about, you know? And *why*? I certainly am not hoping it will someday be read. It's private you know. And besides, no one reads diaries, unless you're a president, or famous writer, or something."

Coop pauses. Cuttingham does not interrupt. "Sometimes, writing in my diary clarifies my thinking when I'm troubled by something and there's value to that I guess. But, that's all beside the point. I decide to keep a diary, my dreary, mundane life notwithstanding, and *bam*! The good Lord throws all of this interesting—distressing, really—stuff at me that gives me more stories and tragedies than I can handle. I've sunk so low, cavorting with naked ladies, and now I'm skipping out of rehearsal … The director's going to kill me, and maybe Millie too … Well if anyone complains, I'll just say I was detained by the FBI!" He chuckles lamely. Cuttingham smiles wanly.

Coop finds his pipe and pouch, and begins packing and tamping. "I can't believe you're an FBI agent, a G-man ... all this time! ... But, you know, thinking about it, I thought it was strange that when Broughton said 'FBI' and we all jumped up shocked beyond belief, only Mr. Rossi said nothing. He already knew! And now, looking back on the last few months, your frequent appearances when Cushing and I were being questioned by Marshal Cutler, and I know you met with that heavyset FBI guy in Des Moines, and your interest in Violet's case, it all adds up in hindsight. I don't know why I didn't guess it sooner, well, I didn't guess it at all, but then, how many female G-men are there?" His pipe goes in his mouth and he strikes a match and begins puffing.

"I suppose there aren't any female G-*men*," Cuttingham says wryly, blowing a stream of smoke into the haze around Coop's pipe. She reaches in her bag and withdraws her pocket purse and opens it. "Here, Coop, take a look." She slides the wallet toward Coop. It shows her FBI credentials. Coop lifts it to his face to read it better in the dim light. In large bold type he sees the acronym, F.B.I. A seal is affixed to the side. Beneath these letters is Cuttingham's name, and beneath her name in small type are the words: Federal Bureau of Idiots. Below this line is a brief descriptive paragraph the contents of which Coop would never read out loud in polite company or even impolite company. He looks up at Cuttingham in wonderment, "Oh, boy, aren't you in trouble now, impersonating a cop!"

Cuttingham says: "Yeah, it's a pretty pickle, alright, although I never said I was FBI. Broughton said that. I simply showed her my credentials. Not my fault she didn't read them."

"Yeah but you said you were going to arrest her, and made claims about shenanigans at the bank—"

"All true by the way, which is why she's not going to say anything, and as for arresting her, I could have arrested her as a citizen, or at least detained her, and allowed the marshal and feds to investigate."

"I don't know ... I think she can get you in trouble. She's a formidable woman—" At this Cuttingham frowns. "—but not as formidable as you, of course, but still, there's bound to be trouble ..."

"I don't think so, but you were right about this: Our time here in Bathington is coming to a close. The only messy part is how to pull it

off—I got to give that some thought and talk to the chilblains about it."
She lights another cigarette. Coop looks around. The place has filled up,
mostly out-of-towners for the centennial, Coop imagines. A couple
across the way is slow-dancing to a melancholy tune on the jukebox. The
bartender's wife, Dottie, is helping him at the bar, tending to three guys
and one woman at the bar. Coop does not recognize the woman. A bar-
maid is working the floor. No one appears to be drunk—yet. No sign of
Jules—yet. *He's bound to show up to give a limerick performance for a free beer or
two. It's probably too early. Boy, he sure created a ruckus the last time I was here with
Violet. We had to help him back to the hotel!*

"Hey!" Coop says suddenly. "I think the last time I was here was with
Violet!"

"You don't get out much, Coop," Cuttingham says smoothly.

"Well, I drink at home," he says lamely.

"The worst kind of drunk," she says, laughing quietly.

"Can I ask you something?" he asks, leaning forward. Cuttingham
nods, and takes a drag on her cigarette. "How come you got a pair of
handcuffs in your purse? When I saw those I thought you were an FBI
agent for sure!'

Cuttingham smiles and almost laughs. She leans toward her companion. "Coop, dahling, do you really want to know why I have a pair of
handcuffs in my purse and what I do with them." Her gaze meets his directly. Her eyes are light and eager, her mouth and red lips parted, awaiting his answer. She does not move. In that moment, Coop thinks she is
beautiful, her toney skin, the hair falling appealingly around her ears, her
features fine and pleasing. Coop breaks her gaze and sits back and shakes
his head. "No, no, I guess not. I don't think I want to know." He has no
idea why this is a line of conversation it would be wise not to pursue, but
whatever Cuttingham's answer might be, for some inexplicable reason
Coop thinks it might be naughty. How or why he has no idea. "No," he says,
"Don't tell me."

Cuttingham takes another drag on her cigarette and flicks the ash into
the ashtray with the Hamm's bear logo. "You're a memory weaver, Coop."

He stares at her. "What?"

"It's why you keep a diary, Coop. You're like a weaver sitting at a
loom. Each day is a thread and each thread is a different color or hue.
Every day you sling the shuttle across the warf and woof of your life and
thread by thread, day by day, a pattern emerges, and someday, you'll stand

back and look at 1952, and you'll see a tapestry, a tapestry of memories, and you'll look at it and it will give you pleasure. You're a writer—a weaver—of memories, and that's one of many things I like about you."

Coop nods and sucks on the pipe stem, and exhales. "Been a lot of warf and even more woofing in my life lately, seems like … and speaking of memories … I remember when I first applied for the typist job—volunteered is a better word—I walked into the church office and Violet was on the phone. She was talking to someone, and that someone was you, Mrs. Cuttingham. So my question, one I've been struggling with, is: How is it that you know Violet Crenshaw?"

Now, Coop is the one who grabs her gaze and holds it. Her eyes widen and her mouth shuts. She sits back, takes a sip of her scotch and pulls on her cigarette. "Why on *earth* would you ask me such a question?"

"I'd like to think," Coop says earnestly and quietly, "that while you might lie to others, perhaps you would not lie to me. I know you know, or knew, Violet, Penny. I just can't figure out how."

Cuttingham is silent and Coop decides not to press his advantage—for now. At that moment, Coop sees that Jules has arrived. *Here we go!* He turns back to Mrs. Cuttingham who is putting out her cigarette. She folds her hands on top of the table and looks directly at Coop and says, "You're confused about me, aren't you Coop? You don't know what to make of me. You don't know if you like me, maybe even love me. You're a little bewildered. One moment you refer to me as Mrs. Cuttingham; the next moment it's Penny. Am I Mrs. Cuttingham to you, or am I Penny?"

"Well—" Coop is nonplussed but quickly regains the edge. "You're changing the subject, a transparent avoidance tactic."

Cuttingham laughs nervously. "Yes, Coop, I know Violet, I will not lie to you, but, but—" Coop is about to interject. "—I don't want to discuss this *now*, okay?"

"If not now, when?" Coop says, agitated. "This could be crucial to the investigation!"

"No it's not, trust me," she says firmly, lips tight. "But right now it's late, and it's a long story, and I'm going back to the farmhouse. I will tell you all about it within a couple of days—before I blow this town, okay? Promise."

"No, please, Penny! You can't leave this way—and if it's possible I'd rather you not leave at all, not now or in a couple of days!" Cuttingham stands and picks up her handbag and then her scotch and throwing her head back takes the rest of the glass and sets it back hard on the table. She takes but a couple steps to Coop and lets a hand rest on his shoulder. She leans toward him slightly.

"Coop," she says faintly, as though she's about to utter a dying declaration, "You're sweet. That's the nicest thing anyone, anyone, has said to me in *years!* And I love you for it. Now I will tell you this: Violet Crenshaw was—and is—my sister."

And with that she is gone.

Chapter XXX

AS THE BATHINGTON CENTENNIAL BEGINS TO roll toward the glorious gathering Saturday afternoon in the park, other matters are likewise being resolved as inexorably as most things in life are. Cuttingham and Broughton are passing through a valley of decision and, for both of these dowagers, the way seems dark and uncertain.

Mrs. Penelope Cuttingham returns to the farmhouse and into the hours of that same night, and throughout the following day, discussions continue as to the best course of action for the Publications Ministry team and their other business and publication ventures. They must leave; the question is when. Cuttingham does not believe Broughton will keep quiet. She counsels an early departure, perhaps Saturday morning or afternoon. A good time to slip out of town might be in broad daylight when thousands of people will be drawn to the park where the Centennial conclave will be held. Leaving at night is a problem because discovery is more likely then, lights, prying neighbors, and so on, than were they simply to back up the truck and load the pages they had printed awaiting binding and stitching, and load the boxes onto the truck and head for Davenport. Perhaps they could get the press later. Who knows?

Deep in an inner room of her three story, varnished Victorian house, Mrs. Clarice Broughton weighs her options. She sits soddenly in a wing-back chair beneath a portrait of her late husband. She does not know how Cuttingham knows what she knows, but she knows. She is not troubled by Cuttingham's threat to arrest her or to call in the F.B.I. She recognizes a con when she sees one, and it didn't hurt that when Cuttingham flashed those phony F.B.I. credentials that Broughton knew immediately the badge was a fake. A woman like her, with the banking connections she has, certainly has met a federal officer or two in her day. No, Cuttingham is a rotten tomato in a patch of rotten tomatoes and if Broughton has her way, she is going to make a spicy tomato soup. As for her business affairs at the bank, there isn't a judge or jury in the county that won't believe that if there were improprieties, they were transgressions of ignorance not of intent. Yes, she might have to pay some fines, re-file some papers, but there would be no arrest, and certainly, she shuddered at the thought, no incarceration! Yes, she would call the F.B.I. alright. Fortunately we live in a Christian country and where the law of the land still frowns on immorality; where adultery, sodomy and the dissemination of vulgar and obscene literature are still crimes. She is quite certain that a further investigation will no doubt reveal that Cuttingham and her little Chinese friend are card-carrying Communists!

And so, two decisions are made. A flight and a fight. Cuttingham and gang begin preparations to flee, aiming for a departure by Saturday noon to the sound of the umphas of the tubas, the trills of flute and fife and the rattling of snare drums as the marching band kicks it up in the parade and city park. Broughton places an urgent phone call to Des Moines. The earliest authorities can be in Bathington, she is told, is Saturday morning.

# # #

Saturday morning breaks sunny and warm, although breezy. It's a perfect day for travel, for an arrest, for a parade.

The parade is scheduled to begin 11 a.m. Already two days into the Centennial observance, the town, but for the mechanized vehicles, telephone poles and lines, electric signs and lights, and thousands of outside visitors, looks as though it has been brought forth from the mid-nineteenth century. This impression is fortified by the fact that not a living being appears in modern dress. Men are in old-fashioned work clothes and boots or gussied up in plus fours, or suits and vests. The women wear bonnets and high-collared blouses with wide skirts, pantaloons and hooped underskirts. Even Baxter the beagle has on a pair of overalls with tiny, short pants, and a red bandana around his neck.

Providing security for the events of the day is the responsibility of the marshal's office. Several thousand people are expected to be in town for the day and that's too many folk for the marshal and his deputy to handle by themselves. Most of the visitors will be well-behaved, but in a crowd this size, odds are that a certain number of "undesirables" will show up, and others will drink too much and cause a lot of mischief. That's why the marshal in such cases turns to the Bathington Brigade, a posse of roughly a dozen local citizens who meet regularly for some basic law enforcement training. They do target practice, ride their horses, and then mostly sit around and shoot the breeze, drinking beer and talking about their wives. Today, the Bathington Brigade has mounted up. They're easy to spot because they are a mounted unit, and wearing cowboy gear: white hat, black pointy boots spit-shined, a gun belt without the gun, Levi's, bolos in front and a red bandana in back. Their shirts are short-sleeved and green bearing the name of their unit on the back, and the initials BB on the flap of the breast pocket. They have been assigned to the parade and will accompany it into town until it gets to city park, whereupon they are to disperse and patrol the area and take care of problems as they may arise.

The "jail" is already filling up, mostly with men who have violated the whisker code in some way, although Mrs. Lottie Kemp is incarcerated for dressing like a man. Coop, himself, is scheduled to do time for an hour on account of his absence from pageant rehearsal Wednesday night, after which he'll be released upon paying a fine.

The parade, however, is the main attraction. It is a gigantic affair that includes more than 100 units, counting floats, cars, tractors, marching bands, ox-teams and various horse-drawn contrivances. Hoping to get First Prize in the float division is the church entry, a cooperative project of all the local churches, except for Sacred Heart. The float, pulled by a little gray Ford tractor, is of a quintessential white country church with a steeple over the doors. Of course it is just a replica and was made with two by fours and lathe wood with chicken wire stretched over a frame. The chicken wire has been stuffed with tissues to create the effect of a white church. The "stained glass" effect of the windows, two on each side of the church, was created by a variety of flower blossoms to make the shape of a cross. Thaney Waite, who also plays a hefty Santa Claus at the department store, stands in front of the church door dressed up as the Good Shepherd, arguably the oldest and heaviest Lord and Savior Good Shepherd ever to reprise the role. To complete the image he's carrying a squirming and bleating lamb in his arms. The area around the "church" and the "congregation" area had been sodded with fescue, and periodically the lamb on a leash is let down to do its business in the grass.

In front of the church are three pews of folding chairs, three chairs to a row. On these chairs sit the "congregation" which consists of the town pastors. In front of the float and the "congregation" is a large pulpit at which one of the pastors stands, taking a shift of five minutes before being replaced by a different man of the cloth. While at the pulpit the pastor *pro tem* waves to the cheering crowds along the parade route who are sitting on the curbs, or in folding chairs, or on blankets under an elm or oak. Perhaps they are drinking lemonade offered by Vic and Missy Chambers who have set up a series of "ade stations" along the parade route hoping to turn Bathington's thirst into a small fortune, a windfall, Millie told Vic, that would be tithed to the church.

While the parade units assemble on the north end of town, Cuttingham, Carlo, Wason and Alice appear at the Publications Ministry about 9:30 a.m. Broughton is nowhere to be seen. They do not expect to see her, but they enter the offices warily. Failing to find her, Alice leaves in search of the same whom they suspect is at the city park. Alice is to keep watch on her, and on the look out for long black shiny cars coming through town occupied by serious middle-aged men in dark suits. After she leaves, they get to work off-loading some empty cardboard liquor boxes in which to stuff reams of printed pages of naked girls. They will collate and staple later in Davenport. Larger boxes are used to stuff supplies and equipment such as ink, cameras, filters, light stands, backdrops and more. Some of it will be thrown into the back of the truck as is.

Broughton is already at the city park. She is aware that officers are en route from Des Moines and has no desire to be around the Publications Office when arrests are made. In fact, it gives her more pleasure to think of herself as someone removed from the dirtiness of this affair, keeping her gloves clean as it were, orchestrating events from a lofty loge in the balcony.

Thousands, even at mid-morning, are milling around in the park, setting up picnics, or visiting the nearby runway where games of chance are taking place, or listening to some of the early "acts" which are taking place on stage. They have chosen to be in the park when the parade goes by on Main Street, rather than set up somewhere along the route itself.

Coop is here too. He has not talked to Cuttingham since the startling revelation of Wednesday night. He assumes Cuttingham is still in town because she promised to see him again and explain more of her relationship with Violet Crenshaw whom she revealed is her sister. But now, as one of the senior citizens of this town, and indeed, the last surviving male with Bathington blood in him, he strolls about the park in his snappy plus fours, white cotton shirt and red suspenders, visiting with long time friends and residents, enjoying his role as the face of Bathington. He smiles and nods at friendly faces, people whom he presumes are nodding at him with knowing glances, aware of his illustrious forebears. They whisper and he laughs inwardly because they are unaware that he can divine what they're thinking and saying. He sees Alice. She is wearing a long, ankle-length red cotton skirt with a matching blouse. It has high-cut short sleeves in the Chinese style with a Mandarin collar, butterfly fasteners, with an elaborate dragon pattern running from stem to stern. On one side, her left side, the skirt is slit from the hem to well above the knee, mid-thigh, perhaps. Coop did not want to dwell on it much. Over her shoulder she carries a black handbag. She seems to be looking for someone. He waves. She waves back, smiles and moves on. Occasionally he sees Millie and Frankie, sometimes walking together, other times not. They're dressed in old-fashioned garb as are all the Bathington residents, both in outfits made for the Sunbonnet Sues.

The wind has kicked up and some of the bunting on the bandstand has whipped loose. Workers are trying to fasten it down. But the zephyr doesn't seriously dampen the fun and enthusiasm. Grady Neilson and his boy are playing catch. Old men are playing horseshoes. The band is still playing, and once again the cooks are at work on the west end of the park with barbecue drums and ten fat hogs that have been roasting since last night. The menu includes corn on the cob, baked beans, pork, potato chips and lemonade. The eating will begin around noon after the parade has passed by, after which people will be invited to listen to the band and some speeches, sit on their blankets, and also to hear Miss Frances Katherine Cooper deliver her speech about Bathington.

In fact he sees Frankie now across the crowd on the south side of the park. She's talking to someone, a man. Coop walks in her direction, still so far away that even if he were to call out to her, she'd not hear him because of the crowd noise, the band playing and children crying. It was curious, though, to see her in this way. Then he realizes that she is speaking with Ronald Harmon! Not again! What is he doing? Is he backsliding into his former habits? Why can't he leave her alone? But Frankie is not running away. She is gesturing and leaning forward into Ronald's face. Harmon is saying something. Frankie is talking back, agitated. Then they turn away and begin walking to the street and incredibly, Frankie climbs up into a pickup while Ronald strolls around to the driver's side. They sputter away.

Coop is fully alarmed, yet cannot imagine why Frankie would leave willingly with Ronald. Something is not right. He starts running to the spot where they'd been talking, and as he does so runs smack dab into Alice. She's surprised by the sudden jolt, whirls around and sees Coop and her appearance softens.

"Alice, Frankie just left in a pickup with Rondo, and I don't know where on earth they're going, but something's wrong because she's supposed to give her speech in a couple of hours and besides it's lunch time." Coop is breathless and feels a tightness in his chest.

"Oh *s**t*, he's up to no good, Coop," Alice says grimly. "We've got to find them. Where's Millie?" Their first task is to get Millie and discuss what they're going to do. They agree that Frankie's in trouble. They spot Millie over by the Centennial Jail. Alice runs on ahead of Coop and reaches her first and explains the situation. By the time Coop arrives, Millie is already in tears. "Frankie was right!" she wails. "A leopard can't change his spots." She wants to know where they might have gone? Back to his house? No, too obvious. In fact they could be out on a country road anywhere. Perhaps at the Clearwater County park on the river? That is just a guess. Millie reminds Alice that she'd found the boys after the prom at the equipment shed on the high school athletic field. Maybe they were there. That lights up a memory in Alice's mind.

"I remember when the boys had been released, that Rondo went after it with me, wanting Lester to tie me up and he said he was going to take me to tracks by the depot because he had a nice place there he'd used before for girls like me, the creep!"

Coop says, "There are a couple of abandoned railroad cars on the south siding. That could be where he is!"

"That's it alright," Alice said. To Millie she says, "Do you want to run and get Marshal Cutler and meet us out there? Coop and I can go right now in Cuttingham's car. I saw the marshal by the band stand. Look for him there. If he's not there, someone will know where he is."

"Okay," Millie says. She's still crying. Alice grabs her and shakes her by the shoulders. "Millie! Snap out of it. Your daughter needs a mother who's isn't falling apart. Now, where's Vickie?"

"She's with ... Oh dear! I lost track of her. I shouldn't leave her, too!"

"She'll be fine. She's probably playing with some friends, let's go, and *you*—get the marshal!"

Coop and Alice run for Cuttingham's car parked on Main Street on the east edge of City Park. As they approach, Alice sees a State Patrol car approaching from the south. "Oh crap," she mutters.

They get in the car and Alice peels out and roars down Main Street as the patrol car, cruising slowly approaches. Suddenly she veers into the center of the street, and blocks the way, and gets out of the car. "Alice, what are you doing?" Coop yells, leaning out of the window.

He watches as Alice runs toward the startled officer in the patrol car. The patrolman has reacted quickly, jumping out of the car, using the front door of the car as a shield and has drawn his weapon. Alice keeps her hands free and in sight and approaches. "Officer, my friend was just abducted. Her grandfather witnessed it. Attempts like this have been made before by this guy and we think we know where he is." Coop sees the office holster his gun as Alice fumbles around in her handbag. She appears to show the trooper some kind of identification—identification?—and then hears her explain where the depot and tracks are. He gets back in the car and takes off down the road. "I told him we'd join him in a minute because Rondo might respond better to familiar voices."

"Sorry, but I got to make a quick stop," Alice says grimly. She's headed for the church and the Publications Ministry. The car speeds into the lot and comes to a screeching halt by the pickup which looks to be completely loaded now. She finds Cuttingham whom Coop now realizes is about to flee town—without saying a word to him. He's bitterly disappointed. Alice tells Cuttingham that a state cop is in town, but that she's diverted him to the depot for a real emergency: Frankie's gone and Rondo's got her.

When they arrive at the depot in West Bathington they spot Millie and the marshal. Parked nearby is the patrol car and the state trooper. "I'm going to go down to those cars on the siding to see what's up," says the trooper. He has his gun drawn.

"Right!" Alice says. "The marshal and I will take the other side." The trooper jogs across some track and then follows them to the railroad cars so that he is not visible from the open doors of the cars. Alice, to Coop's amazement, retrieves a revolver from somewhere within her skirt, and runs stealthily in a crouching position to the far side of the track—gun ready. The marshal follows. There are three railroad cars, doors open, one on the nearest track, and two on the far tracks. The single car is beside one of the other two on the adjacent track.

It doesn't take long for them to realize that no one is here.

They hear the sound of hoof beats. They see someone in black riding hard toward them. It's the preacher! Cushing rides up and comes to a quick halt, and dismounts. "Is everyone safe?" he asks breathlessly. He is then apprised of the situation. Millie comes to him. She hugs him and lays her bonneted head against his chest and sobs. "Thank you for being here, Reverend."

"Of course, Mrs. Cooper," he says awkwardly. "Line of duty, line of duty. Stiff upper lip, now, eh?"

"Oh, Archie! Where could they BE!" she wails.

Just then, they're distracted by an approaching rattle-trap of a pickup truck. It speeds to the patrol car and pulls up so fast that it slides for a couple of feet on the gravel as the brakes are applied. Leaning out the window is Ronald Harmon. He's wearing a baseball cap that says CO-OP on it in yellow letters.

"Come on," he hollers. "Mr. Bandy is holed up in Shimel's house and has Nomes, and Victoria. He has a gun!" The group rushes to the truck in a move that almost looks practiced: Alice, Coop, Millie, Cushing, the marshal, and the State patrolman.

"Where's Frankie?" Coop asks tersely.

"She's out front of the house, yelling at Bandy, hiding behind a car or something. She's getting wild. She's trying to talk Bandy out of this whole idea. He says he is going to set the whole place on fire, that he'll kill the girls and kill himself."

The State patrolman speaks: "What's your name, son?"

"Ronald Harmon."

"Mr. Harmon, I want you to go back into town, and locate the fire chief, and tell him to get to the scene as soon as possible with a fire truck, okay? Mr. Cooper, and Agent Wang, you can come with me in the patrol car if you'd like or go with Marshal Cutler. You, too, Ma'am."

Millie looks at Cushing for a moment, who nods, and she says, "I'm with the Reverend." Whereupon Ronald Harmon flies away for Sully's bridge and East Bathington, Coop rushes for the front seat of the patrol car, and they speed off. Cushing mounts his horse, and then offers a hand to Millie. She places a foot in the stirrup and a hand in Cushing's and swings to mount the horse behind the Reverend. Then with a shout and dig in the horse's flanks, they gallop down the dirt road, the country preacher in his black frock, and the country lady in her prairie dress and sun bonnet. They disappear in a cloud of dust.

Chapter XXXI

THE WIND IS GUSTING. CUTTINGHAM, DRESSED in a fancy royal blue gay nineties dress with bustle, hoops and stays, looks to the sky. Her hat, a broadbrimmed purple affair with a white band and peacock feathers, shades her eyes. She guesses there's going to be a 3 p.m. thundershower. Maybe it will be later. She can hear the parade passing nearby on Main Street. They'll be hitting downtown and the park right about noon. She watches Alice whip out of the parking lot. She turns left to avoid Main Street and the parade. Cuttingham feels badly about Coop. She saw his face. He looked like he'd just swallowed a bottle of Castor oil. *Could you just have a little faith in me, Cooper?* She knows that he thinks she's leaving town without the promised elaboration regarding Violet. She sighs and turns back to the office and the truck, an old beater, 1940 Chevy. It is dark green with black fenders and wheels with red rims. The bumpers are chrome, as is the front grille which angles to a point like the prow of a boat. The spare tire is attached to the passenger side of the truck bed. The windshield wipers hang from above the two panes; one is broken, hanging limply on the glass. The sidewalls of the truck bed are built up with wooden slats to make it possible to stack a load of goods higher and secure the load to the extended wooden frame on both sides. The truck is getting full. It's starting to look like a family from the Ozarks is hitting the road. All that's missing is a rocking chair on top of the paraphernalia.

Wason and Carlo emerge from the office. Wason has some rope with which to tie down the load. They stand by the over-burdened little truck. Carlo leans laconically on the spare tire. Cuttingham reviews the plan. They are to head south, southwest to Davenport and wait. She will join them in a few days. In her absence they can rent a garage for storage and off load the truck. As they are talking Cuttingham sees a state trooper cruise by on Maple. "We've got company," she says grimly. She nods in the direction of the passing car up at the far intersection. "He's looking for the office, and couldn't use Main Street. We don't have much time." Wason begins to unravel his rope. "No time to tie it down. You guys get out of here, and when the coast is clear, stop and tie it down then." Wason is the driver. He gets in behind the wheel. "Is this thing gassed up?" he asks.

"Yes, yes," Cuttingham says urgently. She simply wants to get the truck out of the parking lot and clear of the Publications Ministry. Then it's just another beat up pickup truck. She checks the intersection. The trooper is not in sight. But she knows he's going to find this church soon and probably within another five minutes. "Get out of here!"

Wason starts up the truck and it rattles to life. They pull out of the lot and turn right toward Main Street. Cuttingham returns to the office to retrieve a few items she needs which she puts in her satchel. She closes the door and leaves the Publications Ministry for the last time and begins to walk in the direction of downtown and the city park. *Coop has not seen the last of me.*

Wason drives up to Main Street which is blocked by the parade moving snail-like toward downtown and the park. One of the Bathington Brigade clops by on a high horse. Wason looks for an opening to cross the street, but then has a better idea. "I've always wanted to be in a parade," he says. He sees a float coming. It's got a white church on it and there's a good space behind it. The church and its "congregation" rolls to the intersection. Cushing is riding by the white church on his black circuit-riding preacher horse, dressed in his stern 19th-century western preacher garb, including broad, flat-brimmed hat. He is a study in black and white. His long-sleeved shirt is white, open at the collar. The rest of him is black. He's not wearing the black coat because it's August and it's hot, but his shoes are black, the trousers are black, and supported by black suspenders. The Assembly of God preacher is at the pulpit waving to people and speaking in tongues.

Wason recognizes Cushing and gives him a little wave. Then he pulls the truck laden with folio sheets of Sally Hildebrand, the Emerson Sisters and Naomi Shimel—a bevy of bare backs, breasts and buttocks—on to Main Street, turning right, and moves into the parade itself right behind the toilet paper church with a Good Shepherd, lost lamb and the town preachers. It's an unlikely conjunction of the sublime and the ridiculous, the holy and the profane. "We can break away when we get past the park," Wason says calmly. "No one will know the difference." Carlo lights a cigarette. Wason rolls down his window, and, steering with his right hand, he begins to wave to the children and families along the parade route. "What are you doing?" Carlo hisses. Wason laughs.

And so they motor on. Children point at the dilapidated truck and yell. Oldsters applaud and cheer. They proceed in this fashion for several minutes until they reach the Fulton Street intersection just a block away from the downtown business area. Waiting for the parade to pass by is a car, a state trooper. "Uh-oh," Wason says. He pulls in his hand and grasps the steering wheel with both hands. He's made eye contact with the trooper. He wishes he hadn't, but it had happened in an instant. He averts his eyes and turns to the white church in front of him. He thinks about options. He wonders if perhaps they shouldn't peel off at the next intersection. He checks his side mirror. The trooper has pulled his patrol car in behind them. The red bubble light is flashing, but he doesn't hear a siren. "We got trouble," he says. Carlo can see the trooper in his side mirror which is cracked. "Play it cool," he says, lighting up another cigarette. "We can't outrun a trooper in this jalopy."

"No, but we might be able to get some distance and, with some luck, ditch this truck and get out of here." The plan formulating in his head is to break from the pack at the next intersection. The trooper will probably follow. They'll swing around the block, head back for Main Street and try to time it so that they can speed through the parade, cutting the trooper off and on the other side of the parade at the city park, jump out of the truck abandoning it, and disappear into the crowds of the park and worry about getting out of town later. They'd lose everything but they've had to start over before. They could do it again.

At the next intersection, Wason pulls the wheel and turns left, breaking from the parade. He turns slowly because his truck is top-heavy with pornography. They lumber down a tree-lined street. The trooper turns with them, siren wailing. "Oh, s**t!" Wason says. He continues to the next block, turns right and motors down to the next corner, turning right again, and sees the parade crawling down Main Street. He increases speed hoping to catch the opening behind the white church that they and the trooper vacated. The gray Ford tractor is in sight and then the church itself. Wason puts the metal to the floor and accelerates sharply which causes several of the boxes in the rear to bounce around and then fall off the truck, hitting the pavement and momentarily obstructing the progress of the state trooper following. This does not concern Wason as they're planning to ditch the whole load anyway. Wason approaches the parade as the congregation and white church enter the intersection. He times his speed and pushes hard. A woman and a little girl then begin to cross the street. Carlo removes his cigarette and shouts, "Look out!" Wason cannot continue forward without hitting the couple. Rather than braking, he accelerates and swerves but the burst of speed has removed all possibility that he can clear the intersection behind the white church, so he jerks the steering wheel hard left and spins the truck around the woman and child so that the truck and white church are parallel, but Wason's speed is too great, and he feels the driver side wheels lifting off the ground. He counter-steers, but it's not enough to slow the momentum of the top-heavy pickup. Carlo tosses his cigarette and hangs on for dear life. The vehicle traveling now on two right wheels teeters and collapses on its side into the white church and slides for a few feet, the metal on asphalt creating a screeching commotion like a thousand donkeys braying. It doesn't go far as the truck has caught the flatbed on which the white church is perched and together they twist and grind until both come to a full stop. The float has not overturned, but the impact of the pickup with the float causes the toilet paper church of flimsy construction to tilt, and then to collapse to the street in a tangled mess of lattice, chicken wire and tissue. It quickly becomes a church afire, lit either by Carlo's errant cigarette or some sparks jumping from the collision itself.

The effect of the accident upon their cargo is dramatic, for the boxes are now strewn hither and yon and because of impact have yielded their contents, spewing folios of salacious material all over Main Street. And at the same time, the wind which has been flustering all morning seems stronger here at this intersection than anywhere. With a dust devil here and a gust there, the wind acting like an atmospheric Hoover, as though to clean up the street of the indecent debris, sucks the paper from the street causing the pages to flutter and twist in the wind. Some alight here and others there; some float over the parade; others sail on to the city park, flying high over the trees; some flap low over the sidewalk where pedestrians grab at them; some are thrown against visitors hitting them in the face or legs. People swat at the papers, bat them away or kick them to the side. Not a few pick them up to peruse the contents and it's safe to say that on this night there is many a home in which a Bathington teenager or a husband has squirrelled away a photograph of Sally Hildebrand, the Emerson Sisters, or the anonymous vixen peering at them through sunglasses and a fan.

The accident and fire are a sensation. Thousands of curious fill the street. The parade comes to a standstill. The floats in the rear of centennial train have no idea what is causing the delay, although rising smoke from the downtown area is readily visible, as are what appears to be leaflets filling the air like confetti. The Bathington Brigade rides to the scene of the calamity and move on horseback into the crowd, to disperse the people so that emergency vehicles, including the volunteer fire department, can access the area. By the time the fire people show up to put out the toilet paper conflagration, the fire is spent and nothing is left of the white church but twisted chicken wire. The Good Shepherd has lost his lamb. No one in the congregation is injured.

The intersection is in a state of uproar. The trooper asks one of the Brigade if the posse could do three things: establish a perimeter around the accident scene, disperse the crowd, and arrange for the removal of the overturned Chevy pickup and the church float. Manning, the captain of the brigade, agrees and confers with his colleagues, and the push begins to move the milling crowd away from the scene.

Cushing is off his horse, and he along with the state trooper as well as some passersby converge on the pickup truck and assist in the removal of the two young men from the wreckage. The boys are dazed but otherwise unharmed. Cushing assists them to the ground where they lean against the wreckage. Carlo denies all knowledge of the contents of the cargo, and Wason says nothing. Robbing banks is easier, he thinks.

Remarkably, Broughton has appeared, pushing through onlookers like a bear catching a scent. She, like Cuttingham, is dressed to the nines in purple georgette and a hat as broad and feathery as Cuttingham's. She accosts the trooper and identifies Carlo as a driving force undermining the morals of the Bathington community. She reminds the trooper, who listens politely, that two of the "gang" are missing and must be apprehended.

At this very moment, Cuttingham materializes before their eyes as though she'd ridden the wind. Seeing her, Broughton says "You!" This one word alone and the tone with which it is conveyed expresses both surprise and an accusation without elaborating on either. Surprise: "You! (You have the misfortune to show up at the very moment when the mask comes off, when you are shown to be who you really are.)" Accusation:

"You! (You are the guilty party who has caused so much trouble in this town and you're not going to get away with it)!"

Turning to the trooper she exclaims, "Why, officer, this trollop is the very woman about whom I was speaking. She's the one that ran this outfit that produced this vile and filthy material that's littering our streets right now, not to speak of polluting the hearts and minds of the people. I demand that you arrrrrest her immediately!"

The two doyens of Bathington stand a mere three feet away from each other. The trooper is to the side but between the two like the referee of a heavyweight fight. Cushing lurks nearby as a spiritual presence. With a crooked smile, Broughton says to Cuttingham. "Oh! You thought I wouldn't make the call, didn't you? That I wouldn't call your bluff? That I wouldn't see through that phony—and terrible, I might add— impersonation of an FBI agent, didn't you? Well, you were wrong."

"I wasn't sure," Cuttingham says calmly. "It could have gone either way, I guess, but in the end it didn't really matter. It wasn't the smartest move you've made. Best wishes to you in the future, Mrs. Broughton."

At this blatant and embarrassing show of patronization, Broughton bristles. "Now see here—" But Cuttingham turns to the officer and gives him a large manila envelope. "Here you go, officer. I think you'll find everything you need right there."

"Thank you, ma'am." He takes the envelope from Cuttingham and begins to peruse the contents. Broughton continues to sputter. While the trooper is inspecting the documents, Cuttingham approaches Cushing and sidling up to him, says *sotto voce*: "Thought you'd want to know that Rondo grabbed Frankie and they are believed to be holed up in a railroad car down at the depot. The marshal and another trooper are there, as well as Alice, Millie and Coop."

The Reverend nods, and thanks her and dashes to his steed, mounts the beast, spurs the animal and rides off, one hand on his hat and the other on the reins.

"Beg your pardon, ma'am," the trooper says to Broughton, "would you know where the marshal is?"

"I certainly do not, but I am sure you can use the services of one of these fine men of the Bathington Brigade, and I know he will be glad to escort this harlot to the Centennial jail for the time being—Shorty Hoffman will do it." speaking louder for Hoffman's benefit: "Won't you, Shorty?"

"Why ma'am, that's an excellent idea," the trooper replies to Broughton. He motions to Shorty to approach. He does so on foot, leading his horse. Turning to Broughton he says, "Ma'am, I am placing you under arrest for misuse of public funds, and misappropriation of funds at Bathington State Bank, and other charges as well, which will be explained in full later. For the time being, I am going to ask you to go with—what's your name?"

"Shorty Hoffman."

"—Mr. Hoffman, here to the Centennial Jail, and stay there until the marshal returns and we can provide proper transfer to the City Jail and from there you'll probably go to county lockup until your arraignment or your attorney can arrange for bail. Mr. Hoffman, if you would take these two young men with you and stay at the jail. Keep these three incarcerated there until the marshal returns and we'll take it from there. Understood?"

"Yes, sir!"

"And we need to locate the whereabouts of a Mr. Arthur Bandy," he says.

At first, Broughton is speechless. Then she's incensed. She bellows: "This is rrrrrrridiculous! If this is your idea of a joke, some sort of prank, yes that's what it is. Centennial humor! Very funny. Well, enough of this claptrap. Enough! Do you understand me? BeHOLD the woman! This is the person you want." She fingers Cuttingham.

The trooper moves to Broughton and places a firm hand on her elbow as a suggestion that she move along. "Ma'am, do not make this difficult. Please go now with Shorty, and when the marshal returns, more can be explained."

At this, Broughton can scarcely be restrained. The litany of abuse goes roughly along these lines: "This is a travesty! I am innocent! You'll pay for this! I had nothing to do with this! It was all Art Bandy's idea. He's the bank officer. He's the one. You'll rrrrrot in hell for this! You are the devil's seed! I will not be treated like a common criminal! I will not be publicly humiliated!"

But she is. At first, many people think she is spending time in jail as a benevolent gesture, albeit somewhat out of character, on behalf of the "Have a Cow" charity. But news of the charges traveled fast, and it is not long before the truth is out.

Chapter XXXII

WHEN THE REVEREND AND MILLIE GALLOP up to Shimel's house, they see a small crowd of people have gathered across the lane to observe the goings-on. Millie dismounts but Cushing stays on his mount.

"Reverend, could you get these people to move down to the end of the block?" the state patrolman asks. "We have a hostage situation here, and a man with a gun. He's already fired shots. We need to get them out of here." Alice and Coop have exited the car, and Millie now rushes to Coop's side. Frankie is in the Shimel's yard, standing behind their old truck parked on the lawn, and she's barking at Bandy telling him to give up the girls and come outside and fight like a man, because she's going to beat the crap out of him.

"Mrs. Cooper, could you ask your daughter to please step back and get in or behind the patrol car?" the officer says.

Alice says, "I'll take care of it, officer." With her gun drawn, she approaches the truck, keeping her eye on the house. She can see Bandy at a window on the left side of the gabled front door. She reaches Frankie. "What are you doing?" she hisses.

"I'm getting my sister and my best friend out of there," she says grimly.

"No, you're not." Alice says. "Let me handle this, and officer Nelson. We'll take care of it." Frankie says nothing. Just then Bandy fires a shot in their general direction. The bullet shatters the glass in the windshield. The girls duck. They hear shrieks and screams from the group behind them. "Frankie, you stay here and hide on this side of the truck, and get down behind this tire and you stay here, do you hear me?" Frankie nods. "Look at me!" Alice commands. Frankie looks at her solemnly. "Promise?" She nods.

"Now, Frankie, you know this house, right?"

"Yes, I know this house."

"Is there a way to get in the back way without him seeing me?"

"Well there's a back porch that has a door on it, and then there's a door on the inside of the porch and that door opens up into the kitchen," she says.

"Any other way into the house?"

"The coal chute. They used to have a coal furnace, but now there's a trap door on the west side with some interior steps that lead into the basement, and then there's steps up to the main floor. You'd have to be quiet, though. And the fifth step from the top creaks."

"It creaks? How would you know? ... Never mind ... okay, I'm going to scoot over to the garage and then backtrack out of Bandy's line of sight a couple of houses, and then come back to the house, and get in through that coal chute. You stay here, okay?"

"Okay."

About five minutes later, Alice is at the coal chute. Once again, she wishes she was not wearing her fancy long Chinese-style skirt. "How am I going to get through this hole?" Meanwhile, Marshal Cutler arrives, siren on, at the same time as a fire truck. Ronald Harmon follows in his pickup. Cutler gets out of his vehicle, and shouts at the people to move back. The only people allowed within the perimeter now are Mr. Watson and his wife who are watching with Tink from afar, and Cushing, Millie, Coop and Ronald. Frankie is hunkered down behind a tire. And Alice is God knows where.

"What's the situation, officer?" Marshal Cutler asks.

"Well, we've got a man with a gun inside, Bandy, I think his name is, and he has two girls with him. He's threatening to kill the girls, kill himself, or he wants a car and ten thousand dollars. I think he wants to get up into Canada. Shots have been fired. I think he's confused. Frankie Cooper is pinned down over there by the truck. And I believe Miss Wang is making an attempt to get inside the house."

"She's what!?"

"She's going in, Marshal," Officer Nelson says. "At least I think that's her plan."

"Criminey!"

"Oh, she's pretty good at this, Marshal. I wouldn't worry too much about Miss Wang."

"So what are our options?"

"Well, we could wait this out," Nelson says. "He's got a limited amount of food. He's going to get tired soon ... or at least sometime. We can keep talking to him. I think he knows that this is not going to turn out well for him."

"What is getting into people these days?" Cutler asks. "I think they've been eating stupid pills or something. Durnest thing I've ever saw."

"I think for now, that we talk when he talks, and in the meantime keep our eye on Miss Wang and watch for developments inside the house."

"Does someone have some field glasses on Bandy?"

"Good idea, Marshal," Nelson says. "There's some in the glove compartment of my patrol car."

# # #

Inside the house, Vickie Cooper is sitting in the living room in an uphol-stered chair with her knees up to her chin, grasping her Teddy bear. Bandy is at the window. He nudges a curtain aside with the barrel of his revolver to peek through the broken window at what's transpiring in the lane in front of the house. In his other hand he has Naomi Shimel's neck, hold-ing her firmly in his grasp. He sees Shimel's truck down front and to his left, and beyond that Marshal Cutler's car and to his right a patrol car where he sees an officer and behind the car he counts four or five people including Mrs. Cooper, Mr. Cooper and Rondo Harmon. The Reverend is on a horse down the street.

He releases the curtain and turns back to the room. As he does so, he hears a door slam. "Who's there?" he yells. He pulls Naomi within his grasp, standing her before him, places his arm across her chest and puts his gun to her head. "Who's there? Come out now or I will shoot this girl for sure!"

"It's just me, Mr. Bandy, Alice Wang, the typist. The temporary typist at church. Remember me?"

"The typist? What the hell are you doing in here?"

"Just came to get the girls, Mr. Bandy, and to save your life, that's all."

"Come out here where I can see you!"

She appears quietly, softly, moving into the room like a cloud drifting across the sky. Bandy is slack-jawed when he sees the apparition now standing before him. He sees a Chinese girl, medium height, with coal black short hair, a face of white polished skin that has not a flaw or a line on it, and looking at him from behind this mask with the fire-engine red lips are the most attractive slanted eyes he's ever seen. She's wearing a red silk blouse with a high Mandarin collar accented with embroidered dragons and lilies of black and gold. Her arms are extended in front of her, pointing toward him and in her right hand is a silver pistol. He can see directly down the barrel. But what's even more astonishing is that she is standing in front of him half naked, in nothing but that beautiful blouse and a pair of deep red panties! She is barefoot.

Vickie and Nomes are likewise stunned beyond words. Nomes is staring at her with eyes that are both anguished and surprised.

"What do you think, Mr. Bandy?" Alice says, keeping her pistol trained on him. She is about twelve feet away from him. "Did your mother ever tell you when you were little to be sure to wear clean underwear every day 'cause you never knew when you might be in an accident or some other embarrassing situation? Sure glad I put on some clean underwear today, that's for sure."

Bandy's been staring at her legs and thighs. Now he looks up and says, "You're a crazy woman, you know that?"

"No, not crazy, Art, just someone who wants everyone to be safe. Now here's what I want you to do. Put down your gun, let the girls run right out that door. Then I will arrest you and you will spend a few years in jail. Then you'll get out and you can start your life over again."

"No, that's not going to happen!" Bandy cries. "You're nuts."

"Okay, Art," Alice says smoothly. "If you don't do what I just said, your life will take an alternative path. You're at a fork in the road right now. You've made some really stupid decisions in the past, and now you have an opportunity to make a smart one. You thought inflating the value of those loans was a smart idea. You thought partnering up with Broughton was a smart move. It wasn't so smart. So now you have a chance to do something smart. If you don't, here's what will happen. You may die right here in this room. Or be seriously injured. You will be prosecuted to the fullest extent of the law since you failed to take advantage of an opportunity to release the girls. You will be in prison a long, long time. In short, if you don't make the smart choice right now, your life is over. So what will it be?"

"This wouldn't be happening if it weren't for those Jews," Bandy rages. His eyes have shrunk and the flesh around the ocular orbits is reddish and pasty. He is mad and his appearance supports the effect. "—always nosing around, making deals, cutting me out—"

"—Is *that* what this is about?" Alice asks coolly. "Joel Shimel is a *tailor*, not a banker."

"Crenshaw gave the files to him!" Bandy yelled. "To *him*! Butting in, nosing around. He had no business interfering."

"I gotta say, Mr. Bandy, I don't think the Jewish lobby or the Jewish influence is so big here in Bathington, you know? Northeast Iowa, not so many Jews."

"What do you know, anyway?" Bandy sneers. "You're like the rest of them, foreigners, a cheap ass Chink whore."

"Really, Mr. Bandy, we got children here," Alice says, not angered in the slightest by Bandy's remarks, but inwardly astonished at the depth of his darkness.

"So what is your plan, Mr. Bandy?" Alice continues to point her gun at him.

"Well, well, I came here to find Mr. Shimel. Thought I could tie him up, and then burn this place down, and next door too. Purifying fire, isn't that what the good book calls it? Refiner's fire, that's right. Refiner's fire. But Shimel wasn't here, and, well—" Bandy tightens his grip on Naomi. He's sweating. The moisture rolls down his cheeks and into his sparse scratch of a beard. "—Well, I had to improvise. You people just need to leave, NOW! or I'll kill her! I'll kill myself, nothing left."

"You like starting fires, huh, Bandy? Is that what you did to the Fremont Hotel, Bandy? You are not thinking this through, Mr. Bandy. If you shoot Naomi, then I will put a bullet through your head. So if you want to kill yourself at your own hand, you need to let Naomi and Victoria leave, and then I promise, I will not interfere and you can go ahead and kill yourself."

"SHUT-UP!"

"Whatever scenario you choose, Mr. Bandy, the girls are useless to you now. If you hold onto them, I'll kill you. If you let them go, you can kill yourself. But, if you drop the gun now, you just spend a few years in jail and then start over. I know you're a banker and all and that most of the time you financial wizards get things ass-backwards and all, but you're not that stupid, Mr. Bandy. You're just not that stupid."

Bandy has his gun at Naomi's head, and Alice has her gun pointed at Bandy's head. "Looks like we got a Mexican standoff here, Miss Wang," Bandy says after a moment of thought.

"No we don't, Mr. Bandy. Your life is in my hands. I can put a bullet in your head at any second, even as I am talking. I am a dead shot. I can shoot the dick off a mosquito from twenty yards. So you're only alive at this moment because I think there's still a chance that no one needs to die. But my finger's getting tired and itchy, and my patience is running thin, and worse, here's the thing, Mr. Bandy, I got to pee. I don't know what happened, but I got to pee bad. And I can't hold this much longer. So you're going to have to decide pretty quick, or I'm just going to shoot you."

At this very moment, Vickie pulls the string. "Hello! My name is Teddy. What's yours?" The sudden noise and strange voice startles Mr. Bandy and he whirls around removing the gun from Naomi's head in order to point it somewhere else—in the direction of the voice, no doubt. But when the gun leaves Naomi's head, Alice fires and catches Bandy in the elbow causing his arm to jerk, and the gun falls to the floor harmlessly as does Bandy himself. Naomi screams and cowers.

Alice dashes to the gun, kicking it away while yelling at Naomi: "Nomes, get Vickie and get out the front door, NOW!"

# # #

Outside, Cutler and Nelson have field glasses and are monitoring the activity inside the house. "He's talking to someone," Cutler says. "It must be Alice." Cushing has dismounted, and has rejoined the group behind the patrol car, i.e. Millie, Coop and Ronald. Then they see a flash of gunfire and hear a report and a scream. Millie herself begins wailing. But moments later, they see Naomi plunge through the front door with Vickie in tow who's got her Teddy bear, and they run and run until they reach the group which has dashed to meet them. Millie sweeps Vickie into her arms and presses her close. She's crying. Likewise, the Shimels embrace their daughter, their only child. There are many tears, and many smiles. Frankie dashes from the pickup to join the group and she and Nomes embrace. Hugs fly all around. Except for Ronald Harmon. He doesn't get any hugs. Frankie sees him leaving for his truck. She sees her grandfather call out after him and watches as the two of them converse briefly. Then they shake hands. Coop turns back to join the group but Ronald stays where he is.

"Where in tarnation is Alice?" Marshal Cutler asks. "What happened in there?"

"Oh she's coming, Marshal," Naomi says. "I think she had to pee."

Moments later, Alice appears from behind the house, fully clothed, with Art Bandy staggering in front of her. "He's going to need some medical attention," Alice says, as Officer Nelson and Marshal Cutler approach. "Got nicked in the elbow here, just a flesh wound." Bandy is handcuffed and escorted to the squad car.

"Mom, I am supposed to give my speech," Frankie says. "What time is it? How am I going to get there?"

"Well, Miss Cooper," says Officer Nelson, "I can get you there with my siren going, and take two additional passengers as well."

"I am going back into town with Mr. Harmon," Coop says. "Vickie can go with me, or ride in the fire truck back. And Miss Alice, Frankie and Nomes can ride with Officer Nelson or Cutler. I believe Reverend Cushing and Mrs. Cooper have an alternative form of transportation."

"Sounds swell to me," Nelson says. Cushing and Millie smile at each other. Once again he helps Millie to get on the horse. She puts her arms around his waist, and leans against him. They ride away slowly, toward Sully's Bridge and the city park beyond.

Chapter XXXIII

OFFICER NELSON STOPS NEAR THE BANDSTAND and the three ladies exit the vehicle quickly. Frankie immediately heads for the stairs leading to the stage—the same platform on which she had given her mock oration not too long ago and following which she'd had her encounter with Rondo Harmon. The newly born-again Christian has also arrived with Coop and Vic and parks his pickup with the front wheels on the grassy edge of the park lawn. Coop and Vic leave hand in hand for the grandstand while Ronald hangs back to watch from a distance.

By Coop's reckoning, there are thousands of people in the park to hear the Senator, eat the food, drink the beer, and listen to a speech by some kid who wrote an essay. The air is scented with the sweet smell of barbecued pork and buttered corn. The charcoal smoke lingers, too, and evokes memories of picnics of yore. An ensemble version of the high school band is now ensconced in the bandstand, back in the shell itself and are playing a song. Dignitaries have taken their seats. The high school glee club is seated on risers at the base of the grandstand and below the lectern. They are dressed in their school colors, black and gold. Coop can see Frankie being shown to her place on the dais. The red-white-and-blue bunting around the stage area looks festive and patriotic. Suddenly, Coop is filled with a sense of loss. He rues the absence of Johnny. He should be here to see this moment, to take pride in the accomplishments of his oldest daughter. And Antonia, too, how thrilled she'd be and how grandmotherly she'd be carrying on today. But, oh well, it is not to be. Coop's acceptance of what happens in his life borders on the fatalistic.

# # #

At 2 p.m. an electronic screech suddenly halts conversation throughout the park. A tapping is heard and a voice saying, "Is this thing on?" Two loud speakers are attached to the grandstand themselves, and additional speakers are strategically located in trees throughout the park, using cable and wiring laid out on the ground to an elm here or a maple there. The thousands standing shoulder to shoulder, some still eating pork sandwiches or chewing on corncobs, do not hear a voice from a burning bush as did Moses in the wilderness, but they hear a voice coming as from the heavens through the trees. This creates a startling effect. At the sound of a human voice coming from above and the beyond, the loud engine-hum of the collective conversation in the city park stills to a few whispers as if a motor has been shut off. The mayor, a portly gentleman who's taken pains to develop a fine set of lamb chop whiskers, addresses the crowd and announces the "Star-Spangled Banner." Immediately the band begins to play. Coop and Vic are standing near the front and off to the side with a clear view of the lectern. He is holding Vic's hand. Millie and Cushing are in the same area. Coop notices the Bathington Brigade patrolling on their chestnut horses, looking sharp. He sees that some of the crowd are still picking up folio pages from the Publications Ministry and examining them closely. The band concludes its rendition and the crowd revs up once again, roaring, shouting and whistling enthusiastically.

The program begins. The mayor welcomes the crowd, and then introduces the Rev. James Connors of the E & R church to give the invocation, which he does. The vice-chair of the Centennial Committee then steps to the podium and reads brief letters of welcome and congratulations from Governor Beardsley and President Truman. The glee club sings "America, the Beautiful," but interjected between stanzas three and four is a solo written for the occasion and offered by a pale high school student whose face is beaded with perspiration and whose hands are shaking; a prairie child who has never seen four hundred people gathered in one place, let alone four thousand. She grips the lectern and with the glee club humming and the band providing a soft accompaniment, she lifts her quavering voice to sing—

O Bathington, our home so dear,
with trees and skies so fair,
Our people strong, our voices clear,
with freedom in the air.
O Bathington, we stand for thee,
forever now we dare,

To *live in peace and harmony,*
and pledge our love and care.

After the applause following this performance, brief words of welcome are offered by politicians from Des Moines and Clearwater County's Congressional representative. The vice-chair then recognizes Editor-in-Chief Theodore Hughes of the *Bathington Beacon-Gazette*. Hughes explains the nature of the county-wide essay contest and identifies the winners in each division, including the second and third place entries. "The winner of the First Prize of the Bathington Beacon-Gazette Centennial Essay Contest in the High School Division in the amount of fifty dollars is … Miss Frances Katherine Cooper." This announcement is greeted with appropriate, if not subdued, applause and cheers. "Please give Miss Cooper now your undivided attention." He turns to Frankie who rises and with one hand smoothes her dress while holding her speech in the other. "Miss Cooper, congratulations" he says, making a big show of handing her an oversized check for $50, and posing with her before the crowd.

"Thank you, Mr. Hughes," she says softly. Coop feels his chest tightening. The air seems dead; the breeze has died. He watches as Frankie steps up to the lectern and lays the fake check and her manuscript on the podium. She waits for what seems like five hours before saying a word. Then she lifts her head and looks out at the masses.

"My name is Frances Katherine Cooper, and my great-great-great-great-grandfather was Adonijah Bathington, one of the Bathingtons who founded this great town of ours. He was the last of the Bathingtons, dying in the town he loved in 1865, only thirteen years after the town was born. Adonijah Bathington was an Iowan. He was an American, a descendant of the English who landed on the shores of America in Massachusetts hundreds of years ago in the seventeenth century. What you may *not* know is that the Bathingtons who founded our fair city were not only English, but were also … part Pocumtuk Indian! Ladies and gentlemen, I stand before you as Frances Cooper. I am English. I am Pocumtuk Indian. I am Bathington. I am America."

Coop is surprised that Frankie is not afraid of the microphone and seems instead to regard it as her friend. Rather than leaning into the microphone as so many speakers do, she lets it do its job of amplification so that she doesn't need to bend, lean or otherwise contort her body. She seems to understand the need to project her voice. Her face is up as she speaks, not buried in her manuscript, and she's looking out across the sea of people beneath her. Her chin is set, and he imagines her eyes are flashing. Her voice has no quaver, but rings clear and true. The crowd reacts to these opening words in general astonishment and a few boos, but mostly cheers.

She then outlines the results of her research establishing the mixed cultural heritage of the Bathington bloodline. In doing so, she recounts the travels, the hard work, the successes and failures of some of the Bathingtons as they created a life in their new home, and moved westward across the mighty Mississippi to the Clearwater River. Coop observes that the crowd is more attentive than they'd been when listening to the Senator, or any of the other speakers. This is only right, he thought. This child is one of our own. Then Frankie concludes using repetitive phrasing for emphasis and effect. Her script looks like this:

My friends, I am Frances Cooper.
 But I am also Bathington. I am America!
I am the Negro who camped along the Clearwater fleeing from slavery en route to freedom.
 I am Bathington. I am America.
I am the farmer, tilling the soil and reaping the harvest.
 I am Bathington. I am America.
I am the black, the red, the white, the yellow who want nothing more than an equal opportunity and to live in mutual respect.
 My fellow Americans, you are Bathington. You are America. You are the Swede, the German, the English, the Italian, the Irish.
 You are the young, the middle aged, the elderly.
You are the child, the mother, the father, the brother, the sister, the aunt, the uncle, the grandmother, the grandfather.
You are the merchant, the teacher, the police officer, the doctor, the dentist, the lawyer, the mechanic, the tailor, the tinker and candlestick maker.
Ladies and gentleman, I am Bathington. I am America. You are Bathington. You are America. Ladies and gentlemen, WE ARE BATHINGTON AND WE ARE AMERICA!

The band and the glee club immediately strike up the final chorus of "America, the Beautiful":
America, America,
God sheds its grace on thee,

And crown thy good with brotherhood,
From sea to shining sea.

The speech, followed by the song, is a *tour de force*. The crowd erupts in an ocean roar of shouting and applause that begins even before she concludes the final cadence of her speech and continues and swells through the anthem. Parents hug their children, sweethearts embrace, people turn to each other clapping, smiling and nodding. At that moment, Frances Katherine Cooper can be elected to any political office to which she aspires. The atmosphere is pulsing. Coop's pride knows no bounds. Millie is in tears and trying to speak. "Oh my precious girl!" Cushing is searching for a handkerchief. In the Centennial jail, even Mrs. Clarice Broughton, felon, is moved, and dabs at a tear. Only Carlo and Wason seem unmoved.

After Rev. Manning of the Assemblies of God church pronounces the benediction, Coop and Vic, Millie and Cushing, Alice and Cuttingham, Joel and Ruth Shimel and Naomi and Tink are at the bottom of the steps to greet her. Descending these steps, Frankie does not lose her footing as she did the night of the Spring Formal, but glides down as an angel into the waiting arms of her mother. "You're crying, Mother!" Frankie says, laughing.

She has other admirers. "That was so swell, Frankie!" says Tink, who came with the Shimels.

"Oh, thank you, Tinkerbell! You're the best!" Congratulations are offered by many, and she receives the hugs of each in turn, and soon other well-wishers appear, and a small mob begins to develop. "Let's get to the cars," Alice says. As they filter through the crowd, Frankie and Naomi embrace again. "Here, take this," Frankie says.

"What's this?" Naomi asks, surprised.

"It's the fake check. I don't want it. I got so much out of this already—"

"No, Frankie, really—"

"Yes, don't be a doofus. You can't cash this check. They're probably going to give me the cash later. Just take this off my hands now and I will get the cash to you when I get it … Oh, Nomes! I could not have done this without you, and your dad. You could give some of the money to Tink if you want." She wraps her arms around Naomi again and holds her. "I love you, Nomes," she said.

Nomes cries and nods.

They all tramp to Cuttingham's car in which Frankie and Vic had been transported earlier, their grandfather at the wheel. Alice says, "Marshal Cutler wants a meeting with all of you present at Cushing's office tonight if that's possible and okay with you, Reverend."

"Sure, that's jolly fine with me. I don't think I have anything going on ... can you think of anything, Coop?"

"Nope. Except—"

"What?"

"It's Saturday night of the Centennial weekend ... We're both in the pageant ... Remember?"

Cushing's eyebrows arch in recognition. He adjusts his eyeglasses, and says, "Oh, right, quite right old boy, there's that."

"Okay, then it's a *late* meeting," Alice says crisply, "Ten o'clock sharp, the vicar's office."

"A meeting?" Millie asks nervously. "What for?"

"Loose ends," Alice says.

Chapter XXXIV

THE WEATHER HAD BEEN FICKLE ALL day. Morning sun and soft breezes had skittered by the forenoon to clouds and unpredictable winds. Then the air quieted and the heat rose during the afternoon, and the moisture that had been accumulating in towering pillowy late afternoon clouds returned to the earth in torrents of biblical proportions during intermittent evening showers.

So it is a soggy group that gathers in Cushing's office after the final pageant performance. When Coop arrives, he sees that the Reverend is still attired in his prairie preacher outfit while Coop himself is still the frontier judge in a dark vested suit, with a gold chain with a watch attached—his railroad watch. Marshal Cutler is in uniform. Alice appears in a lightweight gray raincoat which she removes—Coop is irritated that he wasn't alert enough to assist her—and is dressed in a tight blue skirt, and a smart, matching cotton blouse with a wide flared and high collar. In her ears are pearl stud earrings. Around her fine neck is a single strand of pearls. Coop thinks the Buddhist beauty looks lovely but perhaps overdressed. Her face is pale, her lips red and her black hair, falling straight almost to her shoulders, is razor cut across her forehead a half inch above her eyebrows in a line that is as straight as the Chinese horizon. Messrs. Jard and Rossi are likewise present, caps in hand, and are invited to sit on some folding chairs brought into the office for the occasion. Mrs. Cuttingham, who conveyed the boys from the jailhouse to the church house, is a picture of Chicago *haute couture*, the weather notwithstanding. Finally, Mrs. Mildred Cooper is present. She is finely dressed, clutching a black handbag, but looks like a nervous wreck. She comes with Coop. These, then, are the principals at the meeting.

The furniture in the parson's book-lined study consists of a wide oak desk behind which is a large comfortable desk chair which is occupied by the marshal. He's taken off his white felt Stetson cowboy hat and plunked it atop a nearby Revised Standard Version of the Bible. The marshal's silver badge in the shape of a star is pinned to his shirt, left side. He's chewing on a toothpick. Sitting on the corner of the desk in front of the marshal but to his right side is Alice, a view which the marshal particularly enjoys. To his left, situated on the other corner of the desk is a thick, squat lilac candle, lit by Cushing to mitigate the lingering scent of Cavendish. In the preacher's two wing-backed wine-colored leather chairs are Mrs. Cuttingham and Reverend Cushing. These chairs are across the study and facing the pastor's desk. To the left of the marshal is a loveseat on which are Millie and Coop, and across from them are two folding chairs, one on either side of a small table, occupied by Wason and Carlo. In the center of the room is a low tea table on which is a tea service and a tray laden with a variety of tea bags, a silver pot which sits on a small stand under which is a votive candle keeping the tea water hot. Cups and saucers are on another tray, and beside this is a fancy plate of cookies and shortbread. Cushing invites everyone to help themselves but the only ones who avail themselves of the parson's hospitality are the parson himself, Millie and Mrs. Cuttingham.

The room, which is carpeted and warm, is not dark by any means, but the ceiling light is not switched on as it would be too bright, too glaring and irritating in Cushing's opinion. So the overhead lamp is off, but a floor lamp between the loveseat and one of the wing-backed chairs is on and a pair of sconces on the book-shelved wall behind the desk are also lit; a small table lamp in the shape of the horned Moses that's between Wason and Carlo is likewise on.

Marshal Cutler clears his throat and says, "Well, Reverend, maybe we could get on with it?"

Cushing, playing an English butler, has proffered the tray of cookies and shortbread to his guests. He is arched over in front of Wason who decides he wants a piece of shortbread after all. Cushing looks up but does not straighten up, glancing at Cutler. "Uh, of course, of course. Straightaway, then." He steps back from Wason, replaces the tray on the tea table and returns to his soft chair after retrieving his tea cup and saucer. He sits down, crossing his legs. There's a light tinking and clinking of china before Cutler speaks again.

"If I mighten review the events of tuhday as well as a few of the goings-on of the past few months …" Rather than leaning forward to address the parties in the room, he eases back in the preacher's chair, his arms are raised above him and his fingers are interlocked to provide support for his head. The toothpick is still a-bobbin' in his mouth. There's a decided Midwestern twang in his voice—pitched mid-range with a slight gravelly timber. He doesn't speak loud or soft, just normal-like as though chatting with a friend easy as can be. Coop thinks that considering the tilt in his posture, coupled with the marshal's expansive girth, that the tea service, now resting on the tea table in the center of the room, could be perched instead on the marshal's belly with no danger to the china itself.

"Tuhday alone, we've discovered a porno operation which has been running out of this here church, the said contents of which have been distributed willy-nilly to the residents of Bathington thanks to some help from Mother Nature—the wind and all—and a reckless driver." He glances in Wason's direction. "We've had one of the parade floats, again, sponsored in part by this here church, collapse and burst into flames, and a lamb set on the loose and this is again due to some reckless driving. We have arrested a suspect in an embezzling scheme at Bathington State Bank which I'm figuring has been going on for some time. Doesn't look like it's going to be much of my business as outside enforcement agencies are going to handle the criminal aspect of this with respect to Broughton and Bandy, but as I was saying, we've apprehended two prominent citizens of this town, both of whom are members of this here church. We've arrested these two young men here and are holding them until we find out what, if any, charges are going to be pressed against them. And we had the abduction of two children. Now, to go back a few months, we've also had a landmark in this town, the Fremont Hotel, burn down, and we've had what we thought was the murder of one of the hotel's residents, Violet Crenshaw, a citizen of Bathington, and a member—again—of this here church and the church typist for a number of years—"

Cutler shifts his position, sits up straight and leans forward, placing his arms on the desk, his hands folded together, fingers interlocked. He raises his voice and looks around the room: "Only we find out that she *didn't* die in the fire, she *wasn't* murdered, that it *wasn't* a she but a he, and we don't know who the he is who died, who was murdered or why. And whether any of these events are connected to the other. So that's where we are today, ladies and gentlemen. I reckon we've had more commotion in this town in the last 100 days than we've had in Bathington the last 100 years! The purpose of this here little gathering—the primary purpose—is to see if we can establish who was killed and who was the killer that night of the fire, and second of all, to establish some facts as to this here porno operation and get the record straight so that everyone here in this room knows the truth and we can cut down rumors as they might arise. This is not a formal hearing or inquiry. No minutes are being taken. You can think of this conversation as part of the investeegation which, I'm happy to say, we're close to wrappin' up."

Coop finds Cutler's assessment and review of events riveting stuff. He surmises, from the demeanor of the others in the room, that they do as well. There's a sense, he thinks, that things have come to a head, that everything's so a-jangled and mussed up, that some straightening and tidying is in order. Coop approves of this.

Just then there's a flash of lightning and a crack of thunder so loud that everyone skitters a bit and comments. Rain pelts the windowpanes behind the boys. Cutler unlocks his hands and sits back as before and then speaks again. "We got ourselves a good Midwestern storm brewing out there tonight, doncha think? I reckon the Good Lawd's saying that it's 'bout time we wuz addressing this sitcheation here. And I think that Miss Wang might be the first person to get the ball rollin', so Alice why don't you take it from here."

Alice glances back at Cutler, nods, and says, "Okay," and turns back to face the group. She's sitting on the corner of the desk. Her feet dangle and do not touch the floor. She's kicked off her high heels which lay on the carpet a few inches below her feet. Her arms are straightened out so that her hands grip the desk on either side of her body to provide support as she sits erect and leans toward her audience. "I'll start by explaining now—I couldn't before—that I am C.S.I. Alice Wang attached to the Chicago office of the Federal Bureau of Investigation. I am not an F.B.I agent. The F.B.I. does not have female agents for some insane reason, and will not have female agents for the foreseeable future. C.S.I. stands for Consulting Special Investigator. I am not on the F.B.I. payroll, but I am hired by the F.B.I. for special operations that call for—shall we say— the *special* talents that only a female can provide. We've had a couple of— well three, to be precise—investigations ongoing for about eighteen months now that have involved the upper Midwest. One focused on a ring of pornographers operating out of Chicago with connections to Des Moines, Davenport, and Duluth, the Triple D's we called them. Another was a bank case that came to light through a tip that our office received concerning the Bathington State Bank, and the third had to do with a cold case concerning some events in Chicago in the late 1920s. All of these together brought me to Bathington."

Alice's announcement is met with dropped jaws, quiet gasps and shared glances. Coop does not see this coming. So is Cuttingham also a C.S.I.?, a fake G-man after all?

Millie says, "Well, what does 'special talents' mean? I am not sure I understand?"

"I've checked this out, people," Cutler drawls, back now in a supine position. "She's legit and she's the only female C.S.I. agent in the Midwest and the youngest C.S.I. between Chicago and San Francisco and darn sure the prettiest, I'll tell ya what!"

"I'll try to make this as concise as possible," Alice continues unfazed. "Based on the intel we'd gathered, we developed a sting scenario in which we would use a team of informants by which we could engage a three-pronged strategy to get at the truth in all three of these cases at the same time. But it would take some time, too. The Chicago field office agreed to put me 'undercover' and to send this team to Bathington where we'd set up shop and work. We were given a six-month time frame, and so basically, we're ahead of schedule. The team consisted of myself, Mrs. Cuttingham and Mr. Rossi and Mr. Jard. These three are not C.S.I. people but rather interested parties who for reasons of their own agreed to cooperate in this mission.

"In a moment, Mrs. Cuttingham will add some details, I'm sure, to this account, but for now let me say that when we came to town we needed to set up some kind of legitimate reason for being here. Fortunately we learned of the situation here at the church, with the need for a typist, and with Rossi and Jard's professional skills, and Cuttingham's connections we established a 'business' as it were, which, as you know, was known as the Publications Ministry. Reverend Cushing, we were aware of the risk to the reputation and witness of the church, but felt that it was worth the risk and believed, and still believe, that as these facts become known, the church will be applauded for its role in bringing wrongdoers to justice. We couldn't just open up a business on Main Street—it would have invited too many questions. But as an arm of the church's ministry, the sting operation suddenly took on an aura of righteous plausibility. Our objective was to establish relationships with the smut-peddlers in this region, catch them red-handed in their operations and round up the ring-leaders. This we have done. Major operations are being shut down in ten Midwestern cities as I speak, thanks to the work of this team. But to make this work, we had to go into the 'business' ourselves, and to make it convincing. We had hoped to be able to close down the operation quietly and get out of town, but some unfortunate decisions were made that resulted in today's accident and mayhem and the littering of the town—well, for this I abjectly apologize. And we will do everything in our power to set the record straight on this.

"The second matter has to do with the bank. We received a tip that there were some serious irregularities going on at the BSB. This came to us from Mrs. Cuttingham via Violet Crenshaw who was an employee of the bank. Our objective was to sort out this information, and apprehend the suspects. But before this information could come into focus, there was the fire at the Fremont Hotel, and our informant, Violet Crenshaw, had apparently died in the fire. Of course we immediately thought this to be suspicious, and as it turns out, the victim was not Crenshaw at all. More about this from Mrs. Cuttingham in a moment. But she did leave us with enough documentation that we were able to put the pieces together and make an arrest.

"The third matter, concerning a cold case that emerged back in the late 1920s, also came to us via Mrs. Cuttingham—and perhaps this is where I should hand things off to Mrs. Cuttingham."

For a moment no one says anything, as though the room has been sucked of all its oxygen and no one has the energy to speak. Heads turn in Cuttingham's direction. Rain still patters on the windowpanes. The lights flicker briefly. Beyond the window, the landscape brightens now and then from distant lightning. Thunder is now a low rumble. The storm is passing.

"Anyone for more tea, eh?" Cushing asks, leaping out of his chair. He grabs the tea pot and fills Millie's cup. No one else wants anything. He retreats quietly to his chair after re-filling his own cup.

Then Cutler speaks, "Ah, I guess I'll have some of that stuff." Cushing jumps up again with alacrity and begins to pour. "I don't suppose you have anything stronger to put in that, do you?" he asks.

"Oh, well, as a matter of fact—" He looks around the room at his guests. Coop knows he's wondering whether—or how much—to confess. "I have a small bottle of brandy that might—would that do?"

"Would that do? Why of course it will do! Why didn't you say so earlier?" Cutler roars.

"Well, then, I'll—just a moment." Cushing begins to scurry about going first to a cupboard below the bookshelves behind his desk and retrieves a bottle, and whirls to ask, "Anyone else interested?"

Coop says, "I'll have some."

Cuttingham says, "Me, too." And Carlo, Wason and Alice request a glass as well, and Cushing gets one for himself. He scuttles back and forth to deliver the shot glasses, and then pours for each and with the shortbread and brandy, as though the Reverend's serving Holy Communion. He sits down. The supplicants whom he has just served have all taken a taste. Cuttingham clears her throat and begins.

"I'm not quite accustomed to this sort of thing—it's so confessional, you know, but we Catholics are good at guilt and confession, so off we go, I guess. Violet Crenshaw, as Coop already knows—he was my first Confessor!—" She breaks off in a pleasant giggle. She takes another sip of brandy. "Violet was—is—my sister." The only one who seems surprised at this news is Millie. "We were born and raised in Chicago. It was just she and I—no brothers. Of course her name then was Elizabeth Morley. I was older, married first, married well—a Lakeshore drive doctor—and she married, but didn't marry so well. He was just a bootlegging punk, really, who got involved with a bad crowd during Prohibition—and I am leaving out a lot of details here—and she, being raised Catholic was not going to divorce and especially not after they had a little girl ... Amelia they named her, Amy for short. Gus—her husband—ran a blind pig called the Four Aces. There were hundreds of speakeasies back in those days, most of them operating in a basement, or secret room behind some legit business, like a café, flower shop or bookshop. The Four Aces was below a hardware store and was basically a Mafia hangout like all the speakeasies. Gus had Lizzy serving up cocktails, beer and bathtub gin, keeping the customers happy, you know. The Four Aces wasn't a big club or anything like that—no fancy orchestra, and rooms with tables—but there was a small stage, and there'd be a singer or two or someone playing sax, and a small dance floor. Ten to fifteen tables, white tablecloths, ash trays, you know. It was nice. Lizzy tried to do all this and be a mother too. Most of the time, Amelia would be in a pram behind the bar—she'd wheel it in from the alley—where Lizzy could keep an eye on her. And as she grew, Lizzy would let her toddle about and the regulars got to know her as if she was their own kid. One day, it was in September of 1927, guess who comes busting in? Not the cops, but some goons from Johnny 'The Fox' Torrio, head of 'The Chicago Outfit' who was trying to muscle in on the north side and the Gold Coast. The Four Aces was in control of the Genna brothers at the time, and I don't know how the trouble started, but Torrio's guys came busting in through the alley door with Chicago typewriters rat-a-tat-tating. Gus' guys engaged with Tommy guns as well and when it was all over, there were bodies everywhere. Lizzy had been behind the bar at the time, but the baby was out stumbling around the tables. Lizzy screamed for her and got on her hands and knees and crawled around the end of the bar, scrambling like crazy to find her, but when the smoke cleared, Amelia was dead—caught in the crossfire.

"Well, Lizzy was never the same after that. I was close to Lizzy in those days. She was inconsolable. Even after she gave birth to a little boy a year or so later, the emptiness never seemed to be filled. Oh, she loved that boy alright, but she knew that she could never give him the life he deserved. So she started to think of a way out. Gus was still working for the Genna brothers, but now he was set up in the Blue Sky Lounge which, unlike the Four Aces, was a street front lounge. You couldn't get a drink there except tea or coffee or iced tea, and they had sandwiches and the like. So people would come, smoke, socialize, but if they wanted the hard stuff there was a room in the back, larger than the Blue Sky itself. Gus kept the booze in a locked vault and brought out only what might be need on a per hour basis. Very security conscious, Gus was. But Lizzy contacted the police. It took several months of negotiating, but in the end, they tipped her off to an impending raid, and that's when Lizzy went into action. When the cops arrived, she was ready. The baby was already in the pram. She knew where the money and diamonds were and she was prepared to grab the stash and skedaddle. And she did. She strolled out the back door of the Blue Sky with more than $150,000 and a small bag of diamonds. She stashed this below the baby's bed in the pram, and camouflaged it and put the baby on top, and what's more threw in a dirty, really dirty diaper. Good thing. She got stopped on the sidewalk as she exited the alley behind the Blue Sky, and the cop bends over to take a look at the baby and got a whiff of that dirty diaper and that was that. Lizzy disappeared into the wind.

"But I knew where she was and what she was doing. The first thing she did was to leave the baby with a note and some supplies at St. Joseph's Catholic Church. They ran an orphanage in those days. She knew this baby would have a good, calm life there. At least that was her hope and prayer. It was the hardest thing she ever did in her life. And I think it was the right decision. She was not emotionally able to raise a child and she didn't have the means to do so, not to speak of the danger to herself and the child, and I could not be involved because it would then be assumed I knew what was going on. I was grilled by the cops as it was. As for Gus—he went to prison and was killed there in a prison fight. My husband died about ten years ago of a massive heart attack. In the meantime, I kept my eyes on that baby. Over the years I would visit the orphanage when they had a Christmas program, and I made sure he got presents on his birthday and at Christmas time, and some of these were from his mother. I would watch him play at the park, and I even chatted with the nuns occasionally about his progress—as an interested patron of the orphanage, because I contributed an amount each year to its general fund. The baby grew up to be a fine young man, a handsome fellow, and that young man is Mr. Rossi, whom all of you know. Until a few days ago, he had no idea he had a mother and an aunt who'd been watching him all these years. He learned a trade, photography, but unfortunately, after Carlo got out of the orphanage, he fell in with the wrong crowd. He'd rob a bank now and again, and the last one got him caught.

"That's when I met Special Agent Wang. I think she was just sizing me up at first. She had learned of my relationship with the missing Elizabeth Morley—actually she didn't even know anything about that cold case. Lizzy's name just came up and when she dug around a bit, she found a whole new case that was yet unsolved. Where is Morley and where is the money and diamonds? Because at the time, the cops were steamed that their informant had not only fled but had fled with the goods. And of course, the bad guys were likewise interested—more interested than the cops really—to find her. I knew if they did, they'd kill her.

"Agent Wang wanted a crew. She had met Carlo at Donovan's and had been impressed by him. But she needed leverage with him, so the bank job was arranged and their subsequent capture—basically, they were set up—so she thought that she could leverage a deal so that he could avoid a trial and certain incarceration if he agreed to help. Well, what's not to like about a deal where you're using your gift and photographing naked girls—all due respect, Reverend. Besides, he'd been doing this already for a guy called Lefty Donovan. Agent Wang had already gone undercover at Donovan Printing as I said and knew that Donovan wanted to break up the operation and expand further into the Midwest, west of the Mississippi. So she believed this was an opportunity not only to get Donovan but some of the major smut peddlers in the region. She explained the plan and wanted me to be a part of it. I suggested Bathington because I knew that's where Lizzy had landed, and I thought it would be a great opportunity for us to be together, even if it was a short while. I had not seen Lizzy for more than 20 years for fear of compromising her identity. I didn't realize that Agent Wang and her superiors were hoping that I might do just as I did: lead them to Lizzy.

"Well Lizzy did not like the idea at all. She was afraid of meeting her son, thinking that would complicate his life not to speak of hers. And she feared exposure. Moreover, given what she was finding out at the bank, and that they were prepared to fingerprint all employees, she figured it was time to move on.

"I was introduced to the boys as a 'consultant' with the FBI and that our cover was that I was their aunt, helping them out for the time being until they could get their business set up. You can see the irony. After all, I was Carlo's aunt.

"I'll skip now to the night of the fire. Lizzy had decided as you know to leave, and having developed a fondness for Coop here, spent her last evening with him at Bud's Tavern. She came back to her room in an absolute panic. She'd run into the fellow who was tending bar at the Blue Sky the night of the raid and the night she disappeared back in '29. Joseph Craglione. She thought it was a coincidence. Coincidence, my ass! 'Cuse me. Mr. Craglione was a damn good bartender, but he also had an eye for the ladies, and he and Violet had a one-night fling in a moment of weakness—Gus Morley was a putz?—and, the baby boy? Craglione, not Gus, was the father. Is the father. Carlo's father is still alive, and if Carlo wants to meet him, I am sure it won't be hard to arrange. Anyway—I suppose smoking is not allowed in here, eh?"

The occupants of the room automatically deferred to the reverend on this matter: "Well, Mrs. Cuttingham, I light up my pipe from time to time, and if a cigarette would sooth the nerves, feel free."

The office is completely silent as Cuttingham goes through the ritual of getting her cigarette lit. "I had a room on a lower floor," she continues, after exhaling a long strand of blue smoke, "and went up to see her. You can imagine my surprise that when I got to the door I heard noise inside her room. It sounded like an argument between a man and a woman. I didn't knock. I tried the door. It was unlocked, so I burst in. Standing there in the room was Lefty Donovan, Joseph Craglione and of course Lizzy! I closed the door. Lefty had managed to follow me from Chicago. He was an old friend of Gus' and still had mob connections in Chicago. He had said nothing to his associates. He had a sister who was a sister, a nun, at St. Joseph's. Once at a program, he'd spotted me—he knew who I was because I had been around Four Aces back in those days, and I knew who he was too, obviously. He made some discreet inquiries, learned of my interest in one of the boys. Found out when the boy had been born and put two and two together. When I left with the team to peddle smut in Iowa, he was curious, followed us, and that led him right to Lizzy, who was now Violet Crenshaw. Craglione came with him because he was Lefty's silent partner. Craglione who'd done well for himself after graduating from the U of Chicago, gave Lefty his startup money in exchange for a cut of the business.

"So they were having an argument. Lefty wanted the money and the diamonds, and when she refused, he said he'd settle for a 60-40 split. Craglione didn't say much, but it was clear that he was of the same opinion as Lefty. She still refused. He threatened to expose her to the authorities. She was resolute. Then Lefty grabbed me and put a gun to my head and said he'd blow my brains to kingdom come if she didn't come up with the cash. So she asked for just a moment, told him to calm down, and stooped down to a drawer in the bureau along the wall, opened it, and then turned around to face Lefty and I with a .38 Smith & Wesson Model 10 revolver in her own hand before you could say Jack Sprat. She waved the gun at Craglione to keep him at bay, too.

"I guess she figured she didn't have much to lose, because he started yelling and was sounding irrational. I could feel the cold steel of the gun barrel against my temple—I thought I was going to die right then and there—and Lizzy just raised that pistol and shot him right through the forehead. A clean shot. He fell back against the bedframe and then on to the bed itself. And that's how a body came to be in Violet Crenshaw's bed."

"I thought there were *two* bullet holes in the skull," Coop asks.

Alice speaks quickly: "I'll get to that in a minute."

Cuttingham continues her narrative: "Craglione went beserk. Violet shoved the pistol in his face and got him calmed down real fast. She told him to vamoose and to get his old jalopy and rattle out of town immediately. He did. We watched him through the window throw his grip in the back seat of his Chevy and pull out. Now, Violet had arranged with Joel Shimel to have some dresses delivered, and had called him asking him to come over. He could have shown up at any time, but he shows up shortly after Craglione departs. She wouldn't let him in, but she delivered a packet of documentation concerning the bank and told him to hang on to this, guarding it with his life. She didn't want to leave it with me, as my plans were uncertain, but she said that if Mr. Cooper or myself were ever to specifically ask for it, he was to hand it over."

Millie speaks up: "What about the fire? Did you set fire to the hotel?"

"No, of course not. Lizzy and I have done some bad things in our lives, but we're not murderers. We could never put the lives of other people at risk like that. You people knew Violet, she wouldn't hurt a flea—well, okay, she could if that flea was a low-down scum-sucking bastard like Lefty Donovan. You know what I mean. We had nothing to do with that fire. Let me back up. After Lefty was shot, we both just about went nuts—it was all crashing down on poor Lizzy. As calm as she was when the chips were down, now that the immediate danger had passed, she went to pieces. I sat her down, gave her a shot of bourbon which I, well, happened to have in a little flask. She calmed down and we discussed the situation. We decided to dress Lefty in some of Lizzy's clothes, which we did. Put one of Lizzie's wigs on him—"

"A wig!" Millie exclaims.

"Yes, Mrs. Cooper, a wig. Lizzie had escaped from Chicago to Bathington and was living a different life. A wig was sometimes necessary to maintain the subterfuge."

"What an awful way to have to live," Millie says, looking about at the others.

Cuttingham continues: "So we threw a blanket over him. Then I gave Lizzy a quick trim and we made her up to look like a man, and she put on Lefty's clothes and his shoes—the whole outfit, I know it sounds bizarre and ghoulish, but we're talking about a person's life here. We went out, walked out of the Fremont Hotel, each of us carrying a grip and I took her in my car to the depot so she—he—could catch the 11 o'clock Rocket and she was gone.

"The fire happened in the early hours of the morning. I believe the Fire Marshal got it right. I read the report. I don't think there's anyone in Bathington who could set fire to one of its old historic landmarks like that especially and possibly cause the deaths of innocent people. Just don't think there's anyone in Bathington that evil."

"The fire was started by Arthur Bandy," says Alice, breaking in. "He went to the Fremont hotel to kill Crenshaw and cover the murder with the fire. He arrived after Violet had left. Donovan was already dead in the bed, covered with a blanket and a wig on his head. Bandy, thinking he was Crenshaw, shot him in the head accounting for the second bullet hole. After ransacking the room and failing to find the incriminating documents he needed, he doused the bed in gasoline and sprayed it all around, because he wanted whatever evidence he couldn't find to be destroyed. He ignited that fire, and dashed down the stairs and left a trail of gasoline in the front hall and then tossed the can inside and lit that fire, and the hotel was a gonner."

"My gracious sakes!" Millie exclaims. "Do you know where Violet is now?—I'm afraid I can't call her Lizzy," asks Millie.

Mrs. Cuttingham shrugs. "Don't know. Can't tell you. That's the truth."

"Do you know, Mr. Rossi?" Cutler asks.

"Have no idea, Marshal," Carlo says, shrugging.

"I know where she is," Coop says quietly. He says this to no one in particular and hardly anyone in general hears him.

"Say what?" Cutler bellows.

"Oh, I just said that I know where she is—sort of."

"And where is that?" the marshal asks tersely.

"I'll let you know when I find her," Coop says, looking up, speaking directly to the marshal.

"So," Millie says, "she's on the run, and I suppose the police are after her, now that we know she is the one who killed the person in the bed and who was in the coffin—imagine! Having a funeral service for Violet and all this time it was this—whatshisname? Lefty Donovan! So the police will be after her, right?"

"Well you can't just kill someone and not have to answer for it," Marshal Cutler drawls. He sits up erect and leans forward. "But in this case, I suspect her lawyer could argue self-defense or mitigating circumstances. That would depend, however, on how believable a witness Mrs. Cuttingham makes, since she is the only person, other than Violet herself, who witnessed what happened in that room." He takes another sip of brandy.

"So where's all the money?" Millie asks.

Cutler laughs. "I swear to God, Mrs. Cooper, you ask more questions than a first grader in September, eh?"

Cushing steps in, "I say! I was wondering the same thing," he says thoughtfully. Addressing Mrs. Cuttingham, "Surely in your conversation that day or in your previous interactions the subject came up, did it not?"

"It did not. I never brought up the subject of the money. When we left she had about a thousand dollars in cash which she'd kept in her room, but that's money she probably saved over the years from her work at the bank."

"And she left with a suitcase?"

"Yes, and the clothes on her back—which weren't of much use, as she was dressed as a man—and I am quite sure she did not intend to continue that masquerade for long, unless she found that going through life as a man is easier than doing it as a woman, which as we know is quite true."

"It must have been so hard for her to leave everything behind," Millie says wistfully.

"All that she had was in the hotel room," Cuttingham replies, "and yes, I am sure there are things she's going to miss, books, a few knick knacks. And it was not easy to say goodbye to the friends she'd made in Bathington—she'd been here quite a while. But when you lose a child and have to give up another, you've already given up that which is most priceless. Leaving behind material possessions wasn't that hard."

"So there's nothing left of Violet Crenshaw," Millie muses. "How odd, sad in a way, to live for twenty years in a place, or however long she was here, and then to disappear without a trace as though you were never here, to just vanish—it's like a death in a way. She may not have died physically in the fire, but in a sense Violet Crenshaw did die that night. I felt this same way, had this same feeling after Johnny left, got on that train, and then … just never came back. You live your life and then it's just erased as though—"

"But it's not like she was never here," Cushing says. "Listen to us. We're all talking about Violet. We remember her. We remember the jolly good things she did in this town, and in this church. She was a good person and she helped to protect the assets of a lot of good people in this town at the bank. She was kind to a fault … is the way I remember her. And Johnny—well he's gone, but he left a lot behind. There are traces of Johnny, not only in his two daughters, but in the many good things he did in this town. No, I think that we all leave a footprint when we live on this earth ... We make an impression ... for good or for ill."

"She gave me her crucifix," Coop says absent-mindedly. "The night before the fire, she gave me the crucifix as a going-away memento."

"Yes, she did, didn't she?" Cuttingham says. "That crucifix was no doubt part of a little altar she had in her room, with a picture of the sacred heart of Jesus, some candles, and she'd say the rosary every morning and every evening—"

"Why didn't she attend the Catholic church?" Millie asks.

"Oh, she often did," Cushing says. "She'd go to an early mass Sunday morning, or a Saturday evening mass, or one during the week. I don't think a week went by that she wasn't at mass at least once."

"That crucifix was probably the most precious artifact she had," Cuttingham says. "She had that crucifix custom made in Chicago ... in Chinatown, by a Chinese woodcarver and craftsman, she loved that crucifix and that she gave it to you, Coop, is a measure of the high regard and affection she had for you."

Alice has been listening quietly throughout all of Cuttingham's story and the subsequent conversation, but now she asks, "Where is the crucifix now?"

Coop says, "Why, I gave it to Reverend Cushing. I thought he'd have better use for it. For a while I kept it on the desk in the church office, but when the Publication Ministry was formed, I thought it would be safer if he had it—I didn't want it to get lost in the shuffle of things, and I really didn't think of taking it home with me. Somehow it belonged in a church, a house of God, so I gave it to the Reverend."

"It's right over there, on my bookshelf," Cushing says, pointing to a shelf behind Cutler.

Alice now hops off her perch and pads around the desk in her bare feet to the bookshelf and reaching high, removes the crucifix from the shelf.

"You can see," says Cuttingham, "that the Christ is almost oriental in his face."

Alice returns to the center of the room with the crucifix. It's about seven inches high and sits on a base about five inches long, two or three inches high and two inches wide.

"This base is heavy," she says. She shakes it, holding it up to her ear. There's a slight rattling sound that's audible to everyone in the room. "Didn't you ever hear that?" she asks of Coop.

"Yes," he says. "I assume it's some kind of weight to provide a solid foundation for the crucifix to make it steady."

"Yes, true," Alice says. "But the Chinese have a fondness for boxes, and they usually have a secret method of being opened. Anyone of you want to give it a go?"

This news is treated with surprise and wonderment. Carlo and Wason shift in their chairs. Millie and Cushing exchange glances. Alice is extending the crucifix to everyone in turn to see who will volunteer to have a closer look.

"Here, give it to me," the marshal says, holding out his hand. Alice gives him the crucifix. He moves it around, examining the base from all sides and angles. Then he turns it upside down and attempts to slide the bottom one way or the other, but nothing gives. "I've seen these things before," he says. "Usually you have to slide the top or sides of the dang thing—" He gives the back panel a tug without success. "—They're very clever, the Chinese, yuh know ..." He gives up and hands the crucifix back to Alice.

"Anyone else?" she asks. Cushing motions for her to give the object to him. "Puzzles are solved by the rigid application of reason and logic," he says suavely. "Thus, they collapse before me like a house of cards, dashed by the simple power of ..." He glances about the room, and then completes his thought: "... logic." Not wanting to paw at the box recklessly, he takes a more scholarly approach, examining the lines and seams of the base carefully. Then he stands and moves toward the floor lamp to his right and holds the artifact under the lampshade, touching the shade to tilt it so that more light shines upon the cross itself. He rotates it from side to side, then, grasping the crucifix itself, attempts to slide the cross as though to separate the cross from the box itself, to no avail. "Even the powers of the rational mind are no match for this vexatious little box," he cried.

"We could take it to it the hospital and put it under an x-ray machine," says Cutler. "That would show if there's anything inside anyway ... not that there is. What could be in there anyway?"

Cushing hands the crucifix back to Alice who receives it and then drops to her knees in front of the tea table. With the crucifix in her lap, she likewise examines it, and then says, "The sides are actually a molding for the box itself." She grasps the crucifix in one hand and then sharply raps the base of it on the fist of her other hand, and then with a thumb on the top of the box at the base of the crucifix, she pulls and the frame of the box lifts upward in a pivot motion, leaving the box intact below. She then turns it upside down and draws the bottom piece forward. It moves slightly. Her audience gasps. She then draws the base out completely.

Now everyone leaves their position and gathers around the table and likewise drop to their knees. Cushing alone remains standing above them. Alice reveals the contents of the box—the crucifix is still upside down—a black velvet pouch which she removes. It is tied by a small, delicate drawstring. She unties in, and then, gently releases the contents on to the table. A group of about 15-20 shiny gems, what appears to be diamonds, tinkle forth. More gasps. And a key clatters to the surface as well.

"Goodness sakes!" Millie exclaims.

"So there you have it!" Alice proclaims, beaming. "She kept those diamonds all these years."

"Ah wonder how many there were to begin with," Cutler observes. "Better count them right now with y'all as witnesses." There are nineteen stones.

"What is the key for" Millie asks.

"I suspect it is to a safety deposit box at the bank," says Alice.

"And that," says Cushing, "is where the money is!"

"Wait," says Alice, fingering the inside of the pouch. "There's something else." She withdraws a small piece of paper that's been folded twice. She unfolds it until it becomes a rectangular sheet measuring roughly four by six inches. "There's a note," she says.

"Read it," Millie cries.

"Okay." Alice tilts the paper to catch the best light. "It's addressed to you, Coop," she says, surprised. "Do you want to read it?"

"Oh no," he says. Then he reconsiders. "Maybe you should read it to yourself and if there's nothing incriminating, then you can read it out loud!" The others giggle nervously. Alice peruses the contents. "I think it's okay, Coop."

"You go right ahead," he says. Alice begins to read:

"Dear Mr. Cooper, I don't know when you are reading this, or if you ever will. The key opens a safety deposit box in the bank. There you will find roughly $135,000. As far as I know, this is ill-gotten gain that Johnny Torrio and his outfit collected from bootlegging and prostitution. Certainly it cannot be returned to the Mob. Therefore, if the authorities permit, I'd like you to act as the executor of these funds and disperse them as follows. Twenty thousand to Mrs. Penelope Cuttingham. Five thousand to

Mr. Jules Joyce. Ten thousand to Ruth and Joel Shimel, ten thousand to yourself. Five thousand to Bob Watson for him to keep for Tink's college education. Fifty thousand to St. Joseph's Orphanage in Chicago, and the balance, about $35,000 to Bathington Community Church with the stipulation that the funds not be used for capital improvements, but rather on programs or outreach to benefit the needy. The diamonds are to be sold through a dealer, and the proceeds given to Mr. Carlo Rossi, a diamond-in-the-rough. God bless you, and I apologize for any hardship or inconvenience I may have caused. Sincerely,— and it's signed 'Elizabeth Morley'"

Chapter XXXV

Saturday, September 27, 1952
Chicago, Illinois

"YOU CAN PULL UP OVER HERE and stop at the corner," says Coop to the cab driver. Coop pays the driver and gets out and looks around to get his bearings. He shivers. It's cool on this September day in the Windy City. Coop has on his dark brown suit, brown shoes, spit polished only this morning, argyle socks, white shirt and bowtie. Over this he has drawn a light top coat to protect from the wind. Behind him is a corner bar, the Pale Moon Lounge. On the other corner is Martin's Drug Store. These are the only two corners at this intersection because across the street is the Hillsdale Cemetery.

Coop steps off the curb and, dodging two bicycles and a Chevy, crosses the street and enters the cemetery via a small ascending roadway. Old headstones in row upon row here are quite old, more than a hundred years old. Some markers are slight thin slabs that look like wafers punched into the sod. Other decedents are remembered with impressive monoliths, or a white obelisk, or even a single family mausoleum.

The grass is green but not so green as one would expect in spring or mid-summer. The trees are tall and mature: oaks, elms and maples, mostly, some fir and blue spruce. It's mid-morning. The color seems washed out of the landscape. The sky is pale, the color of ash.

Coop hasn't been in Chicago for many years, and the last time he was here, he was with Antonia. Chicago was their first home. This is where he brought her after they'd married in Cedar Rapids. They set up housekeeping about 400 miles east in Chicago where Coop took a position for Western Union in a branch office at 53rd and Lake Street in the Hyde Park area downtown. Three years later they left and Coop took up with the railroad and they'd started their family. Had Johnny. Dear Antonia.

They'd been in high school for two years together, after he moved to Cedar Rapids from Ashland, Nebraska. He chased her around the bandstand in the park. They went to concerts together. Already she was playing the organ at the First Congregational Church. Coop took a part-time job doing janitor work there just so he could listen to her practice on that pipe organ. And she'd sing solos in church, and he worshiped her from afar, and then not so far. What a beautiful bride she was! Her perfectly oval face with soft, alabaster complexion, doe-like eyes slightly sad, and rounded features—she surely could have captured the heart of many a young swain in Cedar Rapids at the turn of the century. But Antonia chose him. A long, long time ago. Coop is walking with his head up, appreciating his surroundings as though they provided the visual backdrop for the silent film that is playing in his mind.

Coop reaches another path and notes the marking, turns to his right and walks now, more resolutely, and then steps off the path onto the grass, and climbs a gentle swell until he arrives at a row of markers where he stops. He walks down this row, noting markers as though he's reading book titles in Farley's Bookshop. Then he stops before a gravestone. The marker is small and of red polished granite. The name reads: AMELIA LOUISE MARLEY. Below this name is the tragic information: Born, February 11, 1925 — Died, September 27, 1927. And below this the words: "Suffer the little children to come unto me." St. Mark X:14.

Coop remains at Amelia's grave for about an hour. He had thought that he might find Violet here on the 25th anniversary of her death. It's almost noon. Coop pulls out a deli sandwich. It's cocooned in butcher paper. He tugs at the wrapping and takes a bite. He doesn't regret coming. He understands Violet's pain, and he's surprised and not a little embarrassed that he had not surmised the nature of Violet's restraint and pain over the years he knew her in Bathington. The gaunt face and line-tracings like tear-worn tracks. The hollowness of her voice at times, and the way her mind seemed to be somewhere in a distant place. He comprehended now, too, something of the refining fire that had purified her character, that had molded her into the gracious and understanding person she'd become, someone who wasn't upset by ordinary day-to-day trials. Violet was not a complainer. He knew that when you lose a child, other disruptions, however major they might be to someone else, are nothing to you. Burdens that are onerous to most are a light thing. He should have known that this kind of peace and equanimity does not come without great suffering, and yet he had been so self-absorbed, he had never paused to consider what sorrows had forged such a fine and delicate spirit as hers had been.

Coop wraps the butcher paper into a small wad and tucks it into one of the pockets of his topcoat, and then arises, pushing off the top of Amelia's stone. He bends over slightly, to pat the top of the stone, and then turns and walks away, continuing down the row, past HENSON, STOWBRIDGE, FARRER, HARRISON and others until he's in a small grove of spruce, beyond which is a path that leads back to the front gate. Here there are no graves, as the trees are thick, and their wide-spreading boughs form a barrier but for the small path sodden with pine needles that winds through them. He pauses to look up at the canopy and the pale sky beyond, and draws in a deep breath of the cool, pine-scented air.

Then, as though a hand had been laid upon his shoulder, he turns to look back and he sees a solitary figure approaching the spot where he'd rested only moments earlier. It is Violet, he is sure of it! His heart is racing now. He stands motionless. She's in a dark blue coat, and has tied a babushka over her head and is wearing dark glasses. In her hands are a bouquet of flowers that look to be chrysanthemums. Coop takes a tentative step toward her, but stops. Although he'd traveled from Bathington to Chicago on nothing but a hunch, he is hesitant to interrupt what must be a sacred moment. But, nonetheless, he walks through the grove and out into the open and stops again. Then, he raises his arm to wave and says, "Hey!"

The figure looks up immediately in the direction of the voice and sees Coop. She stands abruptly, turns about and begins to walk briskly away. Coop walks now, too. But the woman begins to run, not wildly, nor fast, but she's running away from him. Coop engages in pursuit, but he quickly realizes he cannot overtake her. He stops and cups his hands around his mouth and shouts, "Violet!"

The woman stops. Slowly she turns to face her pursuer. She begins to walk toward him, slowly at first, and then faster. "Coop! Is that you?"

"Violet!"

They meet at Amelia's grave and embrace. Violet buries her head in his shoulders. She is crying. Her body shakes. And when she pulls away and looks at him, she sees that his eyes are moist as well. "Oh Mr. Cooper, what are you doing here? Whatever are you doing here?"

"Ah, Miss Crenshaw, I had a question about the Gestetner. It's not inking properly, and there's only one person I know who can help me with that, you know."

Violet laughs and cries at the same time. She wipes her face of her tears but does not stop looking at him. He has not let her go. But he helps her down. They sit on the grass by Amelia's marker.

"Bathington has been in an uproar since you left, Violet," he says kindly.

She laughs quietly. "So I've heard."

They huddle on Amelia's grave for two hours. Then they leave and go into the city.

Epilogue

October 25, 1952,
Saturday

Up at 7:15 a.m. 45° at Des Moines. Down to Millie's
at 8:15 a.m. Millie and Frankie to Waverly this
morning. Millie called unexpectedly to spend the afternoon on "Band mothers" work having to do getting
out the tickets for another dance sponsored by the
club for next Friday evening, in an effort to raise
money for new band suits.

   Vic had her boyfriend, David Denton, in the second
grade at school, over for dinner this evening, even
though she's been over to his place all afternoon.
She startled everybody when she asked her mother
what a dick was. Millie just about choked on the
spot. Rev. Cushing said, "Why do you ask, sweetheart?" And she said, "Because Miss Wang said she
could shoot the dick off a mosquito." Millie said
that she'd explain later. Thought I was going to get
out of doing the dishes as Frankie insisted that she
would do them while I cleaned up the plates, etc.,
and took care of the food. But she got sidetracked
and ended up in the bathtub, preparatory to going to
the movie "Singing in the Rain." Then it developed
that Vic was to go to the show, Millie taking her up
after squeezing in a bath. Millie is also making
pumpkin pies for Sunday dinner and for Cushing who
is making his usual Saturday evening appearance at

the house, but I gather this time they're staying in, eating pumpkin pie, having tea and listening to some Scaldi and Galli-Curci duets.

Today I've written to Alta, cousin Waldo, and the Mackenzies of Omaha ... Death of Hattie McDaniels announced over the radio last night. Cancer! Today I also did the lunch dishes, and then peeled the spuds, had a little rest, listened to my two operas, and when they were over at 3:15 p.m., I took a walk to make a call on Les Davis, North Main Street, the old Carl Scharpff house, a semi-invalid from a stroke of some standing. Also called on Fred Smith who is much better, and Virgil Perry who is recovering from a broken hip.

It was 6:50 p.m. when I left for my room at Hemmings for an evening of music, starting off with the Railroad Hour. May deviate a bit by taking in Arthur Godfrey and Bob Hawk. Will not care to listen to The Beulah Show any more.

Cut out my sulfas for today.

After the Railroad Hour, I tuned in from my Stewart Warner to my old Majestic, still going strong on thirteen new tubes for Godfrey with four wonderful "talents," one being a quartet from McAllister College, a Presbyterian school in St. Paul, then back to NBC for an hour with "Telephone Hour" and "Band of America" and then at 9 p.m. to CBS with Bob Hawk.

I guess, since we got some word from the marshal only yesterday, that a summary of developments since the events of August last would be in order. Marshal Cutler said that a judge in Chicago has released from escrow the money that was found in a safety deposit box as per Miss Crenshaw's instructions. I doubt that I will have much use for the money Violet gave me, but I may give it back to her, or, more likely, save it toward Frankie and Vic's college education. I would like to help Naomi Shimel too. And speaking of Shimels, they will be glad to get this

news. They plan to open a Main Street business, and
I am sure they will do well. Jules, in a burst of
remarkable, yea brilliant, insight, has made me the
custodian of his windfall, knowing the truth of the
proverb that a fool and his money are soon parted. I
shall put him on an allowance.

Miss Alice Wang, my "xiao hua" and for whom I have
a great deal of affection, has returned to Chicago.
She has not written to me, but she called only last
week. Says she's off the porno case and working undercover—again—tracking smuggling operations involv-
ing the sale of fake merchandise coming in from China via Shanghai which she may visit sometime. She
invited me to go with her. I hope she stays in
touch.

Let's see. Mrs. Penelope Cuttingham has likewise
returned to Chicago. She is in no need of work, but
she is helping her nephew, Mr. Carlo Rossi establish
a photography studio, focusing on weddings, individual portraits, golden anniversaries, family portraits and the like. She also arranged a meeting between Mr. Rossi and his mother—more on her in a moment. It was quite an emotional scene. Mrs. Cuttingham is in her element, orchestrating reunions, man-
aging Carlo's business, communicating with her sister, and arranging clandestine rendezvous for Violet
and me.

Wason Jard has remained in Bathington! He is slowly building up a printing business. I think he's going to do quite well. And, he's taken up with Naomi
Shimel whose parents are quite delighted, them being
Jewish and all. Wason and Naomi are the only Jewish
kids in town and who'd thought they'd connect?

Oh, Mrs. Clarice Broughton and Art Bandy have been
indicted on bank fraud. They are both free at the
moment on bail. Don't know when the trial date is;
twill happen in Des Moines at any rate which is
where Broughton now spends most of her time.

Ronald Harmon has enrolled in St. Paul Bible In-
stitute up in St. Paul. He wants to become a preacher. I think he might make a good one.

Bathington Community Church has a new typist! 'Tis
Miss Frances Katherine Cooper, who's far too young
and beautiful for the job, but I keep a watch out
for her. I taught her everything I know about the
Gestetner, and she's doing a fine job. Very proud of
her. She, Naomi and Tink are still best friends, and
Frankie and Nomes are starting to think of where
they will be going to college next year.

And Violet. Sometimes I think I'm a character in a
film _noir_ scene. The last time I saw Violet at our
secret rendezvous spot in X-, she was still fearful
of exposure. She believes her life will be in danger
if she steps forward. She does not trust the Chicago
Police Department. But I am helping her with that
through some contacts I have via the railroad. We'll
see. She enjoys seeing Carlo—she's seen him three
times. She must be very careful, and Penny arranges
the meetings. She and Violet do not communicate via
letters or phone, thinking that letters can be
opened and phones can be wire-tapped. They have a
bank security deposit system worked out whereby they
leave notes for each other in the box.

I am to see her tomorrow on Sunday, the Lord's
Day. Des Moines WOI says it will be 65° and clear. I
shall awaken early, and 'twill be a morning glorious
and fair!

THE END

Author's Note

The idea of a novel set in Iowa in the 1950s began to emerge as I typed up my grandfather's diaries from the same period. Frank Dexter Merrill (1879-1957) kept a daily diary from 1947 to 1957 right up to the day he died. The research for the novel comes primarily from these diaries — which are a record of post-war public and private life in a small town in northeast Iowa. Although the Carlton Cooper character is a loose image of my grandfather, the other characters are pure fiction and none of the events in this novel can be found in the diaries except for the hotel fire, and the abduction chapter. The material about Sachem of Nahant, Poquanum, is based on research done by Frank Merrill's brother, Willard (a librarian in the Los Angeles School District for 40 years), who prowled around in the public libraries of Boston and Lynn, Massachusetts, in the 1940s and 1950s, looking for information about his ancestors. It is from his hand-written notebooks that the story of Black Will is derived. The 17th-century Thomas Bathington is much like my ancestor, Thomas Dexter.

My cousins in Iowa, Galen and Alice Jones and Betty Boyd Kiefer, have been very helpful in the publication of my grandfather's diaries. I am grateful to Jane France who read my manuscript and made many valuable suggestions and corrected the proof. My wife, Jeanie, also helped me immeasureably by being less than enthusiastic about my first draft. I threw it away and started over. She was very pleased with subsequent drafts and improved the book by sharing some important observations.

I thank you, my readers, for reading this novel. If you can, share your enthusiasm with your friends via social media networks, etc. Visit "The Temporary Typist" on Facebook. This book is also available as a Kindle download for $5.99. Search by author's name or book title at www.amazon.com. You may find the website at http://thetemporarytypist.com under construction. My second novel, *The Reluctant Crusader*, is complete, and now going through a final revision. It will be available soon. And, FYI, I am putting together some notes and ideas for a second "Bathington" novel which I hope I can deliver in 2016.

Again, thank you. I am so grateful and humbled that you've read something I've written.

Timothy Merrill
Shanghai, China
August 4, 2013